"WELL, HERE WE GO," said Japhy.
When I get tired of this big rucksack we'll swap."

"I'm ready now. Man, come on, give it to me now. I feel like carrying something heavy. You don't realize how *good* I feel, man, come on!" So we swapped packs and started off. . . .

"Look over there," sang Japhy, "yellow aspens. Just put me in mind of a haiku . . . 'Talking about the literary life—the yellow aspens.' " Walking in this country you could understand the perfect gems of haikus the Oriental poets had written, never getting drunk in the mountains or anything but just going along as fresh as children writing down what they saw without literary devices or fanciness of expression. We made up haikus as we climbed, winding up and up now on the slopes of the brush.

from "Dharma Bums," by Jack Kerouac

# West Coast Fiction

## Modern Writing from California, Oregon and Washington

Edited and with an Introduction by
**JAMES D. HOUSTON**

## RL 8, IL 9+

WEST COAST FICTION
MODERN WRITING FROM CALIFORNIA, OREGON
AND WASHINGTON

*A Bantam Book / December 1979*

ISBN 0-553-13138-9

*Published simultaneously in the United States and Canada*

Bantam Books are published by Bantam Books, Inc. Its trademark, consisting of the words "Bantam Books" and the portrayal of a bantam, is Registered in U.S. Patent and Trademark Office and in other countries. Marca Registrada. Bantam Books, Inc., 666 Fifth Avenue, New York, New York 10019.

PRINTED IN THE UNITED STATES OF AMERICA

# Contents

# Introduction

The west coast is a territory of the earth and of the mind. As a literary region it has its roots in that much larger realm called the American West. But during the past fifty years a body of fiction has taken shape that deals more directly with the life and landscape and mystique of this farthest reach of the continent—never entirely separate from the vast western world, yet clearly a world of fiction that has mapped its own geography.

The West begins with James Fenimore Cooper. Its stories and legends can occur anywhere between Appalachia and Puget Sound, between Saskatchewan and Mexico. It is peopled by cowhands, miners, trappers, pioneer mothers, Union soldiers, Sioux warriors, sheriffs and sharpshooters. The west coast as a literary region begins with Mark Twain, then heads rather quickly toward modern times. The fiction tends more to deal with contemporary events than to reach back into history. Its heroes fight city traffic as well as blizzards. The physical territory includes, with a little flexibility at the borders, the Pacific states of California, Oregon and Washington, that side of America which faces the far east. You will find some of those same cowhands and miners and pioneers among the characters, but you will also find migrant Okies, zany Armenians, scab lumberjacks, zen poets, talking trout streams, existentialist private eyes, second-rate film stars and undocumented aliens recently smuggled in from Nogales on their way to work in the Central Valley.

From the earliest days of settlement, this has been a region of abundance, excess, and high energy. It has also been a region of tremendous variety in ethnic origins and religious beliefs, as well as in terrain and resources, that kind of uncontainable variety that resists all patterns. Like the life out west, literature nowadays is moving in all directions at once. This is due partly to the so-called open society for which the far west is notorious, and partly to the multitude of writers. It happens that more writers live along the west coast than in any other part of the United States, outside the Boston-Washington megalopolis. Thus a lot of fiction is produced there. Not all of it deals with the region. Many writers choose to live near the Pacific Coast, drawn by the climate or the movies or a campus job or the available space, but write about other climes, other cultures, sometimes other planets and other galaxies.

The first aim of this collection is to gather some of those modern works that have emerged from the experience of the west coast, from the terrain, from the legends, from the dreams dreamed and the lives lived. There are of course many more stories and writers to select from than can possibly be included in a single volume. Hopefully these selections represent the range of what has been done. Most of the writers are native to the coastal states. The others have lived there a while and have also in some way incorporated this experience into their writing. Alice Adams, for example, is a southerner by birth, from Virginia by way of North Carolina. She has explored the south in her fiction, but since the early 1950s she has lived in San Francisco, and some of her strongest work, such as "The Swastika on Our Door," deals with southerners or easterners who for one reason or another find themselves out west, and whose destinies are fulfilled or concluded there. In southern fiction a frequent theme is the play between present time and some resonant moment in history, such as the Civil War. In the far west the more frequent situation is a character's present played against a past from another region, like the south, or the east, or Mexico, or the China

Maxine Hong Kingston reaches back to in "No Name Woman." It is a feature of the Pacific Coast that people arrive continually from somewhere else, with high hopes, or no hopes, to start over, or to play the final card. Because the coastline is both a physical and a psycho/spiritual boundary, this interplay between the far west and the realms left behind is among the recurrent themes.

About half the selections have been published as stories, while the others are taken from longer narratives. West coast writers have not practiced any one form as consistently as writers from the south, for instance, have practiced and excelled at the short story. In the south, with its own rich oral tradition and much closer ties to England and Europe, the short story seems an authentic mode, built into that region's history. Out west a more characteristic impulse has been toward expansiveness and large works stirred to life by the astonishing scale and richness of the landscape, such as: *The Octopus* by Frank Norris, *The Grapes of Wrath* by John Steinbeck, *Sometimes a Great Notion* by Ken Kesey, *Angle of Repose* by Wallace Stegner, *Another Roadside Attraction* by Tom Robbins.

The impulse to expand sometimes manifests itself as a renegade western refusal to be penned in by anyone's expectation of what a narrative should or should not look like, a habit William Everson has called "the repudiation of received forms." We see examples in the chronic digressions of William Saroyan, in Kesey's layer cake of voices and time-zones, in Richard Brautigan's short, surreal, unclassifiable takes on trout fishing, and in the runaway prose of Jack Kerouac, who found a landscape to suit his tastes when he finally reached the same coastal ranges that had inspired Robinson Jeffers to extend his poetic line far past what most publishers had come to accept as the tolerable width of a printed page.

Repudiation of received forms, of course, has long been an American pastime. This may be typical of life and literature in the far west, but not exclusively so. If anything gives definition to this fiction, it is not the forms so much as the available material writers have had access to, such elements as the unique history and geography, with its resulting role in the imagery and mythology of the western world, and thus that endless fund of dreams and aspirations funneled toward the far west from every direction;

some of them fulfilled, some of them demolished, some of
them twisted beyond recognition.

The far west was dreamed about before anyone really
knew it was there. It was foreshadowed in a Spanish novel
of the sixteenth century called *The Adventures of Esplan-
dian*, a romance—that era's equivalent of science fiction—
by Garcia Ordoñez de Montalvo. In that novel, published
in Madrid in 1510, thirty-two years before the Cabrillo
expedition first sighted and identified the west coast, twenty-
five years before Hernando Cortez named what is now the
tip of lower California, Montalvo sent his hero and his
readers on a fantastic journey:

> Know then, that on the right hand of the Indies, there
> is an island called California, very close to the side of the
> Terrestrial Paradise, and it was peopled by black women,
> without any man among them, for they lived in the fashion
> of Amazons. They were of strong and hardy bodies, of
> ardent courage and great force. Their island was the
> strongest in all the world, with its steep cliffs and rocky
> shores. Their arms were all of gold, and so was the harness
> of the wild beasts which they tamed and rode. For, in the
> whole island, there was no metal but gold. (from the 1872
> translation by Edward Everett Hale, for *The Atlantic
> Monthly*)

This island of Montalvo's was an invention, a fantasy, a
dream that actually influenced the expectations of the earliest Spanish adventurers. And this sequence, the dream running well in advance of the reality, has affected the life and
the literature of the region from the outset.

But for two and a half centuries the far west remained
as a beguiling and fabulous place in the mind. Apart from
a few scattered sightings and landings by sea-roving ex-
plorers, the Pacific Coast was uncharted and unaltered by
Europeans until the small band led by Gaspar de Portolá
made the first overland expedition, following the coastline
north from San Diego five hundred miles to what is now
San Francisco Bay. The year was 1769, late in the days of
conquest, settlement, and the advances of the written word.
Elsewhere on the continent, Benjamin Franklin had already published numerous editions of *Poor Richard's Almanac*. Mr. William Byrd, Virginia surveyor and prominent
man of letters, had accumulated a personal library of

3,600 volumes. Settlers in New Mexico had been performing Spanish miracle plays annually for over two hundred years. But on the Pacific Coast, as of 1769, there were only the diaries of a few men like Portolá and his chaplain, Juan Crespi, a Franciscan friar from the island of Mallorca. From these have come the earliest writings about the life and look of the region. Making daily entries as they crept up the coast, Crespi was the first to report at length on the fauna and the flora, the climate, the habits of the local tribes, and the habits of the land.

For the next hundred years the writings came from other travelers—missionaries, adventurers, soldiers and trappers, fortune hunters and homesteaders—trekking overland or shipping around the Horn. Like Crespi, Lewis and Clark kept remarkable diaries describing their progress westward toward the mouth of the Columbia River and the Pacific Ocean, which they reached in November 1805. Richard Henry Dana sailed the sparsely settled coast of California in the 1830s and recorded his impressions in *Two Years Before the Mast* (1840). In 1861 Mark Twain left St. Louis, Missouri, on a trip to the Mother Lode, the Sacramento Valley and eventually out to San Francisco, all of which he recounted ten years later in *Roughing It* (1872).

It is in Twain's early writings that we can observe the point where far west travel narrative began to take the shape of fiction. *Roughing It* is rich with tall tales and outrageous gold country escapades. One such tale became "The Celebrated Jumping Frog of Calaveras County," written while he was working as a journalist in San Francisco. It was published in *The New York Saturday Press* in November 1865 and brought him national attention. At the same time Bret Harte was also working in San Francisco, editing *The Overland Monthly* and beginning to write short stories. In 1868 he published "The Luck of Roaring Camp," another mining country tale, and in 1869, "The Outcasts of Poker Flat," a haunting and poignant story, which does what numerous west coast fictions have done since. It plays *against* the prevailing myth of boundless opportunity by recounting the fate of several people forced out of a mining camp, who meet their death in a Sierra snowstorm they aren't prepared for. Reputed to be a realm of mineral wealth and rich promise, the terrain, for these hapless exiles, is deceptively hostile. Describing the sun's look after a storm, Harte wrote, "It was one of the peculiarities of that mountain climate that its rays diffused a kindly warmth over the wintry landscape, as if in regretful commiseration of the past. But it revealed drift on drift of snow piled high around the hut—a hopeless, uncharted, trackless sea of white lying below the rocky shores to which the castaways still clung."

These stories established Harte and Twain together as the new voices from the far and fabled west. And this is the starting point for west coast fiction, the small gang of journalists centered in San Francisco in the 1860s, which also included Ambrose Bierce and a few others. Twain and Harte soon left for the east, never to return, but San Francisco was to remain a literary center from then on, for many years the only literary town of any consequence west of the Mississippi. In the 1880s Robert Louis Stevenson lived there, eventually married there, and recounted his honeymoon travels around northern California in *The Silverado Squatters*. The first notable fiction writers native to the west coast—Gertrude Atherton and Jack London— were both born there in the second half of the nineteenth century. Both began to publish in the 1890s, in the company of Frank Norris, who had come to California from Chicago with his family at the age of fourteen. Norris studied at Berkeley, and for a while at Harvard, returning to San Francisco as a newspaperman and then, after the success of his fiction took him to New York, as a novelist researching material for his most famous book, *The Octopus* (1901).

The central issue of this novel—the struggle for control of the land and for shares of its bountiful produce—had figured earlier in the original west coast novel, Helen Hunt Jackson's *Ramona* (1884) which depicts the plight of southern California Mission Indians caught in the crossfire between Mexican landowners and Yankee entrepreneurs. Similar concerns would continue to turn up in such varied works as Steinbeck's *In Dubious Battle* (1936), José Antonio Villareal's *Pocho* (1959), and *Rabbit Boss* (1973) by Thomas Sanchez.

Based on actual events, the main story of *The Octopus* deals with a group of independent wheat ranchers defending their interests against a land-greedy, tariff-wielding railroad combine, the octopus of the title. Some features of the novel are typically western: the time is 1880, the land is recently settled, the railroad is the villain, and the law is hard to find. Other features give it a distinctly far-western flavor: the San Joaquin Valley setting, a side trip into San Francisco's already thriving Bohemian subculture, the presence of a long-haired wandering mystic who hears voices and believes in reincarnation, and the aspiring poet, Presley, who observes the unfolding drama. Presley dreams of writing an epic, a poem "of the west, that world's frontier of romance, where a new race, a new people—hardy, brave and passionate—were building an empire. . . . He strove for the diapason, the great song that would embrace in itself a whole epoch. . . ." Throughout the novel this vision preoccupies Presley, who is in many ways Norris's own voice in the story. What emerges is another kind of octopus, as the brutal power struggle gradually surrounds and overwhelms the rhapsody Presley dreams of.

Published in the first year of the twentieth century, this ambitious, sprawling novel signals many things to come. Economically, ecologically, the history of the far west has continued to be a saga of exploitation, land abuse, bloody struggle, and enormous thefts. It has been the same, of course, in other parts of the world during the past two hundred years. What makes the difference, especially in California, are the deathless legends of what the far west holds in store—first, the legend of gold and riches, later, the legend of golden opportunities and the Golden Gate, the legend of open space and oranges, a land of promise, some final haven for the granddaddy of all such legends, the Great American Dream. Such expectations can move people to try things they might not otherwise try, and sometimes achieve things they might not otherwise achieve. They can also lead to particularly sharp, often crippling disappointment. Experiences that might be viewed elsewhere as reality are viewed out west as a failure of the dream. This dream, it should be pointed out, has seldom been promoted by the serious fiction. Other media have kept it alive—word of mouth, popular songs, chambers of commerce, real estate campaigns. What modern fiction has provided, time and time again, is counterpoint, playing under or around or against the legends, as Harte did, prophetically, in "The Outcasts of Poker Flat," as Norris did in *The Octopus*. Presley's yearning for "the frontier of romance" is always there, somewhere, in the foreground, or lurking in the background, yet it is usually surrounded, sometimes choked silent, by the various struggles for power. Very often the source for both the dream and the viciousness of the struggle is the same, the extraordinary abundance and dizzying worth, the formidable expanse of the western landscape and the fertility of the land, together with the expectations brought to it by the throngs it has magnetized.

During the 1930s west coast fiction broadened in range and became rather suddenly more "visible." While a modern generation of native writers found new ways to tap the power of the natural resources, some transplanted writers began to examine the cities in ways they had not been looked at before.

In Oregon the frontier had lasted longer than almost anywhere else in the U.S. H.L. Davis was the first novelist to bring his home state wide literary recognition. In the late 1920s he began publishing stories in H.L. Mencken's *American Mercury*. In 1936 his first novel, *Honey in the Horn*, won the Pulitzer Prize. For his material Davis had dipped into Oregon's recent past, the homesteading period in the decade after 1900, much as Norris had reached back into a similar period in the tumultuous past of California's central valley.

In the mid-1930s, from the town of Fresno in that same rich valley came the voice of William Saroyan, cocky, flamboyant, and instantly famous, upon the publication of his first book, a collection of free-wheeling tales and monologues called *The Daring Young Man on the Flying Trapeze* (1934). For Saroyan the farm country of his birth was not a battle zone. It was a warm, generally benevolent place where his Armenian family struggled to set down roots in a new land. *My Name is Aram* (1940) is still one of his best known books. In its approach to immigrant culture, it is also a landmark book. Only in the past twenty years—since the Civil Rights movement began to unlock minority literatures—has the unique mix of ethnic groups in the far west begun to find full expression in poetry and fiction. In stories like "The Summer of the Beautiful White Horse," Saroyan gives us one of the earliest examples from the west coast of an ethnic minority written about from the inside. This is the source of that love of family and the deeply felt compassion for human effort and human error that mingles with his innate charm and whimsy and perfect timing.

John Steinbeck's first book, *Cup of Gold*, appeared in 1929 and was soon followed by *The Pastures of Heaven* (1932), *To a God Unknown* (1933), *Tortilla Flat* (1935), *Of Mice and Men* (1937), an outpouring of novels and stories and plays that continued for nearly forty years and won him the Nobel Prize for Literature. He was, among other things, one of America's most territorial writers. Like Faulkner and Mississippi, Steinbeck and his region have become inseparable. He laid such powerful claim to a specific piece of central California that nowadays all the land between the Gabilan Range and the ocean, between San Jose and the southern end of the long Salinas Valley is referred to fondly as "Steinbeck country." Like Saroyan he too grew up in a farming community, which gave him an abiding affection for the soil and for those who lived by the work of their hands. But Steinbeck's view of the world was much darker. With a biologist's eye he saw the relentless process of natural cycles at work, in the tide pools off Cannery Row, as well as in the mammoth labor battles he dramatized. Though active in the proletarian movement of the 1930s, he saw an awesome danger in the mass demonstrations that could swallow all individual identity. He also felt deep dangers in the land, and said as much in the opening pages of *East of Eden* (1952). The Gabilan Mountains, to the east of his valley, were so light and sunny, "you wanted to climb into their warm foothills almost as you want to climb into the lap of a beloved mother. They were beckoning with a brown grass love. The Santa Lucias stood up against the sky to the west and kept the valley from the open sea, and they were dark and brooding—unfriendly and dangerous." Those fearful Santa Lucias provide the setting for his story, "Flight," which traces the final days of a young Californio, as he sets out to prove his manhood and ends up consumed by the very mountains he thought would protect him.

"Flight" was included in *The Long Valley*, a collection of his best short fiction, published in 1938. The following year saw the publication of *The Grapes of Wrath*, as well as Nathanael West's *The Day of the Locust*, Aldous Huxley's satirical look at a Hearst-like family in southern California, *After Many a Summer Dies the Swan*, and Raymond Chandler's first novel, *The Big Sleep*. In 1939 F. Scott Fitzgerald was living in Los Angeles doing much of the work on his Hollywood novel, *The Last Tycoon*; and eastern magazines were publishing the Saroyan stories that would appear a year later in *My Name Is Aram*. This confluence of now-famous west coast classics at the end of the decade suggests the improbable variety of fictions the region would continue to deliver—raw challenges from the back country, struggles for shares of produce in the lowlands, immigrant and minority experience, tales about Hollywood, and a new kind of detective story.

This new detective story, as it was reshaped by Dashiell Hammett and Raymond Chandler, originated in San Francisco. If we take things chronologically, Hammett actually provided the first popular hero of modern west coast fiction. Five years before *The Daring Young Man on the Flying Trapeze*, ten years before *The Grapes of Wrath* and the Joad family's epic journey west from Oklahoma, there was *The Maltese Falcon* (1929) with its Satan-faced private eye, Sam Spade, whose prototype, The Continental Op, had been rubber-soling around the city's streets for years. Soon after World War I Hammett had left his native Maryland and traveled out to San Francisco where he worked for Pinkerton's Detective Agency. He lived there for eight years, writing stories that developed from his own experience as a private investigator. To this he brought a post-World War view that changed the history of detective writing.

The hard-boiled private eye, epitomized by The Op and Sam Spade in San Francisco and by Chandler's Phillip Marlowe in Los Angeles, inhabits a world much different from the world that produced Sherlock Holmes and Hercule Poirot. In the traditional detective tale, crime is an aberration, murder will out, justice will be done, and order will probably be restored in a more or less reasonable society. In the stories of Hammett and Chandler, crime is the norm, justice is not expected, and any order is temporary because their jaded heroes live, as Chandler wrote in the introduction to his collected stories, "in a world gone wrong," where "the law was something to manipulate for profit and power." A cynical, unflappable, world-weary survivor, the hard-boiled detective might have been spawned in just about any American city of the 20s or 30s. But San Francisco and Los Angeles served as well, perhaps better than most. Both cities have baroque histories of violence and corruption inseparable from the politics and plundering of the wide open west—and this seems to be the way Sam Spade viewed it in 1929. "Most things in San Francisco," he remarks in *The Maltese Falcon*, "can be bought, or taken."

Among the numerous detectives who have continued down these far-western streets, the most prominent is Ross Macdonald's Lew Archer, hero of some nineteen novels. Like Spade and Marlowe, Archer is a man in mid-life, a loner who expects little from the people he deals with, and whose domain is the California coastline. He too is boiled, but not as hard. In the first scene of *The Underground Man* (1971), he is feeding the birds outside his window and making friends with a five-year-old boy. With a kind of guarded decency, Archer moves through a world that is gradually going to pieces around him. What Chandler caught was the tawdry, tarnished glow of 30s and 40s L.A. Bringing southern California into the 70s, Macdonald shows a man living on the edge of imminent social disintegration, somehow continuing with business as usual and, in a strangely archaic way, morality as usual. In *The Underground Man* the backdrop for Archer's investigations is a mountain range on fire. It has turned Santa Teresa (read Santa Barbara) into a field of war. "The flames that from a distance had looked like artillery flashes were crashing through the thick chaparral like cavalry." This invasion from the landscape echoes other threats he sees everywhere, in collapsing relationships, and in the sad fraudulence depicted by houses with elaborate Tudor facades and nothing in the backyard but weeds.

This is where the west coast detective story intersects with the fictions from in and around Hollywood, which began to proliferate during the 1930s. Both incline toward urban or suburban settings, city worlds almost always characterized by deceit, artificiality, shallow values, and corrupt habits. Nathanael West, Aldous Huxley, F. Scott Fitzgerald, Christopher Isherwood, and Horace McCoy were in the first wave of literary writers lured to the coast by the prices being paid for film scripts. They were then lured, by the very nature of the bizarre and contradictory world they found themselves in, to write about it. In these books the movies merge with a titillating but doomed southern California concoction of fantasy, eccentricity, self-delusion and excess. *The Day of the Locust*, which is still the standard of measurement in this genre, makes Hollywood a place where the worst possibilities of the far west find their most grotesque expression, where movie sets mirror hollow lives, where people driven wild by disappointment turn to violence, where the dream becomes a nightmare. Similarly, the L.A./Hollywood depicted in Joan Didion's *Play It As It Lays* (1970) is brittle, shallow, faithless, destructive. One difference is that West's novel, like several later books, is a satire, weighted with derision. Didion's account of Maria Lang's downward spiral—in taut, surgical prose, and chopped into cuts and takes, like the film Maria usually thinks she's living through—is in its way a more harrowing view of the sundrenched danger zone. In both these novels, however, and in the numerous others that have now made L.A./Hollywood a literary realm unto itself, a good part of the power and the appeal derives from the fact that the dream is always there—if only to be betrayed—the ongoing western promise of the Big Romance, the Second Chance, which is a given in the environment, as potent and as insistent as the coastline.

In these fictional cities survivors have to be toughly plated, like Spade or Marlowe, or L.A. Police Lt. Tom Spellacy in John Gregory Dunne's *True Confessions* (1977), who outlives his priest/brother not because he is better or tried harder, but because he is meaner and trusts no one. In *The Last Days of Louisiana Red* (1974), Ishmael Reed's kaleidoscope morality play and detective novel parody, the city is Berkeley and it is afflicted with a malady called Louisiana Red. The symptoms are malice, bitterness, hypocrisy. At the end the one who comes out smiling is private eye La Bas, the worldly veteran and voodoo investigator. Meanwhile, the soft, the sensitive, the vulnerable—if they don't escape—are liable to get consumed or seriously damaged. At the end of *The Day of the Locust*, Todd Hackett is driven away in a police car, screaming, unable to face the mob violence outside a film premiere. At the end of *Play It As It Lays*, Maria Lang is in a sanitarium where "nothing applies." Up north, in a different kind of story but in the same kind of city, the woman in Ella Leffland's expertly crafted "Last Courtesies" makes the costly mistake of letting her guard down to the wrong person at the right time.

During the 1950s San Francisco once again became the gathering place for an important group of writers. The

poets and novelists of the Beat Generation saw themselves
as a resistance movement, taking a stand against forces in
America that were dehumanizing the cities, stifling the
imagination and spreading a gloss of false complacency
across the land. The San Francisco Bay Area was their
headquarters because the spacious far west seemed well
suited to experiment, expansiveness, release and renewal.
At the center of this movement was Jack Kerouac, a writer
born and bred in Massachusetts, whose life and prose was
ignited by what he discovered in the Berkeley hills, the San
Jose railyards, the mountain ranges between Big Sur and
Washington's North Cascades where he worked one season
as a fire lookout.

Kerouac's books pointed the way for a generation of
American writers, as well as for a generation or two of
American seekers, and it was among these mountains that
he reached a climax point in his long, erratic spiritual
journey. He describes this in *Dharma Bums* (1958), which
like all his fictions is thinly veiled autobiography. Ray
Smith, the easterner, neophyte Buddhist and student of
mountain lore, is Kerouac. Japhy Ryder, his west coast
mentor, is Oregon-born poet and zen scholar, Gary Snyder.
In this novel Kerouac announces what we might call *the
second discovery*. The first discovery had been often described, as Steinbeck did in *East of Eden*, taking his characters into the Salinas Valley in the 1860s to settle and
then to work the virgin soil. For Kerouac in 1955, a valley
was not something you worked for crops; a mountain was
not to be mined for minerals. He came to the high country
more like a poet than a dramatizer, and what he found was
spiritual sustenance and renewal.

A revitalizing force in fiction and poetry, the Beat writers explored the boundaries of language and rhythm and
styles of life. In the history of the west coast, it might be
said that, in ways both actual and symbolic, they reopened
the territory; to an enormous audience they reaffirmed the
west coast as a literary location. During the twenty years
since their heyday, west coast fiction has seen an unprece-
dented flourishing. The Beat legend itself has played a role
in this, drawing writers toward the coast. So has the constant pull of Hollywood, as well as general population
growth and population shift westward, and a new and now
sizable generation of writers native to the region, born

during the 30s and 40s, who began to publish extensively
in the 60s and 70s. The result is an ever-widening spectrum
of lives and voices, from Tillie Olsen's unanchored merchant seamen in "Hey Sailor, What Ship?" (1957), to the
marooned, sadly comic Central Valley cruisers in Leonard
Gardner's "Christ Has Returned to Earth and Preaches
Here Nightly" (1965), to Al Young's fast-talking street
philosopher, "Sitting Pretty," (1976), whose Mississippi-
flavored monologues shine fresh light on unredeemed
districts of suburbia.

The range of contemporary writing can be seen in the
ways writers have continued to make use of the land's
riches, both economic and spiritual, and the powers inher-
ent in the western terrain. These elements are boldly present in such novels as Don Berry's *Trask* (1960), which
explores the meeting of Indian culture and the earliest
white settlers on the Oregon coast during the 1840s; Ken
Kesey's *Sometimes a Great Notion* (1964), and Thomas
Sanchez's *Rabbit Boss*. Sanchez writes of the Washo tribe
who inhabited the Tahoe basin at the time of the first white
penetration of the Sierras. The story begins in 1846, as a
lone Washo hunter comes upon the Donner Party. From
there we follow this tribe's fate through four generations,
experiencing profoundly what has been lost—not simply
land, but an identity, a culture and an entire belief system
tied to the land. Sanchez evokes the complex consciousness
that once pervaded the continent, wherein individual and
tribe and every feature of the natural environment were
physically and spiritually integrated.

For the Stamper family in *Sometimes a Great Notion*,
life is an equally intense bonding of kinship, work, and
soil. Self-reliant loggers, they are fighting a union that
wants to intrude upon their right to grapple with the land.
For Hank Stamper, the larger-than-life hero, it is the final
struggle of the individual to preserve what he considers a
rightful relationship to timber country, which is both a
source of sustenance and an awesome adversary. The great
forests that dominate this terrain are lush and fertile and
inspiring and demonic. The ferocious Wakonda River can
define a man's worth, can uplift his body and his spirit, can
bear his ancestors and his memories along with its currents,
and can also swallow whatever he loves the most.

In Richard Brautigan's *Trout Fishing in America* (1967),

a feature of the western landscape becomes the central character, has a voice, and suffers a terrible fate. It is a burlesque lament for the ways civilization has punished the great outdoors. We see trout streams that become stairways, water faucets, a row of telephone booths, and at last just a collection of scrap for sale in a San Francisco wrecking yard.

*Another Roadside Attraction* (1971) by Tom Robbins, is set farther north, near Puget Sound and the Canadian border. Here the peaks, the mushroom glades and waterways dwarf the towns; yet this spectacular landscape is not being used for produce or for the spiritual renewal of the characters in the story as much as it serves to launch the author's stoned and vaulting inventiveness, a means to explore another zone of reality. The novel offers its own metaphor, in the huge and marvelous hot dog that rises above the roadside restaurant and contains within its surreal borders, rivers, fields, valleys, a baseball stadium, a view of Kilimanjaro, and the gas rings around the planet Saturn—"the perfect emblem," the narrator tells us, "for the people and the land."

In William Kittredge's story "The Van Gogh Fields," Oregon's grain country is something to be possessed not with the hands but with the memory. No longer real fields that Robert Onnter will plant and plough, they still offer him a valuable grounding. The fields of earlier years beckon from afar, dusty with boredom and hard-earned death, but shimmering before the eye of the mind like the Van Gogh painting that once hung in the family living room. In a related way Mary Beal, in her story "Gold," takes some traditional elements of western landscape and legend—a wilderness community of pioneers, the search for a purer life, prospecting, and mountaineering—and transmutes these into a mystical vision. Through some alchemy of prose and human digestion the old-time quest for gold and homestead is linked, again, to that never-ending quest for inner purity.

Among those writers native to the region who have emerged since the 1950s, there are a number of Chicanos and Asian Americans whose stories have begun to illuminate lives crucial to the west coast's past and present. Asian American experience has been principally west coast experience, centered there since the 1850s when men like the great-grandfather in Shawn Wong's "All in the Night without Food" crossed the Pacific to seek his fortune in a land the Chinese called Gold Mountain. The Chicano presence goes back even further to the earliest days of exploration. Mexican Americans, in fact, became an ethnic minority not by immigration but by conquest, since all the states along the border were once northern provinces of Mexico. A fellow like Chato de Shamrock in Danny Santiago's "The Somebody" grew up in a city that has had a continuous Spanish-speaking population since it was founded in 1781. This is a very different Los Angeles from the L.A. of Raymond Chandler and the Hollywood novelists. Here the cultural continuum extends not toward Washington D.C. and London, but south, toward Guadalajara.

The growing number of stories and novels by such writers invites another look at some of the prevailing imagery. Because the Anglo voice dominates the literature, one looming presence has been the Pacific coastline as terminus, as some final limit of that great surge outward from Europe that began in the fifteenth century. Yet for Asian American writers like Maxine Hong Kingston, Shawn Wong, Hisaye Yamamoto, and the late John Okada, whose uncompromising World War II novel, *No-No Boy* (1957) dramatizes the turmoil of a Seattle Nisei caught between two cultures, history has also been pushing toward this coastline from the other direction, eastward, across the Pacific. In the works of Chicano writers like Danny Santiago, José Antonio Villareal, Ronald Arias, J.L. Navarro, Edmundo Villaseñor, and Richard Vasquez, the coastline is not felt much at all. For them history is pushing northward, from the south, across a border that oftentimes seems artificial, into a land their ancestors once held title to. And for Native Americans, like the Washo in *Rabbit Boss*, the ancestry pushes not from west or east or south, but straight up from the soil beneath their feet. Thus, in these past twenty-five years the fiction has finally begun to reflect what this region is, in fact—not only a terminal zone for the westering thrust, but a crossroads where an extraordinary mix of cultures has met, clashed, intermingled: Native American, Spanish, Mexican, Filipino, Chinese, Japanese, Black, Okie, Scots-Irish, Armenian, and Steinbeckian German, along with the various other strains out of northern and Mediterranean Europe. This is one of the sources of hope, because in diversity—if it can be preserved—there is always a richness. Moreover, it is yet another indication that, in a part of the world so recently settled, where the literature is still unfolding, there are still some regions for writers of fiction to explore.

James D. Houston
Santa Cruz, California
March 1979

# ALICE ADAMS

# The Swastika on Our Door

Normally, Karen Washington took a warmly nostalgic interest in stories about and especially pictures of her husband's former girls. They had all been pretty, some beautiful. And they reminded her that her very successful and preoccupied lawyer husband had once been a lively bachelor, vigorously engaged in the pursuit of women. But the large glossy picture of Roger and his brother Richard, who was now dead, and a girl that she found on the top shelf of her husband's shirt closet disturbed her considerably. Why had Roger put it there? She was not jealous; she did not suspect that he perpetuated an old liaison, but she felt left out. Why had he chosen not to tell her about this particular beautiful girl in her high-collared coat?

To the left was fat Roger, grinning and blinking into the flashbulb, having raised his glass of wine to the nightclub camera: a man out on the town, celebrating, having a good time. "The jolly Roger": with his peculiar private irony Richard had sometimes called his brother that. On the right was skinny tortured Richard, who was staring at his brother with a gaze that was at the same time stern and full of an immoderate love. Between them, recessed into half shadow, was the long-necked beautiful dark girl, who was looking at Richard as though she thought he was either

1

marvelous or crazy. Or perhaps she herself looked crazy.
In the bright flat light her collar made an odd shadow on
her cheek, and her eyes were a strange shape—very narrow
and long, like fish.

Karen sighed heavily, and then sneezed from the dust.
Although of German extraction she was a poor housekeeper, and did not like to be reminded of that fact, of
which both the dust and the presence of that picture on an
untouched shelf did remind her. Retreating from the closet,
she put the picture on her husband's dressing table, meaning to ask him about it that night. She was a big dark
handsome girl, descended from successful generations of
Berlin bankers; her father, the last of the line, had come to
San Francisco in the Twenties, well before Hitler, and had
been prominent in the founding of a local bank. Karen had
already, in ten years of marriage to Roger, produced five
sons, five stalwart big Washingtons who did not remember
their difficult doomed Southern uncle, Uncle Richard, car-
tons of whose books were still unpacked in the basement.

Karen remembered Richard very well, and she thought
of him for a great deal of that day as she moved about the
enormous unwieldy and expensive house on Pacific Street,
bought when Richard died and they inherited his money.
The house from its northern windows had mammoth views
of the Bay, and the bridge, Sausalito, the hills of Marin
County. That day, that March, there were threatening rain
clouds, a shifting kaleidoscope of them, an infinite variety
of grays.

Karen had felt and still did feel an uncomfortable mixture
of emotions in regard to Richard, one of which was certainly
the guilty impatience of the healthy with the sick. Richard
had been born with a defective heart, ten months after
Roger's healthy and very normal birth, and had suffered
greatly during his lifetime. But beyond his irremediable
physical pain he had seemed, somehow, to choose to be
lonely and miserable. He lived in a strange hotel even after
he got his money; he was given to isolated, hopeless love
affairs, generally with crazy girls. ("Affairs with psycho-
paths are a marvelous substitute for intimacy," he had been
heard to say.) He only bought books and records; his
clothes were impossible.

Like many very secure and contented people, Karen
tended to be somewhat unimaginative about the needs,
emotional and otherwise, of those who were not content,

of those who were in fact miserable. To her credit she knew this, and so she sighed as she moved incompetently about her house with the vacuum cleaner; she sighed for Richard and for her own failure to have understood or in any way to have helped him.

Karen's deficiencies as a housekeeper were more than made up for by her abilities as a cook, or so her greedy husband and most of their greedy friends thought. That afternoon, as heavy dark rains enshrouded the city and the Bay, Karen made a superior moussaka, which was one of Roger's favorites. It had also been a favorite of Richard's, and she was pleased to remember that she had at least done that for him.

Then, just as she had finished, from upstairs she heard the youngest child begin to whimper, waking up from his nap, and she went up to get him, to bathe and dress him before the older boys all tumbled home from school.

The maid would come at three and stay until after dinner, since Roger liked a formal evening meal.

Karen was dressing, and lost in a long skirt that she tried to pull down over big breasts, down over her increasing thighs, when Roger came in and asked her about the picture.

"What's that doing out here?" "Here" was "heah"; Roger had kept his Southern voice, though less strongly than Richard had.

Her head came out of the dress, and she bridled at the annoyance in his tone. "Why not? It was up on your top shirt self." At worst, in some atavistic Germanic way, Karen became coy. "Some old girl friend you haven't told me about?" she said.

Roger was holding the picture, blinking at it in the harsh light from Karen's makeup lamp, holding it closer and closer to the bulb as though he would burn it if the picture did not reveal all that he wanted to know. He was not thinking about Karen.

"She's beautiful," said Karen. She came to look over his shoulder, and pressed her cheek against his arm. She knew that he loved her.

"She was Richard's girl. Ellen. After that." He pointed unnecessarily at the picture. "We were celebrating his money, after he finally sold his land. That was the night he met her."

Karen was quiet, looking at the peculiar girl, and at

Richard, whom no large sums of money had cheered, and at jolly Roger.

"What a creepy girl," Roger said. "Richard's worst. She finally had to be locked up. Probably still is."

"Oh." Karen shuddered.

Roger put the picture down with a heavy sigh. He was fatter now than when it was taken; his neck was deeply creased with fat, and his big cheeks drooped.

Then abruptly he turned around and embraced Karen with unaccustomed vigor. "What's for dinner?" he asked. "Did I smell what I think I did?"

Because Richard had been sick so much and had been tutored, he and Roger ended by finishing high school in the same June of 1943, and that July they entered Harvard together, two Southern 4-F's in giddy wartime Cambridge, fat Roger, who also had a punctured eardrum, and thin sick Richard. They both reacted to that scene with an immediate and violent loneliness. Together they were completely isolated from all those uniforms, from the desperately gay urgency of that war, that bright New England climate.

Roger's fat and Richard's illnesses had also isolated them in childhood; they were unpopular boys who spent most of their afternoons at home, reading or devising private games. But to be isolated and unpopular in a small town where everyone knows you is also to be surrounded—if not with warmth at least with a knowledge of your history. There is always the old lady approaching on the sidewalk who says, "Aren't you Sophie Washington's boys? I declare, the fat one is the living spit of your grandfather." Or the mean little girl in the corner grocery store who chants softly, "Skinny and fat, skinny and fat, I never saw two brothers like that."

They had too an enormous retreat from the world: that huge house full of books everywhere. And the aging pale parents, Josiah and Sophie Washington, who had been and continued to be surprised at finding themselves parents, who retreated from parenthood to long conversations about the histories of other Southern families. "It was a perfect background for eccentrics of the future," Richard later told Ellen.

Both Roger and Richard had chosen history as their field

of concentration at Harvard. During those summer afternoons, and into the gaudy fall, while R.O.T.C. units drilled
in the Yard and pretty Radcliffe girls—in sloppy sweaters
and skirts, white athletic socks and loafers—lounged on
the steps of Widener Library, Richard and Roger studied
furiously in their ground-floor rooms in Adams House, and
at night they went to movies. Every night a movie, in
suburbs as far-lying as the subway system would carry
them, until one night when the only movie they had not
seen twice was *I Wanted Wings*, in Arlington. So they
stayed home and for a joke read chapters of *Lee's Lieuten-
ants* aloud to each other, which was not one of the texts
for History I but which was the only book in the room
they had not already read. It had been an off-to-college
present from their not very imaginative mother. In stage
Southern accents they read to each other about Fredericksburg and Chickamauga, Appomattox and Antietam.

Roger had a photographic memory, of which Richard
was wildly proud. His own memory was erratic; he easily
memorized poetry but he had a lot of trouble with names
and dates, with facts. As they walked across the Yard in
the brilliant September air, Roger recited several pages
from that book, still in that wildly exaggerated accent: ". . .
and before the Northern armies could marshal their forces
. . ." while Richard gamboled beside him, laughing like a
monkey.

They were taking a course called Philosophic Problems
of the Postwar World. With everyone else they stood
around outside Emerson Hall, waiting for the hour to
sound. Richard was overheard to say to Roger, in that
crazy Southern voice, "As I see it, the chief postwar problem is what to do with the black people."

At the end of the summer Roger had four A's and Richard had two A's, a C and a D, the D being in Biology.
They had no friends. Richard regarded their friendlessness
as a sign of their superiority; no one else was as brilliant,
as amusing, as his brother, and thus they were unappreci-
ated. Roger didn't think much about that sort of thing
then. He was solely concentrated on getting top grades.

Those Harvard years were, or perhaps became in memory, the happiest of Richard's life. Completely isolated
from their classmates and from the war that for most people dominated the scene, he and Roger went about their

scholarly pursuits; he had Roger's almost undivided attention, and it was a time when Roger laughed at all his
jokes.

Aside from the Southern joke, which was their mainstay,
they developed a kind of wild irony of their own, an irony
that later would have been called sick, or black. Roger's
obesity came into this. "You must have another hot dog,
you won't last the afternoon," Richard would say as Roger
wolfed down his seventh hot dog at lunch at the corner
stand. And when Roger did order and eat another hot dog
they both thought that wildly funny. Richard's heart was
funny too. At the foot of the steps of Widener Roger
would say, "Come on, I'll race you up to the top," and they
would stand there, helplessly laughing.

That was how Richard remembered those years: big fat
Roger, tilted to one side chuckling hugely, and himself,
dark and wiry and bent double laughing, in the Cambridge
sun. And he remembered that he could even be careless
about his health in those years; he almost never hurt. They
went for long walks in all the variously beautiful weathers
of Cambridge. Years later, in seasonless California, Richard would sigh for some past Cambridge spring, or summer
or fall. Roger remembered much less: for one thing he was
in later life so extremely busy.

They were reacted to at Harvard for the most part with
indifference; other people were also preoccupied, and also
that is how, in general, Harvard is—it lets you alone.
However, they did manage to be irritating: to the then current remark, "Don't you know there's a war on?" both
Roger and Richard Washington had been heard to respond,
"Sir, the War has been over for almost a hundred years."
Also, those were very "liberal" years; racism, or what
sounded like it, was very unpopular. No one made jokes
about black people, no one but Roger and Richard.

Therefore, it is not too surprising that one night Roger
and Richard came back from the movies (a revival of
*Broadway Melody* in Dorchester: Roger loved musicals)
to find that someone had put a swastika in black chalk on
the door to their room. Richard was absolutely enchanted;
in a way it was the highest moment of his life. All his sense
of the monstrosity of the outside world was justified, as
well as his fondness for drama; he was persecuted and
isolated with his brother. "Roger," he said very loudly and

very Southernly, "do you reckon that's some kind of Indian sign they've gone and put on our door?"

Roger laughed too, or later Richard remembered Roger
as laughing, but he recalled mainly his own delight in that
climactic illuminated moment. They went into their room
and shut the door, and after them someone yelled from
down the stairwell, "Southern Fascists!" Richard went on
chortling with pleasure, lying across the studio couch,
while Roger walked thoughtfully about the room, that big
bare room made personal only by their books and some
dark curtains now drawn against the heady Cambridge
spring night. Then Roger put a Lotte Lenya record on the
player.

That was more or less that. The next day the janitor
washed the chalk off, and Roger and Richard did not spec-
ulate as to who had put it there. Anyone could have.

But a week or so later Roger told Richard that he was
tired of history; he was switching his field of concentration
to economics. And then he would go to law school. "Fat
makes you already eccentric," he said. "And eccentrics
have to be rich."

"In that case I'll switch to Greek," Richard countered
furiously, "and remain land poor."

And that shorthand conversation made perfect sense to
both of them.

They both did what they said they would, except that
soon after their graduation (Roger *summa cum laude* and
Phi Beta) Richard had a heart attack that kept him in the
hospital at home in Virginia, off and on for a couple of
years, fending off his anxious mother and writing long
funny letters to Roger, who seemed to be enjoying law
school.

So it worked out that by the time Richard went back to
Harvard for his master's in Greek literature, Roger had got
out of law school and gone out to San Francisco, where he
began to succeed as a management consultant to increasingly important firms. He was too busy even to come home
for the funerals of his parents, who died within a month of
each other during his first winter in San Francisco—Joseph
and Sophie Washington, who had, they thought, divided
their land equally between their two sons. Roger sold his
immediately for thirty thousand, and thought he had done
very well. He urged Richard to do the same, but Richard

lazily or perversely held on to his, until the advent of a freeway forced him to sell, for a hundred thousand.

Richard did not enjoy his second time at Harvard, except in the sense that one does enjoy a season of mourning. He was terribly lonely, he missed Roger vividly, everywhere in Cambridge, and his heart hurt most of the time.

Thus it was not until the early fifties that Richard got his teaching job in the boys' school in San Francisco, and came out to see his brother again. And then came into his money, and met Ellen.

In those days, even after getting his money, Richard lived in a downtown hotel—his eccentricity. He had a large room that the maid was not allowed to enter. ("In that case why live in a hotel?" practical Roger had asked.) The room was stacked everywhere with books, with records and papers. Richard took most of his meals in the hotel dining room; after he came home from a day of teaching he rarely went out. He was not well; much of the time he felt dizzy, and he ached, but again it was hard to gauge the degree to which his loneliness was chosen. If Roger, for example, had had a bad heart he would undoubtedly have had it continually in the midst of a crowd.

Indeed, in the years since his Harvard isolation Roger had become extremely gregarious. Professionally he was hyperactive; his entire intelligence and energy were occupied. And a vivid social life grew out of professional contracts. People whose adviser he was in a legal economic sense also asked him to dinner, and he became known as a very courtly, if somewhat ponderous bachelor, as well as an astute businessman. Roger was greedy for company; he reveled in his invitations, his cocktails and dinners and his girls.

Girls who fell in love with Richard were always girls with whom Roger had not been successful; that was how Richard met girls. In one of their rare conversations about relationships with women, Roger remarked on Richard's perfect score with women; Richard had never been turned down.

"But with how many ladies have I—uh—attempted to prove my valor? Richard asked, in the parody Southern manner that he sometimes tried to continue with Roger. "Four, or is it three? I sometimes lose track of these—uh—astronomicals."

Ellen made five.

One March afternoon, a few months after they had met, Richard lay across some tufts of new grass on the bank of a duck pond in Golden Gate Park, watching Ellen, who was out wading among the ducks. Like a child, she held her skirt bunched up in front of her, at the top of her long thin childish legs. Water still had spattered the shabby gray flannel; Ellen visibly didn't care. She splashed out toward some brown ducks who were peacefully squatted on the surface of the pond. They fled, scuttering across the water, submarining under, as Ellen screamed out, "See! They know I'm here!"

Her long fish eyes that day were almost blue with excitement. When she was unhappy or simply remote they were gray. After she finally went mad they were gray all the time.

At the farther edge of the pond were willows, now thickly green with spring; they grew out into the water in heavy clusters. And all about the pond were tall eucalyptus, scenting the air with lemon, shedding their bark in long strips, as the breeze fluttered their sad green scimitar leaves above Richard's heavy head.

Out of the water, out of her element, Ellen became a detached and languorous girl who sat on the grass not far from Richard, clutching her arms about her knees and watching him curiously, listening to that tormented and violent Southern talk.

"Interest! *Interest!*" was what Richard was saying. "My own brother, my *heir*, and he offers me interest on a loan. My God, I told him, 'You're my brother, take all the money, but for God's sake don't offer me interest.' "

Above the trees pale-gray clouds drifted ceremoniously across the sky. Half closing her eyes, Ellen turned them into doves, flocks and flocks of pale soft gray doves.

"God, if I'd only sold the bloody land when Roger sold his," said Richard for the tenth or perhaps the hundredth time that day. "And got only thirty thousand like him instead of this bloody hundred."

Richard's wildness and the intensity of his pain had oddly a calming effect on Ellen. Unlike most people, who were frightened or impatient or even—like Roger—bored, Ellen experienced with Richard a reduction of the panic in which she normally lived. Rather reasonably she asked him what she had often been told but had forgotten: "Why didn't you sell it then?"

"I preferred to be land poor." This was in the old stage Southern voice. "Ah pruhfuhd." Then, "Christ, I didn't want the money. I still don't. If I could only just give it to him. Without dying, that is." And he laughed wildly.

By this time pain had deeply lined Richard's face. There were heavy lines across his forehead, lines down the sides of his nose and beside his wide, intensely compressed mouth. Many people, expecially recent friends of Roger's, considered Richard to be crazy, but even they were aware that what sounded like madness could have been an outcry against sheer physical suffering.

"I may not even go to New York," Ellen said. "It takes so much nerve."

Ellen was a mathematician—"of all things," as most people said. Especially her Oakland-Baptist-John Birch Society mother said that, and often. Ellen was talented and had been offered a fellowship at Columbia.

"Stay here," Richard said. "Let me keep you. God, won't anybody take my money?"

The melodramatic note in that last told Ellen that Richard was going to talk about Roger again, and she sighed. She liked it better when he was reading poetry to her, or when he didn't talk at all and played records, Telemann and Boccherini, Haydn and Schubert, in his cluttered and most personal room.

But Richard said, "Roger wants to invest in some resort land at Squaw Valley, with some of his rich new German friends. Do you know the altitude at Squaw Valley? Six thousand feet. I wouldn't last a minute there. How to explain why his brother is never invited for weekends or summer vacations. I am socially unacceptable to my brother—isn't that marvelous?"

Richard's eyes were beautiful; they were large and clear and gray, in that agonized face. Those eyes exposed all his pain and anger and despair, his eyes and his passionate deep Southern voice. He was really too much for anyone, and certainly for himself. And there were times, especially when he ranted endlessly and obsessively about Roger, when even Ellen wanted to be away from him, to be with some dull and ordinary person.

Ellen had met Roger, who always retained a few intellectual friends, at a Berkeley cocktail party, and she had had dinner with him a couple of times before the night they celebrated Richard's money at the silly expensive restaurant where the picture was taken. Ellen had not liked Roger very much. He was exceptionally bright; she recognized and responded to that, but she was used to very bright people, and all the money-power-society talk that Roger tried to impress her with alarmed her. "You could marry extremely well if you wanted to," Roger told her. "With your skin and those eyes and those long legs. And no one should marry on less than thirty thousand a year. It can't be done." Then he had laughed. "But you'd probably rather marry a starving poet, wouldn't you? Come and meet my crazy brother, though, even if he has just come into money."

And so Richard and Ellen met, and in their fashions fell in love.

Now, feeling dizzy, Richard lay back on the bright green grass and stared up through the lowering maze of silvered leaves to the gray procession of clouds. Sickness sometimes made him maudlin; now he closed his eyes and imagined that instead of the pond there was a river near his feet, the Virginia James of his childhood, or the Charles at Harvard, with Roger.

Not opening his eyes but grinning wildly to himself, he asked Ellen, "Did I ever tell you about the night they put the swastika on our door?"

Of course Richard lent Roger the money, with no interest, and their dwindling relationship continued.

Sometimes even in the midst of his burgeoning social life Roger was lonely; he hated to be alone. Sometimes late at night he would telephone Richard, who always stayed up late reading and playing records. These conversations, though never long, were how they kept in touch.

At some point, a couple of years after Richard had met Ellen, Roger began to talk about a girl named Karen Erdman, and Richard knew that she was the one he would marry. But Roger took a long time deciding—Karen was a patient girl. Richard did not meet Karen until the engagement party, but he was so intuitively attuned to his brother that he could see her and feel the quality of her presence: that big generous and intelligent girl who adored his brother. After all, Richard also loved Roger.

"The question seems to me," advised Richard, "as to whether you want to marry at all. If you do, obviously Karen is the girl you should marry."

"I have a very good time as a bachelor," Roger mused.

"But it takes too much of my time. You break off with one girl and then you have to go looking for another, and at first you have to spend all that time talking to them."

"God, what a romantic view. In that case perhaps you should marry."

"But she wants children. I find it almost impossible to imagine children."

"Sir, what kind of a man would deplore the possibility of progeny?" Richard asked, in their old voice.

"I can't decide what to do," said Roger. Then, as an afterthought: "How is Ellen?"

"Marvelous. She has managed to turn down four fellowships in one year."

"She's crazy."

"You're quite right there."

"Well. Good night."

"Good night."

A heavy engraved invitation invited Richard to the Erdmans' engagement party for their daughter. "Oddly enough," Richard said to Ellen. "Since they're being married at Tahoe I'm surprised they didn't do the whole thing up there. Or simply not mention it until later. God knows I don't read the society pages."

Richard was not asked to bring Ellen.

The Erdman house, in Seacliff, was manorial. Broad halls led into broader, longer rooms; immense windows showed an enormous view of the Bay. And the décor was appropriately sumptuous: satins and velvets and silks, walnut and mahogany and gilt. Aubusson and Louis XV. For that family those were the proper surroundings. They were big dark rich people who dressed and ate and entertained extremely well.

In those crowded, scented, overheated rooms Richard's pale lined face was wet. He went out so infrequently; the profusion and brilliance of expensive clothes, in all possible fabrics, of jewels—all made him dizzily stare. The acres of tables of incredibly elaborate food made him further perspire. He stood about in corners, trying to cope with his dizziness and wildly wondering what he could find to say to anyone there. Lunatic phrases of gallantry came to him. Could he say to the beautiful blonde across the room, "I just love the way you do your hair, it goes so well with your shoes"? Or, to the tall distinguished European, who was actually wearing his decorations, "I understand you're in money, sir. I'm in Greek, myself. Up to my ass in Greek." No, he could not say anything. He had nothing to say.

Roger's new circle included quite a few Europeans, refugees like his father-in-law to be, and Mr. Erdman's friends, and transients: visiting representatives of banks, commercial attachés and consuls. The rest were mainly San Francisco's very solid merchant upper class: German Jewish families who had had a great deal of money for a long time. They were very knowledgeable about music and they bought good paintings on frequent trips to Europe. Among those people Roger looked completely at home; even his heavy Southern courtliness took on a European flavor.

Mrs. Erdman was still a remarkably pretty woman, with smooth dark hair in wings and round loving eyes as she regarded both her husband and her daughter. Richard found this especially remarkable; he had never known a girl with a nice mother and he imagined that such girls were a breed apart. Ellen's mother had jumped under a train when Ellen was thirteen and miraculously survived with an amputated foot.

Mrs. Erdman was a very nice woman and she wanted to be nice to Richard, once it was clear to her who he was. The two boys were so unlike that it was hard to believe. "I'm so sorry that you won't be able to come up to the lake for the wedding," she said sympathetically.

"But who'd want a corpse at a wedding?" Richard cackled. "Where on earth would you hide it?" Then, seeing her stricken face and knowing how rude he had been, and how well she had meant, he tried again: "I just love the way you do your hair—" But that was no good either, and he stopped, midsentence.

Mrs. Erdman smiled in a vague and puzzled way. It was sad, and obvious that poor Richard was insane. And how difficult for poor Roger that must be.

Roger was beaming. His creased fat face literally shone with pleasure, which, for the sake of dignity, he struggled to contain. Having decided to marry, he found the idea of marriage very moving, and he was impressed by the rightness of his choice. People fall in love in very divergent ways; in Roger's way he was now in love with Karen, and he would love her more in years to come. He was even excited by the idea of children, big handsome Californian children, who were not eccentric. He stood near the middle of the enormous entrance hall, with Karen near his side, and beamed. He was prepared for nothing but good.

Then suddenly, from the midst of all that rich good will, from that air that was heavy with favorable omens, he heard the wild loud voice of his brother, close at hand. "Say, Roger, remember the night they put the swastika on our door?"

There was a lull in the surrounding conversations as that terrible word reverberated in the room. Then an expectant hum began to fill the vacuum. Feeling himself everywhere stared at, and hearing one nervous giggle, Roger attempted a jolly laugh. "You're crazy," he said. "You've been reading too many books. Karen, darling, isn't it time we went into the other room?"

It is perhaps to the credit of everyone's tact that Richard was then able to leave unobtrusively, as the front door opened to admit new guests.

And a month later, two months before the June wedding at Lake Tahoe, Richard had a severe heart attack and died at Mount Zion Hospital, with Ellen and Roger at his bedside.

They had been watching there at close intervals for almost the entire past week, and they were both miserably exhausted. Even their customary wariness in regard to each other had died, along with Richard.

"Come on, let me buy you some coffee," said Roger, fat and paternal. "You look bad."

"So do you," she said. "Exhausted. Thanks, I'd like some coffee."

He took her to a quiet bar in North Beach, near where she was then living, and they sat in a big recessed booth, in the dim late-afternoon light, and ordered espresso. "Or would you like a cappuccino?" Roger asked. "Something sweet?"

"No. Thanks. Espresso is fine."

The waiter went away.

"Well," said Roger.

"Well," echoed Ellen. "Of course it's not as though we hadn't known all along. What was going to happen."

The flat reasonableness of her tone surprised Roger. Ellen was never reasonable. So he looked at her with a little suspicion, but there was nothing visible on her white face but fatigue and sadness. The strain of her effort at reasonableness, at control, was not visible.

Roger said, "Yes. But I wonder if we really believed it. I mean Richard talked so much about dying that it was hard to believe he would."

The coffee came.

Stirring in sugar, regarding her cup, Ellen said, "People who talk about jumping under trains still sometimes do it. But I know what you mean. We somehow didn't behave as though he would die. Isn't that it?" She lifted her very gray eyes to his blinking pale blue.

He took the sugar, poured and stirred. "Yes, but I wonder what different we would have done."

In her same flat sensible tone Ellen said, "I sometimes wouldn't see him when he wanted to. I would be tired or just not up to it, or sometimes seeing someone else. Even if the other person was a boring nothing." She looked curiously at Roger.

But he had only heard the literal surface of what she had said, to which he responded with a little flicker of excitement. "Exactly!" he said. "He was hurt and complained when I went to boring dinners or saw business friends instead of him, but I had to do that. Sometimes for my own protection."

"Yes," said Ellen, still very calm but again with an oblique, upward look at Roger, which he missed.

"People grow up and they change." Roger sighed. "I could hardly remember all that time at Harvard and he always wanted to talk about it."

"Of course not," she said, staring at him and holding her hands tightly together in her lap, as though they contained her mind.

Roger was aware that he was acting out of character; normally he loathed these intimate, self-revelatory conversations. But he was extremely tired and, as he afterward told himself, he was understandably upset; it is not every day that one's only brother dies. Also, as he was vaguely aware, some quality in Ellen, some quality of her listening, drove him on. Her flat silence made a vacuum that he was compelled to fill.

"And remember that time a couple of years ago when I wanted to borrow the money?" Roger said. "He was so upset that I offered him interest. Of course I'd offer him interest. Otherwise it wouldn't have been fair."

"Of course not," said Ellen, looking deeply into his eyes. "Everyone has to pay interest," she reasonably said.

"It was the least I could do," Roger said. "To be fair to him. And I couldn't spend the rest of my life thinking and talking about how things were almost twenty years ago."

"Of course not," Ellen said again, and soon after that he took her home and they parted—friends.

But in the middle of that night Roger's phone rang, beside his wide bachelor bed, and it was Ellen.

"Pig pig pig pig pig pig pig pig pig!" she screamed. "Horrible fat ugly murdering pig, you killed him with your never time to see him and your wall of fat German business friends always around you and your everything for a purpose and your filthy pig-minded greed and your all-American pig success and your so socially acceptable ambitions. Richard was all Greek to you and you never tried to learn him, how lovely he was and suffering and you found him not socially acceptable to your society and your new pig friends and I would even rather be thin and miserable and ugly me than fat you with your blubber neck and your compound interest and you couldn't believe his heart and now you can get filthy blubber fatter on his money—"

She seemed to have run down, and into the pause Roger asked, "Ellen, do you need money? I'd be more than happy—"

She screamed, but it was less a scream than a sound of total despair, from an absolute aloneness.

Then she hung up, and a few weeks later Roger heard that she had had a complete breakdown and was hospitalized, perhaps for good.

After the excellent dinner of moussaka, salad and strawberries in cream, Karen and Roger settled in the living room with strong coffee and snifters of brandy. It was an attractive, comfortable, if somewhat disheveled room, very much a family room. Karen's tastes were simpler than those of her parents. Her furnishings were contemporary; the fabrics were sturdy wools or linen; the broad sofa was done in dark-brown leather.

Roger leaned back; he blinked and then sighed, looking up to the ceiling. Karen could tell that he was going to say something about Richard.

"I sometimes wish," said Roger, "that I'd taken the time somewhere along the line to have learned a little Greek. It seemed to give Richard so much pleasure."

"But, darling, when would you ever have had the time?"

"That's just it, I never had the time." Roger's tone when talking about or in any way alluding to his brother was one of a softly sentimental regret; Karen gathered that he regretted both his brother's death and their lack of rapport in those final years.

Roger also sounded sentimentally regretful when he referred to anything cultural—those soft pleasures which he valued but for which he had never had time.

"I wonder what's ever happened to that girl. Ellen," said Karen.

"I'm not sure I'd even want to know," said Roger. "Did I ever tell you that she called me the night he died?"

"Really? No."

"Yes, she was quite hysterical. I think she was angry because she knew I was Richard's heir." By now Roger had come to believe that this was indeed the case. He was convinced that other people's motives were basically identical to his own. "Yes," he said. "She probably thought I should give her some of his money."

In the large safe room, beneath other large rooms where her sons were all sleeping, Karen shuddered, and together she and Roger sighed, for Richard's pain and death and for poor lost Ellen's madness.

"Here," said Karen, "have more coffee. Poor darling, you look as though you need it."

"You're right. I do." And Roger reached out to stroke his big wife's smooth dark cheek.

# M. F. BEAL

# Gold

## Where, When, What:

I've been here almost two months now. I've been staying most of the time, all but the warmest nights, with friends: Evelyn and Peter. Friends, but not old friends; they're far far away, some dead, even. Some might not realize I count them that. I'm hoping to see Ruth. I came here in the first place looking for Ruth. It doesn't make me proud to say that; but it's true. I had been looking for her up and down the coast when I heard she was here, too, on the opposite hillside. So I stayed.

Settling down like this has set me to thinking for the first time about why I—we—all left the city. It's almost as if a whole generation has seen itself unable to cope, or as if there has been some sort of pestilence to which certain people are hideously sensitive. That's how it must seem, at any rate, to those deserted. For me it was a simple decision: one night returning from work I realized if I opened the door to my apartment I would be there till I died; so I spent the night with a friend, thinking of how I had, now, to abandon the city and look for Ruth. Or perhaps the search for Ruth was a motive I attached to my decision to justify it.

18

Her name comes up, of course, fairly often, although generally people on this side of the valley do not visit with and are not overly concerned with the people on the other side of the valley. A curious business. Is it jealousy? It really doesn't seem so. Call it preoccupation with the everyday; life itself is the big preoccupation here—except, of course, for gold. Gold. Continual talk of gold.

But though I am so little interested in that part of this life, everyone is very polite. No one pays too much attention to me; or rather, just enough. The attention, when it comes, is practical, relating to the business of the valley (life): Evelyn dispenses it mainly, and indirectly, like this: "Did you notice?" she asks, or "Have you ever tried? . . ." Of course it's perfectly reasonable to presume I'm here for salvation—all the rest are.

Ruth and the Mountain:

I've been trying, today, to remember the hike I took up the mountain the first week here. I have a bad memory. I believe I wanted to orient myself; but I may have been feeling bored, and trapped—isn't that really more likely? It was still May. The nights were cold. I had quite a lot of equipment I'd brought with me in a leather satchel I got in a secondhand store down the street from where I lived the day I decided to start looking for Ruth; a Gladstone bag, the proprietor called it. The evening before my hike up the mountain I went from shack to cabin to shelter and begged a packboard, a hand axe, a canteen; Evelyn gave me rice, my sneakers would do, Peter lent me a sweater to wear under my shirt, so I wouldn't have to lug my jacket along. I also had a bail-handled pot, remnant from a boy scout kit; ditto spoon, extra socks, tea, matches, a geologist's pick, several small bags for collecting specimens of rock and plants, a magnifying glass, a handbook of minerals and one of birds, cigarettes, a blanket roll. What else?

It was a fine day but I got a late start. The mountain was very impressive, bleak with sunlight. Our two hillsides fingering down from her and the rope of water most think is responsible for the gold stood clearly on her flank like children against their mother. But this mother was no insipid aproned lady; rather a sturdy black woman, basalt heaped from her brow, scoria trailing dark hair streaks in a perfect forty-five-degree cape. Only where our creek cut was orange limonite exposed like a tear. A track led to her top.

## A Snapshot:

I could not help but think that in other days there would have been a snapshot of me, standing by the last trees, sunlight splashed on the gray dust. It would have shown me in Levis, slender, looking not at the camera but into the branches above. The only thing I cannot see as I develop this snapshot in my mind is the expression my face would wear.

## Now the Mountain Herself:

Suddenly the mountain loomed enormous. Where water cut rock the newly exposed basalt was like gashes in her flesh. Viewed afar, from the hillside, she was after one week already familiar; but now as I loomed on her she loomed back. There was a quality in the air like lemon—thin, sharp. It had been only minutes since I decided not to pack the canteen's two pounds of water; but now it had receded in my awareness as if I were some Eocene horse with his three toes who had decided not to wear a man's saddle on his back. I was dislodged, unbraced, over-mounted.

## A Lava Flow to Negotiate:

I knew man had been here before me by the brightness of the track. But the black lava flow, dodging from the mountain's broken top, left behind a blanket twenty, thirty feet thick, a blanket to bury the sandals of an Indian out away from his camp hunting elk. I sat to smoke and imagine what I would have done in his place.

## Some Sort of Rabbit:

As I sat virtually immobile, my cigarette just inches from my face and setting free fine veils of smoke, I saw dots of movement, points, shifts of light in the ropy black rock. At first I thought it was some peculiarity of the rough-surfaced lava flow; but then I realized it was a number of small animals, many of them shifting and moving in their burrows and runs as my presence faded from their memories. Or had they been moving right along, simply counting on me not to notice them in my preoccupation with being myself? The lava face was shimmering with them, finally, going about their business of living in the crisp, decaying rock. There was an occasional tiny piping, and once a landslide of such delicate proportions it could not have consisted of more than three or four grains of cinder. The longer I watched, the more clearly I could see these little animals: their large bright eyes; a habit of squatting briefly on hind legs every few steps; even visits from one to another and small courtesies of the path—nose-touching, touching of feet, squeaking. Suddenly it became embarrassing, almost frightening to eavesdrop and I stood, sending them instantly to ground.

A Banging:

I was now aware of all sorts of life signs as I continued. The path wound at the lava flowside for a bit, the dust pocked with footprints of birds, of the tiny animals; then it climbed steeply in a series of rough steps, finally coming out on a plateau. From this height I hoped to have my first sensation of having covered ground.

The trees, unfortunately, hid the valley below with its hillsides, and the stream which cut the valley was hidden too. It seemed I would have to cut back around the flank of the mountain to be above the valley again. So I was pleased when the track turned not much farther on and headed to a fair-sized clump of wizened alpine fir.

Then, as I reached the firs, I heard a banging. The wind was fresher the higher I climbed, and sound traveled more distinctly in the clear air, so as I walked the rustle and clatter of tree limbs far below drafted to me. But the banging was definitely extraordinary.

Not much farther I discovered the cabin. It was more of a shed, really, the tiniest house I had ever seen, and weathered deep-gray like rock. It stood in a level spot almost in the center of the trail; on all sides the ground sloped, which made it seem that someone's hand had flattened the spot. The door was open, banging; it was such a startling sound I had to go shut it immediately.

Inside was a bed, almost full-size, *made up with sheets and blankets*. Yet, where the sheets had been turned down were brown sausages of pack-rat droppings. There was a rocker, badly weathered, the back repaired with strips of rawhide, one rocker resting in a clutter of old clothing which seemed to have been dropped in flight, then rained on, then dried again and again to a stiff bas-relief. On a small oil-drum stove was a coffeepot. A table held a single cup with tacky rime of coffee residue, and (by far the neatest, most considered item of all) a white handkerchief heaped with nuggets of a metallic mineral. Now I say, "a metallic mineral," but actually it was clear to me it was a pile of gold nuggets. And yet it couldn't be a pile of gold, for that defied logic; who would leave gold like that? So it became immediately in my mind "a metallic mineral," probably iron pyrites: "fool's gold."

I sat in the chair, before the empty, dirty cup and the neat pile of nuggets, as if that would make of me somehow the anchorite who had lived in this shack, and tried to imagine why he had left, abandoned his retreat. What had he seen, what thought had driven him from his haven?

A heavy depression came over me. I shut the door firmly, and put my face to the trail.

### I Think I Took Water from the Spring Nearby:

Or I may have gotten it as I crossed the stream somewhat farther on. I was preoccupied the whole time thinking of the apartment that first Ruth and then I had abandoned, leaving, I remember, some of my clothes, letters (not Ruth's—those I gave her late one night), books, records; everything whose ideas had been outgrown and, just as important, for which there wasn't room in the back of the car. These thoughts had the effect of deadening me to the passage of time and the weight of the pack and it was not too long before I came to the rock fault.

### A Big Smile:

I came suddenly on the crack, first narrow but opening over the next hundred feet surprisingly fast, as if the mountain were a vast chocolate pudding which had dried and split. The gash, with its delicate edges—tiny replicas of the larger split—was deep as well, perhaps twenty feet as it opened out. It lay along the mountainside like a big smile, bisected by the stream which must have teased it forth, and from which came the water the people below thought was the catalyst for the formation of gold. . . .

Still, I'm remembering this—I'm sure at the time I didn't think it all. I wanted to get to the top. It had become a passion, and I had an hour's walking to go. I dropped my pack, setting it beside the mountain's smile. Immediately I felt a foot taller and as if my stride were a yard long. Even the ache in my calves diminished. The tuff slid as I dug my toes into it, but still I made good progress; and before I thought it possible, I was within a few feet of the basalt nipple of the mountain peak. Then, like a gift, I found the track again, winding with footholds to the very summit. There, with the heavy blasting wind of early evening on my back, I stood in the fading sun and surveyed what I had done.

Where:

For the first time I could see the valley and the hillsides. The distortion of distance and the shadow which had overtaken them already leached all color from the tiny cabins; there were a few dots I thought might be people, but unlike the conies on the lava flow, concentration didn't bring them into clearer focus. Again I felt the depression of eavesdropping, of seeing aimless patterns in what must be to the people purposeful actions. I forced myself to watch, however, until the notion of patterns separated from the rest of my perceptions as tangerine skin does from the pulp, and the dots that were people came to represent something akin to points of electricity, energy. This perception gave me pleasure, a feeling of inward smiling. I could feel it travel through my organs as a tightening and warming, until my extremities tingled pleasantly. I was not able to refine my perceptions further.

So I turned on my heels and enjoyed the sensation of being clearly higher than anyone or anything for miles and miles. To the east, I saw flat plains and yellow desert; to the west, snow-tendriled peaks, lower than mine, shadowed. The sun, setting into the sheeted ocean, was pure gold.

Below, the gash in the mountainside was a definite smile —deep, black-toothed. The creek which split it moved with white leapings and a foamy urgency from an unprepossessing lens of snow that I realized must be deeper than it seemed. Then farther down, the beard of trees, with a cheek-patch to the side that entirely hid the cabin; and far, far below, the valley, the hillsides where the people, where Ruth was. Overall, a monumental sighing of the wind, blasting at the mountain's bald summit-nipple. I shivered. I started down.

When:

That was in May. I have described it at length, because
now it seems to have been responsible for all that has
followed—it must be what is responsible. But it is a mystery and you must interpret; I know no more about it than
I've just told. When I point to the smiling gash of the fault
and ask a friend what he thinks of *that*, he smiles and turns
away, as if I am still, unfortunately, too preoccupied with
appearances.

This Is Really a Diary:

But even a diary is selective: in the interval between the
event and the transcription of it the mind closes itself to
much. I could write as if I had rushed from each event to
these pages, and then you might *feel* the immediacy; but it
would be no more honest than to allow you a sensation of
interval. So that is what I have done. Now here is something that happened today: one of the women who has
been on the other hillside quite awhile without success, but
who has followed the diet, meditated, etc., thought she
passed some gold. By the time the story got to our hillside,
she was said to have passed a nugget. Evelyn and Peter
came up to tell me. I was working on my shelter, having
gotten together, somehow, enough tools all at one time to
nail up a few boards. But they were so excited (neither has
passed any crystals yet) it was really unthinkable to continue pounding, so we talked the afternoon out. Very little
gold has been passed on our hillside—why, no one knows.
A few theories:

  The average age of the people over here is higher; we are
    more uptight and can't release body-energy in pure form;
    some of us take too mechanical an attitude toward the
    formation of gold.
  The chemical balance of the herbs, etc., which are con-
    sidered vital to production of gold, is not the same as on
    the other hillside.
  The chemical balance of the water is different.
  We get more sunlight than they do.
  Etc., etc.

I was also told to use the correct terminology: the crystals
are called *calculi*; they are small regular crystals of gold,
sometimes occurring with traces of chemically bonded
minerals. I can understand the importance of correct ter-

minology: because of the nature of what is occurring here, it is necessary to have a rational approach to the dissemination of information about it, especially with outsiders.

Late in the afternoon a messenger came over to say it had been a false alarm. The woman had not passed a gold calculus, but rather a common ammonium one.

Thinking of the woman on the other hillside made me wonder about Ruth. Among the things I ask myself often: is she living with someone? (Sometimes this is so painful a thought I can only hold it in my head for a moment at a time. Sometimes it doesn't bother me at all.) Does she think of me? Is she happy? (Also sometimes a painful thought.) As the messenger spoke of the woman's failure to produce a gold calculus I wanted to ask him whether the woman's name was Ruth. But I couldn't. Yet I immediately decided it was Ruth, and I thought of her trying, failing to pass a gold calculus. I was sorry for her pain, but I was happy she had failed; I must admit that. I was happy. That quality about Ruth, her solidness around some center of self-understanding, or if you will, self-acceptance, was always so painful to me, such a reproach. When I was most miserably unsure, she closed around her center like a clam. It served her right that she had failed, for once.

Gold!

Now here is what happened, what it is like to pass a calculus of gold. On the night described above, tired, sick with loneliness, I decided to fast for a week. Evelyn gathered a bitter weed she calls *pooha* and I ate it; it cleaned my system. The following day I did little but sit in the sun, defecate, try not to think about food. I could feel my body drying, the tissues squeezing from them the excess fluids and poisons of my life. I drank, all day, two cupfuls of water from the creek.

The next day I still thought of food, but it was a vague concern. I felt weak, and when I came out of the sun, chill. My body shook with chill at night; but, strangely, I slept deeply between the waking moments, and had no bad dreams.

Toward evening of the third day, I felt my hunger drop from me like a weight and my head became so clear it was painful. I was able to concentrate fully on parts of my life that have shamed me most: on my time with Ruth, and the

things she and I did to each other, on my fear of my mother
and father, my fear of becoming a father. I found also
that if I turned toward the mountain and looked uphill, I
got again the inward smiling sensation I had had that day
on her top. As if she was trying—ridiculous as it looks on
paper—to tell me something. Some linkage, some congru-
ence of mountain/humans whose meaning would fall open
like a Chinese puzzle at the right touch—but I could only
look and enjoy the tingling warmth on my limbs, focusing
my thoughts occasionally on the colony of conies I had
seen and thinking how I related to them as the mountain to
us. This clarity lasted almost an hour. Afterward, I fell
asleep in the sun and slept for a long time, waking only
after sunset with a racking chill. Fortunately Evelyn and
Peter came up to check on me, and immediately dressed
me in all my clothing. Peter brought up some extra blankets and sat with me until I slept. I remember fragments of
what he said: He was depressed about his inability to pass
a calculus, even a common one. I tried to reassure him, to
tell him how much I admired his relationship with Evelyn,
and how solid he seemed to me. This time, in my fever and
the clarity given me by the fasting, I was able to admire
without also hating; and I told him as final reassurance
something which leapt to my head, and which I suddenly
realized my father used to say to me: *To him who hath, it
shall be given . . . and from him who hath not, it shall be
taken away.*

The fourth day I slept.

The fifth day I felt great energy and walked to the
stream, where I washed myself with the fine black sand
that bedded the shallows and rinsed myself over and over
with the icy water. Then I sat shielded by a shadberry
bush and let the sun dry me. I found myself remembering
the neatly heaped pile of gold (it seemed clearly that, now)
I had seen in the cabin on the mountain. Why had I not
taken it? Because it belonged to *him*. But then why had he
abandoned it?

The morning of the sixth day I woke in pain, cramps in
my abdomen so severe I could not stretch out. Evelyn
rubbed my back, which helped for a while; but then the
pain became so deep and cutting that I couldn't stand to be
touched. I tried not to cry out; but the pervasive cramps
made me moan and I begged a hand to hold. There were
many hands; there were many visitors. Evelyn bathed my

face with cloths wrung out of water from the stream. At night a fire was built and the waiting continued. Finally the pain assumed a pulse; bad moments but then better ones during which I caught my breath. During the bad times I cried out freely, and the better times were such a relief that tears came to my eyes. At the end, Peter helped me to stand and we moved to the outer circle of firelight. There the calculus tore my body and passed out.

I slept.

When I woke I had a porridge, a thick gruel of some kind, and slept again.

To be without pain, to be able to sleep, is like divinity.

The Responsibility of Producing a Calculus:

Some of the people who have been here a long time produce calculi once a week, or a series of calculi over a period of hours every month or so. This is why, of course, it is possible for all of us to devote ourselves to the production of calculi; the gold is exchanged for what we need, and while there isn't an abundance there is enough for everyone to be comfortable. Peter also told me I can get money to visit the city, if I want to. He pointed out with considerable pride that while the colony has been in existence for almost fifteen (!) years, no one has had to work out for wages for almost ten. This is not true of other colonies which you may have heard about.

On the other hand, even a regular producer of calculi can undergo a change which stops the process. Everyone seems to believe the deposition begins with a "seed," perhaps a particle of silt. Some claim more calculi are produced in the rainy season, when the stream is slightly cloudy. Some even eat small quantities of silt from the limonite clay bank exposed by the stream. No one knows anything definite about the rest of the process. It may be the water which acts as a catalyst, or something in the *pooha* herb we all eat; it may be the rice, the fasting, the meditation. There are a few who refuse to discuss the process at all, saying it is mystical and not to be plumbed at risk of unbalancing the active forces.

One final point of agreement is that the crystallization process takes a while to get going; all the calculi so far have been regular crystals ranging in size from barely visible to an inch across. This tends to place a value on patience, and in fact the regular producers have all been here many months, if not years. If you lack patience, you move on, for it is an ascetic life; perhaps this, too, has something to do with producing.

## So It's Clear I Am an Initiate:

Today people visited me as if I were some kind of display. Many of them—other initiates—take my hand and grasp it lingeringly to tell me something they cannot put into words, looking me in the eyes, almost kissing me. Once or twice this has given me a chill, as if they know something about this business of producing calculi I don't yet know; they are so deeply into this gold thing—more, much more, than I am. It is almost as if they realize we are all only vessels. One of the men (young, though with broad streaks of gray at his temples and fingered into his beard) drew me schemata of the arrangement of atoms within a calculus. It is a crystalline conglomerate, not a pure crystal (in which the pattern of atoms is repeated without variation), nor amorphous (with no regularity of pattern), but something between: small clusters of crystals oriented in different ways. I was taken by his fluency in describing the phenomenon. This was certainly virtually all there was to know in terms of description. But what of all that lay beyond the naming? What of the why or how? When I framed my observations I got a quick, sharp, almost cautionary look back. So I turned to watching his mouth as he talked, the upper teeth hitting his lower lip and at the junction, beads of opaque spittle, almost a foam, springing up, stretching with the next mouth movement, breaking as if he were a fevered dog, a froth of fever working its way into the corner of the mouth before it was licked away.

But most who come to see me wear a face of fatigued gentleness.

## Ruth: At Last.

I was sitting on the stoop in front of my half-completed shelter and my eyes were drawn by the form of a woman, heavy-bellied, slow, moving herself and her unborn child up the hill to visit me. Her legs beneath the hem of her dress were slender and she held her arms around her stomach as if trying to carry her load in a more wonted fashion. Her brown hair swept from side to side like the pendulum of a clock. I recognized her immediately: Ruth.

In the instant of recognition I was horrified to think my desire for her might flood back, but lowering myself into consideration of my state of mind, I found instead a clean emptiness. (By the time I knew this she had greeted me.) We sat side by side on the stoop like acquaintances on a park bench; I couldn't see her eyes.

"I'm living on the other hillside with John," she announced. She leaned back against the shelter frame when I said nothing and with the set of her shoulders added: *this thing I am doing now is not conditional.*

Conditional. I understood a great deal suddenly about her and me: and how our being together was never anything but conditional. Then she turned her face to me and her eyes said: *I am no longer an object.*

I said with my arms opening and resting on my thighs: *do you remember the warmth of my body, my presentness?*

"You can see a lot here we can't see on the other hillside," she said. "You can see up the mountain where the stream begins; the hill hides that from us."

"There is a fault up there, where the stream comes out of the ice-pack."

"A fault?" But she had already said what she came to say and did not want to learn anything; she turned her head aside.

"What sort of person is John?"

She hesitated a long time—about a month, I guess, or at least a season of the mind, something like passing from spring into summer. "I have passed calculi. I am pregnant. I am happy."

I had to laugh. "You don't sound very happy."

"Well, I am. It's hard to explain, but I think more deeply about these things now. I don't just answer the first thing that enters my head."

This made me very sad. I sat looking up to the gashed smile at the mountaintop, at the black and wrinkled lips of the old lady with her basalt brow.

We talked for a long time, but that is all we said; and when the sun tilted over the old lady's head, Ruth went back to her man.

Pilgrim's Progress:

I awoke desperate to read. There wasn't so much as a book at Peter and Evelyn's, but they said there might be some down in the valley. I went from cabin to cabin: nothing. Finally, hard by the stream I saw a young man— really a child—whose face I knew, and introduced myself; and he took me to his shelter (which in its simplicity and starkness reminded me so much of my own, yet seemed so poor it almost made me cry) and on a shelf, next to his shaving mirror and razor, was *Pilgrim's Progress*.

"I got that because it has such far-out pictures in it, and here, look at this—" He took down a small reproduction of a painting by Gauguin that stood tilted against the wall behind his razor: *Jacob Wrestles with the Angel or Vision After the Sermon*. We stood and looked at it. The left side of the canvas held a curve of Breton peasant women, their white headcloths and dark dresses like the uniforms of a religious order, their superstitious faces open in wonder, while on the right Jacob wrestled with the Angel. The Angel's wings were strong, sweeping over Jacob, whose arms, inferior wings, knotted in the effort of fending off God's Angel. There wasn't even a suggestion that Jacob would win.

I took *Pilgrim's Progress* and headed back to my shelter thinking about the boy who had somewhere found this book and the Gauguin print. Just old enough to have been born in the valley, he was one of the few children there. Like them, he couldn't read. I had never been bothered by this: what need, really, was there for reading? But now it distressed me. How would it be possible to understand what happened, knowing less than man did already? As I read, Peter and Evelyn's three dogs came sniffing uphill to see what I was doing and sat down with me. I saw them as distinctly, then, as I would humans: Sam (for Samuel Gompers), Emmett (for Emmett Till), and the puppy, Ché. Sam, oldest of the three, thrust his nose in my hand and moved along under its weight, humping his back and groaning to me to scratch the thick fur of his rump, beating his tail against my leg when I stopped, squinting his eyes shut and panting when I scratched. Ché tumbled whining, clicking his milk teeth together, stump tail furiously beating the stones; Sam snapped, Ché fell back abashed; Emmett set to licking himself noisily, tonguing the bald gloves of his testicles, sniffing, inspecting, scratching, yawning. In the city, I had had a dog who smelled sour, strong; these dogs, with their diet of brown rice and *pooha*, smell like a child's stuffed toy. As I saw them in this manner, so vividly, it seemed for a long moment that they were wise in some inscrutable way, that they were teachers. And that was delightful, but frightening, too, because it seemed to tell me about myself. Was I mad? Or had I stumbled on some perfectly reasonable awareness? The word *conditional* leapt to the front of my thoughts; these animals seemed anything but conditional, so firmly were they tied to everything around them. They were dependent and yet independent, accepting the warmth of the sun and my hand as if sun and hand were equal in some equation.

But a Man Is Not a Dog:

I am unable to avoid setting down how Peter died. Quite a while ago he confided to me he was distressed because he had had pain but had not passed a calculus. I should have seen what having been here over a year without producing a calculus was doing to his head. Somehow he decided he could vomit these calculi he believed had formed; so he got hold of some ipecac. Apparently he took the whole bottleful. He began vomiting early yesterday; at sunset when he hadn't stopped, though there was no longer anything to vomit up, Evelyn came and got me. I hadn't even known what he was going to do. He was very weak, but peaceful —so convinced of the rightness of what he was doing that I hesitated to interfere. So Evelyn and I sat with him, helping him when the nausea overcame him, bringing him water to moisten his mouth. The moon had canted down when we first noticed the blood. Less than an hour later he was hemorrhaging, waves of blood that spattered us, the walls, the bed, and he died soon after. Now it seems selfish somehow in the face of his death to have any feelings of my own about it: as if that represented a kind of annexation of his essence to my own. And yet all I could think to do when his body had lost all tone and began to take to itself that freight of dust all dead things—deer, dogs, fish— take up at the end; all I could think to do was to stand in the dark and scream at the valley and its safe fires: *Why doesn't anyone think about these things?*

And then later, the following correlations erected themselves in my head. I do not yet understand their significance, if any:

(A reduction formula)
GOLD = DISCIPLINED ASCETICISM (INWARD SHAPING)
↕
FREE CONTACT WITH COSMIC CHAOS (UNDERSTANDING
ESSENTIAL CREATIVE/CHAOTIC CONFIGURATIONS) = GOLD?
(An expansion formula)

The Mountain Again:

It had been raining. Ruth, fulfilled, is on the opposite hillside, an abyss away. Peter is dead. The summer is gone. I am staying with Evelyn now. We live, we pass calculi of gold, we chink our shelters against the winter winds. The dogs, Sam, Emmett, and Ché, sniff the cooking pot after it has been licked clean, dreaming on the odors which reside in the metal, promising new sustenance. The stream is silted, rich. Ruth will bring her new baby and John to my shelter in the depth of the dozy winter; we will talk. I will be even more alone. I am trapped; trapped to pain and the gold calculi. Everything is very easy. I have been thinking again about the pile of gold in the abandoned cabin. Why did he abandon it? *He*, I say, coming to know him through his act. Because he understood it was a beginning, not an end? Do I really believe that? Gold—a beginning?

Or is it simply that he looked up at that enormous smile gashed into the mountain, and at the boulder-landslide premonitions which dribble from her lips moment by moment, now that the autumn rains are here?

In the book I borrowed from the child of this valley it is written:

## FLY FROM THE WRATH TO COME

# GINA BERRIAULT

# Nights in the Gardens of Spain

The boy beside him was full of gin and beer and wine and of the figure he had cut at the party as the great guitarist at seventeen, and he had no idea where he was until he was told to get out. His profile with that heavy chin that he liked to remind everybody was Hapsburg hung open-mouthed against the blowing fog and the cold jet-black ocean of night.

Berger had no intention of forcing him out, but to command him to get out was the next best way of impressing his disgust on his passenger. "I asked you when you got in, friend, if you had twenty-five cents for the bridge toll and you haven't answered me yet. You want to get over this bridge tonight and into your little trundle bed you look for two bits because I'm sick of paying your way wherever we go and getting kicked in the face for a thank you. What the hell did I hear you say to Van Grundy? That you got bored by musicians because all they could talk about was music?" His breath smelled of cheese and garlic from all the mounds of crackers and spread he had eaten, not the kind of breath to accuse anybody with. "And that meant me, of course, because I'm what's known as your constant companion, that meant old ignoramus Berger. For a guy who's got all the famous relatives you're always bragging about—

big dam builders, big mummy diggers, big marine commandants—you ought to be able to come up with a miserable nickel once in a while." He held out his hand for the coins that David was searching for and found.

"What the hell." David gripped his guitar between his knees again, settling back uncomfortably. "You sore because they wanted *me* to play?"

He shifted into low to start the car again. "You don't know what anybody wants, you're too busy playing all night."

The boy waited a minute then sprang the big psychological question with a rare timidity in his voice: "You sore because it's me that's going to play for Torres tomorrow?"

"Jaysus Christ, I'm sittin' next to Freud here!" he cried, disgusted.

They went on in silence over the long bridge. The deputy at the toll gate reached out his hand to take the coins that Berger pressed into it with his gray-gloved fingers, suede driving gloves to keep his hands warm so that he could commence to play soon after entering a room, but David wore no gloves, came with cold, thin hands into a room and played slickly, charmingly, his first number and afterward blew on his fingers to impress upon the audience how cold they were still and how much they had accomplished even so.

Along under the neons of the motels, assured by the rainbow lights and the traffic signals that the time had passed for his abandonment on the bridge, the boy spoke again. "Listen, nobody's destroying you but yourself," his voice empty of experience.

Berger gave a whooping laugh. "Listen yourself. I ain't the one who's destroying himself, you worry about yourself. Someday you're going to explode, a hundred different colors and a sonic boom. Big little David, folks will say for miles around, got too big for himself. God, you slaughtered that Purcell. If you play that for old Torres he'll ask for a change of rooms after you're gone." He unloaded now all the complaints accumulated against the boy—criticism of his teacher-companion that David had made to friends: *Berger could be the best, good as Thomas Torres, but he doesn't look the part, hasn't got the urbanity, short you know, big shoulders, like a wrestler's that don't fit him, big face, and the way he telegraphs his mistakes to you before he makes them, like "this hurts me worse than you, dear*

*audience." But the best, really the best, could have been
the best, but came to it too late, a jazz musician until he
was thirty, still got the mannerisms of a jazzman in a
nightclub, smiling at the audience, smiling at himself. You
can't do that with a classic guitar. He's good all right but
he should have come to it at eighteen, twenty, then he
would have been great.* "Things come back to me!" Berger
was shouting. "For a man of few friends, like you say I
am, they come back to me!"

He drew the car to the curb, leaned across the boy to
open the door. "Get out here, man. From here it's just a
mile to your mother's place. I'd take you there but it's a
mile out of my way."

Under the green-blue motel neon, David stepped out to
the sidewalk, knocking his guitar case against door and
curb and hydrant.

"You're doing it to yourself," said David again, warn-
ingly.

"You keep knocking that guitar around like a dumb
bastard with a normal IQ!" he bellowed, slamming the
door.

He went through the amber lights of intersections as if
they were red and he was drunk. Somebody else on the
verge of fame, somebody else awaiting the encircling arm
of the already great sent him, Berger, over the edge, down
into the abyss of his own life. It was not fame he wanted
for himself, he would never have it now, anyway, at thirty-
seven, with all the faults that David had so meticulously
listed for everybody. Not that, but what? The mastery, the
mastery, play without telegraphing the errors, play without
the errors, play with the mastery of the great yet indifferent
to fame if it came. Palermo was nothing, that mecca of all
the world's guitar students where Torres, old Torres of the
worldly jowls, laid his arm across the jaggedy, humped
young shoulders of the most promising. The photos of the
students in the guitar magazines made him laugh. They
came from everywhere to study under Torres at the *ac-
cademia,* they stood around the silk-jacketed Tommy like
fool disciples: a middle-aged woman with a Russian name;
a young curly-locks guy from Brazil, making hot amorous
eyes at the camera; a stiff-elbowed kid from England who
looked as if he stuttered; and the girls with their big naïve
eyes and their skirts full to make it easier to part their legs
for the correct position of the guitar. He saw them gather-

ing in the hallways of some musty building in Palermo
after school, saw them descend the street into the town
with the stiff-swinging walk of youth attempting youth, and
he had no desire to be among them, to be twenty again and
among them. The older he got the less he wished for a new
beginning and the more he wished for a happy ending. But
sometimes, as in these last few weeks, the wish for that
beginning laid him low again like a childhood disease.

Before his apartment house he let the car door swing
heavily open and lifted his guitar case from the back seat.
The slam of the door reminded him that there was something else in the car that ought to be brought in, but unable
to recall what it was he concluded that it was nothing
stealable and went up the stairs in his neat, black, Italian-
style moccasins, wishing that he were lurching and banging
against walls. Not since he fell down somebody's stairs six
years ago, cracking a vertebra and breaking his guitar in its
case, had he taken a drink, not even wine, and he had
taken none tonight though everybody was awash around
him, but he felt now that drunkenness again, that old exaltation of misery. Sick of black coffee after a dozen cups
through the night, he found a cupful in a saucepan, heated
it to boiling, poured it into a dime-store pale green mug
and willfully drank, scalding the roof of his mouth. He
opened his mouth over the sink and let the black coffee
trickle from the corners, too shocked to expel it with force,
bleating inside: *To hell with all the Great, the Near Great,
the Would-be Great, to hell with all the Failures.*

From the windowsill he took his bottle of sleeping pills,
put two on his tongue, drank down half a glass of water.
He dropped his tie on the kitchen table, his jacket on the
sofa, stepped out of his moccasins in the middle of the
living room. He put on his tan silk pajamas (Who you
fooling with this show of opulence?) and crawled into his
unmade bed. At noon he was wakened by a street noise
and drew the covers over his ear to sleep until evening, until
the boy's interview with the Great Tommy was over.

At four, moving through the apartment in his bare feet,
in his wrinkled pajamas, he tore up the memory of himself
that early morning as he had once, alone again, torn up a
snapshot of himself that someone had thrust upon him: a
man with a heavy face in the sun, hair too long and slick, a
short body and feet small as a dandy's. For with no remind-
ers he was the person he fancied himself. But, dumping

coffee grounds into the sink, he realized suddenly that the
jawing he had given the boy had been given as a memento
of himself, something for the boy to carry around with him
in Palermo, something to make him feel closer to Berger
than to anybody else, because Berger was the man who
had told him off, a jawing to make him love and hate
Berger and never forget him because it is impossible to
forget a person who is wise to you. If the boy never got to
first base as a guitarist then the jawing lost its significance,
the triumph was denied to Berger. It was on David's fame
that he, Berger, wanted to weigh himself. *Jaysus,* he wailed,
*what kind of celebrity chasing is that?* He smelled of
cheese and bed and failure, sitting at the table with his
head in his hands. The interview was over an hour ago and
now he would hear from friends the words of praise, the
quotations from Torres, as if these friends of David had
been there themselves to hear the words drop like jewels
from his lips, all of them closer to God because they were
friends of him who sat up there in God's hotel room,
playing music to enchant God's ears.

So he stayed away from his friends, who were also David's friends; for almost two weeks he eluded any knowledge
of that interview. He gave lessons to his students in his
own apartment or in their homes and in this time it was as
if he were seventeen again, living again that period of
himself, and sometimes during the lessons his hands or his
voice shook with shyness. He felt as if he were instructing
them without having learned anything himself first, and he
hated his students for exacting more of him than he was
capable of giving. Once again he was in that age of terrible
self-derision and of great expectations: Somebody great
would recognize him and would prove, once and for all to
himself and to everybody, his nobility. After every lesson
his armpits were sticky and he would have trouble in civilly
saying good-bye.

On the evening of the twelfth day he drove across the
bridge to visit the Van Grundys. They were still at supper,
Van and his wife and the two kids, eating a kind of crusty
lemon dessert, and they made a place for him to pull up a
chair. He had coffee and dessert with them and joked with
the boy and the girl, finding a lift in the children's slapstick
humor, the upside-down, inside-out humor, and in the
midst of it he turned his face to Van Grundy at his left, the
smile of his repartee with the children still on his lips, the

hot coffee wet on his lips, his spoon, full of lemon dessert, waiting on the rim of his bowl—all these small things granting him the semblance of a man at ease with himself —and asked, "Well, did Torres flip over our Davy?"

"You don't know?" Van Grundy replied. "He told everybody as fast as if it were good news," raising his voice above his children's voices demanding the guest's attention again. "Torres kept interrupting. Every damn piece Davy played, Torres didn't like the way he played it. What's the matter you haven't heard? Something like that happens to a person he's got to spread it around, along with his excuses, as fast as he can."

The coffee he sipped had no taste, the dessert no taste. "Is he going to Palermo anyway?"

"Oh," said Van Grundy, stretching back, finding his cigarettes in his shirt pocket, offering one to his wife by reaching around behind the guest's chair, "he won't go to Palermo now. He can if he wants to, he's okayed as a pupil, but since Torres isn't throwing down the red carpet for him he won't go as less than a spectacular. You know David."

"Even if he doesn't like old Tommy anymore he can learn a thing or two from him, if he went," Berger said, sounding reasonable, sounding as if all his problems were solved by bringing reason to bear.

"He's already taken off for Mexico City. A week ago. He's going to study under Salinas down there if he can get that cat to stay sober long enough. Says he's always said that Salinas was better than Torres. He's stopping off in Los Angeles to ask a rich uncle to subsidize him. He was going to do it anyway to get to Palermo on, so now he'll need less and maybe get it easier. Hasn't seen his uncle since he was twelve. Got a lot of nerve, our Davy."

"What did you think of that Rivas woman?" Van Grundy's wife was asking, and he turned his face to hear, regretting, for a moment, that he heard her, usually, only with his ears and not his consciousness. He had known her for ten years now, she had been the vocalist with a combo he'd played string bass in and it was he who had introduced her to Van Grundy—a tiny woman with short, singed-blonde hair and an affectation of toughness. "Rivas?" he asked.

"Rivas, Maruja Rivas. The girl on the record we lent you. Last time you were here." The smoke hissed out from between her thin, orange lips, aimed into her empty coffee cup. "Don't tell me she didn't mean anything to you."

"Did you play the record?" Van Grundy asked.

"I can't remember borrowing it," he said.

The last student was gone. He had come home from the Van Grundy's to find the first student waiting in the apartment and he had put aside the record on a pile of sheet music and there she had waited in the silence of the confident artist. He had noticed that proud patience of hers when, in the streetlight that shone into his car parked before the Van Grundys' gate, he had looked for the record and found it on the floor, under the seat, where David had slipped it so he could sit down. After she had waited for so many days she had waited again until the last student was gone, and when he picked up the record cover, the racy cover with orange letters on purple background and the woman in the simple black dress, there was that unsmiling serenity again.

He turned his back to the record going around, half-sitting on the cabinet, chin dipping into his fingers, elbow propped in his stomach. He cautioned himself to listen with his own ear, not Van Grundy's, but with the first emerging of the guitar from the orchestra, the first attack on the strings, he found himself deprived of caution. His head remained bowed through all the first movement, and at the start of the second he began to weep. The music was a gathering of all the nostalgia of his life for all the beautiful things of the earth, it was his desire to possess the fire, to play so well that all the doors of the world would spring open. Wiping his nose with his shirt sleeve, he sat down on the sofa.

With the cover in his hands he watched her as she played, though he knew that the photo was taken while her hands were still, the left-hand fingers spread in a chord. He watched her, the pale face and arms against some Spanish wall of huge blocks of stone and a gate of wrought-iron whorls. Her hair was olive-black, smoothed back from the brow, the face delicately angular, the black eyebrows painted on, the nose short, straight, high-bridged, and the lips thin and soft and attuned to the fingers that plucked the strings. He knew the sensation in the lips, the mouth wanting to move over the music as if it were palpable.

*Concierto de Aranjuez*, and the fine print on the back of
the cover told him that Aranjuez had been the ancient
residence of the Spanish kings. *I believed myself in some
enchanted palace. The morning was fresh, birds singing on
all sides, the water murmuring sweetly, the espaliers loaded
with delectable fruit.* Why did they quote some French-
woman back in 1679? He knew the place without any help.
The memory of another Aranjuez came to him, the party
he'd played for last summer down the Peninsula, the sun
hot on the pears and the plums even at six in the evening,
and the shade waiting along with everything else for the
cooling night. He had played all night under the paper
lanterns of the brick patio and tiny bells were tied to the
trees and tinkled in the night's warm winds, and, early in
the morning when all the guests were gone, that party-
thrower, that divorcee with a dress the color of her tan,
had told him her checkbook was in her purse and her purse
in her bedroom, and he had awakened at noon in a sweat
from the heat of the day and the fiery closeness of her little
body. He had phoned her in the evening from the city, but
she had spoken to him as to an entertainer who has already
been paid and who says he hasn't. Years ago it would have
been a pleasure and a joke. He had known a lot of women
briefly like that, a pleasure and a joke, but for some reason
—what reason?—that time had hurt him. Was it because it
had shown him, graying, smiling, almost forty, the truth
that he was no more than an entertainer, not artist but
entertainer, one who drove up the hedge-lined driveway in
his 1950 magazine solicitor's Chevy, one for whom the
door was closed after the glasses and ashtrays were cleared
away and the woman had bathed away his odor and his
touch. The music from the fingers of that woman on the
record cover caused the ache of his mediocrity to flare up
and then die down. He needed nobody now to blame for
that mediocrity, neither himself nor that middle-class
woman who had withheld greatness from him by withhold-
ing everything owing to him, for that Madrid woman went
in everywhere and took him along. The great went in doorways hung across with blankets and they went in the gates
of palaces, and everywhere they were welcomed like one of
the family.

The disc went around all night, except for the hours he
himself played, and he had another two cups of coffee and,
along about four o'clock, stale toast with stringy dark apri-

cot jam which he did not taste as he ate and yet which tasted in his memory like a rare delight that he could, paradoxically, put together again easily. His shoes were off, he was more at home than he had ever been in his rented rooms anywhere, and the woman with him was like a woman he had met early in the evening and between himself and her everything had been understood at once. The disc went around until the room was lighted from outside and the globes drew back their light into themselves, and water began to run through the pipes of the house.

He heated the last of the coffee, sat down at the kitchen table and pushed up the window, and through the clogged screen the foggy breath of morning swept in. What was morning like in Madrid? What was her room like, what was she like with her hair unbound, in what kind of bed did she sleep and in what gown?—the woman he had spent the night with.

He tipped his chair back against the wall and the thought of David Hagemeister struck him like somebody's atonal music. Now in the morning whose silence was like the inner circle of the record there returned to him the presence of David, but the discord was not a response anymore from his own being, the discord was in David himself.

Davy's mother must be up by now, he thought. One morning he had brought the boy home at six, after a Friday night of playing duets here and there, and she was already up in a cotton housecoat, dyed yellow hair up in curlers, having tea for breakfast and not a bit worried. She was the kind who would have sent him to Europe at seven by himself because he was the kind who could have done it fine. Carrying his cup to the phone in the living room, he sat on the sofa's arm, and after he had dialed the number he pulled off his socks, for his feet were smothering from the nightlong confinement.

"Edith, this is Hal Berger. Did I wake you?" his voice as thickly strange to himself as it must be to her.

"I was just putting my feet in slippers." Her voice sailed forth as if all mornings were bright ones. She always spoke on the phone as if her department manager at the Emporium picked up his phone whenever hers rang, a third party on the line listening for signs of age and apathy.

"Where's David? Somebody said he's zooming down to Mexico," massaging the arch of his pale foot.

"He's in Nogales. It's on the border."

"What's he on the border for?"

"He's waiting for some money from me."

"What about the uncle in Los Angeles?"

"He gave him supper and twenty-five dollars to come back north on and buy himself a new pair of cords. He went to Nogales, instead, wearing the same pants and sent me a telegram from there."

"You sending him something?"

"Yes."

He began to subtract several dollars from the substance of himself, and fear was left like a fissure where the amount was taken away. But then why phone her at quarter to six in the morning, rushing his voice at her with its big, benevolent question? "Send him an extra fifty for me," he said, "and I'll drop you a check in the mail to cover it." Overcome by a great weariness, he hung up.

He lay down on the sofa. His shirt stung his nostrils with the night's nervous sweat and he tried not to breathe it. In the Nogales Western Union the boy would pick up the check, the total drawn from the days of his mother's captivity behind the counter, drawn from the hours of Berger's teaching, but since it had come to him, this money, then was it not his due because he was David Hagemeister? Poor Davy H.! Maybe the boy would be always on borders, always on the border of acclaim waiting for something to come through and get him there. But once in a while as he grew older and envious of those who had got across the border, he would hear somebody great and lose all envy. It might be, he thought, that this Rivas woman wasn't as great as he thought she was, but he had needed, this night, to think that she was great.

His crossed arms weighting down his eyes, he fell asleep to the sound of someone running lightly down the carpeted interior stairs, some clean-shaven and showered clerk running down into the day.

# RICHARD BRAUTIGAN

# Trout Fishing in America

### KNOCK ON WOOD
### (PART ONE)

As a child when did I first hear about trout fishing in America? From whom? I guess it was a stepfather of mine.

Summer of 1942.

The old drunk told me about troutfishing. When he could talk, he had a way of describing trout as if they were a precious and intelligent metal.

Silver is not a good adjective to describe what I felt when he told me about trout fishing.

I'd like to get it right.

Maybe trout steel. Steel made from trout. The clear snow-filled river acting as foundry and heat.

Imagine Pittsburgh.

A steel that comes from trout, used to make buildings, trains and tunnels.

The Andrew Carnegie of Trout!

The Reply of Trout Fishing in America:

I remember with particular amusement, people with three-cornered hats fishing in the dawn.

### KNOCK ON WOOD
(PART TWO)

One spring afternoon as a child in the strange town of Portland, I walked down to a different street corner, and saw a row of old houses, huddled together like seals on a rock. Then there was a long field that came sloping down off a hill. The field was covered with green grass and bushes. On top of the hill there was a grove of tall, dark trees. At a distance I saw a waterfall come pouring down off the hill. It was long and white and I could almost feel its cold spray.

There must be a creek there, I thought, and it probably has trout in it.

Trout.

At last an opportunity to go trout fishing, to catch my first trout, to behold Pittsburgh.

It was growing dark. I didn't have time to go and look at the creek. I walked home past the glass whiskers of the houses, reflecting the downward rushing waterfalls of night.

The next day I would go trout fishing for the first time. I would get up early and eat my breakfast and go. I had heard that it was better to go trout fishing early in the morning. The trout were better for it. They had something extra in the morning. I went home to prepare for trout fishing in America. I didn't have any fishing tackle, so I had to fall back on corny fishing tackle.

Like a joke.

Why did the chicken cross the road?

I bent a pin and tied it onto a piece of white string.

And slept.

The next morning I got up early and ate my breakfast. I took a slice of white bread to use for bait. I planned on making doughballs from the soft center of the bread and putting them on my vaudevillean hook.

I left the place and walked down to the different street corner. How beautiful the field looked and the creek that came pouring down in a waterfall off the hill.

But as I got closer to the creek I could see that something was wrong. The creek did not act right. There was a strangeness to it. There was a thing about its motion that was wrong. Finally I got close enough to see what the trouble was.

The waterfall was just a flight of white wooden stairs leading up to a house in the trees.

I stood there for a long time, looking up and looking down, following the stairs with my eyes, having trouble believing.

Then I knocked on my creek and heard the sound of wood.

I ended up by being my own trout and eating the slice of bread myself.

The Reply of Trout Fishing in America:

There was nothing I could do. I couldn't change a flight of stairs into a creek. The boy walked back to where he came from. The same thing once happened to me. I remember mistaking an old woman for a trout stream in Vermont, and I had to beg her pardon.

"Excuse me," I said. "I thought you were a trout stream."

"I'm not," she said.

### TOM MARTIN CREEK

I walked down one morning from Steelhead, following the Klamath River that was high and murky and had the intelligence of a dinosaur. Tom Martin Creek was a small creek with cold, clear water and poured out of a canyon and through a culvert under the highway and then into the Klamath.

I dropped a fly in a small pool just below where the creek flowed out of the culvert and took a nine-inch trout. It was a good-looking fish and fought all over the top of the pool.

Even though the creek was very small and poured out of a steep brushy canyon filled with poison oak, I decided to follow the creek up a ways because I liked the feel and motion of the creek.

I liked the name, too.

Tom Martin Creek.

It's good to name creeks after people and then later to follow them for a while seeing what they have to offer, what they know and have made of themselves.

But that creek turned out to be a real son-of-a-bitch. I had to fight it all the God-damn way: brush, poison oak and hardly any good places to fish, and sometimes the canyon was so narrow the creek poured out like water from a faucet. Sometimes it was so bad that it just left me standing there, not knowing which way to jump

You had to be a plumber to fish that creek.

After that first trout I was alone in there. But I didn't know it until later.

## TROUT FISHING IN AMERICA

The creek was made narrow by little green trees that grew too close together. The creek was like 12,845 telephone booths in a row with high Victorian ceilings and all the doors taken off and all the backs of the booths knocked out.

Sometimes when I went fishing in there, I felt just like a telephone repairman, even though I did not look like one. I was only a kid covered with fishing tackle, but in some strange way by going in there and catching a few trout, I kept the telephones in service. I was an asset to society.

It was pleasant work, but at times it made me uneasy. It could grow dark in there instantly when there were some clouds in the sky and they worked their way onto the sun. Then you almost needed candles to fish by, and foxfire in your reflexes.

Once I was in there when it started raining. It was dark and hot and steamy. I was of course on overtime. I had that going in my favor. I caught seven trout in fifteen minutes.

The trout in those telephone booths were good fellows. There were a lot of young cutthroat trout six to nine inches long, perfect pan size for local calls. Sometimes there were a few fellows, eleven inches or so—for the long distance calls.

I've always liked cutthroat trout. They put up a good fight, running against the bottom and then broad jumping. Under their throats they fly the orange banner of Jack the Ripper.

Also in the creek were a few stubborn rainbow trout, seldom heard from, but there all the same, like certified public accountants. I'd catch one every once in a while.

They were fat and chunky, almost as wide as they were long. I've heard those trout called "squire" trout.

It used to take me about an hour to hitchhike to that creek. There was a river nearby. The river wasn't much. The creek was where I punched in. Leaving my card above the clock, I'd punch out again when it was time to go home.

I remember the afternoon I caught the hunchback trout.

A farmer gave me a ride in a truck. He picked me up at a traffic signal beside a bean field and he never said a word to me.

His stopping and picking me up and driving me down the road was as automatic a thing to him as closing the barn door, nothing need be said about it, but still I was in motion traveling thirty-five miles an hour down the road, watching houses and groves of trees go by, watching chickens and mailboxes enter and pass through my vision.

Then I did not see any houses for a while. "This is where I get out," I said.

The farmer nodded his head. The truck stopped.

"Thanks a lot," I said.

The farmer did not ruin his audition for the Metropolitan Opera by making a sound. He just nodded his head again. The truck started up. He was the original silent old farmer.

A little while later I was punching in at the creek. I put my card above the clock and went into that long tunnel of telephone booths.

I waded about seventy-three telephone booths in. I caught two trout in a little hole that was like a wagon wheel. It was one of my favorite holes, and always good for a trout or two.

I always like to think of that hole as a kind of pencil sharpener. I put my reflexes in and they came back out with a good point on them. Over a period of a couple of years, I must have caught fifty trout in that hole, though it was only as big as a wagon wheel.

I was fishing with salmon eggs and using a size 14 single egg hook on a pound and a quarter test tippet. The two trout lay in my creel covered entirely by green ferns, ferns made gentle and fragile by the damp walls of telephone booths.

The next good place was forty-five telephone booths in. The place was at the end of a run of gravel, brown and slippery with algae. The run of gravel dropped off and disappeared at a little shelf where there were some white rocks.

One of the rocks was kind of strange. It was a flat white rock. Off by itself from the other rocks, it reminded me of a white cat I had seen in my childhood.

The cat had fallen or been thrown off a high wooden sidewalk that went along the side of a hill in Tacoma, Washington. The cat was lying in a parking lot below.

The fall had not appreciably helped the thickness of the cat, and then a few people had parked their cars on the cat. Of course, that was a long time ago and the cars looked different from the way they look now.

You hardly see those cars any more. They are the old cars. They have to get off the highway because they can't keep up.

That flat white rock off by itself from the other rocks reminded me of that dead cat come to lie there in the creek, among 12,845 telephone booths.

I threw out a salmon egg and let it drift down over that rock and WHAM! a good hit! and I had the fish on and it ran hard downstream, cutting at an angle and staying deep and really coming on hard, solid and uncompromising, and then the fish jumped and for a second I thought it was a frog. I'd never seen a fish like that before.

God-damn! What the hell!

The fish ran deep again and I could feel its life energy screaming back up the line to my hand. The line felt like sound. It was like an ambulance siren coming straight at me, red light flashing, and then going away again and then taking to the air and becoming an air-raid siren.

The fish jumped a few more times and it still looked like a frog, but it didn't have any legs. Then the fish grew tired and sloppy, and I swung and splashed it up the surface of the creek and into my net.

The fish was a twelve-inch rainbow trout with a huge hump on its back. A hunchback trout. The first I'd ever seen. The hump was probably due to an injury that occurred when the trout was young. Maybe a horse stepped on it or a tree fell over in a storm or its mother spawned where they were building a bridge.

There was a fine thing about that trout. I only wish I could have made a death mask of him. Not of his body though, but of his energy. I don't know if anyone would have understood his body. I put it in my creel.

Later in the afternoon when the telephone booths began to grow dark at the edges, I punched out of the creek and went home. I had that hunchback trout for dinner. Wrapped in cornmeal and fried in butter, its hump tasted sweet as the kisses of Esmeralda.

### THE CLEVELAND WRECKING YARD

Until recently my knowledge about the Cleveland Wrecking Yard had come from a couple of friends who'd bought things there. One of them bought a huge window: the frame, glass and everything for just a few dollars. It was a fine-looking window.

Then he chopped a hole in the side of his house up on Potrero Hill and put the window in. Now he has a panoramic view of the San Francisco County Hospital.

He can practically look right down into the wards and see old magazines eroded like the Grand Canyon from endless readings. He can practically hear the patients thinking about breakfast: *I hate milk*, and thinking about dinner: *I hate peas*, and then he can watch the hospital slowly drown at night, hopelessly entangled in huge bunches of brick seaweed.

He bought that window at the Cleveland Wrecking Yard.

My other friend bought an iron roof at the Cleveland Wrecking Yard and took the roof down to Big Sur in an old station wagon and then he carried the iron roof on his back up the side of a mountain. He carried up half the roof on his back. It was no picnic. Then he bought a mule, George, from Pleasanton. George carried up the other half of the roof.

The mule didn't like what was happening at all. He lost a lot of weight because of the ticks, and the smell of the wildcats up on the plateau made him too nervous to graze there. My friend said jokingly that George had lost around two hundred pounds. The good wine country around Pleasanton in the Livermore Valley probably had looked a lot better to George than the wild side of the Santa Lucia Mountains.

My friend's place was a shack right beside a huge fire-

place where there had once been a great mansion during
the 1920s, built by a famous movie actor. The mansion
was built before there was even a road down at Big Sur.
The mansion had been brought over the mountains on the
backs of mules, strung out like ants, bringing visions of the
good life to the poison oak, the ticks, and the salmon.

The mansion was on a promontory, high over the Pacific.
Money could see farther in the 1920s, and one could look
out and see whales and the Hawaiian Islands and the
Kuomintang in China.

The mansion burned down years ago.

The actor died.

His mules were made into soap.

His mistresses became bird nests of wrinkles.

Now only the fireplace remains as a sort of Carthaginian
homage to Hollywood.

I was down there a few weeks ago to see my friend's
roof. I wouldn't have passed up the chance for a million
dollars, as they say. The roof looked like a colander to me.
If that roof and the rain were running against each other at
Bay Meadows, I'd bet on the rain and plan to spend my
winnings at the World's Fair in Seattle.

My own experience with the Cleveland Wrecking Yard
began two days ago when I heard about a used trout
stream they had on sale out at the Yard. So I caught the
Number 15 bus on Columbus Avenue and went out there
for the first time.

There were two Negro boys sitting behind me on the
bus. They were talking about Chubby Checker and the
Twist. They thought that Chubby Checker was only fifteen
years old because he didn't have a mustache. Then they
talked about some other guy who did the twist forty-four
hours in a row until he saw George Washington crossing
the Delaware.

"Man, that's what I call twisting," one of the kids said.

"I don't think I could twist no forty-four hours in a
row," the other kid said. "That's a lot of twisting."

I got off the bus right next to an abandoned Time Gasoline filling station and an abandoned fifty-cent self-service
car wash. There was a long field on one side of the filling
station. The field had once been covered with a housing
project during the war, put there for the shipyard workers.

On the other side of the Time filling station was the

Cleveland Wrecking Yard. I walked down there to have a look at the used trout stream. The Cleveland Wrecking Yard has a very long front window filled with signs and merchandise.

There was a sign in the window advertising a laundry marking machine for $65.00. The original cost of the machine was $175.00. Quite a saving.

There was another sign advertising new and used two and three ton hoists. I wondered how many hoists it would take to move a trout stream.

There was another sign that said:

THE FAMILY GIFT CENTER,
GIFT SUGGESTIONS FOR THE ENTIRE FAMILY

The window was filled with hundreds of items for the entire family. *Daddy, do you know what I want for Christmas? What, son? A bathroom. Mommy, do you know what I want for Christmas? What, Patricia? Some roofing material.*

There were jungle hammocks in the window for distant relatives and dollar-ten-cent gallons of earth-brown enamel paint for other loved ones.

There was also a big sign that said:

USED TROUT STREAM FOR SALE
MUST BE SEEN TO BE APPRECIATED

I went inside and looked at some ship's lanterns that were for sale next to the door. Then a salesman came up to me and said in a pleasant voice, "Can I help you?"

"Yes," I said. "I'm curious about the trout stream you have for sale. Can you tell me something about it? How are you selling it?"

"We're selling it by the foot length. You can buy as little as you want or you can buy all we've got left. A man came in here this morning and bought 563 feet. He's going to give it to his niece for a birthday present," the salesman said.

"We're selling the waterfalls separately of course, and the trees and birds, flowers, grass and ferns we're also selling extra. The insects we're giving away free with a minimum purchase of ten feet of stream."

"How much are you selling the stream for?" I asked.

"Six dollars and fifty-cents a foot," he said. "That's for the first hundred feet. After that it's five dollars a foot."

"How much are the birds?" I asked.

"Thirty-five cents apiece," he said. "But of course they're used. We can't guarantee anything."

"How wide is the stream?" I asked. "You said you were selling it by the length, didn't you?"

"Yes," he said. "We're selling it by the length. Its width runs between five and eleven feet. You don't have to pay anything extra for width. It's not a big stream, but it's very pleasant."

"What kinds of animals do you have?" I asked.

"We only have three deer left," he said.

"Oh . . . What about flowers?"

"By the dozen," he said.

"Is the stream clear?" I asked.

"Sir," the salesman said. "I wouldn't want you to think that we would ever sell a murky trout stream here. We always make sure they're running crystal clear before we even think about moving them."

"Where did the stream come from?" I asked.

"Colorado," he said. "We moved it with loving care. We've never damaged a trout stream yet. We treat them all as if they were china."

"You're probably asked this all the time, but how's fishing in the stream?" I asked.

"Very good," he said. "Mostly German browns, but there are a few rainbows."

"What do the trout cost?" I asked.

"They come with the stream," he said. "Of course it's all luck. You never know how many you're going to get or how big they are. But the fishing's very good, you might say it's excellent. Both bait and dry fly," he said smiling.

"Where's the stream at?" I asked. "I'd like to take a look at it."

"It's around in back," he said. "You go straight through that door and then turn right until you're outside. It's stacked in lengths. You can't miss it. The waterfalls are upstairs in the used plumbing department."

"What about the animals?"

"Well, what's left of the animals are straight back from the stream. You'll see a bunch of our trucks parked on a road by the railroad tracks. Turn right on the road and follow it down past the piles of lumber. The animal shed's right at the end of the lot."

"Thanks," I said. "I think I'll look at the waterfalls first. You don't have to come with me. Just tell me how to get there and I'll find my own way."

"All right," he said. "Go up those stairs. You'll see a bunch of doors and windows, turn left and you'll find the used plumbing department. Here's my card if you need any help."

"Okay," I said. "You've been a great help already. Thanks a lot. I'll take a look around."

"Good luck," he said.

I went upstairs and there were thousands of doors there. I'd never seen so many doors before in my life. You could have built an entire city out of those doors. Doorstown. And there were enough windows up there to build a little suburb entirely out of windows. Windowville.

I turned left and went back and saw the faint glow of pearl-colored light. The light got stronger and stronger as I went farther back, and then I was in the used plumbing department, surrounded by hundreds of toilets.

The toilets were stacked on shelves. They were stacked five toilets high. There was a skylight above the toilets that made them glow like the Great Taboo Pearl of the South Sea movies.

Stacked over against the wall were the waterfalls. There were about a dozen of them, ranging from a drop of a few feet to a drop of ten or fifteen feet.

There was one waterfall that was over sixty feet long. There were tags on the pieces of the big falls describing the correct order for putting the falls back together again.

The waterfalls all had price tags on them. They were more expensive than the stream. The waterfalls were selling for $19.00 a foot.

I went into another room where there were piles of sweet-smelling lumber, glowing a soft yellow from a different color skylight above the lumber. In the shadows at the edge of the room under the sloping roof of the building were many sinks and urinals covered with dust, and there was also another waterfall about seventeen feet long, lying there in two lengths and already beginning to gather dust.

I had seen all I wanted of the waterfalls, and now I was very curious about the trout stream, so I followed the salesman's directions and ended up outside the building.

O I had never in my life seen anything like that trout stream. It was stacked in piles of various lengths: ten, fifteen, twenty feet, etc. There was one pile of hundred-foot lengths. There was also a box of scraps. The scraps were in odd sizes ranging from six inches to a couple of feet.

There was a loudspeaker on the side of the building and soft music was coming out. It was a cloudy day and sea-gulls were circling high overhead.

Behind the stream were big bundles of trees and bushes. They were covered with sheets of patched canvas. You could see the tops and roots sticking out the ends of the bundles.

I went up close and looked at the lengths of stream. I could see some trout in them. I saw one good fish. I saw some crawdads crawling around the rocks at the bottom.

It looked like a fine stream. I put my hand in the water. It was cold and felt good.

I decided to go around to the side and look at the animals. I saw where the trucks were parked beside the railroad tracks. I followed the road down past the piles of lumber, back to the shed where the animals were.

The salesman had been right. They were practically out of animals. About the only thing they had left in any abundance were mice. There were hundreds of mice.

Beside the shed was a huge wire birdcage, maybe fifty feet high, filled with many kinds of birds. The top of the cage had a piece of canvas over it, so the birds wouldn't get wet when it rained. There were woodpeckers and wild canaries and sparrows.

On my way back to where the trout stream was piled, I found the insects. They were inside a prefabricated steel building that was selling for eighty-cents a square foot. There was a sign over the door. It said

**INSECTS**

# RAYMOND CARVER

# So Much Water So Close to Home

My husband eats with good appetite but seems tired, edgy.
He chews slowly, arms on the table, and stares at something across the room. He looks at me and looks away
again, and wipes his mouth on the napkin. He shrugs, goes
on eating. Something has come between us though he
would like to believe otherwise.

"What are you staring at me for?" he asks. "What is
it?" he says and lays his fork down.

"Was I staring?" I say and shake my head stupidly,
stupidly.

The telephone rings. "Don't answer it," he says.

"It might be your mother," I say. "Dean—it might be
something about Dean."

"Watch and see," he says.

I pick up the receiver and listen for a minute. He stops
eating. I bite my lip and hang up.

"What did I tell you?" he says. He starts to eat again,
then throws the napkin onto his plate. "Goddamn it, why
can't people mind their own business? Tell me what I did
wrong and I'll listen! It's not fair. She was dead, wasn't
she? There were other men there besides me. We talked it
over and we all decided. We'd only just got there. We'd
walked for hours. We couldn't just turn around, we were

55

five miles from the car. It was opening day. What the hell,
I don't see anything wrong. No, I don't. And don't look at
me that way, do you hear? I won't have you passing judgment on me. Not you."

"You know," I say and shake my head.

"What do I know, Claire? Tell me. Tell me what I know.
I don't know anything except one thing; you hadn't better
get worked up over this." He gives me what he thinks is a
*meaningful* look. "She was dead, dead, dead, do you hear?"
he says after a minute. "It's a damn shame, I agree. She
was a young girl and it's a shame, and I'm sorry, as sorry
as anyone else, but she was dead, Claire, dead. Now let's
leave it alone. Please, Claire. Let's leave it alone now."

"That's the point," I say. "She was dead—but don't you
see? She needed help."

"I give up," he says and raises his hands. He pushes his
chair away from the table, takes his cigarettes and goes out
to the patio with a can of beer. He walks back and forth
for a minute and then sits in a lawn chair and picks up the
paper once more. His name is there on the first page along
with the names of his friends, the other men who made the
"grisly find."

I close my eyes for a minute and hold onto the drainboard. I must not dwell on this any longer. I must get over
it; put it out of sight, out of mind, etc., and "go on." I
open my eyes. Despite everything, knowing all that may be
in store, I rake my arm across the drainboard and send the
dishes and glasses smashing and scattering across the floor.

He doesn't move. I know he has heard, he raises his
head as if listening, but he doesn't move otherwise, doesn't
turn around to look. I hate him for that, for not moving.
He waits a minute, then draws on his cigarette and leans
back in the chair. I pity him for listening, detached, and
then settling back and drawing on his cigarette. The wind
takes the smoke out of his mouth in a thin stream. Why do
I notice that? He can never know how much I pity him for
that, for sitting still and listening, and letting the smoke
stream out of his mouth. . . .

He planned his fishing trip into the mountains last Sunday, a week before the Memorial Day weekend. He and
Gordon Johnson, Mel Dorn, Vern Williams. They play
poker, bowl, and fish together. They fish together every
spring and early summer, the first two or three months of

the season, before family vacations, little league baseball,
and visiting relatives can intrude. They are decent men,
family men, responsible at their jobs. They have sons and
daughters who go to school with our son, Dean. On Friday
afternoon these four men left for a three-day fishing trip to
the Naches River. They parked the car in the mountains and
hiked several miles to where they wanted to fish. They carried
their bedrolls, food and cooking utensils, their playing cards,
their whisky. The first evening at the river, even before they
could set up camp, Mel Dorn found the girl floating face
down in the river, nude, lodged near the shore against
some branches. He called the other men and they all came
to look at her. They talked about what to do. One of the
men—Stuart didn't say which—perhaps it was Vern Williams, he is a heavy-set, easy man who laughs often—one
of them thought they should start back to the car at once.
The others stirred the sand with their shoes and said they
felt inclined to stay. They pleaded fatigue, the late hour,
the fact that the girl "wasn't going anywhere." In the end
they all decided to stay. They went ahead and set up the
camp and built a fire and drank their whisky. They drank a
lot of whisky and when the moon came up they talked
about the girl. Someone thought they should do something
to prevent the body from floating away. Somehow they
thought that this might create a problem for them if she
floated away during the night. They took flashlights and
stumbled down to the river. The wind was up, a cold wind,
and waves from the river lapped the sandy bank. One of
the men, I don't know who, it might have been Stuart, he
could have done it, waded into the water and took the girl
by the fingers and pulled her, still face down, closer to
shore, into shallow water, and then took a piece of nylon
cord and tied it around her wrist and then secured the cord
to tree roots, all the while the flashlights of the other men
played over the girl's body. Afterwards, they went back to
camp and drank more whisky. Then they went to sleep.
The next morning, Saturday, they cooked breakfast, drank
lots of coffee, more whisky, and then split up to fish, two
men upriver, two men down.

That night, after they had cooked their fish and potatoes
and had more coffee and whisky, they took their dishes
down to the river and washed them a few yards from
where the girl lay in the water. They drank again and then

they took out their cards and played and drank until they couldn't see the cards any longer. Vern Williams went to sleep but the others told coarse stories and spoke of vulgar or dishonest escapades out of their past, and no one mentioned the girl until Gordon Johnson, who'd forgotten for a minute, commented on the firmness of the trout they'd caught, and the terrible coldness of the river water. They stopped talking then but continued to drink until one of them tripped and fell cursing against the lantern, and then they climbed into their sleeping bags.

The next morning they got up late, drank more whisky, fished a little as they kept drinking whisky, and then, at one o'clock in the afternoon, Sunday, a day earlier than they'd planned, decided to leave. They took down their tents, rolled their sleeping bags, gathered their pans, pots, fish and fishing gear, and hiked out. They didn't look at the girl again before they left. When they reached the car they drove the highway in silence until they came to a telephone. Stuart made the call to the sheriff's office while the others stood around in the hot sun and listened. He gave the man on the other end of the line all of their names—they had nothing to hide, they weren't ashamed of anything—and agreed to wait at the service station until someone could come for more detailed directions and individual statements.

He came home at eleven o'clock that night. I was asleep but woke when I heard him in the kitchen. I found him leaning against the refrigerator drinking a can of beer. He put his heavy arms around me and rubbed his hands up and down my back, the same hands he'd left with two days before, I thought.

In bed he put his hands on me again and then waited, as if thinking of something else. I turned slightly and then moved my legs. Afterwards, I know he stayed awake for a long time, for he was awake when I fell asleep; and later, when I stirred for a minute, opening my eyes at a slight noise, a rustle of sheets, it was almost daylight outside, birds were singing, and he was on his back smoking and looking at the curtained window. Half-asleep I said his name, but he didn't answer. I fell asleep again.

He was up that morning before I could get out of bed, to see if there was anything about it in the paper, I suppose. The telephone began to ring shortly after eight o'clock.

"Go to hell," I heard him shout into the receiver. The telephone rang again a minute later, and I hurried into the kitchen. "I have nothing else to add to what I've already said to the sheriff. That's right!" He slammed down the receiver.

"What is going on?" I said, alarmed.

"Sit down," he said slowly. His fingers scraped, scraped against his stubble of whiskers. "I have to tell you something. Something happened while we were fishing." We sat across from each other at the table, and then he told me.

I drank coffee and stared at him as he spoke. I read the account in the newspaper that he shoved across the table . . . unidentified girl eighteen to twenty-four years of age . . . body three to five days in the water . . . rape a possible motive . . . preliminary results show death by strangulation . . . cuts and bruises on her breasts and pelvic area . . . autopsy . . . rape, pending further investigation.

"You've got to understand," he said. "Don't look at me like that. Be careful now, I mean it. Take it easy, Claire."

"Why didn't you tell me last night?" I asked.

"I just . . . didn't. What do you mean?" he said.

"You know what I mean," I said. I looked at his hands, the broad fingers, knuckles covered with hair, moving, lighting a cigarette now, fingers that had moved over me, into me last night.

He shrugged. "What difference does it make, last night, this morning? You were sleepy, I thought I'd wait until this morning to tell you." He looked out to the patio: a robin flew from the lawn to the picnic table and preened its feathers.

"It isn't true," I said. "You didn't leave her there like that?"

He turned quickly and said, "What'd I do? Listen to me carefully now, once and for all. Nothing happened. I have nothing to be sorry for or feel guilty about. Do you hear me?"

I got up from the table and went to Dean's room. He was awake and in his pajamas, putting together a puzzle. I helped him find his clothes and then went back to the kitchen and put his breakfast on the table. The telephone rang two or three more times and each time Stuart was abrupt while he talked and angry when he hung up. He called Mel Dorn and Gordon Johnson and spoke with them, slowly, seriously, and then he opened a beer and smoked a cigarette while Dean ate, asked him about school, his friends, etc., exactly as if nothing had happened.

Dean wanted to know what he'd done while he was gone, and Stuart took some fish out of the freezer to show him.

"I'm taking him to your mother's for the day," I said.

"Sure," Stuart said and looked at Dean who was holding one of the frozen trout. "If you want to and he wants to, that is. You don't have to, you know. There's nothing wrong."

"I'd like to anyway," I said.

"Can I go swimming there?" Dean asked and wiped his fingers on his pants.

"I believe so," I said. "It's a warm day so take your suit, and I'm sure your grandmother will say it's okay."

Stuart lighted another cigarette and looked at us.

Dean and I drove across town to Stuart's mother's. She lives in an apartment building with a pool and a sauna bath. Her name is Catherine Kane. Her name, Kane, is the same as mine, which seems impossible. Years ago, Stuart has told me, she used to be called Candy by her friends. She is a tall, cold woman with white-blonde hair. She gives me the feeling that she is always judging, judging. I explain briefly in a low voice what has happened (she hasn't yet read the newspaper) and promise to pick Dean up that evening. "He brought his swimming suit," I say. "Stuart and I have to talk about some things," I add vaguely. She looks at me steadily from over her glasses. Then she nods and turns to Dean, saying "How are you, my little man?" She stoops and puts her arms around him. She looks at me again as I open the door to leave. She has a way of looking at me without saying anything.

When I returned home Stuart was eating something at the table and drinking beer. . . .

After a time I sweep up the broken dishes and glassware and go outside. Stuart is lying on his back on the grass now, the newspaper and can of beer within reach, staring at the sky. It is breezy but warm out and birds call.

"Stuart, could we go for a drive?" I say. "Anywhere."

He rolls over and looks at me and nods. "We'll pick up some beer," he says. "I hope you're feeling better about this. Try to understand, that's all I ask." He gets to his feet and touches me on the hip as he goes past. "Give me a minute and I'll be ready."

We drive through town without speaking. Before we reach the country he stops at a roadside market for beer. I notice a great stack of papers just inside the door. On the top step a fat woman in a print dress holds out a licorice stick to a little girl. In a few minutes we cross Everson Creek and turn into a picnic area a few feet from the water. The creek flows under the bridge and into a large pond a few hundred yards away. There are a dozen or so men and boys scattered around the banks of the pond under the willows, fishing.

*So much water so close to home, why did he have to go miles away to fish?*

"Why did you have to go there of all places?" I say.

"The Naches? We always go there. Every year, at least once." We sit on a bench in the sun and he opens two cans of beer and gives one to me. "How the hell was I to know anything like that would happen?" He shakes his head and shrugs, as if it had all happened years ago, or to someone else. "Enjoy the afternoon, Claire. Look at this weather."

"They said they were innocent."

"Who? What are you talking about?"

"The Maddox brothers. They killed a girl named Arlene Huby near the town where I grew up, and then cut off her head and threw her into the Cle Elum River. She and I went to the same high school. It happened when I was a girl."

"What a hell of a thing to be thinking about," he says. "Come on, get off it. You're going to get me riled in a minute. How about it now? Claire?"

I look at the creek. I float toward the pond, eyes open, face down, staring at the rocks and moss on the creek bottom until I am carried into the lake where I am pushed by the breeze. *Nothing will be any different. We will go on and on and on and on. We will go on even now, as if nothing had happened.* I looked at him across the picnic table with such intensity that his face drains.

"I don't know what's wrong with you," he says. "I don't—"

I slap him before I realize. I raise my hand, wait a fraction of a second, and then slap his cheek hard. This is crazy, I think as I slap him. We need to lock our fingers together. We need to help one another. This is crazy.

He catches my wrist before I can strike again and raises his own hand. I crouch, waiting, and see something come into his eyes and then dart away. He drops his hand. I drift even faster around and around in the pond.

"Come on, get in the car," he says. "I'm taking you home."

"No, no," I say, pulling back from him.

"Come on," he says, "Goddamn it."

"You're not being fair to me," he says later in the car. Fields and trees and farmhouses fly by outside the window. "You're not being fair. To either one of us. Or to Dean, I might add. Think about Dean for a minute. Think about me. Think about someone else besides yourself for a change."

There is nothing I can say to him now. He tries to concentrate on the road, but he keeps looking into the rearview mirror. Out of the corner of his eye, he looks across the seat to where I sit with my knees doubled under me. The sun blazes against my arm and the side of my face. He opens another beer while he drives, drinks from it, then shoves the can between his legs and lets out breath. He knows. I could laugh in his face. I could weep.

## 2

Stuart believes he is letting me sleep this morning. But I was awake long before the alarm sounded, thinking, lying on the far side of the bed, away from his hairy legs and his thick, sleeping fingers. He gets Dean off for school, and then he shaves, dresses, and leaves for work himself soon after. Twice he looks into the bedroom and clears his throat, but I keep my eyes closed.

In the kitchen I find a note from him signed "Love." I sit in the breakfast nook in the sunlight and drink coffee and make a coffee ring on the note. The telephone has stopped ringing, that is something. No more calls since last night. I look at the paper and turn it this way and that on the table. Then I pull it close and read what it says. The body is still unidentified, unclaimed, apparently unmissed. But for the last twenty-four hours men have been examining it, putting things into it, cutting, weighing, measuring, putting back again, sewing up, looking for the exact cause and moment of death. And the evidence of rape. I'm sure they hope for rape. Rape would make it easier to understand. The paper says she will be taken to Keith & Keith Funeral Home pending arrangements. People are asked to come forward with information, etc.

Two things are certain: 1) people no longer care what happens to other people, and 2) nothing makes any real difference any longer. Look at what has happened. Yet nothing will change for Stuart and me. Really change, I mean. We will grow older, both of us, you can see it in our faces already, in the bathroom mirror, for instance, mornings when we use the bathroom at the same time. And certain things around us will change, become easier or harder, one thing or the other, but nothing will ever really be any different. I believe that. We have made our decisions, our lives have been set in motion, and they will go on and on until they stop. But if that is true, what then? I mean, what if you believe that, but you keep it covered up, until one day something happens that should change something, but then you see nothing is going to change after all. What then? Meanwhile, the people around you continue to talk and act as if you were the same person as yesterday, or last night, or five minutes before, but you are really undergoing a crisis, your heart feels damaged. . . .

The past is unclear. It is as if there is a film over those early years. I cannot be sure that the things I remember happening really happened to me. There was a girl who had a mother and father—the father ran a small cafe where the mother acted as waitress and cashier—who moved as if in a dream through grade school and high school and then, in a year or two, into secretarial school. Later, much later—what happened to the time in between? —she is in another town working as a receptionist for an electronic parts firm and becomes acquainted with one of the engineers who asks her for a date. Eventually, seeing that's his aim, she lets him seduce her. She had an intuition at the time, an insight about the seduction that later, try as she might, she couldn't recall. After a short while they decide to get married, but already the past, her past, is slipping away. The future is something she can't imagine. She smiles, as if she has a secret, when she thinks about the future. Once, during a particularly bad argument, over what she can't now remember, five years or so after they were married, he tells her that someday this affair (his words: "this affair") will end in violence. She remembers this. She files this away somewhere and begins repeating it aloud from time to time. Sometimes she spends the whole morning on her knees in the sandbox behind the garage playing with Dean and one or two of his friends. But every afternoon at four o'clock her head begins to hurt. She holds her forehead and feels dizzy with the pain. Stuart asks her to see a doctor and she does, secretly pleased at the doctor's solicitous attention. She goes away for a while to a place the doctor recommends. His mother comes out from Ohio in a hurry to care for the child. But she, Claire, Claire spoils everything and returns home in a few weeks. His mother moves out of the house and takes an apartment across town and perches there, as if waiting. One night in bed when they are both near sleep, Claire tells him that she heard some women patients at DeWitt discussing fellatio. She thinks this is something he might like to hear. She smiles in the dark. Stuart is pleased at hearing this. He strokes her arm. Things are going to be okay, he says. From now on everything is going to be different and better for them. He has received a promotion and a substantial raise. They have even bought another car, a station wagon, her car. They're going to live in the here and now. He says he feels able to relax for the first time in years. In the dark, he goes on stroking her arm. . . . He continues to bowl and play cards regularly. He goes fishing with three friends of his.

That evening three things happen: Dean says that the children at school told him that his father found a dead body in the river. He wants to know about it.

Stuart explains quickly, leaving out most of the story, saying only that, yes, he and three other men did find a body while they were fishing.

"What kind of a body?" Dean asks. "Was it a girl?"

"Yes, it was a girl. A woman. Then we called the sheriff." Stuart looks at me.

"What'd *he* say?" Dean asks.

"He said he'd take care of it."

"What did it look like? Was it scary?"

"That's enough talk," I say. "Rinse your plate, Dean, and then you're excused."

"But what'd it look like?" he persists. "I want to know."

"You heard me," I say. "Did you hear me, Dean? Dean!" I want to shake him. I want to shake him until he cries.

"Do what your mother says," Stuart tells him quietly. "It was just a body, and that's all there is to tell."

I am clearing the table when Stuart comes up behind and touches my arm. His fingers burn. I start, almost losing a plate.

"What's the matter with you?" he says, dropping his hand. "Tell me, Claire, what is it?"

"You scared me," I say.

"That's what I mean. I should be able to touch you without you jumping out of your skin." He stands in front of me with a little grin, trying to catch my eyes, and then he puts his arm around my waist. With his other hand he takes my free hand and puts it on the front of his pants.

"Please, Stuart." I pull away and he steps back and snaps his fingers.

"Hell with it then," he says. "Be that way if you want. But just remember."

"Remember what?" I say quickly. I look at him and hold my breath.

He shrugs. "Nothing, nothing," he says and cracks his knuckles.

The second thing that happens is that while we are watching television that evening, he in his leather reclining chair, I on the couch with a blanket and magazine, the house quiet except for the television, a voice cuts into the program to say that the murdered girl has been identified. Full details will follow on the eleven o'clock news.

We look at each other. In a few minutes he gets up and says he is going to fix a nightcap. Do I want one?

"No," I say.

"I don't mind drinking alone," he says. "I thought I'd ask."

I can see he is obscurely hurt, and I look away, ashamed and yet angry at the same time.

He stays in the kitchen for a long while, but comes back with his drink when the news begins.

First the announcer repeats the story of the four local fishermen finding the body, then the station shows a high school graduation photograph of the girl, a dark-haired girl with a round face and full, smiling lips, then a film of the girl's parents entering the funeral home to make the identification. Bewildered, sad, they shuffle slowly up the sidewalk to the front steps to where a man in a dark suit stands waiting and holding the door. Then, it seems as if only a second has passed, as if they have merely gone inside the door and turned around and come out again, the same couple is shown leaving the mortuary, the woman in tears, covering her face with a handkerchief, the man stopping long enough to say to a reporter, "It's her, it's Susan. I can't say anything right now. I hope they get the person or persons who did it before it happens again. It's all this violence . . ." He motions feebly at the television camera. Then the man and woman get into an old car and drive away into the late afternoon traffic.

The announcer goes on to say that the girl, Susan Miller, had gotten off work as a cashier in a movie theater in Summit, a town 120 miles north of our town. A green, late model car pulled up in front of the theater and the girl, who according to witnesses looked as if she'd been waiting, went over to the car and got in, leading authorities to suspect that the driver of the car was a friend, or at least an acquaintance. The authorities would like to talk to the driver of the green car.

Stuart clears his throat then leans back in the chair and sips his drink.

The third thing that happens is that after the news Stuart stretches, yawns, and looks at me. I get up and begin making a bed for myself on the couch.

"What are you doing?" he says, puzzled.

"I'm not sleepy," I say, avoiding his eyes. "I think I'll stay up a while longer and then read something until I fall asleep."

He stares as I spread a sheet over the couch. When I start to go for a pillow, he stands at the bedroom door, blocking the way.

"I'm going to ask you once more," he says. "What the hell do you think you're going to accomplish?"

"I need to be by myself tonight," I say. "I just need to have time to think."

He lets out breath. "I'm thinking you're making a big mistake by doing this. I'm thinking you'd better think again about what you're doing, Claire."

I can't answer. I don't know what I want to say. I turn and begin to tuck in the edges of the blanket. He stares at me a minute longer and then I see him raise his shoulders. "Suit yourself then. I could give a fuck less what you do," he says and turns and walks down the hall scratching his neck.

This morning I read in the paper that services for Susan Miller are to be held in Chapel of the Pines, Summit, at two o'clock the next afternoon. Also, that police have taken statements from three people who saw her get into the green Chevrolet, but they still have no license number for the car. They are getting warmer, though, the investigation is continuing. I sit for a long while holding the paper, thinking, then I call to make an appointment at the hairdresser's.

I sit under the dryer with a magazine on my lap and let Millie do my nails.

"I'm going to a funeral tomorrow," I say after we have talked a bit about a girl who no longer works there.

Millie looks up at me and then back at my fingers. "I'm sorry to hear that, Mrs. Kane. I'm real sorry."

"It's a young girl's funeral," I say.

"That's the worst kind. My sister died when I was a girl, and I'm still not over it to this day. Who died?" she says after a minute.

"A girl. We weren't all that close, you know, but still."

"Too bad. I'm real sorry. But we'll get you fixed up for it, don't worry. How's that look?"

"That looks . . . fine. Millie, did you ever wish you were somebody else, or else just nobody, nothing, nothing at all?"

She looks at me. "I can't say I ever felt that, no. No, if I was somebody else I'd be afraid I might not like who I was." She holds my fingers and seems to think about something for a minute. "I don't know, I just don't know. . . . Let me have your other hand now, Mrs. Kane."

At eleven o'clock that night I make another bed on the couch and this time Stuart only looks at me, rolls his tongue behind his lips, and goes down the hall to the bedroom. In the night I wake and listen to the wind slamming the gate against the fence. I don't want to be awake, and I lie for a long while with my eyes closed. Finally I get up and go down the hall with my pillow. The light is burning in our bedroom and Stuart is on his back with his mouth open, breathing heavily. I go into Dean's room and get into bed with him. In his sleep he moves over to give me space. I lie there for a minute and then hold him, my face against his hair.

"What is it, mama?" he says.

"Nothing, honey. Go back to sleep. It's nothing, it's all right."

I get up when I hear Stuart's alarm, put on coffee and prepare breakfast while he shaves.

He appears in the kitchen doorway, towel over his bare shoulder, appraising.

"Here's coffee," I say. "Eggs will be ready in a minute." He nods.

I wake Dean and the three of us have breakfast. Once or twice Stuart looks at me as if he wants to say something, but each time I ask Dean if he wants more milk, more toast, etc.

"I'll call you today," Stuart says as he opens the door.

"I don't think I'll be home today," I say quickly. "I have a lot of things to do today, In fact, I may be late for dinner."

"All right. Sure." He wants to know, he moves his brief-case from one hand to the other. "Maybe we'll go out for dinner tonight? How would you like that?" He keeps looking at me. He's forgotten about the girl already. "Are you ... all right?"

I move to straighten his tie, then drop my hand. He wants to kiss me goodbye. I move back a step. "Have a nice day then," he says finally. Then he turns and goes down the walk to his car.

I dress carefully. I try on a hat that I haven't worn in several years and look at myself in the mirror. Then I remove the hat, apply a light makeup, and write a note for Dean.

> *Honey, Mommy has things to do this afternoon, but will be home later. You are to stay in the house or in the back yard until one of us comes home.*
>
> *Love*

I look at the word "Love" and then I underline it. As I am writing the note I realize I don't know whether *back yard* is one word or two. I have never considered it before. I think about it and then I draw a line and make two words of it.

I stop for gas and ask directions to Summit. Barry, a

forty-year-old mechanic with a moustache, comes out from the restroom and leans against the front fender while the other man, Lewis, puts the hose into the tank and begins to slowly wash the windshields.

"Summit," Barry says, looking at me and smoothing a finger down each side of his moustache. "There's no best way to get to Summit, Mrs. Kane. It's about a two, two and a half hour drive each way. Across the mountains. It's quite a drive for a woman. Summit? What's in Summit, Mrs. Kane?"

"I have business," I say, vaguely uneasy. Lewis has gone to wait on another car.

"Ah. Well, if I wasn't all tied up there"—he gestures with his thumb toward the bay—"I'd offer to drive you to Summit and back again. Road's not all that good. I mean it's good enough, there's just a lot of curves and so on."

"I'll be all right. But thank you." He leans against the fender. I can feel his eyes as I open my purse.

Barry takes the credit card. "Don't drive it at night," he says. "It's not all that good a road, like I said, and while I'd be willing to bet you wouldn't have car trouble with this, I know this car, you can never be sure about blowouts and things like that. Just to be on the safe side I'd better check these tires." He taps one of the front tires with his shoe. "We'll run it onto the hoist. Won't take long."

"No, no, it's all right. Really, I can't take any more time. The tires look fine to me."

"Only takes a minute," he says. "Be on the safe side."

"I said no. No! They look fine to me. I have to go now. Barry . . ."

"Mrs. Kane?"

"I have to go now."

I sign something. He gives me the receipt, the card, some stamps. I put everything in my purse. "You take it easy," he says. "Be seeing you."

Waiting to pull into the traffic, I look back and see him watching. I close my eyes, then open them. He waves.

I turn at the first light, then turn again and drive until I come to the highway and read the sign: SUMMIT 117 miles. It is ten-thirty and warm.

The highway skirts the edge of town, then passes through farm country, through fields of oats and sugar beets and apple orchards, with here and there a small herd of cattle grazing in open pastures. Then everything changes, the farms become fewer and fewer, more like shacks now than houses, and stands of timber replace the orchards. All at once I'm in the mountains and on the right, far below, I catch glimpses of the Naches River.

In a little while a green pickup truck comes up behind me and stays behind for miles. I keep slowing at the wrong times, hoping he will pass, and then increasing my speed, again at the wrong times. I grip the wheel until my fingers hurt. Then on a long clear stretch he does pass, but he drives along beside for a minute, a crewcut man in a blue workshirt in his early thirties, and we look at each other. Then he waves, toots the horn twice, and pulls ahead of me.

I slow down and find a place, a dirt road off of the shoulder, pull over and shut off the ignition. I can hear the river somewhere down below the trees. Ahead of me the dirt road goes into the trees. Then I hear the pickup returning.

I start the engine just as the truck pulls up behind me. I lock the doors and roll up the windows. Perspiration breaks on my face and arms as I put the car in gear, but there is no place to drive.

"You all right?" the man says as he comes up to the car. "Hello. Hello in there." He raps the glass. "Are you okay?" He leans his arms on the door then and brings his face close to the window.

I stare at him and can't find any words.

"After I passed I slowed up some," he says, "but when I didn't see you in the mirror I pulled off and waited a couple of minutes. When you still didn't show I thought I'd better drive back and check. Is everything all right? How come you're locked up in there?"

I shake my head.

"Come on, roll down your window. Hey, are you sure you're okay? You know it's not good for a woman to be batting around the country by herself." He shakes his head and looks at the highway and then back at me. "Now come on, roll down the window, how about it? We can't talk this way."

"Please, I have to go."

"Open the door, all right?" he says, as if he isn't listening. "At least roll down the window. You're going to smother in there." He looks at my breasts and legs. The skirt has pulled up over my knees. His eyes linger on my legs, but I sit still, afraid to move.

"I want to smother," I say. "I am smothering, can't you see?"

"What in the hell?" he says and moves back from the door. He turns and walks back to his truck. Then, in the side mirror, I watch him returning, and close my eyes.

"You don't want me to follow you toward Summit, or anything? I don't mind. I got some extra time this morning."

I shake my head again.

He hesitates and then shrugs. "Have it your way then," he says.

I wait until he has reached the highway, and then I back out. He shifts gears and pulls away slowly, looking back at me in his rearview mirror. I stop the car on the shoulder and put my head on the wheel.

The casket is closed and covered with floral sprays. The organ begins soon after I take a seat near the back of the chapel. People begin to file in and find chairs, some middle-aged and older people, but most of them in their early twenties or even younger. They are people who look uncomfortable in their suits and ties, sports coats and slacks, their dark dresses and leather gloves. One boy in flared pants and a yellow short-sleeved shirt takes the chair next to mine and begins to bite his lips. A door opens at one side of the chapel and I look up and for a minute the parking lot reminds me of a meadow, but then the sun flashes on car windows. The family enters in a group and moves into a curtained area off to the side. Chairs creak as they settle themselves. In a few minutes a thick, blonde man in a dark suit stands and asks us to bow our heads. He speaks a brief prayer for us, the living, and when he finishes he asks us to pray in silence for the soul of Susan Miller, departed. I close my eyes and remember her picture in the newspaper and on television. I see her leaving the theater and getting into the green Chevrolet. Then I imagine her journey down the river, the nude body hitting rocks, caught at by branches, the body floating and turning, her hair streaming in the water. Then the hands and hair catching in the overhanging branches, holding, until four men come along to stare at her. I can see a man who is drunk (Stuart?) take her by the wrist. Does anyone here know about that? What if these people knew that? I look around at the other faces. There is a connection to be made of these things, these events, these faces, if I can find it. My head aches with the effort to find it.

He talks about Susan Miller's gifts: cheerfulness and beauty, grace and enthusiasm. From behind the closed curtain someone clears his throat, someone else sobs. The organ music begins. The service is over.

Along with the others I file slowly past the casket. Then I move out onto the front steps and into the bright, hot afternoon light. A middle-aged woman who limps as she goes down the stairs ahead of me reaches the sidewalk and looks around, her eyes falling on me. "Well they got him," she says. "If that's any consolation. They arrested him this morning. I heard it on the radio before I came. A guy right here in town. A longhair, you might have guessed." We move a few steps down the hot sidewalk. People are starting cars. I put out my hand and hold on to a parking meter. Sunlight glances off polished hoods and fenders. My head swims. "He's admitted having relations with her that night, but he says he didn't kill her." She snorts. "You know as well as I do. But they'll probably put him on probation and then turn him loose."

"He might not have acted alone," I say. "They'll have to be sure. He might be covering up for someone, a brother, or some friends."

"I have known that child since she was a little girl," the woman goes on, and her lips tremble. "She used to come over and I'd bake cookies for her and let her eat them in front of the TV." She looks off and begins shaking her head as the tears roll down her cheeks.

### 3

Stuart sits at the table with a drink in front of him. His eyes are red and for a minute I think he has been crying. He looks at me and doesn't say anything. For a wild instant I feel something has happened to Dean, and my heart turns.

Where is he? I say. Where is Dean?

Outside, he says.

Stuart, I'm so afraid, so afraid, I say, leaning against the door.

What are you afraid of, Claire? Tell me, honey, and maybe I can help. I'd like to help, just try me. That's what husbands are for.

I can't explain, I say. I'm just afraid. I feel like, I feel like, I feel like. . . .

He drains his glass and stands up, not taking his eyes from me. I think I know what you need, honey. Let me play doctor, okay? Just take it easy now. He reaches an arm around my waist and with his other hand begins to unbutton my jacket, then my blouse. First things first, he says, trying to joke.

Not now, please, I say.

Not now, please, he says, teasing. Please nothing. Then he steps behind me and locks an arm around my waist. One of his hands slips under my brassiere.

Stop, stop, stop, I say. I stamp on his toes.

And then I am lifted up and then falling. I sit on the floor looking up at him and my neck hurts and my skirt is over my knees. He leans down and says, You go to hell then, do you hear, bitch? I hope your cunt drops off before I touch it again. He sobs once and I realize he can't help it, he can't help himself either. I feel a rush of pity for him as he heads for the living room.

He didn't sleep at home last night.

This morning, flowers, red and yellow chrysanthemums. I am drinking coffee when the doorbell rings.

Mrs. Kane? the young man says, holding his box of flowers.

I nod and pull the robe tighter at my throat.

The man who called, he said you'd know. The boy looks at my robe, open at the throat, and touches his cap. He stands with his legs apart, feet firmly planted on the top step, as if asking me to touch him down there. Have a nice day, he says.

A little later the telephone rings and Stuart says, Honey, how are you? I'll be home early, I love you. Did you hear me? I love you, I'm sorry, I'll make it up to you. Goodbye, I have to run now.

I put the flowers into a vase in the center of the dining room table and then I move my things into the extra bedroom.

Last night, around midnight, Stuart breaks the lock on my door. He does it just to show me that he can, I suppose,

for he does not do anything when the door springs open
except stand there in his underwear looking surprised and
foolish while the anger slips from his face. He shuts the
door slowly and a few minutes later I hear him in the
kitchen opening a tray of ice cubes.

He calls today to tell me that he's asked his mother to
come stay with us for a few days. I wait a minute, thinking
about this, and then hang up while he is still talking. But in
a while I dial his number at work. When he finally comes
on the line I say, It doesn't matter, Stuart. Really, I tell you
it doesn't matter one way or the other.

I love you, he says.

He says something else and I listen and nod slowly. I
feel sleepy. Then I wake up and say, For God's sake,
Stuart, she was only a child.

# RAYMOND CHANDLER

# The Long Goodbye

Back from the highway at the bottom of Sepulveda Canyon were two square yellow gateposts. A five-barred gate hung open from one of them. Over the entrance was a sign hung on wire: PRIVATE ROAD. NO ADMITTANCE. The air was warm and quiet and full of the tomcat smell of eucalyptus trees.

I turned in and followed a graveled road around the shoulder of a hill, up a gentle slope, over a ridge and down the other side into a shallow valley. It was hot in the valley, ten or fifteen degrees hotter than on the highway. I could see now that the graveled road ended in a loop around some grass edged with stones that had been lime-washed. Off to my left there was an empty swimming pool, and nothing ever looks emptier than an empty swimming pool. Around three sides of it there was what remained of a lawn dotted with redwood lounging chairs with badly faded pads on them. The pads had been of many colors, blue, green, yellow, orange, rust red. Their edge bindings had come loose in spots, the buttons had popped, and the pads were bloated where this had happened. On the fourth side there was the high wire fence of a tennis court. The diving board over the empty pool looked knee-sprung and tired. Its matting covering hung in shreds and its metal fittings were flaked with rust.

I came to the turning loop and stopped in front of a redwood building with a shake roof and a wide front porch. The entrance had double screen doors. Large black flies dozed on the screens. Paths led off among the ever green and always dusty California oaks and among the oaks there were rustic cabins scattered loosely over the side of the hill, some almost completely hidden. Those I could see had that desolate out-of-season look. Their doors were shut, their windows were blanked by drawn curtains of monk's cloth or something on that order. You could almost feel the thick dust on their sills.

I switched off the ignition and sat there with my hands on the wheel listening. There was no sound. The place seemed to be as dead as Pharaoh, except that the doors behind the double screens were open and something moved in the dimness of the room beyond. Then I heard a light accurate whistling and a man's figure showed against the screen, pushed it open and strolled down the steps. He was something to see.

He wore a flat black gaucho hat with the woven strap under his chin. He wore a white silk shirt, spotlessly clean, open at the throat, with tight wristlets and loose puffed sleeves above. Around his neck a black fringed scarf was knotted unevenly so that one end was short and the other dropped almost to his waist. He wore a wide black sash and black pants, skin-tight at the hips, coal black, and stitched with gold thread down the side to where they were slashed and belled out loosely with gold buttons along both sides of the slash. On his feet he wore patent-leather dancing pumps.

He stopped at the foot of the steps and looked at me, still whistling. He was as lithe as a whip. He had the largest and emptiest smoke-colored eyes I had ever seen, under long silky lashes. His features were delicate and perfect without being weak. His nose was straight and almost but not quite thin, his mouth was a handsome pout, there was a dimple in his chin, and his small ears nestled gracefully against his head. His skin had that heavy pallor which the sun never touches.

He struck an attitude with his left hand on a hip and his right made a graceful curve in the air.

"Greetings," he said. "Lovely day, isn't it?"

"Pretty hot in here for me."

"I like it hot." The statement was flat and final and closed the discussion. What I liked was beneath his notice. He sat down on a step, produced a long file from somewhere, and began to file his fingernails. "You from the bank?" he asked without looking up.

"I'm looking for Dr. Verringer."

He stopped working with the file and looked off into the warm distance. "Who's he?" he asked with no possible interest.

"He owns the place. Laconic as hell, aren't you? As if you didn't know."

He went back to his file and fingernails. "You got told wrong, sweetie. The bank owns the place. They done foreclosed it or it's in escrow or something. I forget the details."

He looked up at me with the expression of a man to whom details mean nothing. I got out of the Olds and leaned against the hot door, then I moved away from that to where there was some air.

"Which bank would that be?"

"You don't know, you don't come from there. You don't come from there, you don't have any business here. Hit the trail, sweetie. Buzz off but fast."

"I have to find Dr. Verringer."

"The joint's not operating, sweetie. Like it says on the sign, this is a private road. Some gopher forgot to lock the gate."

"You the caretaker?"

"Sort of. Don't ask any more questions, sweetie. My temper's not reliable."

"What do you do when you get mad—dance a tango with a ground squirrel?"

He stood up suddenly and gracefully. He smiled a minute, an empty smile. "Looks like I got to toss you back in your little old convertible," he said.

"Later. Where would I find Dr. Verringer about now?"

He pocketed his file in his shirt and something else took its place in his right hand. A brief motion and he had a fist with shining brass knuckles on it. The skin over his cheekbones was tighter and there was a flame deep in his large smoky eyes.

He strolled towards me. I stepped back to get more room. He went on whistling but the whistle was high and shrill.

"We don't have to fight," I told him. "We don't have anything to fight about. And you might split those lovely britches."

He was as quick as a flash. He came at me with a smooth leap and his left hand snaked out very fast. I expected a jab and moved my head well enough but what he wanted was my right wrist and he got it. He had a grip too. He jerked me off balance and the hand with the brass knucks came around in a looping bolo punch. A crack on the back of the head with those and I would be a sick man. If I pulled he would catch me on the side of the face or on the upper arm below the point of the shoulder. It would have been a dead arm or a dead face, whichever it happened to be. In a spot like that there is only one thing to do.

I went with the pull. In passing I blocked his left foot from behind, grabbed his shirt and heard it tear. Something hit me on the back of the neck, but it wasn't the metal. I spun to the left and he went over sideways and landed catlike and was on his feet again before I had any kind of balance. He was grinning now. He was delighted with everything. He loved his work. He came for me fast.

A strong beefy voice yelled from somewhere: "Earl! Stop that at once! At once, do you hear me?"

The gaucho boy stopped. There was a sort of sick grin on his face. He made a quick motion and the brass knucks disappeared into the wide sash around the top of his pants.

I turned and looked at a solid chunk of man in a Hawaiian shirt hurrying towards us down one of the paths waving his arms. He came up breathing a little fast.

"Are you crazy, Earl?"

"Don't ever say that, Doc," Earl said softly. Then he smiled, turned away, and went to sit on the steps of the house. He took off the flat-crowned hat, produced a comb, and began to comb his thick dark hair with an absent expression. In a second or two he started to whistle softly.

The heavy man in the loud shirt stood and looked at me. I stood and looked at him.

"What's going on here?" he growled. "Who are you, sir?"

"Name's Marlowe. I was asking for Dr. Verringer. The lad you call Earl wanted to play games. I figure it's too hot."

"I am Dr. Verringer," he said with dignity. He turned his head. "Go in the house, Earl."

Earl stood up slowly. He gave Dr. Verringer a thoughtful studying look, his large smoky eyes blank of expression. Then he went up the steps and pulled the screen door open. A cloud of flies buzzed angrily and then settled on the screen again as the door closed.

"Marlowe?" Dr. Verringer gave me his attention again. "And what can I do for you, Mr. Marlowe?"

"Earl says you are out of business here."

"That is correct. I am just waiting for certain legal formalities before moving out. Earl and I are alone here."

"I'm disappointed," I said, looking disappointed. "I thought you had a man named Wade staying with you."

He hoisted a couple of eyebrows that would have interested a Fuller Brush man. "Wade? I might possibly know somebody of that name—it's a common enough name—but why should he be staying with me?"

"Taking the cure."

He frowned. When a guy has eyebrows like that he can really do you a frown. "I am a medical man, sir, but no longer in practice. What sort of cure did you have in mind?"

"The guy's a wino. He goes off his rocker from time to time and disappears. Sometimes he comes home under his own power, sometimes he gets brought home, and sometimes he takes a bit of finding." I got a business card out and handed it to him.

He read it with no pleasure.

"What goes with Earl?" I asked him. "He think he's Valentino or something?"

He made with the eyebrows again. They fascinated me. Parts of them curled off all by themselves as much as an inch and a half. He shrugged his meaty shoulders.

"Earl is quite harmless, Mr. Marlowe. He is—at times— a little dreamy. Lives in a play world, shall we say?"

"You say it, Doc. From where I stand he plays rough."

"Tut, tut, Mr. Marlowe. You exaggerate surely. Earl likes to dress himself up. He is childlike in that respect."

"You mean he's a nut," I said. "This place some kind of sanitarium, isn't it? Or was?"

"Certainly not. When it was in operation it was an artists' colony. I provided meals, lodging, facilities for exer-

cise and entertainment, and above all seclusion. And for
moderate fees. Artists, as you probably know, are seldom
wealthy people. In the term artists I of course include
writers, musicians, and so on. It was a rewarding occupation for me—while it lasted."

He looked sad when he said this. The eyebrows drooped
at the outer corners to match his mouth. Give them a little
more growth and they would be *in* his mouth.

"I know that," I said. "It's in the file. Also the suicide
you had here a while back. A dope case, wasn't it?"

He stopped drooping and bristled. "What file?" he asked
sharply.

"We've got a file on what we call the barred-window
boys, Doctor. Places where you can't jump out of when the
French fits take over. Small private sanitariums or what
have you that treat alcoholics and dopers and mild cases of
mania."

"Such places must be licensed by law," Dr. Verringer
said harshly.

"Yeah. In theory anyway. Sometimes they kind of forget
about that."

He drew himself up stiffly. The guy had a kind of dignity, at that. "The suggestion is insulting, Mr. Marlowe. I
have no knowledge of why my name should be on any
such list as you mention. I must ask you to leave."

"Let's get back to Wade. Could he be here under another name, maybe?"

"There is no one here but Earl and myself. We are
quite alone. Now if you will excuse me—"

"I'd like to look around."

Sometimes you can get them mad enough to say something off key. But not Dr. Verringer. He remained dignified. His eyebrows went all the way with him. I looked
towards the house. From inside there came a sound of
music, dance music. And very faintly the snapping of fingers.

"I bet he's in there dancing," I said. "That's a tango. I
bet you he's dancing all by himself in there. Some kid."

"Are you going to leave, Mr. Marlowe? Or shall I have
to ask Earl to assist me in putting you off my property?"

"Okay, I'll leave. No hard feelings, Doctor. There were
only three names beginning with V and you seemed the
most promising of them. That's the only real clue we had

—Dr. V. He scrawled it on a piece of paper before he left: Dr. V."

"There must be dozens," Dr. Verringer said evenly.

"Oh sure. But not dozens in our file of the barred-window boys. Thanks for the time, Doctor. Earl bothers me a little."

I turned and went over to my car and got into it. By the time I had the door shut Dr. Verringer was beside me. He leaned in with a pleasant expression.

"We need not quarrel, Mr. Marlowe. I realize that in your occupation you often have to be rather intrusive. Just what bothers you about Earl?"

"He's so obviously a phony. Where you find one thing phony you're apt to expect others. The guy's a manic-depressive, isn't he? Right now he's on the upswing."

He stared at me in silence. He looked grave and polite. "Many interesting and talented people have stayed with me, Mr. Marlowe. Not all of them were as level-headed as you may be. Talented people are often neurotic. But I have no facilities for the care of lunatics or alcoholics, even if I had the taste for that sort of work. I have no staff except Earl, and he is hardly the type to care for the sick."

"Just what would you say he is the type for, Doctor? Apart from bubble-dancing and stuff?"

He leaned on the door. His voice got low and confidential. "Earl's parents were dear friends of mine, Mr. Marlowe. Someone has to look after Earl and they are no longer with us. Earl has to live a quiet life, away from the noise and temptations of the city. He is unstable but fundamentally harmless. I control him with absolute ease, as you saw."

"You've got a lot of courage," I said.

He sighed. His eyebrows waved gently, like the antennae of some suspicious insect. "It has been a sacrifice," he said. "A rather heavy one. I thought Earl could help me with my work here. He plays beautiful tennis, swims and dives like a champion, and can dance all night. Almost always he is amiability itself. But from time to time there were— incidents." He waved a broad hand as if pushing painful memories into the background. "In the end it was either give up Earl or give up my place here."

He held both hands palms up, spread them apart, turned them over and let them fall to his sides. His eyes looked moist with unshed tears.

"I sold out," he said. "This peaceful little valley will become a real estate development. There will be sidewalks and lampposts and children with scooters and blatting radios. There will even"—he heaved a forlorn sigh—"be Television." He waved his hand in a sweeping gesture. "I hope they will spare the trees," he said, "but I'm afraid they won't. Along the ridges there will be television aerials instead. But Earl and I will be far away, I trust."

"Goodbye, Doctor. My heart bleeds for you."

He put out his hand. It was moist but very firm. "I appreciate your sympathy and understanding, Mr. Marlowe. And I regret I am unable to help you in your quest for Mr. Slade."

"Wade," I said.

"Pardon me, Wade, of course. Goodbye and good luck, sir."

I started up and drove back along the graveled road by the way I had come. I felt sad, but not quite as sad as Dr. Verringer would have liked me to feel.

I came out through the gates and drove far enough around the curve of the highway to park out of sight of the entrance. I got out and walked back along the edge of the paving to where I could just see the gates from the barbed-wire boundary fence. I stood there under a eucalyptus and waited.

Five minutes or so passed. Then a car came down the private road churning gravel. It stopped out of sight from where I was. I pulled back still farther into the brush. I heard a creaking noise, then the click of a heavy catch and the rattle of a chain. The car revved up and the car went back up the road.

When the sound of it had died I went back to my Olds and did a U turn to face back towards town. As I drove past the entrance to Dr. Verringer's private road I saw that the gate was fastened with a padlocked chain. No more visitors today, thank you.

I drove back to Hollywood feeling like a short length of chewed string. It was too early to eat, and too hot. I turned on the fan in my office. It didn't make the air any cooler, just a little more lively. Outside on the boulevard the traffic brawled endlessly. Inside my head thoughts stuck together like flies on flypaper.

Three shots, three misses. All I had been doing was seeing too many doctors.

I called the Wade home. A Mexican sort of accent answered and said that Mrs. Wade was not at home. I asked for Mr. Wade. The voice said Mr. Wade was not home either. I left my name. He seemed to catch it without any trouble. He said he was the houseboy.

I called George Peters at The Carne Organization. Maybe he knew some more doctors. He wasn't in. I left a phony name and a right telephone number. An hour crawled by like a sick cockroach. I was a grain of sand on the desert of oblivion. I was a two-gun cowpoke fresh out of bullets. Three shots, three misses. I hate it when they come in threes. You call on Mr. A. Nothing. You call on Mr. B. Nothing. You call on Mr. C. More of the same. A week later you find out it should have been Mr. D. Only you didn't know he existed and by the time you found out, the client had changed his mind and killed the investigation.

Drs. Vukanich and Varley were scratched. Varley had it too rich to fool with hooch cases. Vukanich was a punk, a high-wire performer who hit the main line in his own office. The help must know. At least some of the patients must know. All it took to finish him was one sorehead and one telephone call. Wade wouldn't have gone within blocks of him, drunk or sober. He might not be the brightest guy in the world—plenty of successful people are far from mental giants—but he couldn't be dumb enough to fool with Vukanich.

The only possible was Dr. Verringer. He had the space and the seclusion. He probably had the patience. But Sepulveda Canyon was a long way from Idle Valley. Where was the point of contact, how did they know each other, and if Verringer owned that property and had a buyer for it, he was halfway to being pretty well heeled. That gave me an idea. I called a man I knew in a title company to find out the status of the property. No answer. The title company had closed for the day.

I closed for the day too, and drove over to La Cienega to Rudy's Bar-B-Q, gave my name to the master of ceremonies, and waited for the big moment on a bar stool with a whiskey sour in front of me and Marek Weber's waltz music in my ears. After a while I got in past the velvet rope and ate one of Rudy's "world-famous" Salisbury steaks, which is hamburger on a slab of burnt wood, ringed with browned-over mashed potato, supported by fried onion rings and one of those mixed up salads which men will eat with complete docility in restaurants, although they would probably start yelling if their wives tried to feed them one at home.

After that I drove home. As I opened the front door the phone started to ring.

"This is Eileen Wade, Mr. Marlowe. You wanted me to call you."

"Just to find out if anything had happened at your end. I have been seeing doctors all day and have made no friends."

"No, I'm sorry. He still hasn't showed up. I can't help being rather anxious. Then you have nothing to tell me, I suppose." Her voice was low and dispirited.

"It's a big crowded county, Mrs. Wade."

"It will be four whole days tonight."

"Sure, but that's not too long."

"For me it is." She was silent for a while. "I've been doing a lot of thinking, trying to remember something," she went on. "There must be something, some kind of hint or memory. Roger talks a great deal about all sorts of things."

"Does the name Verringer mean anything to you, Mrs. Wade?"

"No, I'm afraid not. Should it?"

"You mentioned that Mr. Wade was brought home one time by a tall young man dressed in a cowboy outfit. Would you recognize this tall young man if you saw him again, Mrs. Wade?"

"I suppose I might," she said hesitantly, "if the conditions were the same. But I only caught the merest glimpse of him. Was his name Verringer?"

"No, Mrs. Wade. Verringer is a heavily built, middle-aged man who runs, or more accurately has run, some kind of guest ranch in Sepulveda Canyon. He has a dressed up fancy boy named Earl working for him. And Verringer calls himself a doctor."

"That's wonderful," she said warmly. "Don't you feel that you're on the right track?"

"I could be wetter than a drowned kitten. I'll call you when I know. I just wanted to make sure Roger hadn't come home and that you hadn't recalled anything definite."

"I'm afraid I haven't been of much help to you," she said sadly. "Please call me at any time, no matter how late it is."

I said I would do that and we hung up. I took a gun and a three-cell flashlight with me this time. The gun was a tough little short-barreled .32 with flat-point cartridges. Dr. Verringer's boy Earl might have other toys than brass knuckles. If he had, he was plenty goofy enough to play with them.

I hit the highway again and drove as fast as I dared. It was a moonless night, and would be getting dark by the time I reached the entrance to Dr. Verringer's estate. Darkness was what I needed.

The gates were still locked with the chain and padlock. I drove on past and parked well off the highway. There was still some light under the trees but it wouldn't last long. I climbed the gate and went up the side of the hill looking for a hiking path. Far back in the valley I thought I heard a quail. A mourning dove exclaimed against the miseries of life. There wasn't any hiking path or I couldn't find one, so I went back to the road and walked along the edge of the gravel. The eucalyptus trees gave way to the oaks and I crossed the ridge and far off I could see a few lights. It took me three quarters of an hour to work up behind the swimming pool and the tennis courts to a spot where I could look down on the main building at the end of the road. It was lighted up and I could hear music coming from it. And farther off in the trees another cabin showed light. There were small dark cabins dotted all over the place in the trees. I went along a path now and suddenly a floodlight went on at the back of the main cabin. I stopped dead. The floodlight was not looking for anything. It pointed straight down and made a wide pool of light on the back porch and the ground beyond. Then a door banged open and Earl came out. Then I knew I was in the right place.

Earl was a cowpoke tonight, and it had been a cowpoke who brought Roger Wade home the time before. Earl was spinning a rope. He wore a dark shirt stitched with white and a polka-dot scarf knotted loosely around his neck. He wore a wide leather belt with a load of silver on it and a pair of tooled leather holsters with ivory-handled guns in them. He wore elegant riding pants and boots cross-stitched in white and glistening new. On the back of his head was

a white sombrero and what looked like a woven silver cord
hanging loosely down his shirt, the ends not fastened.

He stood there alone under the white floodlight, spinning
his rope around him, stepping in and out of it, an actor
without an audience, a tall, slender, handsome dude wran-
gler putting on a show all by himself and loving every
minute of it. Two-Gun Earl, the Terror of Cochise County.
He belonged on one of those guest ranches that are so all-
fired horsy the telephone girl wears riding boots to work.

All at once he heard a sound, or pretended to. The rope
dropped, his hands swept the two guns from the holsters,
and the crook of his thumbs was over the hammers as they
came level. He peered into the darkness. I didn't dare move.
The damn guns could be loaded. But the floodlight had
blinded him and he didn't see anything. He slipped his guns
back in the holsters, picked up the rope and gathered it
loosely, went back into the house. The light went off, and
so did I.

I moved around through the trees and got close to the
small lighted cabin on the slope. No sound came from it. I
reached a screened window and looked in. The light came
from a lamp on a night table beside a bed. A man lay flat
on his back in the bed, his body relaxed, his arms in
pajama sleeves outside the covers, his eyes wide open and
staring at the ceiling. He looked big. His face was partly
shadowed, but I could see that he was pale and that he
needed a shave and had needed one for just about the right
length of time. The spread fingers of his hands lay motionless on the outside of the bed. He looked as if he hadn't
moved for hours.

I heard steps coming along the path at the far side of the
cabin. A screen door creaked and then the solid shape of
Dr. Verringer showed in the doorway. He was carrying
what looked like a large glass of tomato juice. He switched
on a standing lamp. His Hawaiian shirt gleamed yellowly.
The man in the bed didn't even look at him.

Dr. Verringer put the glass down on the night table and
pulled a chair close and sat down. He reached for one of
the wrists and felt a pulse. "How are you feeling now, Mr.
Wade?" His voice was kindly and solicitous.

The man on the bed didn't answer him or look at him.
He went on staring at the ceiling.

"Come, come, Mr. Wade. Let us not be moody. Your

pulse is only slightly faster than normal. You are weak, but otherwise—"

"Tejjy," the man on the bed said suddenly, "tell the man that if he knows how I am, the son of a bitch needn't bother to ask me." He had a nice clear voice, but the tone was bitter.

"Who is Tejjy?" Dr. Verringer said patiently.

"My mouthpiece. She's up there in the corner."

Dr. Verringer looked up. "I see a small spider," he said. "Stop acting, Mr. Wade. It is not necessary with me."

"*Tegenaria domestica*, the common jumping spider, pal. I like spiders. They practically never wear Hawaiian shirts."

Dr. Verringer moistened his lips. "I have no time for playfulness, Mr. Wade."

"Nothing playful about Tejjy." Wade turned his head slowly, as if it weighed very heavy, and stared at Dr. Verringer contemptuously. "Tejjy is dead serious. She creeps up on you. When you're not looking she makes a quick silent hop. After a while she's near enough. She makes the last jump. You get sucked dry, Doctor. Very dry. Tejjy doesn't eat you. She just sucks the juice until there's nothing left but the skin. If you plan to wear that shirt much longer, Doctor, I'd say it couldn't happen too soon."

Dr. Verringer leaned back in the chair. "I need five thousand dollars," he said calmly. "How soon could that happen?"

"You got six hundred and fifty bucks," Wade said nastily. "As well as my loose change. How the hell much does it cost in this bordello?"

"Chicken feed," Dr. Verringer said. "I told you my rates had gone up."

"You didn't say they had moved to Mount Wilson."

"Don't fence with me, Wade," Dr. Verringer said curtly. "You are in no position to get funny. Also you have betrayed my confidence."

"I didn't know you had any."

Dr. Verringer tapped slowly on the arms of the chair. "You called me up in the middle of the night," he said. "You were in a desperate condition. You said you would kill yourself if I didn't come. I didn't want to do it and you know why. I have no license to practice medicine in this state. I am trying to get rid of this property without losing it all. I have Earl to look after and he was about due for a bad spell. I told you it would cost you a lot of money. You still insisted and I went. I want five thousand dollars."

"I was foul with strong drink," Wade said. "You can't hold a man to that kind of bargain. You're damn well paid already."

"Also," Dr. Verringer said slowly, "you mentioned my name to your wife. You told her I was coming for you."

Wade looked surprised. "I didn't do anything of the sort," he said. "I didn't even see her. She was asleep."

"Some other time then. A private detective has been here asking about you. He couldn't possibly have known where to come, unless he was told. I stalled him off, but he may come back. You have to go home, Mr. Wade. But first I want my five thousand dollars."

"You're not the brightest guy in the world, are you, Doc? If my wife knew where I was, why would she need a detective? She could have come herself—supposing she cared that much. She could have brought Candy, our houseboy. Candy would cut your Blue Boy into thin strips while Blue Boy was making up his mind what picture he was starring in today."

"You have a nasty tongue, Wade. And a nasty mind."

"I have a nasty five thousand bucks too, Doc. Try and get it."

"You will write me a check," Dr. Verringer said firmly. "Now, at once. Then you will get dressed and Earl will take you home."

"A check?" Wade was almost laughing. "Sure I'll give you a check. Fine. How will you cash it?"

Dr. Verringer smiled quietly. "You think you will stop payment, Mr. Wade. But you won't. I assure you that you won't."

"You fat crook!" Wade yelled at him.

Dr. Verringer shook his head. "In some things, yes. Not in all. I am a mixed character like most people. Earl will drive you home."

"Nix. That lad makes my skin crawl," Wade said.

Dr. Verringer stood up gently and reached over and patted the shoulder of the man on the bed. "To me Earl is quite harmless, Mr. Wade. I have ways of controlling him."

"Name one," a new voice said, and Earl came through the door in his Roy Rogers outfit. Dr. Verringer turned smiling.

"Keep that psycho away from me," Wade yelled, show-ing fear for the first time.

Earl put his hands on his ornamented belt. His face was deadpan. A light whistling noise came from between his teeth. He moved slowly into the room.

"You shouldn't have said that," Dr. Verringer said quickly, and turned towards Earl. "All right, Earl. I'll handle Mr. Wade myself. I'll help him get dressed while you bring the car up here as close to the cabin as possible. Mr. Wade is quite weak."

"And he's going to be a lot weaker," Earl said in a whistling kind of voice. "Out of my way, fatso."

"Now, Earl—" he reached out and grabbed the hand-some young man's arm—"you don't want to go back to Camarillo, do you? One word from me and—"

That was as far as he got. Earl jerked his arm loose and his right hand came up with a flash of metal. The armored fist crashed against Dr. Verringer's jaw. He went down as if shot through the heart. The fall shook the cabin. I started running.

I reached the door and yanked it open. Earl spun around, leaning forward a little, staring at me without recognition. There was a bubbling sound behind his lips. He started for me fast.

I jerked the gun out and showed it to him. It meant nothing. Either his own guns were not loaded or he had forgotten all about them. The brass knuckles were all he needed. He kept coming.

I fired through the open window across the bed. The crash of the gun in the small room seemed much louder than it should have been. Earl stopped dead. His head slewed around and he looked at the hole in the window screen. He looked back at me. Slowly his face came alive and he grinned.

"Wha' happen?" he asked brightly.

"Get rid of the knucks," I said, watching his eyes.

He looked surprisingly down at his hand. He slipped the mauler off and threw it casually in the corner.

"Now the gun belt," I said. "Don't touch the guns, just the buckle."

"They're not loaded," he said smiling. "Hell, they're not even guns, just stage money."

"The belt. Hurry it."

He looked at the short-barreled .32. "That a real one? Oh sure it is. The screen. Yeah, the screen."

The man on the bed wasn't on the bed any more. He was behind Earl. He reached swiftly and pulled one of the bright guns loose. Earl didn't like this. His face showed it.

"Lay off him," I said angrily. "Put that back where you got it."

"He's right," Wade said. "They're cap guns." He backed away and put the shiny pistol on the table. "Christ, I'm as weak as a broken arm."

"Take the belt off," I said for the third time. When you start something with a type like Earl you have to finish it. Keep it simple and don't change your mind.

He did it at last, quite amiably. Then, holding the belt, he walked over to the table and got his other gun and put it in the holster and put the belt right back on again. I let him do it. It wasn't until then that he saw Dr. Verringer crumpled on the floor against the wall. He made a sound of concern, went quickly across the room into the bathroom, and came back with a glass jug of water. He dumped the water on Dr. Verringer's head. Dr. Verringer sputtered and rolled over. Then he groaned. Then he clapped a hand to his jaw. Then he started to get up. Earl helped him.

"Sorry, Doc. I must have just let fly without seeing who it was."

"It's all right, nothing broken," Verringer said, waving him away. "Get the car up here, Earl. And don't forget the key for the padlock down below."

"Car up here, sure. Right away. Key for the padlock. I got it. Right away, Doc."

He went out of the room whistling.

Wade was sitting on the side of the bed, looking shaky. "You the dick he was talking about?" he asked me. "How did you find me?"

"Just asking around from people who know about these things," I said. "If you want to get home, you might get clothes on."

Dr. Verringer was leaning against the wall, massaging his jaw. "I'll help him," he said thickly. "All I do is help people and all they do is kick me in the teeth."

"I know just how you feel," I said.

I went out and left them to work at it.

# LEONARD GARDNER

## Christ Has Returned to Earth and Preaches Here Nightly

From the small, flat, hot valley town of Tracy, California
—split by a highway and surrounded by fields of sugar
beets, alfalfa, and tomatoes—an enormous pink car one
day departed by the eastern end without previously entering by the western end, this car being the property of a
permanent resident, Ernest Grubb, nineteen, who was in
turn the property of a finance company. Ernest's fingernails were rimmed in black and there were black specks
imbedded in the blemishes on his cheeks. Painted on the
rear fenders of the car, though it was only a week out of
the show room, were the words VALENTINO RETURNS.
Sunk in the passenger side of the front seat were the
meager contours of Harry Ames, also nineteen, who had
just been removed from unemployment insurance rolls in
accordance with a code section under the heading "Failure
to Seek Work." Harry was taking Ernest Grubb, with Ernest furnishing the car and gas, to a rendezvous with two
divorcees in the neighboring town of Stockton. Until that
day he had only mentioned one divorcee (and he mentioned
her at every opportunity), but now it appeared there had
always been two and that he divided his attentions equally
between them, which made it sound as if there were only

one. Ernest felt an innate caution around friends in need of chauffeurs, but as he had yet to score anything with his new car in a week of cruising, he could not decline Harry's proposition.

Once during that week he had almost been successful, but his passenger had passed out before he could take her anywhere. He had driven around as long as he could, waiting for her to revive, but as he had to drive a tractor early the next morning, he left her on the lawn in front of the library. Ernest had thought of leaving her in the car overnight to enjoy during his lunch hour in the fields; however, he had feared he might end up having to marry her, if she knew where he lived. Such things were known to happen in Tracy, as his father often warned him. His father himself had been discovered in front of his future in-laws' house one bright morning, asleep on the back seat of a model A Ford in only a pair of high-top shoes without socks (it was summer) beside the girl who was now the cranky, round-shouldered, double-chinned television fan for whom Ernest bought bubble bath on Mother's Day. Divorcees were better risks; they were also anxious to regain lost delights.

When he had driven no farther than a hamburger stand at the edge of town, however, Ernest had already become skeptical.

"If we can't get hold of yours right away," Harry told him, "you just wait around till I'm through and we'll go find her. She's really fine looking, I swear it."

"I thought it was all fixed up."

"It's all set," Harry assured him. "Only her mother's dying in the hospital and maybe she had to go there for something, you know, to bid farewell. You wouldn't grudge her that, would you?"

"She won't be no fun coming from her mother's death bed," Ernest complained.

Harry answered that he had to have a hamburger, and Ernest felt obligated to stop. Having done so, he was likewise obligated to pay.

The girl behind the glass, who passed the hamburgers through an opening as small as the ticket hole in a box office, refused to speak to them, as it was generally known that certain advertisements penciled on local walls, involving her name and phone number and a very low sum of money, were the work of Harry Ames. Advertising ran in Harry's family; his father was the proprietor of *Neon Signs*.

As the two rode on placidly chewing, Harry said he wanted a donut, but Ernest stated they would stop no more until they picked up the divorcees. Harry alluded to loss of virility from malnutrition, then glumly stared at his tattoos. On one forearm beneath a dagger piercing his profusely bleeding skin was written DEATH BEFORE DISHONOR, and on the other, HARRY AMES and U.S.M.C. curved around the Marine Corps emblem—an anchor and the world with a boil in its northern hemisphere. He had obtained these in his thirteenth year from a Hawaiian who had come up from Stockton on a motor scooter with his needles in the tool box.

Farmers were still out irrigating, but the pickers had all come in. Butterflies and juicy bugs that had somehow eluded the divebombings of crop-dusters smacked against the windshield. Tomato lugs lay scattered between rows in the fields and Ernest, coming upon one in the road, attempted to swerve around it—without success, due to the immensity of his tires. He felt the bump and with a pounding heart heard a rush of air among the cracks and clatters under the car. With resignation he thumped off onto the shoulder.

Upon inspection of the trunk, Ernest discovered that the only accessory he had not been issued was a jack, and so he and Harry were forced to stand at the edge of the road waving at passing cars. Twilight was approaching and with it the opening of the drive-in movie. Ernest and Harry were rocked back on their heels, their clothes flapping like sails, as car after car raced by with a male head behind the steering wheel and a female head so close a two-headed monster appeared to be driving. Finally a low, dull-grey sedan with flames painted on the hood hurled by in a din of loose rods. Wobbling on and off the dusty shoulder, it screeched to a stop and began backing up. A dangling plaque with THE BLOWN GASKETS emblazoned across it identified the vehicle as Count Messner's, for his was the only car in that particular automobile club. The Count stepped out followed by Joe and Wallace Pucci, their hair sweeping upward on the sides in vast glistening arcs like the wings of birds of paradise, and curling down over their foreheads like the necks of swans, the ends in a beak over each of their noses. The Count succeeded in prying open the handleless trunk lid and threw a jack down in the dust. Then, his thumb hooked in the fly of his Levi's, he stood in

a line with the others and watched Ernest flounder with his
tire. Though it was a warm valley evening and the Count
and the Puccis had lived their lives in Tracy, they wore red
wool jackets with

### "THE BLOWN GASKETS"
### "OF"
### "FRISCO"

on the backs in white letters. They were—the Count explained, as the jack began to lean under the sighing corpu-
lence of the car—on their way to Manteca to pick up
Sylvia Fuller, a girl who enjoyed considerable popularity
despite an I.Q. uncoveted by her rivals. As her father, a
Baptist egg producer, had archaic views on dating, it was
necessary for the carloads of Sylvia's admirers to honk
once when passing the farm house, then continue on to a
dirt road leading to an irrigation ditch with grassy banks
and the seclusion of willows where, a few minutes later,
Sylvia would come stumbling to them over the clods.

Ernest bolting on the spare, was somewhat interested in
this outing, but Harry assured him they had better things
awaiting them. The car crashed back to earth, the Count
and the Puccis returned to their flaming sedan, and when
Ernest started his motor they roared away, spraying his
windshield with gravel. He saw their derisive faces looking
back, but as he had hundreds more miles of slow driving
before his engine would be broken in, he had to watch the
ash-colored car shrink away. While Harry sat in scornful
silence, Ernest punched buttons on the radio until he got a
good-music station to his liking. They were all good-music
stations now, but some played better good-music than others.

A sawmill of electric guitars resounded in the car, and
the abdomen of a large grasshopper, clinging desperately to
a windshield-wiper blade, began to pulsate.

"She better not be no pig," Ernest threatened. "I won't
take just anything."

"You won't be disappointed, I promise you. If she was a
pig nobody would of married her in the first place, would
they?"

Ernest was not dull. He had read Shakespeare in high
school—"A Midsummer Night's Dream," in *Classic Comics*
—and earned an A for his report on it. He told Harry he

could hitchhike back if things were not as represented. Harry slid down in the seat and stared out of the window with his nose on the sill.

They crossed the muddy San Joaquin River, where houseboats with smoking stovepipes and clusters of rowboats were tied among the tules, and they passed grain fields and orchards, fruit stands, and packs of erotic dogs. Though Stockton was less than twenty miles from Tracy, Ernest had to stop in French Camp for minor repairs; his sputtering car had consumed nearly a quarter-tank of gas. It died as he was attempting to cross to a station, settling in the center of the highway. After he had ground the starter several minutes with traffic swerving by on both sides, a man in a foreign sports car shouted something as he shot past.

"Come here and say that!" Ernest yelled, leaping out; then with a surge of indignant patriotism he strained against the door frame, as did Harry on the other side, until the car rolled a few inches and Ernest felt a hernia about to detonate. The station attendant, a young man with a sideburn on one side of his face and a small radio against the other, came out to assist.

In the station Ernest watched gloomily as the attendant worked under the hood with a dexterous right hand, his left still holding the radio to his ear.

"I bet you got to beat the women off it with a stick," the young man said when the hood was down again and he and Ernest were standing back gazing at the whole pink panorama, their eyes jumping as if viewing a pinball machine where all the balls had been shot in one giant splurge.

"That's where we're going now," answered Ernest.

"Huh?"

"Divorcees."

"I might of known it," the attendant said enviously. "Huh? I hope they come through for you."

"No hoping about it," replied Ernest.

He drove on, now very anxious to meet his divorcee. He felt so deserving of her it seemed unreasonable to doubt Harry's promises. Ernest Grubb had all the qualities necessary for the successful man about town and it would hardly make sense if they went unrewarded. Even on those occasions when he was outside his car his personal charm was magnetic, as he had once demonstrated in a truckbed full of sugar beets, where a young woman, Sylvia Fuller, had fallen hopelessly in love with him while his friends waited on the running board. He walked with his pants hung low, thumbs in his pockets, heel taps scraping, and when he spoke he mumbled just enough, with his head down and the hint of a sneer on his lips, to give him a suggestion of great suffering, of having a profound soul that had been misunderstood; and though he was swarthy and tended toward plumpness, he could nevertheless discern in his features a certain resemblance to the late James Dean.

"I'm going to make that divorcee cry for more," he said to Harry, who slipped his spine farther down the seat.

Nearing the city limits of Stockton, Ernest and Harry encountered several homemade signs—HAVE *YOU* BEEN CHOSEN? COULD YOU FACE JUDGMENT *TODAY*?—before approaching a large tent sagging next to a wrecking yard. Over the entrance of the tent a banner announced: CHRIST HAS RETURNED TO EARTH AND PREACHES HERE NIGHTLY.

Harry, a student of advertising, approved it as a good gimmick.

"I wonder how they got the guy rigged up," said Ernest, looking over at the tent where a few dilapidated cars and pickup trucks were parked.

"Let's stop and see," suggested Harry, "We don't have to put nothing in the plate."

When Ernest said they didn't have time, Harry assured him they were too early for their appointments. "You don't want to look eager, do you?"

"I'm not eager. I'm just in a hurry."

"But they won't be ready! You get what I mean? I'll have to call and say we're coming early."

"That's okay."

Harry ran his fingers down his face. "Turn in here then, and I'll use their phone."

"There wouldn't be no phone at a revival tent."

"Sure there would. Hurry up, turn! Turn!"

Flustered by Harry's urgency, Ernest turned with misgivings onto the dirt driveway.

"I don't see no phone booth," Harry Ames said after they had climbed out. "I'll tell you what—I'll take the car into town and get the divorcees while you're watching the show, and we'll all come back here and pick you up. How's that?"

"I'll go with you," Ernest answered flatly.

"Well, hell, we might as well see what's going on then," Harry mumbled, kicking the dust.

As they entered the tent, a preacher under a string of dim light bulbs shouted to them in a ringing tenor. "He's not here yet, folks." Long strands of black hair, evidently combed across his bald spot before the sermon, hung down over one ear to his collar. The hair on the other side of his head was clipped short. "But just be patient. He's coming. I got the word from Christ himself that He's coming, and He won't let us down. No He won't. He told me definitely He would be here in this meeting tent tonight to talk to all you good people and come into your hearts, and I know He will, because He don't lie. No, friends, Jesus Christ don't lie—no He don't, no question about that—and He'll be here among us shortly to make us all singing saints in the sixties. I think I can feel Him coming now, folks; I think I can, and you'll feel Him, too—yes you will—if you'll just let yourselves. Won't you let yourselves feel Jesus?"

"Let's get out of here," whispered Ernest, who had at least expected someone in sandals from San Francisco. "There isn't going to be any guy, can't you see what he means? You're supposed to *feel* Him."

When Harry said they had better wait and see, Ernest knew it was a stall; if he waited until Christ came he never would find out about the divorcees.

As the preacher talked on, the rumble of an approaching motorcycle grew outside, finally coming to an idle near the tent flap, then flaring up into one last thunderous blast, and when the roar died away he was wailing: "O, I feel Him, He's coming, I hear Him, yes indeed I feel Him coming." As he rocked with closed eyes, saliva gleaming on his chin, the congregation turned toward the entrance.

A young man in a leather jacket, with a small goatee like armpit hair on the end of his chin, came in and walked unsteadily to the front. Across his back was painted BALLS O' FIRE.

"I feel Him coming," the preacher gasped. "To spread His gospel, yes, His blessed assurance."

The motorcyclist shambled up beside him. Then, spreading his arms, he addressed the congregation, "Verily I say unto you." Knees buckling, sighing, the preacher swooned backward. Women moaned and shrieked; one slumped in her chair speaking words unknown to mortal man.

"Let me talk," the motorcyclist interrupted, raising a hand, light sparkling off the chromium studs of his jacket. "Peace! Verily I am the Christ our Lord, let me tell you. And if none of you believe it you better read up on your Bible, because now I've come whether nobody expected me or not, and I can see by the size of our gathering that not too many did. Well, that's all right. Each man's salvation is up to him. But I could tell by your humble cars outside— all except one that's a vehicle of sin if I ever seen one— that you're the chosen ones. I know you lived clean and righteous lives by looking in your weary faces. And don't think you're going to be forgotten for your sacrifices, because right now, here in this tent tonight, is the Last Judgment. No need telling your friends and neighbors to come tomorrow. They're just out of luck. Only those that were here to greet me have earned them berths up in paradise."

There were cries of spiritual ecstasy. A woman fell on all fours, children wailed in confusion, and a gangling redhaired man was on his knees pleading: "Let me go home and get my daughter. My teen-age daughter, she's led a sinful life." Ernest, recognizing him as LeRoy Fuller, of Fuller's Eggs, Grad B Dirties, and the father of Sylvia, hunched down on his folding chair.

"We don't want no fallen women with us On High, man," replied the motorcyclist. "I bet you're the one that owns that pink car out there, aren't you?"

"No sir, no, I don't," LeRoy Fuller protested. "No, no, just an old pickup. Won't you please wait while I get her?"

"Verily, like I said, only the people that happen to be here get in on the deal, out of all the peoples on the four corners of the earth, see? That's the way things go." He raised his hand to quiet the tumult. "Hark! I ask ye to be quiet, all right? I'll leave you now. Preaching can't do no more when you're as pure like unto a new born lamb. Go in peace to your eternal reward."

He strode out of the tent. Ernest left just as the motorcycle roared off. It was dark outside now, and he saw the single headlight rushing toward Stockton.

"You'd think they'd of dressed him up better than that," said Harry.

Others were leaving the tent. When the preacher came out holding the back of his neck and asking what had happened, everybody answered at once. "Are you sure?" he said in a cautious, puzzled tone, stroking the long sparse hairs back over his head. "You didn't just hear His words? What did He look like?"

"He had a beard."

"Had a *beard*?" he shouted, steadying himself on a tent rope. "What have I done, brothers and sisters? A *beard*! A materialization—God bless you—of the Holy Ghost, amen, His most sacred heart, His lofty brow . . ."

"My daughter's been doing bad things," LeRoy Fuller interrupted, and Ernest crept toward his car.

"Bring her, that her wound may be healed, that she may never again tread the path of sin—no never—and bring a newspaper reporter. Dearly beloved friends, I'm on my way to bigger things—yes I am, I can see that—a great crusade to save Los Angeles, the juvenile delinquents, the moving picture industry . . ."

As LeRoy Fuller was trying to start his pickup truck, marked on the door with the name of his business, and on the hood and fenders with verifications by the hens themselves, Ernest and Harry departed.

LeRoy Fuller, and a covering of dust over the car, had depressed Ernest and when, at the edge of town, Harry returned from a phone booth with regrets that Ernest's divorcee was not home, Ernest mumbled that they were going right back to Tracy.

"No, no," protested Harry. "She left a message with her mother for you to meet her later at my divorcee's place. She said to be sure and wait for her."

Recalling that her mother was at the moment dying in the hospital, Ernest prepared to make a U-turn.

"Just give me an hour," Harry pleaded. "That's all I ask."

Harry Ames' appeal for women was famous. His legend could be found recorded in numerous lavatories with lists of mysterious names often included. Still his arsenal of charms lacked that major one Ernest had so recently acquired. And so Ernest decided to win the remaining divorcee for himself. As he continued into town, the folds subsided from Harry's forehead.

At a stop signal Ernest found himself between two choptop cars, one identified as HITLER'S REVENGE. The hunched drivers peered up at him through slot windows, shouting challenges above the eruptions of their mufflers. But Ernest had to let them, too, screech away without him.

He proceeded with ardent limbs and just a trace of shame to the divorcee's residence—a room, in a transient hotel, that remained silent after·five minutes of pounding. "Maybe she's not home," he suggested, but Harry, calling and kicking, shook the door until an old man with warts and slippers puffed up the stairs to request that Ernest and Harry go elsewhere.

They drove to the bar where the divorcee was employed, in case by some miscalculation she was working on her day off. Crowds of Filipino and Mexican farm workers milled on the sidewalks, and winos were against cars and walls and down in doorways. Ernest parked well away from the bottle-lined gutter, locked all the doors, walked around the car checking them, and then followed Harry into the *Club Aguascalientes*.

A crowd of men stood around a lone woman on a bar stool. Harry, out of the side of his mouth, requested that Ernest not mention the other divorcee, as his divorcee knew nothing about her. "I don't want to make her jealous," he explained, then pushed in among the crowd. Following, Ernest tripped over boots and was jabbed by the leather elbows of the BALLS O' FIRE motorcycle club.

"Hello, sweetie," Harry said, "Did you forget we had a date?"

The woman had orange hair, a bloodred dress, pink high heels with white bobbysocks, and a pallid face that had fallen into pouches. She squinted at him. "Who's that, anyhow?"

"It's me, sweetie—Harry."

"Harry who? Step over in the light, why don't you?"

"Harry Ames, your date and steady," he said in a rising voice as he shoved in closer.

"Watch it, man," somebody warned.

"Oh, it's you, honey. Why didn't you say so? Who's that with you?"

"Ernest Grubb, this is April Humphrey, the Georgia Peach."

"I got a brand new car outside," said Ernest. "You want to take a ride in it?"

The bartender demanded Ernest and Harry's identification, and as they slowly took out their wallets and went through the pantomime of searching for cards that must somehow have been misplaced, April Humphrey began necking with one of the motorcyclists.

"It's here somewhere," Harry said. "Come on, sweetie, let's get out of here."

"Let's you and me sneak off for a ride in my new car—alone," Ernest whispered in her ear, careful not to say it in the motorcyclist's.

Her lipless mouth, surrounded by a liberal red smear, puckered tenderly as she declined. "I'm sorry, honey, can't you see I'm working?" She held up a highball and began swallowing.

"How about afterwards?" Harry asked with a note of desperation, while the motorcyclist nibbled at her throat.

"Better make it some other time, honey."

A heel mashed down on Ernest's toes. When he squirmed to free himself he was cracked under the chin by a five-starred epaulet. "You better fade, man," somebody muttered beside him, and someone else in a loud voice said, "Minors." The bartender then ordered Ernest and Harry out, and as they hung their heads and stalled, mumbling about pickpockets, they were grasped around the shoulders and waists and hauled protesting to the doorway. Ernest felt a foot against his spine just before he was catapulted out into the night. As he rose to his hands and knees, the jukebox inside began to play.

Harry was sitting on the sidewalk with his pants leg pulled up examining his knee. Near him a woman in a black bonnet and dress, with a canvas satchel hanging from her shoulder, held up a magazine, *Awake!*

"There been signs and portents," she said. "A horse give birth to a chicken tonight, and Jesus Christ was seen just outside town in his flowing robes and crown of thorns. Are you ready for the end, young man?" She thrust the magazine at Ernest, and he yelled "No!" as he stumbled up against the car, trying to get the key in the lock. "Has your soul been purified?" He scrambled inside. Harry limped over and joined him, and Ernest started the motor with the woman's voice ringing in his ears. "Tomorrow's too late!"

A band was playing on the corner as Ernest stopped at the signal. Above the thuds and bleats, an old man jangling a tambourine was hysterically chanting that the world was coming to an end. Loiterers leaning against darkened store fronts gave no signs of caring, which seemed to make the man more desperate. He began to plead. Several BALLS O' FIRE motorcyclists parked by the curb were heckling, and one of them Ernest recognized. From his sneer, it also

seemed he recognized Ernest's car as the one he had de-
nounced at the revival.

"Didn't that thing get you there yet?" he yelled. Crouch-
ing for a fast start with his goatee jutting forward, he raced
his motor. When the signal changed, Ernest bitterly roared
off beside him with screaming tires. They buzzed up the
block side by side, shot through the next intersection, then,
as the motorcycle pulled ahead, a sudden great clamor of
blacksmith banging commenced in Ernest's engine. He applied the brakes, his face going pale and his heart seeming
to sink out of him.

Slumped over the wheel, too sick to speak, he drove
slowly out of town. When the car passed the lot where the
revival had been, the tent was already gone. A small gathering of patient people were still waiting by lantern light,
their failing voices raised in song.

Banging and clattering, the car crept on, past fields,
orchards, and lighted farm houses, over the black river,
finally making it back to the glare of Tracy's neon. Ernest
drove straight to his house and told Harry he could walk
home. Leaving him complaining in the car, he trudged
through the weeds to his back door.

But Ernest did not open it. In the night's immense emptiness the thought of his bed was more than he could
bear. Instead, he crouched behind a shrub and peered
through the leaves at the car. The interior light came on as
Harry stepped out, then went off with a slam. Ernest remained among the twigs long after the horseshoe heels had
faded off down the sidewalk. When he returned to the
street it was with a desolation that frightened him.

He drove out of town, and as he neared Manteca the
feeling seemed to lessen, and to his relief it lessened still
more when, knocking past moonlit chicken pens, he gave
his horn a short decorous honk. The feeling continued to
grow less as he bounced over the ruts of a dirt road, and
then, by the willows, as he watched the pajama-clad figure
coming toward him across the field, it was gone altogether.

# JAMES D. HOUSTON

# Continental Drift

## I

From high above, say gazing down from one of our track-ing satellites, he can see it plain as an incision, a six-hundred-mile incision some careless surgeon stitched up across the surface of the earth. It marks the line where two great slabs of the earth's crust meet and grind together. Most of North America occupies one of these slabs. Most of the Pacific Ocean floats on the other. A small lip of the Pacific slab extends above the surface, along America's western coastline, a lush and mountainous belt of land not as much a part of the rest of the continent as it is the most visible piece of that slab of crust which lies submerged. The line where these two slabs, or plates, meet is called the San Andreas Fault. It cuts south from San Francisco, past San Jose, underneath the old San Juan Bautista Mission, on down behind Los Angeles, and back under water again at the Gulf of California.

The Pacific plate, he will tell you, is creeping north and west at about two inches per year, an example of the movement geologists call continental drift. Our globe, which appears to be divided into continents and bodies of water, is actually a patchwork of these vast plates, all

103

floating around on a kind of subterranean pudding. What it resembles most is a badly fractured skull. From time to time the towns and cities along the fault line have been jiggled or jolted by tremors large and small, when sections of it buckle or lock, and then unbend, release, or settle. There are people who predict that one day the ultimate quake is going to send a huge chunk of California sliding into the ocean like Atlantis. They foresee this as one of the worst disasters in the history of the civilized world. They sometimes add that in a land as bizarre and corrupt as California is reputed to be, such a fate has been well earned.

Montrose Doyle will tell you all that is poppycock, both the physics and the prophecy. He will tell you that the earth's crust is three hundred miles thick, whereas the fault line only cuts down for thirty of those miles. He will tell you that if anything is going to undo this piece of coast it will be the accumulated body weight of all the people who have been moving into his part of the world at a steady rate since 1849. But it won't be the San Andreas. He has made it his business to find out what he can about this creature, because he owns fifty-five acres of orchard and grazing land that border it. He grew up on this ranch, will probably die here, and during his forty-six years he has seldom felt more than a tic across the earth's skin, an infrequent shiver in the high cupola which serves as his personal antenna and seismograph.

Montrose has studied with fascination the photographs of rotundas upended in the streets of San Francisco during the famous quake of 1906. He has corresponded with experts. And he has escorted visitors over to Hollister, twenty-five miles east of where his own house stands. An otherwise neat and orderly farm town, Hollister happens to be gradually splitting in two, because it sits in the fracture zone, like an Eskimo village caught on a cracking ice floe. By following cracks you can trace the subtle power of the fault as it angles under the town, offsetting sidewalks and curbstones and gutters, an effect most alarming in the house of a chiropractor which you pass soon after entering Hollister from the west. One half of a low concrete retaining wall holding back the chiropractor's lawn has been carried north and west about eight inches. The concrete walkway is buckling. Both porch pillars lean precariously toward the coast. In back, the wall of his garage is bent into a curve like a stack of whale's ribs. The fact that half his doomed house rides on the American plate and the other half rides the Pacific has not discouraged this chiropractor from maintaining a little order in his life. He hangs his sign out front, he keeps his lawn well mowed and the old house brightly, spotlessly painted.

One afternoon Montrose leaned down to talk with a fellow in Hollister who was working on the transmission of a Chevy pickup. The curb his truck stood next to had been shattered by the ageless tension of those two slabs of earth crust pulling at each other. Five inches had opened in the curb, like a little wound, and someone had tried to fill it with homemade concrete, and that had started to split.

Monty said, "Hey!"

The grease-smeared face emerged, irritably. It was hot. The man said, "Yeah?"

"Hey, doesn't the fault line run through this part of town?"

"The what?"

"The San Andreas . . ."

"Oh, that damn thing." The man waved his wrench aimlessly. "Yeah, she's around somewhere," and he slid back out of sight underneath his pickup.

Montrose regards that man with fondness now. He voiced Monty's own attitude pretty well, which is to say, none of this really troubles him much. Is he a fatalist? Yes. And no. He anticipates. Yet he does not anticipate. What he loves to dwell on—what he savors so much during those trips to Hollister—is that steady creep which, a few million years hence, will put his ranch on a latitude with Juneau, Alaska. He admires the foresight of the Spanish cartographers who, in their earliest maps, pictured California as an island. Sometimes late at night, after he has been drinking heavily, he will hike out to his fence line and imagine that he can feel beneath his feet the dragging of the continental plates, and imagine that he is standing on his own private raft, a New World Noah, heading north, at two inches per year.

Most of the time he doesn't think about it at all. It is simply there, a presence beneath his land. If it ever comes to mind during his waking hours, he thinks of it as just that, a presence, a force, you might even say a certainty, the one thing he knows he can count on—this relentless grinding of two great slabs which have been butting head-on now for millennia and are not about to relax.

## II

Monty's house is redwood, cut from timbers hauled out of the coastal fog eighty years ago. He still isn't certain who built it. They say she was a widow, a Christian Scientist who wanted a high cupola so she could sit up there and contemplate the ocean on a clear day. They say she was a meditator. Monterey Bay is seven miles west. In the summer it makes a distant wedge of burnished metal, like a hypnotist's medallion. This is the only explanation he has been able to find that accounts for the steep angle of his roof, an alpine roof designed to help heavy snows slide over the side. Montrose has lived here since he was eleven, has seen snow seven times, and only twice has it lasted overnight. He calls it white rain. An alpine roof on a Victorian house, its sole function to lift a cupola above the nearest trees.

His wife, Leona, sits up there from time to time with the field glasses, gazing not west, as the Christian Scientist would have done, but east, toward the "river." She calls this a river. The river with no water. And no bottom. She envisions a deep fissure that drops, like a polar crevasse, right to the seething bowels of the earth. She knows better. When he calls it "the Grand Canyon of our dreams," Leona giggles. They used to make love out there. Nowadays she would rather not go near it, not since The Big Scare of 1969. She prefers her vision. It inspires her, she says. Her tapestries are conceived up in the cupola. Alone, with the trap door shut, she sketches baroque and involuted patterns, then brings the sketches downstairs to her workroom, her rainbow of threads and yarns and her armory of needles. Sometimes she does not sketch. Sometimes from the cupola, when the light is soft and indirect and right, she will study shadows and imagine the ground's anger, the muscular rippling that will bend this ungainly house and send her flying as if released from a catapult.

Montrose prefers the shadowy interior, the first-floor living room, cool and quiet, with, at this hour, clean new

light silhouetting indoor plants—begonias, asparagus ferns
—while he moves through his yoga regimen. His dance.
His morning solo. "It's for the lower back," he tells the
fellows in town, who know he has had that kind of trouble.
"Spinal massage," he will say. "Glandular toning." Since
they greet even this much with suspicion, he keeps to himself the larger reason, the appeal of things eternal.

In a headstand, breathing deeply, gazing upside down at
his plants, he feels at once afloat and firmly rooted. He is
alive. The air is alive. The plants are alive. The house is
alive. The grain of the boards in the window casing reminds him once again that these trees lived a thousand
years, in the fog and sunlight, shading giant primeval ferns.
Maybe longer. They are among the olest living things on
earth. In state parks he has seen the cross-cut sections of
patriarch redwoods with rings tagged back through history
to the birth of Jesus Christ, and beyond. To the assassina-
tion of Julius Caesar in 44 B.C. He stares at the grain in his
window casing, each dark stripe a year of aging, a year of
growth. Breathing, he finds himself inside a tree. The hairs
on his head are fibers feeding. His arms are rings embrac-
ing the heart-core of juice sucked up through roots that
tap the deepest troughs of mountain reservoirs. Ancient
Montrose hears the rush of subterranean waters.

Above him, old limbs creak. Leona is heading for the
stairs. One more glance at the window casing, one last
whisper of the taproot sipping, and he lets his feet jack-
knife to the floor. His temples drain.

From the landing she calls down, "Monty! Monty?" And
from midflight, "What do you want for breakfast?"

She knows what he wants for breakfast, but never tires
of discussing these things. Nor does Montrose, when the
appetites are rising. Something about the yoga gives every
appetite an edge. He is ready to be aroused by Leona's
question, which has for years served as a double invitation.
He is astonished at how often he still wants her. For some
reason he never believed such things would last—his own
vitality, this house, her bosom and buoyancy, their orchards, the richness of the sunlight. Long ago he began to
expect everything he valued to give way and collapse. He
has been prepared at any moment for holocaust. For ashes.
When Travis left, Montrose fully expected never to see him
alive again. It took him two years to admit he had killed

his son ahead of time, in his mind, quickly and desperately, before the bus even pulled away, in order to get it over with. Nowadays each sunrise surprises him. He feels the primitive's awe for these inexplicable returns of a son, a moon, a season, the rich craving in his loins when Leona, suddenly behind him, reaches between his legs, teasing.

"You haven't answered my question," she says.

"What's on the menu?"

"You're such a dirty old man."

"Did I say something dirty? Only a mind depraved with lust could find anything dirty in what I just said."

His hands rush around beneath her robe.

"Not *now*."

"Why not?"

"You might miss the . . . . Oh, your fingernails!"

"Sorry."

"What if Trav's plane . . ."

"If that plane lands on time I'll eat the propeller."

"It doesn't have a propeller, hon."

She bends to frown out the front window, as if a plane might at this moment be taxiing through the field between their porch and the first hills. He takes this opportunity to nudge her onto the brocade couch. She turns toward him and her robe falls open. As he straddles her, tendrils of asparagus fern flick his shoulders. Early window light tints her neck and face with the blue-white gloss of porcelain, and Montrose, nude yogi, regards this too with wonder.

The ferns, the light, the gloss of her skin, all bring to mind a wondrous day many years ago when they went romping through that orchard toward their favorite spot. Her eyes this morning are like her eyes were then. Liquid. Intimate. Yet inward. Keeping something. The phone rings. Monty's vision dissolves. He goes limp.

Leona disentangles herself and hurries down the hall to the booth, robe flapping. Monty leans back against his brocade sofa, longing to tear the phone out and stomp it to pieces.

With veiled sarcasm, Lee shouts, "For you-ou!"

He decides to take this final call, then destroy the phone. He vows to do this, while walking naked to the square glass booth where the phone resides. Travis and Grover ripped this booth from its moorings several years ago and brought it home in the pickup. It has remained in the hallway, the words PACIFIC TELEPHONE the first thing you see upon entering the front door. Leona complained at the time, saying it would be a nuisance to clean around, but Monty thought it would be good for the boys to feel they too had contributed to the household, to its design, its overall *effect*.

## III

Watching a 707 taxi in, Monty scans forty opaque portholes for some sign of life. A portable tunnel is plugged into the fuselage, moments later spilling passengers out its near end, into the terminal. Monty keeps thinking the next one will be Travis. The flow is thinning, he is reaching to check the wrinkled airletter with the time and flight number, when he hears a voice, not from the plane, but seemingly from behind him, shouting, "Dad!"

He doesn't turn. So prepared is he to see Trav emerging from the plane, he interprets this as some trick of sound inside the echo-filled terminal, some odd ventriloquy. He peers into the tunnel, ready to smile. He hears the voice again.

"Hey, Dad!"

This time he turns, and sees Travis striding toward him from the direction of the snack bar, his head suddenly dipping to hear a girl just behind him. He wears a Panama hat Monty figures he must have picked up in Manila or Honolulu. Always had a taste for hats. This one sits oddly, as if jostled. Yet it isn't the hat, it's the head, something about the way Travis holds his head. The motion is unfamiliar, nothing like any moves he used to make. Montrose is looking for this, the signs of change. But he wants them to be recognizable—signs of growth, signs of manhood. A spasm of giddiness runs through him. Then Trav's eyes turn from the girl to fix on Monty. He has the look of a man returning from the grave and seeing for the first time his executioner. Monty tastes ashes, can scarcely meet his gaze. He fears his own eyes will falter. Travis blinks, and the gaze is gone, replaced by whimsy, by his cocky grin, as if that last look was just a gag, a phony hate message, to keep Dad on his toes. Monty knows Trav is capable of this. Reaching for the hand, he can't help thinking it may just have been some veteran's sympathy routine. He wavers, fiercely shaking hands, waiting for a sign.

"Travis, did I get the gate wrong? We thought—"

"I took another plane, Dad. Didn't have time to let you know."

Travis has a charming smile, perfected long before he understood how it worked. He uses it now.

Seduced, relieved, exasperated, suddenly drained, Montrose blurts, "You what? For Christ sake, Travis!"

"It was Crystal's idea," he says, urging forward the girl at his elbow. "Dad, I'd like you to meet Crystal. I met her in the Islands. She's interested in land, gardening, fruits and vegetables. I told her she could stay at our place for a few days. Sort of look around. If that's all right."

Like a man caught in crossfire, Monty half hunches, turning to glare at her. She clutches Trav's arm. Monty relaxes, forces himself to smile. She could be younger than Travis. Twenty, he estimates. And very dark, as if from sunning for months in Hawaii. White flared beachcomber's trousers. But not beachy, he is glad to see. Montrose shut the door on beach girls, with their self-serving monologues, when Travis was in high school. Crystal is a different kind of wanderer. A Rolleiflex hangs at her waist. Bright, crafty eyes size him up now while he sizes her up. Eyes like Trav's. On the verge of laughter. An adventuress. With a taste for veterans. That could liven up the place. Monty is a veteran too. Of numerous campaigns. Not that he imagines it would ever come to that. But he can tell he and Crystal will be able to get along. In any case, she's Trav's choice, and you don't start drawing lines the day your son comes home.

He throws an arm around Trav's shoulder. "Well, of course it's all right. Hell. I mean, anything's all right on a day like this. You thirsty? Let's go get a drink before we start back," winking then at Crystal in what he considers hearty welcome. Her glance is so alarmingly seductive he avoids it.

He concentrates on Travis, finding an interval, before the talk begins, to study the profile, the way he moves and conducts himself, suddenly exulting in the sheer fact of his own fatherhood. To have a son returning from . . . from anywhere, full-grown, full-bodied, not at all the son who went away, yet unmistakably that same boy. He is still compact, with Leona's straight back, and a flash of Lee's prancing in his stride. Monty sees the built-up layers of him, the original shape and nature, in ever-widening proportions, the way a tree builds. Seeing all the stages, the inner rings exposed to him as if for the first time, Monty grabs his son by both arms exuberantly, drunkenly, shouting, "Shit fire! You're gettin' to be a husky rascal, Travis!"

He shoves with his shoulder, and Travis shoves back. There among the passengers rushing toward their luggage, they begin to trade light blows, feinting, fist-tapping. It is an ancient game, which always ends when Monty gives him a wide opening, and Travis drives a fist into the tensed abdominals. It always hurt, even when Trav was eight years old, and Monty has always let him do it.

## IV

Three abreast in the front seat, they are speeding down the Bayshore Freeway, heading home. Travis is talking, and Montrose at the wheel in his cowboy hat glances sideways from time to time, still looking for the signs, the changes. He wants to know what happened over there, though he knows it's far too soon to ask, remembering as if it were only last month how long it took before he himself could share with anyone what he'd seen in the South Pacific. It took three or four years, and even today some of his stories have not yet been told, some of his dreams have never been discussed.

Too soon to tell. Too soon to ask. Too soon for much of anything. Travis talks, but he is not with us yet. His mind is elsewhere. He has not entirely landed.

"In Honolulu," he says, "right at the end of the main boulevard that runs through Waikiki, I saw fifty Americans in aloha shirts. It was about eleven o'clock at night. They were on one of these package tours?" His voice inflects upward, his eyebrows raise as each phrase becomes a question. "They hit three clubs a night? With a two-drink guarantee at each club? Well, while they are waiting for their Gray Line bus to pick them up to take them to the next hotel, the surf is crashing in the background and they all start singing 'Swing low, sweet chariot . . .'"

Chuckling, Montrose picks up the song. Crystal joins in too:

> *Swing low, sweet chariot.*
> *Comin for to carry me home . . .*

Then it's silent in the car, just Travis humming under his
breath the next eight bars, which might almost be the
humming within him, that waning buzz of motion, slowly
draining away. This is what Montrose hears as he observes
faint flickers of bewilderment, Travis waiting for something
to replace that buzz. Monty recognizes the symptoms of jet
lag, traveler's hangover. It never ceases to amaze him how
he can live down a country road the way they do, and
nearly every day run into someone just in from Rio or
Manila or Jerusalem, with the smell of foreign cities still
on the clothes. The traveler's soul is always far out over the
water somewhere, booked onto a much slower flight, usually about four days behind the body, which can be sitting
right here next to you, and talking, yet be incomplete.
Sometimes you can almost see through the body. It is a
double wonder—the exotic arrival of the traveler, and the
body-shaped space that waits for the arrival of the soul.
Monty does not yet know how much Travis has in common with those ultimate survivors of jet lag, the astronauts,
who splash down glossy-eyed, their eyes and their lives
out of synch at reentry and somehow forever altered on the
high-speed journey home.

"Hey, Dad," says Travis, urgently, "I have to drive! Do
you mind if I drive the rest of the way?"

Still looking for signs, Monty sees this as a good one. A
sign of recovery. A sign of health. He pulls off onto the
emergency lane. He is tired of driving anyway. Thirty-one
years since he got his first permit. He could use some
relief.

With the engine running, he opens the left-hand door
and climbs out. Travis, sliding behind the wheel, looks up
at him for just an instant with his head cocked in that eerie
way, as if some glare prevents him from seeing Montrose
clearly, and with the look that so disturbed him at the
terminal, that returning-from-the-deepest-pit-of-hell look,
that you're-the-one-who-put-me-there look. This time
Monty is petrified with fear. He is sure Travis plans to
drive away and leave him standing on the freeway. It is one
of those science-fiction moments you cannot quite believe,
a brief scene, with half-caught details that don't add up
until much later. They are underneath the smooth concrete
belly of an overpass, almost noon, yet the belly is slung so
low and spread so wide it is like dusk. The engine roars.

Monty imagines himself marooned under here for days, his
clothes blown to tatters. Papers and candy wrappers have
flown up into the angle where the sloping foundation pillar
meets the arc. Every car that speeds past rattles papers in
its wake of artificial wind. He stands studying a cloudlike
blue-gray construction stain, thinking distantly of an archi-
tect in town who prizes *accidents* like this, who waves his
hands describing the "aesthetic of materials in process." He
is trying to detach himself. He breathes. The moment
passes.

Leaning forward, Travis is testing the controls, giving
Monty just enough time to rush around to the far side and
scoot in next to Crystal. The car's lunge slams the door.
Travis leaves angry horns back there, raising one defiant
finger out the open window, hitting eighty before they've
gone a hundred yards.

It was a mistake to let him drive. Yet something in
Montrose accepts this situation, perhaps a boyish yearning
to give up all responsibility, perhaps his own wish that
Trav's return be appropriately celebrated . . . with wildness,
with appropriate risks. It is among his small regrets that
Travis has missed the taste of actually coming home a
winner. Montrose would bequeath this to him if he could.
But America is too far gone for that. How often has he
seen himself, that August night in 1945, when they celebrated the ending of *his* war. He was fresh off a troop ship,
Sergeant Doyle home from the Pacific, at large in San
Francisco, with Purple Heart and scarlet face. He remembers tipping over a streetcar on Market, then dancing
across the upturned side with a young girl whose breasts,
through the years, have expanded to the size of street-
lamps. In his memory they glow, leaving all her other parts
in shadow. She wanted his Purple Heart for a souvenir,
and he said he'd give it to her if she took her sweater off.
Which she did. Monty's pals joined him on the streetcar
then, half his platoon, followed by a dozen sailors, all
dancing among the windows, then nudging and shoving,
finally sparring and rabbit-punching and side-stepping into
panes of brittle glass. With one arm around the doomed
female, one around a yeoman's neck, Monty watched a
flame bloom behind his eyes—the whiskey's uppercut, not
the yeoman's—and go black. The rest of that night exists
for him only as other men have recounted it, legendary

boozing, legendary brawls, legendary cocksmanship. Triumphant devastation, he would call it now. And yet it was
so much more of a tribute than has been offered up for
Travis's war, the Southeast Asian one. No dancing in the
street. No plaques. No holidays added to the calendar.
Perhaps a manic drive down Bayshore Freeway will help
turn a few of these omissions into trophies.

A pint bottle flashes in the sunlight, on its way to Crystal from inside Trav's denim jacket. She unscrews the top,
sips some and passes it to Monty, who figures this is something else he picked up in Honolulu, along with Crystal
and the hat.

"Fiji Island rum, Dad," he says, glancing over to see
how Monty takes this, a sly glance, like that smile of his,
calculated. He looks now exactly like Leona. Travis and
Leona share a whole armory of smiles and glances. For this
instant he is Lee talking Montrose into something.

Monty raises the flask and says, "Welcome home, Sarge,"
and takes a long pull and gasps like a kid. Firewater.

Travis laughs. "It goes a long way."

Crystal laughs. Monty laughs too, just as they barrel
past a highway patrolman on the far side of the freeway,
whose head snaps in their direction. He would be on their
tail immediately were it not for the divider strip and were
he not surrounded by six matronly women, all wearing
jewelry and Easter bonnets, evidently on their way to the
city for a luncheon date, perhaps at the Clift Hotel, and
very angry about this delay, so that the patrolman is pinned
on all sides and cannot even get to his radio to warn a
colleague farther down the road.

They are still laughing, and Monty is trying to advise
Travis to slow down, when Crystal flips open the cover of
the Rolleiflex slung around her neck and begins snapping
pictures of Montrose sitting next to her. Close-ups. Pro-
files. "Don't pay any attention to this," she says. He turns
away, annoyed, thinking: What right does this girl have?
He yearns for the strength of mind said to be possessed by
certain holy men in Asia who, when photographed, can
will their image not to appear on the developed print. He
would protest aloud, but the shutter's only clicking for
fifteen seconds, then the leather lid flips shut.

Winking thanks, Crystal reaches for the radio. The car
fills up with Roy Acuff's version of "The Wabash Cannonball."

*Listen to the jingle, the rumble, and the roar,*
*As she rolls along the woodland,*
*Through the hills and by the shore . . .*

The dial is set for KEEN, San Jose's country music station. This is not her idea of highway listening. She jiggles the dial till she hits a talk show, turns the volume up, and offers Monty a short grin.

"You can hear country music anywhere in the world these days," she says, "but you can only hear talk shows in the States."

"Why is that?"

"We have more telephones."

The subject is earthquakes. An elderly woman is complaining that if geologists are going to keep predicting earthquakes, she wishes they would get their stories straight. "That is to say," she quavers, "either put up or shut up! Every week one a them fellas tells the newspapers there is going to be a massive shaker all up and down the state, and I want you to know I am a nervous wreck trying to get ready for all these predictions. Packing my bags. Unpacking my bags. Taking Darvon, and calling up people long-distance. I can't pay my phone bill half the time. I tell you, I simply cannot take it one more *minute!*"

She raises her voice, weeping now, shouting into the radio line: "YOU HEAR ME? I CANNOT STAND THIS WISHY-WASHY, BACK-AND-FORTH, NOW-YOU-SEE-IT, NOW-YOU-DON'T . . ."

The emcee cuts her off, saying he knows exactly how she feels and in the same modulated tones becomes the owner of a pet store describing the powers of a new brand of cat food, at which point the flask appears again in front of Montrose. He sips, and gasps again, and admits to himself that it does feel very, very good to be sitting next to Crystal drinking Fiji Island rum with his veteran son and listening to the talk show. He knows, of course, that they are near death. Travis is risking their lives with every flick of the wheel. Given the accumulating effects of jet lag, combat fatigue, one-hundred-proof rum, and perhaps as yet unspecified foreign drugs, Monty wonders how qualified Trav is for this kind of driving. But he wants to allow it, wants the boy to let off steam.

Much later, months from now, he will remember that at the very moment the emcee cut off that caller and the flask appeared, defining Monty's mood, his car was crossing the San Andreas. Perhaps coincidence. Perhaps not. The fault line cuts through these mountains, just above a large dam outside San Jose. Prophets say that when the great quake comes, this dam, like several throughout the state, will burst and the water from the reservoir will flow down to inundate the town. This road, they say, will buckle, perhaps split theatrically, creating two steep cliffs edged with asphalt and facing each other across an open maw. Of the thousands who use this highway daily, from the Santa Clara Valley to the coast, few realize that during the westward climb they cross from the American to the Pacific plate. Few care. Certainly the thought is far from Monty's conscious mind right now, far from Trav's, from Crystal's. They zip along the asphalt, sipping rum, half listening to callers, afloat on the forward motion of their journey. Would anything be revealed if we could read uncharted shadings of the mind as each rider crosses this invisible and seldom noticed boundary line? Take Monty. Who is to say what pressures or magnetisms open certain portals of the memory? Just now the glimmer of a scene began to flash for him. It flickered first this morning as he coupled with Leona. Perhaps that incomplete embrace explains the scene's return. Perhaps it is simply the nearness of Crystal, pressed against him in the front seat as they swing another outside curve. Or perhaps all three—the wife, the adventuress, and that brief acceleration through the zone of power, where two slabs of continental crust join and mate and send forth their vibrations.

As he floats in the front seat, his thigh adjoining hers, the libertine in Montrose is aroused. He begins to think of women, various women, Leona in particular, that look she wore this morning as she lay back on the brocade to receive him. Sweet, sweet Leona. He wonders how she might regard this trip. With reserve, he imagines. More likely, with a tinge of disapproval. She is not a prude. Not a party pooper. Not opposed to every form of abandon. But she practices abandon on her own terms, and does not enjoy anything that smacks of physical danger or material risk. He knows that's one reason he married her. He believes it is true that at least two kinds of women exist in the world. He would never, for example, set up housekeeping with Crystal. Yet during those periods, which vary greatly from man to man, when one wants to be free of limits, Crystal is

just the sort of woman one hopes to meet. Loose. In every
sense of that word. Having her along makes this wild and
soldierly trip that much wilder and more soldierly. He
would like to touch her. But knows he can't. Or knows he
won't. She is, at this point, for him, a kind of pornography,
calling forth his lusts. Savoring Crystal, he dwells the more
upon Leona, her inward look this morning, among asparagus ferns, her neck and face the blue-white gloss of porcelain. The memory the phone's ring interrupted starts again,
and the ferns become spring apple trees, Lee looking back
as she hurtles along between the rows, two arms' lengths
ahead of him. How old was she then? Twenty-two, or
-three? He sees his basket crunch smooth bark as he lets it
swing, grabbing for her with his free hand. She is trying to
be modest about all this, to appear for some nonexistent
audience as if they are merely strolling among the trees
toward a late-in-the-day picnic spot.

"Monty, don't do that," she cautions, fiercely squeezing
her brows. "Not *today*." He trips on a stone-size clod and
lunges, knees and elbows into the dirt, letting his basket
spill like a cornucopia, as he reaches again for Leona. She
leaps back squealing, pulls free from his loose grip
around her ankle and begins to lope down between the
rows, white trousers, pink blouse, her head turning once to
repeat, "Not today, Monty!"

He leaves the wine, the basket, the olives and smoked
oysters and cheese. He gathers up the quilt, rises to his
knees, then waits, watching a moment longer—something
in the flicker of her clothing among the trees. She is a
white-and-pink bloom under dark-green limbs edged with
pinkish-white where ten thousand blossoms wait for one
more day, perhaps one more hour of new heat.

With the quilt flapping like a serape he follows, silent,
bounding over plowed clods toward the low place where he
never plows, a trough of grass, mallow, miner's lettuce,
mustard greens, a weed collector's paradise, where Lee
hides cuddled like a child, feigning childishness until he
finds her and spreads the quilt, and there is no resistance
now. She knows what he is going to do, and wants him to,
wants what he wants, and lets him take it. The taking is
important. His woman. His land. Her blooming is another
of the promises brimming among all these trees. Her pink
blouse shimmers beneath him, out here where everything is
spring-green and pink-rimmed blossoms craving heat, every-

thing, yes, until her eyes turn inward, just at the instant of his possession, of his bursting, as if the season of this blossom he has so many times possessed is now suddenly over. He sees that look and feels the deep regret for taking what he cannot let go. Regret and burning need and conquest, while he watches the eyes in the young face beneath him grow older, grow wistful and inexplicably wise.

# JACK KEROUAC

# Dharma Bums

"Well here we go" said Japhy. "When I get tired of this big rucksack we'll swap."

"I'm ready now. Man, come on, give it to me now, I feel like carrying something heavy. You don't realize how *good* I feel, man, come on!" So we swapped packs and started off.

Both of us were feeling fine and were talking a blue streak, about anything, literature, the mountains, girls, Princess, the poets, Japan, our past adventures in life, and I suddenly realized it was a kind of blessing in disguise Morley had forgotten to drain the crankcase, otherwise Japhy wouldn't have got in a word edgewise all the blessed day and now I had a chance to hear his ideas. In the way he did things, hiking, he reminded me of Mike my boyhood chum who also loved to lead the way, real grave like Buck Jones, eyes to the distant horizons, like Natty Bumppo, cautioning me about snapping twigs or "It's too deep here, let's go down the creek a ways to ford it," or "There'll be mud in that low bottom, we better skirt around" and dead serious and glad. I saw all Japhy's boyhood in those eastern Oregon forests the way he went about it. He walked like he talked, from behind I could see his toes pointed slightly inward, the way mine do, instead of out; but when it came time to climb he pointed his toes out, like Chaplin, to make a kind of easier flapthwap as he trudged. We went across a kind of muddy riverbottom through dense undergrowth and a few willow trees and came out on the other side a little wet and started up the trail, which was clearly marked and named and had been recently repaired by trail crews but as we hit parts where a rock had rolled on the trail he took great precaution to throw the rock off saying "I used to work on trail crews, I can't see a trail all mettlesome like that, Smith." As we climbed the lake began to appear below us and suddenly in its clear blue pool we could see the deep holes where the lake had its springs, like black wells, and we could see schools of fish skitter.

"Oh this is like an early morning in China and I'm five years old in beginningless time!" I sang out and felt like sitting by the trail and whipping out my little notebook and writing sketches about it.

"Look over there," sang Japhy, "yellow aspens. Just put me in the mind of a haiku . . . 'Talking about the literary life—the yellow aspens.'" Walking in this country you could understand the perfect gems of haikus the Oriental poets had written, never getting drunk in the mountains or anything but just going along as fresh as children writing down what they saw without literary devices or fanciness of expression. We made up haikus as we climbed, winding up and up now on the slopes of brush.

"Rocks on the side of the cliff," I said, "why don't they tumble down?"

"Maybe that's a haiku, maybe not, it might be a little too complicated," said Japhy. "A real haiku's gotta be as simple as porridge and yet make you see the real thing, like the greatest haiku of them all probably is the one that goes 'The sparrow hops along the veranda, with wet feet.' By Shiki. You see the wet footprints like a vision in your mind and yet in those few words you also see all the rain that's been falling that day and almost smell the wet pine needles."

"Let's have another."

"I'll make up one of my own this time, let's see, 'Lake below . . . the black holes the wells make,' no that's not a haiku goddammit, you never can be too careful about haiku."

"How about making them up real fast as you go along, spontaneously?"

"Look here," he cried happily, "mountain lupine, see the delicate blue color those little flowers have. And there's some California red poppy over there. The whole meadow is just powdered with color! Up there by the way is a genuine California white pine, you never see them much any more."

"You sure know a lot about birds and trees and stuff."

"I've studied it all my life." Then also as we went on climbing we began getting more casual and making funnier sillier talk and pretty soon we got to a bend in the trail where it was suddenly gladey and dark with shade and a tremendous cataracting stream was bashing and frothing over scummy rocks and tumbling on down, and over the stream was a perfect bridge formed by a fallen snag, we got on it and lay belly-down and dunked our heads down, hair wet, and drank deep as the water splashed in our faces, like sticking your head by the jet of a dam. I lay there a good long minute enjoying the sudden coolness.

"This is like an advertisement for Rainier Ale!" yelled Japhy.

"Let's sit awhile and enjoy it."

"Boy you don't know how far we got to go yet!"

"Well I'm not tired!"

"Well you'll be, Tiger."

We went on, and I was immensely pleased with the way the trail had a kind of immortal look to it, in the early afternoon now, the way the side of the grassy hill seemed to be clouded with ancient gold dust and the bugs flipped over rocks and the wind sighed in shimmering dances over the hot rocks, and the way the trail would suddenly come into a cool shady part with big trees overhead, and here the light deeper. And the way the lake below us soon became a toy lake with those black well holes perfectly visible still, and the giant cloud shadows on the lake, and the tragic little road winding away where poor Morley was walking back.

"Can you see Morl down back there?

Japhy took a long look. "I see a little cloud of dust, maybe that's him comin back already." But it seemed that I had seen the ancient afternoon of that trail, from meadow rocks and lupine posies, to sudden revisits with the roaring stream with its splashed snag bridges and undersea greennesses, there was something inexpressibly broken in my heart as though I'd lived before and walked this trail, under similar circumstances with a fellow Bodhisattva, but maybe on a more important journey. I felt like lying down by the side of the trail and remembering it all. The woods do that to you, they always look familiar, long lost, like the face of a long-dead relative, like an old dream, like a piece of forgotten song drifting across the water, most of all like golden eternities of past childhood or past manhood and all the living and the dying and the heartbreak that went on a million years ago and the clouds as they pass overhead seem to testify (by their own lonesome familiarity) to this feeling. Ecstasy, even, I felt, with flashes of sudden remembrance, and feeling sweaty and drowsy I felt like sleeping and dreaming in the grass. As we got higher we got more tired and now like two true mountain climbers we weren't talking any more and didn't have to talk and were glad, in fact Japhy mentioned that, turning to me after a half-hour's silence, "This is the way I like it, when you get going there's just no need to talk, as if we were animals and just communicated by silent telepathy." So huddled in our own thoughts we tromped on, Japhy using that gazotsky trudge I mentioned, and myself finding my own true step, which was short steps slowly patiently going up the mountain at one mile an hour, so I was always thirty yards behind him and when we had any haikus now we'd yell them fore and aft. Pretty soon we got to the top of the part of the trail that was a trail no more, to the incomparable dreamy meadow, which had a beautiful pond, and after that it was boulders and nothing but boulders.

"Only sign we have now to know which way we're going, is ducks."

"What's ducks?"

"See those boulders over there?"

"See those boulders over there! Why God man, I see five miles of boulders leading up to that mountain."

"See the little pile of rocks on that near boulder there by the pine? That's a duck, put up by other climbers, maybe that's one I put up myself in 'fifty-four I'm not sure. We just go from boulder to boulder from now on keeping a sharp eye for ducks then we get a general idea how to raggle along. Although of course we know which way we're going, that big cliff face up there is where our plateau is."

"Plateau? My God you mean that ain't the top of the mountain?"

"Of course not, after that we got a plateau and then scree and then more rocks and we get to a final alpine lake no biggern this pond and then comes the final climb over one thousand feet almost straight up boy to the top of the world where you'll see all California and parts of Nevada and the wind'll blow right through your pants."

"Ow . . . How long does it all take?"

"Why the only thing we can expect to make tonight is our camp up there on that plateau. I call it a plateau, it ain't that at all, it's a shelf between heights."

But the top and the end of the trail was such a beautiful spot I said: "Boy look at this . . ." A dreamy meadow, pines at one end, the pond, the clear fresh air, the afternoon clouds rushing golden . . . "Why don't we just sleep here tonight, I don't think I've ever seen a more beautiful park."

"Ah this is nowhere. It's great of course, but we might wake up tomorrow morning and find three dozen school-teachers on horseback frying bacon in our backyard. Where we're going you can bet your ass there won't be one human being, and if there is, I'll be a spotted horse's ass. Or maybe just one mountain climber, or two, but I don't expect so at this time of the year. You know the snow's about to come here any time now. If it comes tonight it's goodbye me and you."

"Well goodbye Japhy. But let's rest here and drink some water and admire the meadow." We were feeling tired and great. We spread out in the grass and rested and swapped packs and strapped them on and were rarin to go. Almost instantaneously the grass ended and the boulders started; we got up on the first one and from that point on it was just a matter of jumping from boulder to boulder, gradually climbing, climbing, five miles up a valley of boulders getting steeper and steeper with immense crags on both sides forming the walls of the valley, till near the cliff face we'd be scrambling up the boulders, it seemed.

"And what's behind that cliff face?"

"There's high grass up there, shrubbery, scattered boulders, beautiful meandering creeks that have ice in 'em even in the afternoon, spots of snow, tremendous trees, and one boulder just about as big as two of Alvah's cottages piled on top the other which leans over and makes a kind of concave cave for us to camp at, lightin a big bonfire that'll throw heat against the wall. Then after that the grass and the timber ends. That'll be at nine thousand just about."

Jumping from boulder to boulder and never falling, with a heavy pack, is easier than it sounds; you just can't fall when you get into the rhythm of the dance. I looked back down the valley sometimes and was surprised to see how high we'd come, and to see farther horizons of mountains now back there. Our beautiful trail-top park was like a little glen of the Forest of Arden. Then the climbing got steeper, the sun got redder, and pretty soon I began to see patches of snow in the shade of some rocks. We got up to where the cliff face seemed to loom over us. At one point I saw Japhy throw down his pack and danced my way up to him.

"Well this is where we'll drop our gear and climb those few hundred feet up the side of that cliff, where you see there it's shallower, and find that camp. I remember it. In fact you can sit here and rest or beat your bishop while I go ramblin around there, I like to ramble by myself."

Okay. So I sat down and changed my wet socks and changed soaking undershirt for dry one and crossed my legs and rested and whistled for about a half-hour, a very pleasant occupation, and Japhy got back and said he'd found the camp. I thought it would be a little jaunt to our resting place but it took almost another hour to jump up the steep boulders, climb around some, get to the level of the cliff-face plateau, and there, on flat grass more or less, hike about two hundred yards to where a huge gray rock towered among pines. Here now the earth was a splendorous thing—snow on the ground, in melting patches in the grass, and gurgling creeks, and the huge silent rock mountains on both sides, and a wind blowing, and the smell of heather. We forded a lovely little creek, shallow as your hand, pearl pure lucid water, and got to the huge rock. Here were old charred logs where other mountain climbers had camped.

"And where's Matterhorn mountain?"

"You can't see it from here, but"—pointing up the farther long plateau and a scree gorge twisting to the right—"around that draw and up two miles or so and then we'll be at the foot of it."

"Wow, heck, whoo, that'll take us a whole other day!"

"Not when you're travelin with me, Smith."

"Well Ryderee, that's okay with me."

"Okay Smithee and now how's about we relax and enjoy ourselves and cook up some supper and wait for ole Morleree?"

So we unpacked our packs and laid things out and smoked and had a good time. Now the mountains were getting that pink tinge, I mean the rocks, they were just solid rock covered with the atoms of dust accumulated there since beginningless time. In fact I was afraid of those jagged monstrosities all around and over our heads.

"They're so silent!" I said.

"Yeah man, you know to me a mountain is a Buddha. Think of the patience, hundreds of thousands of years just sittin there bein perfectly perfectly silent and like praying for all living creatures in that silence and just waitin for us to stop all our frettin and foolin." Japhy got out the tea, Chinese tea, and sprinkled some in a tin pot, and had the fire going meanwhile, a small one to begin with, the sun was still on us, and stuck a long stick tight down under a few big rocks and made himself something to hang the teapot on and pretty soon the water was boiling and he poured it out steaming into the tin pot and we had cups of tea with our tin cups. I myself'd gotten the water from the stream, which was cold and pure like snow and the crystal-lidded eyes of heaven. Therefore, the tea was by far the most pure and thirst-quenching tea I ever drank in all my life, it made you want to drink more and more, it actually quenched your thirst and of course it swam around hot in your belly.

"Now you understand the Oriental passion for tea," said Japhy. "Remember that book I told you about the first sip is joy, the second is gladness, the third is serenity, the fourth is madness, the fifth is ecstasy."

"Just about old buddy."

That rock we were camped against was a marvel. It was thirty feet high and thirty feet at base, a perfect square almost, and twisted trees arched over it and peeked down on us. From the base it went outward, forming a concave, so if rain came we'd be partially covered. "How did this immense sonumbitch ever get here?"

"It probably was left here by the retreating glacier. See over there that field of snow?"

"Yeah."

"That's the glacier what's left of it. Either that or this rock tumbled here from inconceivable prehistoric mountains we can't understand, or maybe it just landed here when the friggin mountain range itself burst out of the ground in the Jurassic upheaval. Ray when you're up here you're not sittin in a Berkeley tea room. This is the beginning and the end of the world right here. Look at all those patient Buddhas lookin at us saying nothing."

"And you come out here by yourself. . . ."

"For weeks on end, just like John Muir, climb around all by myself following quartzite veins or making posies of flowers for my camp, or just walking around naked singing, and cook my supper and laugh."

"Japhy I gotta hand it to you, you're the happiest little cat in the world and the greatest by God you are. I'm sure glad I'm learning all this. This place makes me feel devoted too, I mean, you know I have a prayer, did you know the prayer I use?"

"What?"

"I sit down and say, and I run all my friends and relatives and enemies one by one in this, without entertaining any angers or gratitudes or anything, and I say, like 'Japhy Ryder, equally empty, equally to be loved, equally a coming Buddha,' then I run on, say, to 'David O. Selznick, equally empty, equally to be loved, equally a coming Buddha' though I don't use names like David O. Selznick, just people I know because when I say the words 'equally a coming Buddha' I want to be thinking of their eyes, like you take Morley, his blue eyes behind those glasses, when you think 'equally a coming Buddha' you think of those eyes and you really do suddenly see the true secret serenity and the truth of his coming Buddhahood. Then you think of your enemy's eyes."

"That's great, Ray," and Japhy took out his notebook and wrote down the prayer, and shook his head in wonder. "That's really really great. I'm going to teach this prayer to the monks I meet in Japan. There's nothing wrong with you Ray, your only trouble is you never learned to get out to spots like this, you've let the world drown you in its horseshit and you've been vexed . . . though as I say comparisons *are* odious, but what we're sayin now is true."

He took his bulgur rough cracked wheat and dumped a couple of packages of dried vegetables in and put it all in the pot to be ready to be boiled at dusk. We began listening for the yodels of Henry Morley, which didn't come. We began to worry about him.

"The trouble about all this, dammit, if he fell off a boulder and broke his leg there'd be no one to help him. It's dangerous to . . . I do it all by myself but I'm pretty good, I'm a mountain goat."

"I'm gettin hungry."

"Me too dammit, I wish he gets here soon. Let's ramble around and eat snowballs and drink water and wait."

We did this, investigating the upper end of the flat plateau, and came back. By now the sun was gone behind the western wall of our valley and it was getting darker, pinker, colder, more hues of purple began to steal across the jags. The sky was deep. We even began to see pale stars, at least one or two. Suddenly we heard a distant "Yodelay-hee" and Japhy leaped up and jumped to the top of a boulder and yelled "Hoo hoo hoo!" The Yodelayhee came back.

"How far is he?"

"My God from the sound of it he's not even started. He's not even at the beginning of the valley of boulders. He can never make it tonight."

"What'll we do?"

"Let's go to the rock cliff and sit on the edge and call him an hour. Let's bring these peanuts and raisins and munch on 'em and wait. Maybe he's not so far as I think."

We went over to the promontory where we could see the whole valley and the Japhy sat down in full lotus posture cross-legged on a rock and took out his wooden juju prayer-beads and prayed. That is, he simply held the beads in his hands, the hands upsidedown with thumbs touching, and stared straight ahead and didn't move a bone. I sat down as best I could on another rock and we both said nothing and meditated. Only I meditated with my eyes closed. The silence was an intense roar. From where we were, the sound of the creek, the gurgle and slapping talk of the creek, was blocked off by rocks. We heard several more melancholy Yodelayhees and answered them but it seemed farther and farther away each time. When I opened my eyes the pink was more purple all the time. The stars began to flash. I fell into deep meditation, felt that the mountains were indeed Buddhas and our friends, and I felt the weird sensation that it was strange that there were only three men in this whole immense valley: the mystic number three. Nir-manakaya, Sambhogakaya, and Dharmakaya. I prayed for the safety and in fact the eternal happiness of poor Morley. Once I opened my eyes and saw Japhy sitting there rigid as a rock and I felt like laughing he looked so funny. But the mountains were mighty solemn, and so was Japhy, and for that matter so was I, and in fact laughter is solemn.

It was beautiful. The pinkness vanished and then it was all purple dusk and the roar of the silence was like a wash of diamond waves going through the liquid porches of our ears, enough to soothe a man a thousand years. I prayed for Japhy, for his future safety and happiness and eventual Buddhahood. It was all completely serious, all completely hallucinated, all completely happy.

"Rocks are space," I thought, "and space is illusion." I had a million thoughts. Japhy had his. I was amazed at the way he meditated with his eyes open. And I was mostly humanly amazed that this tremendous little guy who eagerly studied Oriental poetry and anthropology and ornithology and everything else in the books and was a tough little adventurer of trails and mountains should also suddenly whip out his pitiful beautiful wooden prayerbeads and sol-emnly pray there, like an old-fashioned saint of the deserts certainly, but so amazing to see it in America with its steel mills and airfields. The world ain't so bad, when you got Japhies, I thought, and felt glad. All the aching muscles and the hunger in my belly were bad enough, and the surrounding dark rocks, the fact that there is nothing there to soothe you with kisses and soft words, but just to be sitting there meditating and praying for the world with another earnest young man—'twere good enough to have been born just to die, as we all are. Something will come of it in the Milky Ways of eternity stretching in front of all our phantom unjaundiced eyes, friends. I felt like telling Japhy everything I thought but I knew it didn't matter and moreover he knew it anyway and silence is the golden mountain.

"Yodelayhee," sang Morley, and now it was dark, and Japhy said, "Well, from the looks of things he's still far away. He has enough sense to pitch his own camp down there tonight so let's go back to our camp and cook sup-per."

"Okay." And we yelled "Hoo" a couple of times reassur-ingly and gave up poor Morl for the night. He did have enough sense, we knew. And as it turned out he did, and pitched his camp, wrapped up in his two blankets on top of the air mattress, and slept the night out in that incomparably happy meadow with the pond and the pines, telling us about it when he finally reached us the next day.

At about noon we started out, leaving our big packs at the camp where nobody was likely to be till next year anyway, and went up the scree valley with just some food and first-aid kits. The valley was longer than it looked. In no time at all it was two o'clock in the afternoon and the sun was getting that later more golden look and a wind was rising and I began to think "By gosh how we ever gonna climb that mountain, tonight?"

I put it up to Japhy who said: "You're right, we'll have to hurry."

"Why don't we just forget it and go on home?"

"Aw come on Tiger, we'll make a run up that hill and then we'll go home." The valley was long and long and long. And at the top end it got very steep and I began to be a little afraid of falling down, the rocks were small and it got slippery and my ankles were in pain from yesterday's muscle strain anyway. But Morley kept walking and talking and I noticed his tremendous endurance. Japhy took his pants off so he could look just like an Indian, I mean stark naked, except for a jockstrap, and hiked almost a quarter-mile ahead of us, sometimes waiting a while, to give us time to catch up, then went on, moving fast, wanting to climb the mountain today. Morley came second, about fifty yards ahead of me all the way. I was in no hurry. Then as it got later afternoon I went faster and decided to pass Morley and join Japhy. Now we were at about eleven thousand feet and it was cold and there was a lot of snow and to the east we could see immense snow-capped ranges and whooee levels of valleyland below them, we were already practically on top of California. At one point I had to scramble, like the others, on a narrow ledge, around a butte of rock, and it really scared me: the fall was a hundred feet, enough to break your neck, with another little ledge letting you bounce a minute preparatory to a nice good-bye one-thousand-foot drop. The wind was whipping now. Yet that whole afternoon, even more than the other, was filled with old premonitions or memories, as though I'd been there before, scrambling on these rocks, for other purposes more ancient, more serious, more simple. We finally got to the foot of Matterhorn where there was a most beautiful small lake unknown to the eyes of most men in this world, seen by only a handful of mountain climbers, a small lake at eleven thousand some odd feet with snow on the edges of it and beautiful flowers and a beautiful meadow, an alpine meadow, flat and dreamy, upon which I immediately threw myself and took my shoes off. Japhy'd been there a half-hour when I made it, and it was cold now and his clothes were on again. Morley came up behind us smiling. We sat there looking up at the imminent steep scree slope of the final crag of Matterhorn.

"That don't look much, we can do it!" I said glad now.

"No, Ray, that's more than it looks. Do you realize that's a thousand feet more?"

"That much?"

"Unless we make a run up there, double-time, we'll never make it down again to our camp before nightfall and never make it down to the car at the lodge before tomorrow morning at, well at midnight."

"Phew."

"I'm tired," said Morley. "I don't think I'll try it."

"Well, that's right," I said. "The whole purpose of mountain climbing to me isn't just to show off you can get to the top, it's getting out to this wild country."

"Well I'm gonna go," said Japhy.

"Well if you're gonna go I'm goin with you."

"Morley?"

"I don't think I can make it. I'll wait here." And that wind was strong, too strong. I felt that as soon as we'd be a few hundred feet up the slope it might hamper our climbing.

Japhy took a small pack of peanuts and raisins and said, "This'll be our gasoline, boy. You ready Ray to make a double-time run?"

"Ready. What would I say to the boys in The Place if I came all this way only to give up at the last minute?"

"It's late so let's hurry." Japhy started up walking very rapidly and then even running sometimes where the climb had to be to the right or left along ridges of scree. Scree is long landslides of rocks and sand, very difficult to scramble through, always little avalanches going on. At every few steps we took it seemed we were going higher and higher on a terrifying elevator, I gulped when I turned around to look back and see all of the state of California it would seem stretching out in three directions under huge blue skies with frightening planetary space clouds and immense vistas of distant valleys and even plateaus and for all I knew whole Nevadas out there. It was terrifying to look down and see Morley a dreaming spot by the little lake waiting for us. "Oh why didn't I stay with old Henry?" I thought. I now began to be afraid to go any higher from sheer fear of being too high. I began to be afraid of being blown away by the wind. All the nightmares I'd ever had about falling off mountains and precipitous buildings ran through my head in perfect clarity. Also with every twenty steps we took upward we both became completely exhausted.

"That's because of the high altitude now Ray," said Japhy sitting beside me panting. "So have raisins and peanuts and you'll see what kick it gives you." And each time it gave us such a tremendous kick we both jumped up without a word and climbed another twenty, thirty steps. Then sat down again, panting, sweating in the cold wind, high on top of the world our noses sniffling like the noses of little boys playing late Saturday afternoon their final little games in winter. Now the wind began to howl like the wind in movies about the Shroud of Tibet. The steepness began to be too much for me; I was afraid now to look back any more; I peeked: I couldn't even make out Morley by the tiny lake.

"Hurry it up," yelled Japhy from a hundred feet ahead. "It's getting awfully late." I looked up to the peak. It was right there, I'd be there in five minutes. "Only a half-hour to go!" yelled Japhy. I didn't believe it. In five minutes of scrambling angrily upward I fell down and looked up and it was still just as far away. What I didn't like about that peak-top was that the clouds of all the world were blowing right through it like fog.

"Wouldn't see anything up there anyway," I muttered. "Oh why did I ever let myself into this?" Japhy was way ahead of me now, he'd left the peanuts and raisins with me, it was with a kind of lonely solemnity now he had decided to rush to the top if it killed him. He didn't sit down any more. Soon he was a whole football field, a hundred yards ahead of me, getting smaller. I looked back and like Lot's wife that did it. *"This is too high!"* I yelled to Japhy in a panic. He didn't hear me. I raced a few more feet up and fell exhausted on my belly, slipping back just a little. *"This is too high!"* I yelled. I was really scared. Supposing I'd start to slip back for good, these screes might start sliding any time anyway. That damn mountain goat Japhy, I could see him running up through the foggy air up ahead from rock to rock, up, up, just the flash of his boot bottoms. "How can I keep up with a maniac like that?" But with nutty desperation I followed him. Finally I came to a kind of ledge where I could sit at a level angle instead of having to cling not to slip, and I nudged my whole body inside the ledge just to hold me there tight, so the wind would not dislodge me, and I looked down and around and I had had it. *"I'm stayin here!"* I yelled to Japhy.

"Come on Smith, only another five minutes. I only got a hundred feet to go!"

*"I'm staying right here! It's too high!"*

He said nothing and went on. I saw him collapse and pant and get up and make his run again.

I nudged myself closer into the ledge and closed my eyes and thought "Oh what a life this is, why do we have to be born in the first place, and only so we can have our poor gentle flesh laid out to such impossible horrors as huge mountains and rock and empty space," and with horror I remembered the famous Zen saying, "When you get to the top of a mountain, keep climbing." The saying made my hair stand on end; it had been such cute poetry sitting on Alvah's straw mats. Now it was enough to make my heart pound and my heart bleed for being born at all. "In fact when Japhy gets to the top of that crag he *will* keep climbing, the way the wind's blowing. Well this old philosopher is staying right here," and I closed my eyes. "Besides," I thought, "rest and be kind, you don't have to prove anything." Suddenly I heard a beautiful broken yodel of a strange musical and mystical intensity in the wind, and looked up, and it was Japhy standing on top of Matterhorn peak letting out his triumphant mountain-conquering Buddha Mountain Smashing song of joy. It was beautiful. It was funny, too, up here on the not-so-funny top of California and in all that rushing fog. But I had to hand it to him, the guts, the endurance, the sweat, and now the crazy human singing: whipped cream on top of ice cream. I didn't have enough strength to answer his yodel. He ran around up there and went out of sight to investigate the little flat top of some kind (he said) that ran a few feet west and then dropped sheer back down maybe as far as I care to the sawdust floors of Virginia City. It was insane. I could hear him yelling at me but I just nudged farther in my protective nook, trembling. I looked down at the small lake where Morley was lying on his back with a blade of grass in his mouth and said out loud "Now there's the karma of these three men here: Japhy Ryder gets to his triumphant mountaintop and makes it, I almost make it and have to give up and huddle in a bloody cave, but the smartest of them all is that poet's poet lyin down there with his knees crossed to the sky chewing on a flower dreaming by a gurgling *plage*, goddammit they'll never get me up here again."

I really was amazed by the wisdom of Morley now: "Him with all his goddamn pictures of snowcapped Swiss Alps," I thought.

Then suddenly everything was just like jazz: it happened in one insane second or so: I looked up and saw Japhy *running down the mountain* in huge twenty-foot leaps, running, leaping, landing with a great drive of his booted heels, bouncing five feet or so, running, then taking another long crazy yelling yodelaying sail down the sides of the world and in that flash I realized *it's impossible to fall off mountains you fool* and with a yodel of my own I suddenly got up and began running down the mountain after him doing exactly the same huge leaps, the same fantastic runs and jumps, and in the space of about five minutes I'd guess Japhy Ryder and I (in my sneakers, driving the heels of my sneakers right into sand, rock, boulders, I didn't care any more I was so anxious to get down out of there) came leaping and yelling like mountain goats or I'd say like Chinese lunatics of a thousand years ago, enough to raise the hair on the head of the meditating Morley by the lake, who said he looked up and saw us flying down and couldn't believe it. In fact with one of my greatest leaps and loudest screams of joy I came flying right down to the edge of the lake and dug my sneakered heels into the mud and just fell sitting there, glad. Japhy was already taking his shoes off and pouring sand and pebbles out. It was great. I took off my sneakers and poured out a couple of buckets of lava dust and said "Ah Japhy you taught me the final lesson of them all, you can't fall off a mountain."

"And that's what they mean by the saying, When you get to the top of a mountain keep climbing, Smith."

"Dammit that yodel of triumph of yours was the most beautiful thing I ever heard in my life. I wish I'd a had a tape recorder to take it down."

"Those things aren't made to be heard by the people below," says Japhy dead serious.

"By God you're right, all those sedentary bums sitting around on pillows hearing the cry of the triumphant mountain smasher, they don't deserve it. But when I looked up and saw you running down that mountain I suddenly understood everything."

"Ah a little satori for Smith today," says Morley.

"What were you doing down here?"

"Sleeping, mostly."

"Well dammit I didn't get to the top. Now I'm ashamed of myself because now that I know how to come *down* a mountain I know how to go *up* and that I can't fall off, but now it's too late."

"We'll come back next summer Ray and climb it. Do you realize that this is the first time you've been mountain climbin and you left old veteran Morley here way behind you?"

"Sure," said Morley. "Do you think, Japhy, they would assign Smith the title of Tiger for what he done today?"

"Oh sure," says Japhy, and I really felt proud. I was a Tiger.

"Well dammit I'll be a lion next time we get up here."

"Let's go men, now we've got a long long way to go back down this scree to our camp and down that valley of boulders and then down that lake trail, wow, I doubt if we can make it before pitch dark."

"It'll be mostly okay." Morley pointed to the sliver of moon in the pinkening deepening blue sky. "That oughta light us a way."

"Let's go." We all got up and started back. Now when I went around that ledge that had scared me it was just fun and a lark, I just skipped and jumped and danced along and I had really learned that you can't fall off a mountain. Whether you *can* fall off a mountain or not I don't know, but I had learned that you can't. That was the way it struck me.

It was a joy, though, to get down into the valley and lose

sight of all that open sky space underneath everything and finally, as it got graying five o'clock, about a hundred yards from the other boys and walking alone, to just pick my way singing and thinking along the little black cruds of a deer trail through the rocks, no call to think or look ahead or worry, just follow the little balls of deer crud with your eyes cast down and enjoy life. At one point I looked and saw crazy Japhy who'd climbed for fun to the top of a snow slope and skied right down to the bottom, about a hundred yards, on his boots and the final few yards on his back, yippeeing and glad. Not only that but he'd taken off his pants again and wrapped them around his neck. This pants bit of his was simply he said for comfort, which is true, besides nobody around to see him anyway, though I figured that when he went mountain climbing with girls it didn't make any difference to him. I could hear Morley talking to him in the great lonely valley: even across the rocks you could tell it was his voice. Finally I followed my deer trail so assiduously I was by myself going along ridges and down across creekbottoms completely out of sight of them, though I could hear them, but I trusted the instinct of my sweet little millennial deer and true enough, just as it was getting dark their ancient trail took me right to the edges of the familiar shallow creek (where they stopped to drink for the last five thousand years) and there was the glow of Japhy's bonfire making the side of the big rock orange and gay. The moon was bright high in the sky. "Well that moon's gonna save our ass, we got eight miles to go downtrail boys."

We ate a little and drank a lot of tea and arranged all our stuff. I had never had a happier moment in my life than those lonely moments coming down that little deer trace and when we hiked off with our packs I turned to take a final look up that way, it was dark now, hoping to see a few dear little deer, nothing in sight, and I thanked everything up that way. It had been like when you're a little boy and have spent a whole day rambling alone in the woods and fields and on the dusk homeward walk you did it all with your eyes to the ground, scuffling, thinking, whistling, like little Indian boys must feel when they follow their striding fathers from Russian River to Shasta two hundred years ago, like little Arab boys following their fathers, their fathers' trails; that singsong little joyful solitude, nose sniffling, like a little girl pulling her little brother home on the sled and they're both singing little ditties of their imagination and making faces at the ground and just being themselves before they have to go in the kitchen and put on a straight face again for the world of seriousness. "Yet what could be more serious than to follow a deer trace to get to your water?" I thought. We got to the cliff and started down the five-mile valley of boulders, in clear moonlight now, it was quite easy to dance down from boulder to boulder, the boulders were snow white, with patches of deep black shadow. Everything was cleanly whitely beautiful in the moonlight. Sometimes you could see the silver flash of the creek. Far down were the pines of the meadow park and the pool of the pond.

At this point my feet were unable to go on. I called Japhy and apologized. I couldn't take any more jumps. There were blisters not only on the bottoms but on the sides of my feet, from there having been no protection all yesterday and today. So Japhy swapped and let me wear his boots.

With these big lightweight protective boots on I knew I could go on fine. It was a great new feeling to be able to jump from rock to rock without having to feel the pain through the thin sneakers. On the other hand, for Japhy, it was also a relief to be suddenly lightfooted and he enjoyed it. We made double-time down the valley. But every step was getting us bent, now, we were all really tired. With the heavy packs it was difficult to control those thigh muscles that you need to go *down* a mountain, which is sometimes harder than going up. And there were all those boulders to surmount, for sometimes we'd be walking in sand awhile and our path would be blocked by boulders and we had to climb them and jump from one to the other then suddenly no more boulders and we had to jump down to the sand. Then we'd be trapped in impassable thickets and had to go around them or try to crash through and sometimes I'd get stuck in a thicket with my rucksack, standing there cursing in the impossible moonlight. None of us were talking. I was angry too because Japhy and Morley were afraid to stop and rest, they said it was dangerous at this point to stop.

"What's the difference the moon's shining, we can even sleep."

"No, we've got to get down to that car tonight."

"Well, let's stop a minute here. My legs can't take it."

"Okay, only a minute."

But they never rested long enough to suit me and it
seemed to me they were getting hysterical. I even began to
curse them and at one point I even gave Japhy hell:
"What's the sense of killing yourself like this, you call this
fun? Phooey." (Your ideas are a crock, I added to myself.)
A little weariness'll change a lot of things. Eternities of
moonlight rock and thickets and boulders and ducks and
that horrifying valley with the two rim walls and finally it
seemed we were almost out of there, but nope, not quite
yet, and my legs screaming to stop, and me cursing and
smashing at twigs and throwing myself on the ground to
rest a minute.

"Come on, Ray, everything comes to an end." In fact I
realized I had no guts anyway, which I've long known. But
I have joy. When we got to the alpine meadow I stretched
out on my belly and drank water and enjoyed myself peacefully in silence while they talked and worried about getting
down the rest of the trail in time.

"Ah don't worry, it's a beautiful night, you've driven
yourself too hard. Drink some water and lie down here for
about five even ten minutes, everything takes care of itself."
Now I was being the philosopher. In fact Japhy agreed
with me and we rested peacefully. That good long rest
assured my bones I could make it down to the lake okay. It
was beautiful going down the trail. The moonlight poured
through thick foliage and made dapples on the backs of
Morley and Japhy as they walked in front of me. With our
packs we got into a good rhythmic walk and enjoying
going "Hup hup" as we came to switchbacks and swiveled
around, always down, down, the pleasant downgoing swinging rhythm trail. And that roaring creek was a beauty by
moonlight, those flashes of flying moon water, that snow
white foam, those black-as-pitch trees, regular elfin para-
dises of shadow and moon. The air began to get warmer
and nicer and in fact I thought I could begin to smell
people again. We could smell the nice raunchy tidesmell of
the lake water, and flowers, and softer dust of down below.
Everything up there had smelled of ice and snow and heartless spine rock. Here there was the smell of sun-heated
wood, sunny dust resting in the moonlight, lake mud, flow-

ers, straw, all those good things of the earth. The trail was fun coming down and yet at one point I was as tired as ever, more than in that endless valley of boulders, but you could see the lake lodge down below now, a sweet little lamp of light and so it didn't matter. Morley and Japhy were talking a blue streak and all we had to do was roll on down to the car. In fact suddenly, as in a happy dream, with the suddenness of waking up from an endless nightmare and it's all over, we were striding across the road and there were houses and there were automobiles parked under trees and Morley's car was sitting right there.

# KEN KESEY

# Wakonda

*You can make a mark across the night with the tip of an embered stick, and you can actually see it fixed in its finity. You can be absolutely certain of its treacherous impermanence. And that is all. Hank knew . . .*

As well as he knew that the Wakonda has not always run this course. (Yeah . . . you want to know something about rivers, friends and neighbors?)

Along its twenty miles numerous switchbacks and oxbows, sloughs and backwaters mark its old channel. (You want me to tell you a thing or two about rivers?) Some of these sloughs are kept clean by small currents from nearby streams, making them a chain of clear, deep, greenglass pools where great chubs lie on the bottom like sunken logs; in the winter the pools in these sloughs are nightly stopovers for chevrons of brant geese flying south down the coast; in the spring the pole willows along the banks arch long graceful limbs out over the water; when an angler breeze baits the tree, the leafy tips tickle the surface and tiny fingerling salmon and steelhead dart up to strike, sometimes shooting clear into the sunshine like little silver bullets fired from the depths. (Funny thing is, I didn't learn this thing about rivers from the old man or any of the

uncles, or even Boney Stokes, but from old Floyd Evenwrite, a couple years ago, that first time Floyd and us
locked horns about the union.)

Some sloughs are flooded spear-fields of cattail and
skunk cabbage where loons and widgeon breed; some are
bogs where maple leaves and eelgrass and snakeweed skele-
ton with decay and silently dissolve into purple, oil-sheened
mud; and some of the sloughs have silted in completely
and dried enough to become rich blue-green deer pastures
or two-story-high berry thickets. (The way it happened I'd
come to town to meet with Floyd Evenwrite that first time
this Closed Shop business came up and instead of taking
the cycle I figured I'd use the boat to try out this brand-
new Johnson Seahorse 25 I'd picked up in Eugene not a
week before, and swinging in toward the municipal dock I
whanged into something floating out of sight; probably an
old deadfall washed loose, and the boat and motor went
down like a rock and I had to swim it, mad as hell and sure
as shooting in *no* frigging mood to talk Labor Organization.)

There is one such berry thicket up river from the Stamper
house, a thicket so dense, so woven and tangled that even
the bears avoid it: from the mossy bones of deer and elk
trapped trying to trample a path rises a wall of thorns that
appears totally impenetrable. (In the meeting Floyd did
most of the talking, but I didn't do my share of the listening. I couldn't get my mind on him. I just sat there looking
out the window where my boat and motor had sunk, feeling my Sunday slacks shrink dry on me.) But when Hank
was a boy of ten he found a way to penetrate this thorny
wall: he discovered that the rabbits and raccoons had tun-
neled an elaborate subway system next to the ground, and
by pulling on a hooded oilskin poncho to protect his hide
from the thorns, he was able to half crawl, half worm his
way through that snarl of vines. (Floyd kept talking on
and on; I knew he was expecting me and the half-dozen or
so other gyppo men to be mowed right over by his logic. I
don't know about them other boys, but for myself I wasn't
able to follow him worth sour apples. My pants dried; it
got warmer; I pulled on my motorcycle shades so's he
couldn't see if I dropped off during his talk; and I leaned
back and sulked about that boat and motor.)

When the spring sun was bright above the thicket,
enough light filtered down through the leaves so he was

able to see, and he would spend hours on his hands and knees exploring the smooth passageways. He frequently came face to face with a fellow explorer, an old boar coon, who, the first time he encountered the boy, had huffed and growled and hissed, then turned loose a musk that put a skunk to shame, but as they met again and again the old masked outlaw gradually came to regard this hooded intruder as something of a partner in crime; in a dim passageway of thorn the boy and the animal stand nose to nose and compare booty before they go on with their furtive ramblings: "What you got, old coon? A fresh wapatoo? Well, look here at my gopher skull . . ." (Floyd talked on and on and on and—what with sitting there half asleep stewing about the boat and river and all—I got to thinking about something that'd happened a long time before, something I'd clean forgot about . . .) He found countless treasures in the passageways: a foxtail caught in the thorns; a fossilized bug that still struggled against a millennium of mud; a rusted ball-and-cap pistol that reeked still of rum and romance . . . but never anything near to equaling the discovery made one chilly April afternoon. (I got to thinking about the bobcats I found in the berry vines, is what; I got to remembering them bobcats.)

There were three kittens at the end of a strange new passageway, three kittens with their blue-gray eyes but a few days open, peering up at him from a mossy, hair-lined nest. Except for the nub of a tiny tail, and the tassels of hair at the tip of each tiny ear, they looked much the same as barn kittens that Henry drowned by the sackful every summer. The boy stared wide-eyed at them playing in their nest, overcome by his remarkable good fortune. "Suck egg mule," he whispered reverently, as though such a find needed the awed respect of Uncle Aaron's expressions instead of the forceful punch of old Henry's curses. "Three little baby bobcats all by theirselves . . . suck egg mule."

He picked up the nearest kitten and began to fight and tear at the vine until he had made a space large enough to turn around in. He headed back the way he'd come, reasoning, without even consciously thinking about it, that the mother would most likely pick a route that he hadn't used, she would most likely steer clear of a tunnel with mansmell in it. He found he was being slowed by holding the hissing and snapping kitten in his hands so he took the scruff of its neck between his teeth. The kitten became immediately calm and swung placidly from the boy's mouth as Hank sped through the blackberries as fast as elbows and knees could carry him. "Beat it out; *beat* it!"

When he emerged from the thicket he was scratched and bleeding from a score of places on his hands and face, but he didn't remember any pain, he didn't remember any of the scratches; all he could recall was the soft flutter of panic beneath his chest. What would have happened had that old bitch bobcat suddenly run smack dab into a boy toting one of her offspring in his mouth? A boy pinned down and practically helpless under fifteen feet of blackberry vines? He had to sit down and breathe deeply before he could manage the ten more yards to the empty blasting-cap crate where he put the kitten.

Then, for some reason, instead of securing the box and beating it back to the house as he advised himself, he hesitated to inspect his catch. Carefully he slid back the lid and bent to look into the box.

"Hey you. Hey there you, Bobby the Cat . . ."

The little animal ceased its frantic scurrying from corner to corner and lifted its fuzzy face toward the sound of the voice. Then uttered a cry so tragic, so pleading, so frightened and forlorn, that the boy winced with sympathy.

"Hey, you lonely, ain't you? Huh, ain't you?"

The kitten's yowled answer threw the boy into an intense conflict, and after five minutes of reminding himself that nobody *no*-body but a snotnosed moron would go *back* in that hole, he gave in to that yowling.

The other two kittens had fallen asleep by the time he reached the nest. They lay curled about each other, purring softly. He paused for an instant to catch his breath, and in the silence that descended, now that the brambles were no longer scratching and resounding on his oilskin hood, heard the first kitten crying from its box at the edge of the thicket; the thin, pitiful wail penetrated the jungle like a needle. Why, a noise like that must carry for miles! He grabbed up the next kitten, clamped his teeth over the fur at the back of the neck, thrashed quickly around in the little turning space that was already beginning to take on a smooth, used appearance, and once more sprinted on elbows and knees for that opening to safety that lay an ever farther distance away through an ever smaller tube of thorns and terror. It seemed to take hours. Time got snagged on a sticker. The vines hissed past. It must have started to rain, for the tunnel had grown quite dim and the ground slick. The boy squirmed through with eyes straining, that bobcat's child swaying and swinging in his mouth, keening a shrill plea for help, the other in the box echoing and relaying the plea. The tunnel got longer as it grew dimmer, he was certain of it. Or the other way around. He gasped for breath through the fur in his teeth. He battled the mud and vine as though it were water drowning him, and when he broke into the clear at the end of the tunnel he drew a huge breath like a swimmer coming after many minutes into the glorious air.

He placed the second kitten in the box with the first. They both hushed their yowling and became quiet and drowsy against each other. They began to purr quietly along with the soft swish of rain through the pines. And the only other noise, through all the forest, was the broken-hearted wailing of that third kitten, alone and frightened and wet, back in that nest at the end of that tunnel.

"You'll be okay." He called assurance toward the thicket. "Sure. It's rainin' now; mama'll be hustlin' back from huntin', now it's rainin'."

And this time even went so far as to pick up the box and walk a few yards toward home.

But something was strange; safe as he knew himself to be—he had picked up the .22 from the hollow log where he always stashed it during his forays into the thicket—his heart still pounded and his stomach still heaved with fear, and the image of that mother cat's wrath still burned in his head.

He stopped walking and stood very still with his eyes closed. "No. No sir, by gosh, I ain't." Shaking his head back and forth: "No. I ain't such a dummy as *that*, I don't care what!"

But the fear continued to shake against his ribs, and it occurred to him that it had been shaking that way constantly from the moment he'd found the three kittens playing peacefully in their nest. Because it had known—it, the fear, *the being-awful-scared-of-something*—had known the boy better than he knew himself, had known all along from that first glance that he wasn't going to be satisfied until he had all three kittens. It didn't make any difference if they were baby dragons and mama dragon was breathing fire on him every step of the way.

So it wasn't until he emerged the third time with the

third kitten between his teeth that he was able to sigh and relax and peacefully start toward the house, triumphantly shouldering the explosives box as if it were spoils of a mighty battle. And when he met the old coon waddling toward him on the muddy path he saluted the inscrutable animal and advised him, "Maybe you better leave off the thickets t'day, Mister Jig; it's fierce in yonder for a old man."

Henry was in the woods. Uncle Ben and Ben, Junior—a boy called Little Joe by everyone but his father, shorter and younger than Hank and already showing his hell-raising father's heavenly good looks—were staying at the house while Uncle Ben's present woman cooled off enough to take them back into her home in town. They saw the kittens and Hank's scratched and bleeding condition and both arrived at the same conclusion.

"Did you really?" asked the boy. "Did you really, Hank, fight a wildcat for 'em?"

"No, not really," Hank replied modestly.

Ben looked at his nephew's scratched and muddy face and triumphant eyes. "Oh, you did. Oh yeah you did, kid. Maybe not head on. Maybe not a wildcat. But you fought something." Then surprised both Hank and his own boy by spending the rest of the afternoon helping build a cage out near the river's edge.

"I don't care much for cages," he told them. "I'm not keen on cages of any kind. But if these cats are ever to get big enough to hold their own against those hounds, it's gonna have to be in protected confinement. So we'll make it a good cage, a comfortable cage; we'll make the world's *best* cage."

And that short, beautifully featured black sheep of the family, who prided himself on never working with more than his wink and his smile, slaved away all afternoon helping two boys build a true paragon among cages. It was made from an old pick-up-truck box that had once been on Aaron's pick-up but had sucked too much dust to suit him. When finished, this box was painted, calked, reinforced, and stood majestically a few feet from the ground on sawn four-by-four legs. Half of it, including the floor, was of wire mesh to make it easy to keep clean, and the door was large enough that Hank or Joe Ben could get right in with the regular tenants. There were boxes for hiding, straw for burrowing, and a burlap-covered post for climbing to the peaked top of the cage, where a wicker basket was lined with an old pair of woolens. There were a little tree to climb and rubber balls hung from the mesh ceiling with string, and a dishpan full of fresh river sand in case bob-cats, like other cats, were inclined that way. It was a beau-tiful cage, a strong cage, and, as comfort in cages went, the goddamned cat cage—as Henry came to call it whenever smell indicated it was past time for cleaning—was as com-fortable as a cage could be.

"The *best* of all possible cages." Ben stepped back to regard the job with a sad smile. "What more can one ask?"

Hank spent a large part of that summer in the cage with the three kittens, and by fall they were all so accustomed to his morning visit that if it was delayed by so much as five minutes there was such a howl raised that old Henry would pardon his son from whatever chore he was doing and send him running to attend to that damned menagerie in the goddam boogering cat cage. By Halloween the cats were tame enough to bring into the house to play; by Thanksgiv-ing Hank had promised his classmates that on Playday, the day before Christmas vacation, he would bring all three to school.

The night before this event the river had risen four feet in response to three hard days of rain; Hank was worried that the boats might be swept loose from their moorings as they had been last year, and prevent him from making it across to the school bus. Or, worse, that the river might even rise clear up to the cage. Before going up to bed he put on rubber boots over his pajamas and pulled on a poncho and went out with a lantern to check. The rain had slowed to a thin, cold spitting that came with occasional gusts of wind; the worst of the storm was over; the white blur above the mountains showed the moon trying to clear a way through the clouds. In the buttery yellow light of the lantern he could see the rowboat and the motorboat cov-ered with green tarpaulins, bobbing in the dark water. They tugged at their ropes, pulling to be away up river, but they were safe. The tides at the river's mouth were flood-ing, and the river was flowing inland instead of toward the sea. The current usually flowed four hours toward the sea, then stood an hour, then turned and flowed two or three hours in the other direction. During this backward upriver flow, as the salt water from the sea rushed to embrace the mud-filled rainwater from the mountains, the river would be at its highest. Hank noted the water's height on the marker at the dock—black water swirling at the number five; five feet, then, above the normal high-tide mark—then he went on to the end of the dock and followed the rickety plank walk around the edge of the jetty to the place where his father was clinging with a crooked elbow to a cable, seemingly glued to the side of the foundation by the sticky light of his lantern while he hammered spikes into a two-by-six he was adding to the tangle of wood and cable and pipe. Henry held his hammer and squinted against the blowing gusts of rain.

"Is that you, boy? What do you want out here this time of night?" he demanded fiercely, then as an afterthought asked, "You come out to give the old man a hand at floodtime, is that it?"

The last thing in the boy's mind was freezing for an hour in this wind, hammering aimlessly on that crazy business of his father's, but he said, "I don't know. I might, then I might not." He hung, swinging outward by the cable, and looked past old Henry's streaking features; by the light coming from his mother's upstairs window he could see the outline of the cat cage against black clouds. "No sir, I just don't know. . . . How much higher you reckon she'll raise tonight?"

Henry leaned out to spit his exhausted wad of snuff down into the water. "The tides'll shift in an hour. At the rate she's risin' now she'll come up two more feet, three at the darnedest, then start easin' back. Especial now that the rain's quittin'."

"Yeah," Hank agreed, "I reckon that's about the way I see it." Looking at the cage he realized that the river would have to rise a good fifteen feet to reach even the legs, and by that time the house, the barn, probably the whole town of Wakonda would be washed away. "So I guess I'll go on in an' hit the sack. She's all yours," Hank called over his shoulder.

Henry looked after his son. The moon had finally made it through, and the boy moving away down the planks in his shapeless poncho, black outlined in glistening silver, was as much a mystery to the old man as the clouds he resembled. "Feisty little outfit." Henry dipped out another charge of snuff, jammed it into the breech, and resumed his hammering.

By the time Hank was in bed the rain had stopped completely and patches of stars were showing. The big moon meant good clamming at the flats as well as colder, drier weather. Before he fell asleep he could tell by the absence of sound from the river that it had crested and from here on would drain back to the sea.

When he woke in the morning he looked out and saw the boats were fine and the river wasn't much higher than usual. He hurried through breakfast, then took the box he had prepared and ran out toward the cage. He went first to the barn to pick up some burlap sacks to put in the bottom of the box. The morning was cold; a light frost was sifted into all the shadows and the cow breath was like skim milk in the air. Hank pulled some sacks from the pile in the feed room, scattering mice, and ran on out through the back door. The chill air in his lungs made him feel light and silly. He turned the corner and stopped: *the bank!* (About the time I went to nodding into my dream about the cats, Floyd and old man Syverson who used to run the little mill at Myrtleville had really got into it about something; they snapped me out of it, hollering back and forth at each other to beat hell.) . . . *The whole bank where the cage stood is gone; the new bank shines bright and clean, as though a quick slice had been made into the earth last night with the edge of a huge moon-stropped razor.* ("Syverson," Evenwrite yells, "don't be so dunder-headed; I'm talkin' sense! And Syverson says, "Bull. What you mean, sense!" "Sense! I'm talking *sense!*" "Bull. You talkin' sign over t' you all the say-so I got of my business is what you talkin'!") *At the bottom of this slice, in the mud and roots, the corner of the cage protrudes above the turgid surface of the river. Floating in the corner behind the wire mesh are the contents of the cage—the rubber balls, the torn cloth Teddy bear, the wicker basket and sodden bedding, and the shrunken bodies of the three cats.* ("How much's it want," Syverson yells, "how much, this organization you tell us about?" "Dang it, Syve, all it wants is what's fair—" "Fair! It wants advantage is what.") *Looking so very small with their wet fur plastered against their bodies, so small and wet and ugly.* ("Okay! okay!" Floyd hollered, getting rattled, "but all it wants is its *fair* advantage!")

*He doesn't want to cry; he hasn't allowed himself to cry in years. And to stop that old scalding memory mounting in his nose and throat he forces himself to imagine exactly*

*what it must have been like—the crumbling, the cage rock-
ing, then falling with the slice of earth into the water, the
three cats thrown from their warm bed and submerged in
struggling icy death, caged and unable to swim to the surface. He visualizes every detail with painful care and then
runs the scene over and over through his mind until it is
grooved into him, until a call from the house puts a stop to
his torture. . . .* (Everybody laughed when Floyd made that
slip, even old Floyd himself. And for some time after folks
kidded him about it. "All it wants is its fair advantage."
But me, not paying attention, nodding on and off; thinking
about my drowned cats and my new Johnson outboard at
the bottom of the drink, I kind of switched what he said to
something else.) *Until the pain and guilt and loss are replaced by something different, something larger . . .*

After putting the box and gunny sacks down I went back
into the house and got my lunch along with that bony little
peck the old lady laid on my cheek every morning. Then I
went out to where old Henry was readying the boat to
ferry me and Joe Ben across to wait for the school bus. I
kept still, hoping neither of them'd notice me not having
the box of cats like I'd planned. (. . . *replaced for good by
something far stronger than guilt or loss.*) And they might
not of, because the motorboat wouldn't start, it being so
cold, and after Henry had jerked and kicked and cussed
and raved at it for about ten minutes he finally barked the
hide off his knuckles and then he wasn't in any shape to
notice anything. We all got into the row boat and I thought
I was gonna make it, but on the way across old bright-eyed
Joe Ben gave a yell and pointed at the bank. "The cat cage!
Hank, the *cat* cage!"

I didn't say anything. The old man stopped rowing and
looked, then turned to me. I frigged around, acting like I
was all wrapped up tying my shoe or something. But pretty
quick I saw they weren't gonna let me off the hook without
I said something or other. So I just shrugged and told
them, cool and matter-of-fact, "It's a dirty deal, is all.
Nothing but just a crappy deal."

"Sure," the old man said. "The way the football
bounces."

"Sure," Joe Ben said.

"Just a tough break," I said.

"Sure," they said.

"But boy, I'll tell ya I'll tell—*you* . . ." I could feel that cool, matter-of-fact tone slipping away, but couldn't do diddle about it. "If I ever—*ever*, I don't care *when*—get me any more of them bobcats—oh, Christ, Henry, that crappy river, I should, I should of—"

And when I couldn't go on I went to beating at the side of the boat until the old man took me by the fist and stopped me.

And after that the whole thing was done and shut and forgot. None of the family ever mentioned it. For a while kids at school asked me how about them *bobcats* I was always blowing about, how come I hadn't brought them *bobcats* to school? . . . But I just told them to fuck off and after I told them enough times and showed them I meant what I said a time or two, *nobody* mentioned it any more. So I forgot it. Leastways the part of a man that remembers out loud forgot it. But years later it used to wonder me just how come I'd sometimes get all of a sudden so itchy to cut out from basketball practice, or from a date. It would really wonder me. To other people—Coach Lewellyn or a drinking buddy, or whatever honey I might have been necking with—I would say that if I waited too long the river would be up too high to cross. "Report of high water," I'd say. "If she gets up too big there's a chance the boat might be pulled loose and there I'd be, you know, up that ol' creek without that ol' canoe." I'd tell buddies and coaches that I had to beat it home "on account of that ol' Wakonda is risin' like a wall between me and the supper table." I'd tell dates just ready to tip over that "sorry kid, I got to up and hustle or the boat might be swamped." But myself, I'd tell myself, Stamper, you got deals going with it, with that river. Face it. You might've put all kinds of stories on the little girlies from Reedsport, but when it comes right down to it you know them stories are so much crap and you got deals going with that snake of a river.

It was like me and that river had drawn ourselves a little contract, a little grudge match, and without me knowing exactly why. "It's like this, sweetie-britches," I might say to some little high-school honey when we was parked someplace, steaming up the windows of the old man's pick-up in some Saturday-night battle of the bra. "It's like if I don't go *now*, then it might be shiver all night long waitin' to get across; it's rainin', *look* out there at it come down like a cow wettin' on a flat rock!" Feed her any dumb tale but know what you meant was you *had to*—for some reason I

didn't know then—*had* to get home and get into a slicker
and corks and get a hammer and nails and lay on the
timbers like a crazy man, maybe even give up a *sure hump*
just to freeze a half an hour out on that goddamned jetty!

And I never understood why until that afternoon in
Wakonda at the union meeting, sitting there remembering
how I'd lost my bobcats, looking out the window of the
grange hall at the spot where my boat had sunk in the bay,
and hearing Floyd Evenwrite say to old man Syverson:
"All it wants is its fair advantage."

So as close as I can come to explaining it, friends and
neighbors, that is why that river is no buddy of mine. It's
maybe the buddy of the brant geese and the steelhead. It is
mighty likely a buddy of old lady Pringle and her Pioneer
Club in Wakonda—they hold oldtime get-togethers on the
docks every Fourth of July in honor of the first time some
old moccasined hobo come paddling across in his dugout a
hundred years ago, the Highway of Pioneers they call it . . .
and who the hell knows, maybe it *was*, just like now it is
the railroad we use to float our log booms down—but it
still is no personal friend of *mine*. Not just the thing about
the bobcats; I could tell you a hundred stories, probably,
give you a hundred reasons showing *why* I got to fight that
river. Oh, *fine* reasons; because you can spend a good deal
of time thinking during those thinking times, when you're
taking timber cruises walking all day long with nothing to
do but check the pedometer on your foot, or sitting for
hours in a stand blowing a game call, or milking in the
morning when Viv is laid up with cramps—a *lot* of time,
and I got a lot of things about myself straight in my mind:
I know, for an instance, that, if you want to play this way,
you can make the river stand for all *sorts* of other things.
But doing that it seems to me is taking your eye off the
ball; making it more than what it is lessens it. Just to see it
clear is plenty. Just to feel it cold against you or watch it
flood or smell it when the damn thing backs up from
Wakonda with all the town's garbage and sewage and dead
crud floating around in it stinking up a breeze, that is
plenty. And the best way to see it is not looking behind
it—or beneath it or beyond it—but dead at it.

And to remember that all it wants is its fair advantage.

So by keeping my eye on the ball I found it just came
down to this: that that river was after some things I figured
belonged to me. It'd already got some and was all the time

working to get some more. And in as how I was well known as one of the Ten Toughest Hombres this side of the Rockies, I aimed to do my best to *hinder* it.

And as far as I was concerned, hindering something meant—had always meant—going after it with everything you got, fighting and kicking, stomping and gouging, and cussing it when everything else went sour. And being just as strong in the hassle as you got it in you to be. Now that's real logical, don't you think? That's real simple. If You Wants to Win, You Does Your Best. Why, a body could paint that on a plaque and hang it up over his bedstead. He could live by it. It could be like one of the Ten Commandments for success. "If You Wants to Win You Does Your Best." Solid and certain as a rock; one rule I was gutsure I could bank on.

Yet it took nothing more than my kid brother coming to spend a month with us to show me that there are *other* ways of winning—like winning by giving in, by being soft, by not gritting your goddam teeth and getting your best hold . . . winning by not, for *damned* sure, being one of the Ten Toughest Hombres west of the Rockies. And show me as well that there's times when the only way you can win is by being weak, by losing, by doing your worst instead of your best.

And learning that come near to doing me in.

# MAXINE HONG KINGSTON

# No Name Woman

"You must not tell anyone," my mother said, "what I am about to tell you. In China your father had a sister who killed herself. She jumped into the family well. We say that your father has all brothers because it is as if she had never been born.

"In 1924 just a few days after our village celebrated seventeen hurry-up weddings—to make sure that every young man who went 'out on the road' would responsibly come home—your father and his brothers and your grandfather and his brothers and your aunt's new husband sailed for America, the Gold Mountain. It was your grandfather's last trip. Those lucky enough to get contracts waved goodbye from the decks. They fed and guarded the stowaways and helped them off in Cuba, New York, Bali, Hawaii. 'We'll meet in California next year,' they said. All of them sent money home.

"I remember looking at your aunt one day when she and I were dressing; I had not noticed before that she had such a protruding melon of a stomach. But I did not think, 'She's pregnant,' until she began to look like other pregnant women, her shirt pulling and the white tops of her black pants showing. She could not have been pregnant, you see, because her husband had been gone for years. No one said anything. We did not discuss it. In early summer she was ready to have the child, long after the time when it could have been possible.

"The village had also been counting. On the night the baby was to be born the villagers raided our house. Some were crying. Like a great saw, teeth strung with lights, files of people walked zigzag across our land, tearing the rice. Their lanterns doubled in the disturbed black water, which drained away through the broken bunds. As the villagers closed in, we could see that some of them, probably men and women we knew well, wore white masks. The people with long hair hung it over their faces. Women with short hair made it stand up on end. Some had tied white bands around their foreheads, arms, and legs.

"At first they threw mud and rocks at the house. Then they threw eggs and began slaughtering our stock. We could hear the animals scream their deaths—the roosters, the pigs, a last great roar from the ox. Familiar wild heads flared in our night windows; the villagers encircled us. Some of the faces stopped to peer at us, their eyes rushing like searchlights. The hands flattened against the panes, framed heads, and left red prints.

"The villagers broke in the front and the back doors at the same time, even though we had not locked the doors against them. Their knives dripped with the blood of our animals. They smeared blood on the doors and walls. One woman swung a chicken, whose throat she had slit, splattering blood in red arcs about her. We stood together in the middle of our house, in the family hall with the pictures and tables of the ancestors around us, and looked straight ahead.

"At that time the house had only two wings. When the men came back, we would build two more to enclose our courtyard and a third one to begin a second courtyard. The villagers pushed through both wings, even your grandparents' rooms, to find your aunt's, which was also mine until the men returned. From this room a new wing for one of the younger families would grow. They ripped up her clothes and shoes and broke her combs, grinding them underfoot. They tore her work from the loom. They scattered the cooking fire and rolled the new weaving in it. We could hear them in the kitchen breaking our bowls and banging the pots. They overturned the great waist-high earthenware jugs; duck eggs, pickled fruits, vegetables burst out and mixed in acrid torrents. The old woman from the next field swept a broom through the air and loosed the spirits-of-the-broom over our heads. 'Pig.' 'Ghost.' 'Pig,' they sobbed and scolded while they ruined our house.

"When they left, they took sugar and oranges to bless themselves. They cut pieces from the dead animals. Some of them took bowls that were not broken and clothes that were not torn. Afterward we swept up the rice and sewed it back up into sacks. But the smells from the spilled preserves lasted. Your aunt gave birth in the pigsty that night. The next morning when I went for the water, I found her and the baby plugging up the family well.

"Don't let your father know that I told you. He denies her. Now that you have started to menstruate, what happened to her could happen to you. Don't humiliate us. You wouldn't like to be forgotten as if you had never been born. The villagers are watchful."

Whenever she had to warn us about life, my mother told stories that ran like this one, a story to grow up on. She tested our strength to establish realities. Those in the emigrant generations who could not reassert brute survival died young and far from home. Those of us in the first American generations have had to figure out how the invisible world the emigrants built around our childhoods fit in solid America.

The emigrants confused the gods by diverting their curses, misleading them with crooked streets and false names. They must try to confuse their offspring as well, who, I suppose, threaten them in similar ways—always trying to get things straight, always trying to name the unspeakable. The Chinese I know hide their names; sojourners take new names when their lives change and guard their real names with silence.

Chinese-Americans, when you try to understand what things in you are Chinese, how do you separate what is peculiar to childhood, to poverty, insanities, one family, your mother who marked your growing with stories, from what is Chinese? What is Chinese tradition and what is the movies?

If I want to learn what clothes my aunt wore, whether flashy or ordinary, I would have to begin, "Remember Father's drowned-in-the-well sister?" I cannot ask that. My mother has told me once and for all the useful parts. She will add nothing unless powered by Necessity, a riverbank that guides her life. She plants vegetable gardens rather than lawns; she carries the odd-shaped tomatoes home from the fields and eats food left for the gods.

Whenever we did frivolous things, we used up energy; we flew high kites. We children came up off the ground over the melting cones our parents brought home from work and the American movie on New Year's Day—*Oh, You Beautiful Doll* with Betty Grable one year, and *She Wore a Yellow Ribbon* with John Wayne another year. After the one carnival ride each, we paid in guilt; our tired father counted his change on the dark walk home.

Adultery is extravagance. Could people who hatch their own chicks and eat the embryos and the heads for delicacies and boil the feet in vinegar for party food, leaving only the gravel, eating even the gizzard lining—could such people engender a prodigal aunt? To be a woman, to have a daughter in starvation time was a waste enough. My aunt could not have been the lone romantic who gave up everything for sex. Women in the old China did not choose. Some man had commanded her to lie with him and be his secret evil. I wonder whether he masked himself when he joined the raid on her family.

Perhaps she encountered him in the fields or on the mountain where the daughters-in-law collected fuel. Or perhaps he first noticed her in the marketplace. He was not a stranger because the village housed no strangers. She had to have dealings with him other than sex. Perhaps he worked an adjoining field, or he sold her the cloth for the dress she sewed and wore. His demand must have surprised, then terrified her. She obeyed him; she always did as she was told.

When the family found a young man in the next village to be her husband, she stood tractably beside the best rooster, his proxy, and promised before they met that she would be his forever. She was lucky that he was her age and she would be the first wife, an advantage secure now. The night she first saw him, he had sex with her. Then he left for America. She had almost forgotten what he looked like. When she tried to envision him, she only saw the black and white face in the group photograph the men had taken before leaving.

The other man was not, after all, much different from her husband. They both gave orders: she followed. "If you tell your family, I'll beat you. I'll kill you. Be here again next week." No one talked sex, ever. And she might have separated the rapes from the rest of living if only she did not have to buy her oil from him or gather wood in the same forest. I want her fear to have lasted just as long as rape lasted so that the fear could have been contained. No drawn-out fear. But women at sex hazarded birth and hence lifetimes. The fear did not stop but permeated everywhere. She told the man, "I think I'm pregnant." He organized the raid against her.

On nights when my mother and father talked about their life back home, sometimes they mentioned an "outcast table" whose business they still seemed to be settling, their voices tight. In a commensal tradition, where food is precious, the powerful older people made wrongdoers eat alone. Instead of letting them start separate new lives like the Japanese, who could become samurais and geishas, the Chinese family, faces averted but eyes glowering sideways, hung on to the offenders and fed them leftovers. My aunt must have lived in the same house as my parents and eaten at an outcast table. My mother spoke about the raid as if she and my aunt, a daughter-in-law to a different household, should not have been living together at all. Daughters-in-law lived with their husbands' parents, not their own; a synonym for marriage in Chinese is "taking a daughter-in-law." Her husband's parents could have sold her, mortgaged her, stoned her. But they had sent her back to her own mother and father, a mysterious act hinting at disgraces not told me. Perhaps they had thrown her out to deflect the avengers.

She was the only daughter; her four brothers went with her father, husband, and uncles "out on the road" and for some years became western men. When the goods were divided among the family, three of the brothers took land, and the youngest, my father, chose an education. After my grandparents gave their daughter away to her husband's family, they had dispensed all the adventure and all the property. They expected her alone to keep the traditional ways, which her brothers, now among the barbarians, could fumble without detection. The heavy, deep-rooted women were to maintain the past against the flood, safe for returning. But the rare urge west had fixed upon our family, and so my aunt crossed boundaries not delineated in space.

The work of preservation demands that the feelings playing about in one's guts not be turned into action. Just watch their passing like cherry blossoms. But perhaps my aunt, my forerunner, caught in a slow life, let dreams grow and fade and after some months or years went toward what persisted. Fear at the enormities of the forbidden kept her desires delicate, wire and bone. She looked at a man because she liked the way the hair was tucked behind his ears, or she liked the question-mark line of a long torso curving at the shoulder and straight at the hip. For warm eyes or a soft voice or a slow walk—that's all—a few hairs, a line, a brightness, a sound, a pace, she gave up family. She offered us up for a charm that vanished with tiredness, a pigtail that didn't toss when the wind died. Why, the wrong lighting could erase the dearest thing about him.

It could very well have been, however, that my aunt did not take subtle enjoyment of her friend, but, a wild woman, kept rollicking company. Imagining her free with sex doesn't fit, though. I don't know any women like that, or men either. Unless I see her life branching into mine, she gives me no ancestral help.

To sustain her being in love, she often worked at herself in the mirror, guessing at the colors and shapes that would interest him, changing them frequently in order to hit on the right combination. She wanted him to look back.

On a farm near the sea, a woman who tended her appearance reaped a reputation for eccentricity. All the married women blunt-cut their hair in flaps about their ears or pulled it back in tight buns. No nonsense. Neither style blew easily into heart-catching tangles. And at their weddings they displayed themselves in their long hair for the last time. "It brushed the backs of my knees," my mother tells me. "It was braided, and even so, it brushed the backs of my knees."

At the mirror my aunt combed individuality into her bob. A bun could have been contrived to escape into black streamers blowing in the wind or in quiet wisps about her face, but only the older women in our picture album wear buns. She brushed her hair back from her forehead, tucking the flaps behind her ears. She looped a piece of thread, knotted into a circle between her index fingers and thumbs, and ran the double strand across her forehead. When she closed her fingers as if she were making a pair of shadow geese bite, the string twisted together catching the little hairs. Then she pulled the thread away from her skin, ripping the hairs out neatly, her eyes watering from the needles of pain. Opening her fingers, she cleaned the thread, then rolled it along her hairline and the tops of her eyebrows. My mother did the same to me and my sisters and herself. I used to believe that the expression "caught by the short hairs" meant a captive held with a depilatory string. It especially hurt at the temples, but my mother said we were lucky we didn't have to have our feet bound when we were seven. Sisters used to sit on their beds and cry together, she said, as their mothers or their slaves removed the bandages for a few minutes each night and let the blood gush back into their veins. I hope that the man my aunt loved appreciated a smooth brow, that he wasn't just a tits-and-ass man.

Once my aunt found a freckle on her chin, at a spot that the almanac said predestined her for unhappiness. She dug it out with a hot needle and washed the wound with peroxide.

More attention to her looks than these pullings of hairs and pickings at spots would have caused gossip among the villagers. They owned work clothes and good clothes, and they wore good clothes for feasting the new seasons. But since a woman combing her hair hexes beginnings, my aunt rarely found an occasion to look her best. Women looked like great sea snails—the corded wood, babies, and laundry they carried were the whorls on their backs. The Chinese did not admire a bent back; goddesses and warriors stood straight. Still there must have been a marvelous freeing of beauty when a worker laid down her burden and stretched and arched.

Such commonplace loveliness, however, was not enough for my aunt. She dreamed of a lover for the fifteen days of New Year's, the time for families to exchange visits, money, and food. She plied her secret comb. And sure enough she cursed the year, the family, the village, and herself.

Even as her hair lured her imminent lover, many other men looked at her. Uncles, cousins, nephews, brothers would have looked, too, had they been home between journeys. Perhaps they had already been restraining their curiosity, and they left, fearful that their glances, like a field of nesting birds, might be startled and caught. Poverty hurt, and that was their first reason for leaving. But another, final reason for leaving the crowded house was the never-said.

She may have been unusually beloved, the precious only daughter, spoiled and mirror gazing because of the affection the family lavished on her. When her husband left, they welcomed the chance to take her back from the in-laws; she could live like the little daughter for just a while longer. There are stories that my grandfather was different from other people, "crazy ever since the little Jap bayoneted him in the head." He used to put his naked penis on the dinner table, laughing. And one day he brought home a baby girl, wrapped up inside his brown western-style great-coat. He had traded one of his sons, probably my father, the youngest, for her. My grandmother made him trade back. When he finally got a daughter of his own, he doted on her. They must have all loved her, except perhaps my father, the only brother who never went back to China, having once been traded for a girl.

Brothers and sisters, newly men and women, had to efface their sexual color and present plain miens. Disturbing hair and eyes, a smile like no other threatened the ideal of five generations living under one roof. To focus blurs, people shouted face to face and yelled from room to room. The immigrants I know have loud voices, unmodulated to American tones even after years away from the village where they called their friendships out across the fields. I have not been able to stop my mother's screams in public libraries or over telephones. Walking erect (knees straight, toes pointed forward, not pigeon-toed, which is Chinese-feminine) and speaking in an inaudible voice, I have tried to turn myself American-feminine. Chinese communication was loud, public. Only sick people had to whisper. But at the dinner table, where the family members came nearest one another, no one could talk, not the outcasts nor any eaters. Every word that falls from the mouth is a coin lost. Silently they gave and accepted food with both hands. A preoccupied child who took his bowl with one hand got a sideways glare. A complete moment of total attention is due everyone alike. Children and lovers have no singularity here, but my aunt used a secret voice, a separate attentiveness.

She kept the man's name to herself throughout her labor and dying; she did not accuse him that he be punished with her. To save her inseminator's name she gave silent birth.

He may have been somebody in her own household, but intercourse with a man outside the family would have been no less abhorrent. All the village were kinsmen, and the titles shouted in loud country voices never let kinship be forgotten. Any man within visiting distance would have been neutralized as a lover—"brother," "younger brother," "older brother"—one hundred and fifteen relationship titles. Parents research birth charts probably not so much to assure good fortune as to circumvent incest in a population that has but one hundred surnames. Everybody has eight million relatives. How useless then sexual mannerisms, how dangerous.

As if it came from an atavism deeper than fear, I used to add "brother" silently to boys' names. It hexed the boys, who would or would not ask me to dance, and made them less scary and as familiar and deserving of benevolence as girls.

But, of course, I hexed myself also—no dates. I should have stood up, both arms waving, and shouted out across libraries, "Hey, you! Love me back." I had no idea though, how to make attraction selective, how to control its direction and magnitude. If I made myself American-pretty so that the five or six Chinese boys in the class fell in love with me, everyone else—the Caucasian, Negro, and Japanese boys—would too. Sisterliness, dignified and honorable, made much more sense.

Attraction eludes control so stubbornly that whole societies designed to organize relationships among people cannot keep order, not even when they bind people to one another from childhood and raise them together. Among the very poor and the wealthy, brothers married their adopted sisters, like doves. Our family allowed some romance, paying adult brides' prices and providing dowries so that their sons and daughters could marry strangers. Marriage promises to turn strangers into friendly relatives —a nation of siblings.

In the village structure, spirits shimmered among the live creatures, balanced and held in equilibrium by time and land. But one human being flaring up into violence could open up a black hole, a maelstrom that pulled in the sky. The frightened villagers, who depended on one another to maintain the real, went to my aunt to show her a personal, physical representation of the break she had made in the "roundness." Misallying couples snapped off the future, which was to be embodied in true offspring. The villagers punished her for acting as if she could have a private life, secret and apart from them.

If my aunt had betrayed the family at a time of large grain yields and peace, when many boys were born, and wings were being built on many houses, perhaps she might have escaped such severe punishment. But the men— hungry, greedy, tired of planting in dry soil, cuckolded— had had to leave the village in order to send food-money home. There were ghost plagues, bandit plagues, wars with the Japanese, floods. My Chinese brother and sister had died of an unknown sickness. Adultery, perhaps only a mistake during good times, became a crime when the village needed food.

The round moon cakes and round doorways, the round tables of graduated size that fit one roundness inside another, round windows and rice bowls—these talismen had lost their power to warn this family of the law: a family must be whole, faithfully keeping the descent line by having sons to feed the old and the dead, who in turn look after the family. The villagers came to show my aunt and her lover-in-hiding a broken house. The villagers were speeding up the circling of events because she was too shortsighted to see that her infidelity had already harmed the village, that waves of consequences would return unpredictably, sometimes in disguise, as now, to hurt her. This roundness had to be made coin-sized so that she would see its circumference: punish her at the birth of her baby. Awaken her to the inexorable. People who refused fatalism because they could invent small resources insisted on culpability. Deny accidents and wrest fault from the stars.

After the villagers left, their lanterns now scattering in various directions toward home, the family broke their silence and cursed her. "Aiaa, we're going to die. Death is coming. Death is coming. Look what you've done. You've killed us. Ghost! Dead ghost! Ghost! You've never been born." She ran out into the fields, far enough from the house so that she could no longer hear their voices, and pressed herself against the earth, her own land no more. When she felt the birth coming, she thought that she had been hurt. Her body seized together. "They've hurt me too much," she thought. "This is gall, and it will kill me." Her forehead and knees against the earth, her body convulsed

and then released her onto her back. The black well of sky
and stars went out and out and out forever; her body and
her complexity seemed to disappear. She was one of the
stars, a bright dot in blackness, without home, without a
companion, in eternal cold and silence. An agoraphobia
rose in her, speeding higher and higher, bigger and bigger;
she would not be able to contain it; there would be no end
to fear.

Flayed, unprotected against space, she felt pain return,
focusing her body. This pain chilled her—a cold, steady
kind of surface pain. Inside, spasmodically, the other pain,
the pain of the child, heated her. For hours she lay on the
ground, alternately body and space. Sometimes a vision of
normal comfort obliterated reality: she saw the family in
the evening gambling at the dinner table, the young people
massaging their elders' backs. She saw them congratulating
one another, high joy on the mornings the rice shoots came
up. When these pictures burst, the stars drew yet further
apart. Black space opened.

She got to her feet to fight better and remembered that
old-fashioned women gave birth in their pigsties to fool the
jealous, pain-dealing gods, who do not snatch piglets. Before the next spasms could stop her, she ran to the pigsty,
each step a rushing out into emptiness. She climbed over
the fence and knelt in the dirt. It was good to have a fence
enclosing her, a tribal person alone.

Laboring, this woman who had carried her child as a
foreign growth that sickened her every day, expelled it at
last. She reached down to touch the hot, wet, moving mass,
surely smaller than anything human, and could feel that it
was human after all—fingers, toes, nails, nose. She pulled
it up on to her belly, and it lay curled there, butt in the air,
feet precisely tucked one under the other. She opened her
loose shirt and buttoned the child inside. After resting, it
squirmed and thrashed and she pushed it up to her breast.
It turned its head this way and that until it found her
nipple. There, it made little snuffling noises. She clenched
her teeth at its preciousness, lovely as a young calf, a
piglet, a little dog.

She may have gone to the pigsty as a last act of responsibility: she would protect this child as she had protected
its father. It would look after her soul, leaving supplies on
her grave. But how would this tiny child without family
find her grave when there would be no marker for her

anywhere, neither in the earth nor the family hall? No one would give her a family hall name. She had taken the child with her into the wastes. At its birth the two of them had felt the same raw pain of separation, a wound that only the family pressing tight could close. A child with no descent line would not soften her life but only trail after her, ghostlike, begging her to give it purpose. At dawn the villagers on their way to the fields would stand around the fence and look.

Full of milk, the little ghost slept. When it awoke, she hardened her breasts against the milk that crying loosens. Toward morning she picked up the baby and walked to the well.

Carrying the baby to the well shows loving. Otherwise abandon it. Turn its face into the mud. Mothers who love their children take them along. It was probably a girl; there is some hope of forgiveness for boys.

"Don't tell anyone you had an aunt. Your father does not want to hear her name. She has never been born." I have believed that sex was unspeakable and words so strong and fathers so frail that "aunt" would do my father mysterious harm. I have thought that my family, having settled among immigrants who had also been their neighbors in the ancestral land, needed to clean their name, and a wrong word would incite the kinspeople even here. But there is more to this silence: they want me to participate in her punishment. And I have.

In the twenty years since I heard this story I have not asked for details nor said my aunt's name; I do not know it. People who can comfort the dead can also chase after them to hurt them further—a reverse ancestor worship. The real punishment was not the raid swiftly inflicted by the villagers, but the family's deliberately forgetting her. Her betrayal so maddened them, they saw to it that she would suffer forever, even after death. Always hungry, always needing, she would have to beg food from other ghosts, snatch and steal it from those whose living descendants give them gifts. She would have to fight the ghosts massed at crossroads for the buns a few thoughtful citizens leave to decoy her away from village and home so that the ancestral spirits could feast unharassed. At peace, they could act like gods, not ghosts, their descent lines providing them with paper suits and dresses, spirit money, paper houses, paper automobiles, chicken, meat, and rice into eternity—essences delivered up in smoke and flames, steam and incense rising from each rice bowl. In an attempt to make the Chinese care for people outside the family, Chairman Mao encourages us now to give our paper replicas to the spirits of outstanding soldiers and workers, no matter whose ancestors they may be. My aunt remains forever hungry. Goods are not distributed even among the dead.

My aunt haunts me—her ghost drawn to me because now, after fifty years of neglect, I alone devote pages of paper to her, though not origamied into houses and clothes. I do not think she always means me well. I am telling on her, and she was a spite suicide, drowning herself in the drinking water. The Chinese are always very frightened of the drowned one, whose weeping ghost, wet hair hanging and skin bloated, waits silently by the water to pull down a substitute.

# WILLIAM KITTREDGE

# The Van Gogh Field

Clyman Teal: swaying and resting his back against the clean-grain hopper, holding the header wheel of the Caterpillar-drawn John Deere 36 combine, a twenty-nine-year old brazed and wired-together machine moving along its path around the seven-hundred-acre and perfectly rectangular field of barley with seemingly infinite slowness, traveling no more than two miles in an hour, harvest dust rising from the separating fans within the machine and hanging around him as he silently contemplates the acreage being reduced swath by swath, a pale yellow rectangle peeling toward the last narrow and irregular cut and the finished center, his eyes flat and gray, squinted against the sun.

Robert Onnter, standing before the self-portrait of van Gogh, had finally remembered Clyman Teal, his expression beneath that limp sweat-and-grease-stained hat, the long round chin and creased, sun and windburned cheeks and shaded eyes, a lump of tobacco wadded under his thin lower lip, sparse gray week-old whiskers, face of a man getting through not just the pain of his last illness and approaching death, but the glaring sameness of what he saw, at least trying to see through.

Changing position every few moments, as if from some not-yet-discovered perspective he would be able to see into an interior space he felt the picture must have, Robert Onnter faced the self-portrait of van Gogh on temporary display in the marble-floored main lower corridor of the Chicago Art Institute and felt the eyes in the portrait as those of a man looking into whatever Clyman Teal must have seen while watching the harvest fields that occupied the sun-colored impenetrable August days of his life, the sheen brilliant and unresolved as light glaring off buffed aluminum: eye of van Gogh.

In the same place the afternoon before, people dressed for winter occasionally passing, Robert had been distracted by the woman, her gloved hand on his sleeve, while trying to visualize something he could not imagine, what lay beneath and yet over the texture of thick blue paint, how the ridged strokes fixed there changed his memories of slick wheatfield prints under glass in frames on his mother's wall. This morning he had left the woman sleeping in her cluttered brown apartment . . . her fragility only appearance . . . curled like a small aging moth on her side of a too-wide bed in a building that overlooked the northern end of Michigan Boulevard and snow-covered ice of the lake, gone by taxi to his room in the Drake Hotel and showered and shaved and changed clothes, and feeling clean as when outdoors on a long-ago summer morning touched by dew, which dampened the leather of his worn-toed childhood boots, caught another taxi and returned to stand again before the picture.

There was a sense in which he had come to Chicago to look the first time at real paintings because of van Gogh. Part of his reaction against the insubstantiality of his life had been founded on those flat wheatfield prints his mother cherished. Robert smoked a cigarette from a crumpled pack, wondered if he should have left a note for the woman, and thought, as when the woman interrupted him the afternoon before, about his mother's life in isolation and her idea of beauty, surely implied by her love of those prints, desolate small loves in the eastern Oregon valley that was his home, the transparently streaked sheen of yellow gold over the ripening barleyfields under summer twilight, views of that and level windblown snow no doubt having something to do with the way he had felt compelled to spend this winter and with what he saw in the eyes of van Gogh, remembered from the simple death of Clyman

Teal, and what he thought of his mother's idea, not so much of beauty but of the reasons things were beautiful. The woman's appearance beside him the day before seemed inevitably part of the education he had planned for this winter, escaping stillness. Except for two and a half years at the University of Oregon in liberal arts, studying nothing, a course urged on him by his mother, four years in the air force, a year and a half of marriage to a girl from Vacaville, California, named Dennie Wilson . . . when he lived in Sacramento selling outboard motors . . . he had always lived in the valley. So there was need to travel.

Twenty-seven when he returned to the valley, he worked for his father as he had always known eventually he would, spending his time at chores and drinking in the town of Nyall at the north end of the valley, seeing whichever girl he happened to meet in the taverns. Lately the calm of that existence had fragmented, partly because of his mother's insistence he was wasting his life, more surely because of constant motionlessness, reflected in the eyes of Clyman Teal and now in the detached and burning eyes of van Gogh. Robert had been disconnected from even his parents since the divorce, and now it seemed there had been no one even then. The girl Dennie, addicted to huge dark glasses with shining amber lenses, so briefly his wife, now lived in Bakersfield with another man and a daughter named Felicity who was nearly six years old and ready for school. Robert could recall his wife's face . . . the girl he married . . . could not imagine her with a child, saw with absolute clarity the slender girl from Vacaville, eyes faintly owllike in the evening because her suntan ended at the rim of her glasses. She had grown up while he had not. By missing knowledge of her strength in childbirth he had missed part of what he could have been. His sense of lost contact was constructed at least in part of that.

The previous year, early spring, before winter broke out of the valley, a morning he remembered perfectly, he called Dennie before daylight, a frantic and stupid mistake finally shattering any sort of relationship they might have carried past divorce. Robert had been reading a book pushed on him by his mother, *The Magic Mountain*, written by a German named Mann, which seemed a strange name for a German, his mother saying the book would tell him something about himself and that if he would only begin reading he would see why he must change. The day was a dead Sunday and he was a little hung over and somehow bored with the idea of another slow afternoon in the bars of Nyall, the blotched snow and peeling frame buildings and the same people as always, aimless Sunday drinkers. So he read because there was nothing else to do and then for reasons he did not understand became fascinated and began to struggle seriously with comprehending what the German meant by writing down his story of sickness and escape, seeing why his mother might imagine it applied to him, yet sure it meant something more.

He spent weeks at it, reading and rereading each page and paragraph, savoring the way it was to be German and writing about sickness, staying in his room and working at it each night, waking in the early morning before daylight and thinking about it again. Until at four o'clock the morning of the phone call he turned on his light and began reading about a beautiful epileptic woman and began to feel as if he were himself at the next breath going to descend into a spasm and ended terrified and unable to focus his eyes on the print, or even more, as if the merest responses of his body might cause the heavy and shrouding weight of stillness to settle like a cloud blotting away all connection, and finally he forced himself and called the girl who had been his wife, Dennie, who he sensed might understand, might not have completely deserted him. She told him he was drunk and hung up quickly, and Robert felt himself alone in his cloud and could think of nothing but awakening his mother, begging her to make it go away, ended going for weeks through the motions of days surrounded by terror of something simple as air.

Now the heavy and vivid symbolic color of the self-portrait seemed reality, the expression and agony of a man abruptly giving up, Clyman Teal who had been dying that last summer, a wandering harvest-following man who could have been van Gogh, who traveled north with the seasons along the West Coast in a succession of gray and rust-stained automobiles, always alone: hard streaked color of the painting ridged and unlike the wheatfield prints, actual as barley ripe before harvest, all bound into the stasis Robert was attempting to escape in this city, while traveling.

The woman's amber-colored hair was long and straight, over her shoulders, contrasting with the natural paleness of her clear oval face. She brushed her hair slowly. "I'd just finished washing it," she said, smiling, "when you called."

So casual she seemed younger, and small and full rather than tiny and drawn together by approaching age; she sat in a black velvet chair by a window overlooking the lake, lighted from behind by gray midwestern sunlight, wearing a deep-and-soft-blue gown, which concealed all but her white shoulders and neck, bare feet curled beneath her. Worn embroidered slippers lay on the pale, almost-white carpet in the room cluttered with sofas covered by blankets and with tables whose surfaces reflected intricate porcelain figures. "I like nice things," she'd said the night before. "Most of these things were my mother's. Is there anything wrong with that?" Robert told her he imagined not, and she smiled. "Call me Goldie," she'd said. "Everyone does." He had read the card inserted in the small brass frame beneath the entry buzzer. *Mrs. Daniel (Ruth Ann) Brown.* Her husband, she explained, was away in Europe. "He's no threat," she'd said. "He's gone for the winter."

They'd come here in the evening at her insistence, sat in flickering near darkness before the artificial fire, and she changed into a dressing gown and served tiny glasses of a thick pale drink that tasted like burnt straw. Finally he kissed her, moving awkwardly across the sofa while she waited with an icelike smile. "He's away," she said, "to Greece, to the islands, to walk and think."

In the soft light of afternoon she was completely serene. Robert asked why her husband had gone. "Because of the clearness," she said. "The light . . . things have gone badly, with the unrest, and he wanted to think. . . ." Perhaps, Robert thought, he would follow, to the pale sunlight and dusty white islands and the water of the sea, New York and then London, Paris, Rome, at last to the islands off Greece, and see the water moving under the light, flow and continuity that might illuminate his vision of a desert stream low in a dry summer and water falling through crevices between boulders, always images of water, the cold Pacific gray beneath winter clouds, waves breaking in on barren sand and the heavy movement of the troopship just after leaving San Francisco for Guam, where he spent a year and a half of his air force time.

In childhood he had imagined the barleyfields were water. After the last meal of the day, while dishes remained stacked in the sink to be washed later, they would all of them go out into the valley and look at the ripening crop, his mother and father, Robert, and his younger brother and even-younger sister all in the old dark-green Chevrolet pickup. Now his brother had been dead eleven years, killed in an automobile crash his second semester of college, and his sister, married directly out of high school, lived distantly with children in Amarillo, Texas. Then they had all been home, and his father had driven them out over the dusty canalbank roads until east of the fields, looking toward the last sunlight glaring over the low rim; and those yellowing fields were luminous and transformed into a magic and perfect cloth for them to walk on, and Robert imagined them all hand in hand, walking toward the sun.

His mother had named the largest field on one of those trips, and because of the prints in the house it had seemed she was only silly. But surely she had been right, however inadvertently. The yellowish, rough sheen of bearded, separate, and sunlighted barley heads matched perfectly the reality of van Gogh, glowing paint, his eyes, texture. "The van Gogh field," she said, repeating it as if delighted. "It's so classic." She would often say that. "It's so classic." They stayed until the air began to cool and settle and then went slowly home, Robert and his brother in the back of the pickup, watching the dust rise soft and gray as flour behind them and hang in the air, streaked and filmy as an unlighted aura even after the pickup was parked beneath the cottonwood trees behind the house.

Robert wondered what those evening trips had meant to his father. Nearly sixty, silently beguiled by sentiment, his father wept openly for a month after Robert's brother was killed, sat abruptly upright drinking the coffee Robert's mother brought, never going outside until spring irrigation forced him to work, after that revealing emotion only with his hands, gesturing abruptly and reaching to pick up a clod of dry and grainy peat, crumbling it to dust between callused fingers. During planting the man would sometimes walk out over the damp tilled ground and kneel, sink his hands and churn up the undersoil, crouch lower like a trailing animal. "Seeing if it's right," he would say. "If it's ready."

The woman returned with drinks. "I didn't think you'd be back," she said. "I hoped, but . . ." She smiled, perhaps wishing she were alone, the last night an incident scarcely remembered. "I went back to the painting," Robert said.

"What are you really doing? I don't think I believe what you told me." She continued smiling. He had lied, unable to admit he had borrowed ten thousand dollars from his father, feeling childish over his search for places and cities missed, and told her he was an insurance salesman. "Looking for islands," he said, wondering if she would take him seriously.

She glanced away, stopped smiling. "The wheatfields," she said, "you should see them, the last particularly." Robert didn't answer. "Before he shot himself, I mean," she said, "when you think of what it meant to him . . . the yellow and that field pregnant, those birds . . . his idea of death, and remember it was there he killed himself, in that field, then you see."

"Yellow?"

"Simply love." The afternoon had settled, blue winter light darkening, her face isolated as if detached from her dark gown. "I don't think you can tell from prints," he said, "we had prints and there's nothing in them . . . my mother must have thought he was pretty and bright." Robert could not explain the insincerity of imitations, falsity.

"So?" The woman leaned forward just slightly perhaps interested and no longer getting politely through an afternoon with a man she'd slept with and would have preferred never seeing again. Her tone was sharper, quick, and she sipped her drink, turned the glass in her hands.

"The way she acted. . . ." Robert stalled.

"Your mother acted improperly." The woman's voice was impatient, dropping the *improperly* as if she had changed her mind while speaking, finishing awkwardly, perhaps not wanting to acknowledge the moral distance implied in her judgment of him and his judgment of his mother.

". . . as if it were an example of something."

"Are you so sure? Perhaps it was all a disguise."

"I don't think she. . . ." Robert hesitated. "A man died and she knew some pictures and so it was beautiful and emblematic of something." His mother had stirred her coffee and smiled with total self-possession. "He finished doing what he loved," she had said. "Until the job was over."

The woman rose from her chair and began walking slowly before the windows, carrying a half-empty glass. "Women see more than you imagine," she said. "Sometimes, perhaps everything."

His mother: Duluth Onnter, what did she see, having come west from Minnesota to marry his father out of college, so taken by color and names? Her parents had moved from Minneapolis to Tucson the year after Robert was born, and although he had visited them as a child, he could not imagine the long-dead people he remembered, a heavy white-haired man and woman, as having lived anywhere not snow covered half the year. His grandfather had been in Duluth the day Robert's mother was born, and because of that had insisted she be named after a cold lakeport city. "Papa always said it was beautiful that morning," his mother told him. "That I was his beauty."

"Maybe the pictures were only warm and nice," Robert said. "Maybe she did see."

"My husband is like that," the woman answered, "imagines he's going to find spirituality in Greece, in some island. I don't. I'm lucky." She continued walking before the windows, gown trailing the carpet, her thin figure silhouetted. "I have what seems necessary and it's not freedom. I'll go Friday and confess having slept with you. That's freedom."

"To a priest?" It seemed totally wrong, sleeping with him and then carrying the news to church, the kind of circularity he had been escaping. "I don't see that at all," he said. "Why do anything in the first place . . . and pretend you didn't?"

"It's not pretending," she said. "It's being forgiven. I go to look as you do, somehow for a moment you helped me see better, look at van Gogh, and even my need to see is a sin, a failure of belief. I sold myself for what you helped me see. If that sounds silly maybe it is, but it wasn't to me then and it's not now. It's my own freedom and I don't need to go anywhere to find it. And it has to be confessed."

Robert wondered if she found himself foolish, in Chicago, planning on Europe, if she wished to be rid of him and would regard his going coldly, as his mother had taken the death of Clyman Teal, if for her anything existed for hope. "I must seem stupid," he said.

"No . . . I just don't think there's anything like what you're looking for."

"Like what?"

"I don't know, but it isn't here . . . or Greece or any-where."

"Perhaps I should stay." There was the easy possibility of a winter in Chicago, walking the street, looking at pictures, going from van Gogh to Gauguin, Seurat, seeing her occasionally, as often as she would permit.

"I wouldn't," she said. "If I were you." Feeling denied some complex understanding she could give if only she would, Robert knew she was right and trying to be kind. "I wouldn't bother you," he said. 'Only once in a while, just to talk."

"No," the woman said. "I'll get your coat." Her face was hard and set and he thought how melodramatic she was with her insistence on futility. Standing in the hallway with her door closed behind he saw how much she believed she was right, her belief founded on quick sliding glances at whatever it was van Gogh and Clyman Teal had regarded steadily in their fields of grain.

The next morning he returned to the Art Institute, and she was there, standing quietly in a beige wool suit with a camel's-hair coat thrown over her shoulders, a thin and stylish, nearly pretty woman who was aging. "You came back," he said. She turned as if surprised and then smiled. "Let's be quiet," she said, "the best part is silence, then we can talk."

Beside her, sensing she now wanted some word from him, Robert was drawn to the fierce and despairing painted face, memories of Clyman Teal in the days before he died. Summer had been humid, with storms in June and a week of soft rain in late July, and the crop the best in years, kernels filled without the slightest pinch and heavy by the time harvest started in August. Clyman Teal arrived the day it began, lean and thick shouldered, long arms seeming perpetually broken at the elbows, driving slowly across the field in the latest of his rusted secondhand automobiles, a gray two-door Pontiac. He rubbed his eyes and walked a little into the field with Robert and his father. Dew was just burning off. "Came last night from Arlington," he said. "Finished there yesterday." He'd been working the summer wheat harvest just south of the Columbia River, two hundred and fifty miles north, for twenty years, always coming when it finished to run combine for Robert's father. After

this job ended he'd go south to the rice harvest in the
Sacramento Valley. Thick heads of barley drooped around
them, and Clyman Teal cracked kernels between his teeth
and chewed and swallowed, squinting toward the sun.
"Going to be fine," he said, "ain't it boy." Leaving the
trunk lid open on the Pontiac, heedless of dust sifting over
his bedroll and tin-covered suitcase, he dragged out his
tools and spent the rest of the morning working quietly and
steadily while the rest of them waited, regreasing bearings
Robert had greased the afternoon before, tightening chains
and belts, running the machine and tightening again, finishing just as the noon meal was hauled to the field in pots
with their lids fastened down by rubber bands. They all
squatted in the shade to eat, then flipped the scraps from
their plates to the sea gulls, and the work began. With the
combine motor running, Clyman Teal motioned for Robert
to follow him and walked to where Robert's father stood
cranking the old D7 Caterpillar, dust goggles already down
over his eyes. "When there's time," he shouted, "I want
this boy on the machine with me." Then he walked away,
climbed the steel ladder to the platform where he stood
while tending the header wheel, and waved for Robert's
father to begin the first round.

So when there was time between loads, Robert rode the
combine, learning to tend the header wheel, what amount
of straw to take in so the machine would thrash properly
and to set the concaves beneath the thrashing cylinder,
adjust the speed of the cylinder according to the heaviness
of the crop, regulate the fans that blew the chaff and dust
from the heavier grain. "Whole thing works on gravity,"
the old man said. "Heavy falls and the light floats away."

Sometimes the old man would walk behind the machine
in the fogging dust of chaff, his hat beneath the straw
dump, catching the straw and chaff, then dumping the
hatful of waste on the steel deck and slowly spreading it
with thick fingers, kneeling and blowing away the chaff,
checking to see if kernels of the heavy grain were being
carried over. "You need care," the old man said. "Otherwise you're dumping money."

But most often he just rode with his back braced against
the clean-grain hopper. The harvest lasted twenty-seven
days, the last swath cut late in the afternoon while Robert
was hauling his final truckload on the asphalt road up the
west side of the valley to the elevator in Nyall. Returning

to the field in time to see the other truck pulling out, a surplus GI six-by-six converted to ranch truck wallowing through the soft peaty soil in low gear, Robert waited at the gate. The other driver stopped. "Claims he's sick," the man said, leaning from the truck window. "Climbed down and curled up and claimed he was sick and said to leave him alone." The combine was parked in the exact center of the field, stopped after the last cut. Tin-eyed and balding, the driver lived in the valley just south of Nyall on a sour alkali-infested 160 acres and now seemed impatient to get all this over and back to his quietude. "Your daddy wants you to bring out the pickup," he said.

Robert drove the new red three-quarter-ton International pickup, rough and heavy, out to the combine. Clyman Teal lay curled on the ground in the shade of the machine. Robert and his father loaded the old man into the pickup, and Robert drove slowly homeward over the rutted field while his father supported Clyman Teal with an arm around his shoulders. The old man grunted with pain, eyes closed tightly and arms folded over his belly. Parked at last before the whitewashed bunkhouse, they all sat quiet a moment, nothing in the oppressive empty valley moving but one fly in dust on the slanting windshield. "We'll take him inside," Robert's father said, and Robert was surprised how fragile and light the old man was, small inside his coveralls, like a child, diminished within the folds, his odor like that of a field fire, sharp and acrid. They left him passive and rigid on the bunk atop brown surplus GI blankets. He opened his eyes and grunted something that meant for them to leave him alone, then drew back into himself. The window shelf above the bed was lined with boxes and pills, baking soda and aspirin and home stomach remedies. Robert's mother carried down soup and toast that evening, and the old man lay immobile while Robert's father washed the dust from his face. They tucked him under the blankets and the next morning the meal was untouched. That afternoon Robert's father called a doctor, the only one in Nyall, and after probing at the curled figure the doctor called an ambulance from the larger town fifty miles west. It was evening when the ambulance arrived, a heavy Chrysler staffed by volunteers, red light flickering at the twilight while Robert helped load the old man on a stretcher. Clyman Teal was sealed inside without ever opening his eyes, and Robert never saw him again. During the brief funeral parlor ceremony six days later he didn't go up and look into the coffin, nor did anyone.

Operated on the night he was hauled away, Clyman died. "Eaten up," the doctor said, shaking his head: "Perforations all through his intestines." Robert remembered his mother's reddened hands gripping the tray she carried down the hill, his father's fumbling tenderness while washing the old man's face, the mostly silent actions. Three days after Clyman died the sheriff's office located a brother in Clovis, New Mexico, who said to go ahead and bury him. Six attended the funeral, Robert and his father and mother and the truck driver and his huge smiling wife and a drifter from one of the bars in Nyall. The brother was a grinning old man in a greenish black suit and showed up a week later. He silently loaded Clyman's possessions into the Pontiac and drove away, heading back to New Mexico. He hadn't seen Clyman, he said, in thirty-eight years, hadn't heard from him in all that time. "Just never got around to anything," he said. But the trip was worth his trouble, he said. He'd found hidden in the old man's tin suitcase a bankbook from Bakersfield showing total deposits of eight thousand some odd dollars. He said he thought he'd go home by way of Bakersfield.

The woman took Robert's arm. "I've had enough," she said. "Let's have a cup of coffee." Seated in the noisy cafeteria, she smiled. "I liked that," she said. "Standing there quietly together . . . that's what I first liked about you, that you knew how to be quiet." Robert wondered how often she did this, picked up some stray; what had driven away her husband. "Is that why?" he said, involved in a judgment of her that seemed finally unfair, perhaps because it came so close to being a judgment of himself.

"You could appreciate stillness . . . the moment I love in church is that of prayer, silence before the chant begins." Her hands moved slowly, touching her spoon, turning her cup. "I've changed my mind," she said. "I'd like you to stay the winter.

"You could go with me on Sundays," she said, "and see how the quiet and perfection . . . the loveliness on Easter."

But he couldn't. It was useless, for her perhaps all right, he couldn't know about that, but stillness would mount while they chanted, and not her church or any city in Europe, even clarity of water, would do more for him than going home to those cold wet mornings in early spring while they planted, the motionless afternoons of boredom while the harvest circled to where the combine parked. "Yes," he said, not wanting to hurt her, knowing he might even stay. "I could do that." Wheatfields reared toward the sky under circling birds, evening dust hung still behind his father's pickup, and his brother's childish face was staring ahead toward lights flickering through the poplar trees marking their home, the light yellow color of love, van Gogh dead soon after, nearby.

# ELLA LEFFLAND

# Last Courtesies

"Lillian, you're too polite," Vladimir kept telling her. She did not think so. Perhaps she was not one to return shoves in the bus line, but she did fire off censorious glares; and, true, she never yelled at the paper boy who daily flung her *Chronicle* to a rain-soaked fate, but she did beckon him to her door and remind him of his responsibilities. If she was always the last to board the bus, if she continued to dry out the paper on the stove, that was the price she must pay for observing the minimal courtesy the world owed itself if it was not to go under. Civilized she was. Excessively polite, no.

In any case, even if she had wanted to, she could not change at this stage of life. Nor had Aunt Bedelia ever changed in any manner. Not that she really compared herself to her phenomenal aunt, who, when she had died four months ago at the age of ninety-one, was still a captivating woman; no faded great beauty (the family ran to horse faces), but elegant, serenely vivid. Any other old lady who dressed herself in long gowns circa 1910 would have appeared a mere oddity; but under Bedelia's antiquated hairdo sat a brain; in her gnarled, almond-scented fingers lay direction. She spoke of Bach, of the Russian novelists, of her garden and the consolations of nature; never of her arthritis, the fallen ranks of her friends, or the metamorphosis of the neighborhood, which now featured motorcycles roaring alongside tin cans and blackened banana peels. At rare moments a sigh escaped her lips, but who knew if it was for her crippled fingers (she had been a consummate pianist) or a repercussion from the street? It was bad form, ungallant, to put too fine a point on life's discomfitures.

Since Bedelia's death the flat was lonely; lonely yet no longer private, since a supremely kinetic young woman, herself a music lover, had moved in upstairs. With no one to talk to, with thuds and acid rock resounding from above, Lillian drifted (too often, she knew) into the past, fingering its high points. The day, for instance, that Vladimir had entered their lives by way of the Steinway grand (great gleaming relic of better times) which he came to tune. He had burst in, dressed not in a customary suit but in garage mechanic's overalls and rubber thong sandals, a short square man with the large disheveled head of a furious gnome, who embellished his labors with glorious runthroughs of Bach and Scarlatti, but whose speech, though a dark bog of Slavic intonations, was distinctly, undeniably obscene. Aunt Bedelia promptly invited him to dinner the following week. Lillian stood astonished, but reminded herself that her aunt was a sheltered soul unfamiliar with scabrous language, whereas she, Lillian, lived more in the great world, riding the bus every day to the Opera House, where she held the position of switchboard operator (Italian and German required). The following morning at work, in fact, she inquired about Vladimir.

Several people there knew of him. A White Russian, he had fled to Prague with his parents in 1917, then fled again twenty years later, eventually settling in San Francisco, where he quickly earned the reputation of an excellent craftsman and a violent crackpot. He abused clients who had no knowledge of their pianos' intestines, and had once been taken to court by an acquaintance whom he had knocked down during a conversation about Wagner. He wrote scorching letters of general advice to the newspapers; with arms like a windmill he confronted mothers who allowed their children to drop potato chips on the sidewalk; he kept a bucket of accumulated urine to throw on dog-

walkers who were unwary enough to linger with their squatting beasts beneath his window. He had been institutional-
ized several times.

That night Lillian informed her aunt that Vladimir was
brilliant but unsound.

The old woman raised an eyebrow at this.

"For instance," Lillian pursued, "he is actually known to
have struck someone down."

"Why?" Her aunt's voice was clear and melodious, with
a faint ring of iron.

"It was during a conversation about Wagner. Apparently
he disapproves of Wagner."

Her aunt gave a nod of endorsement.

"The man has even had himself committed, aunt. Several times, when he felt he was getting out of hand."

The old woman pondered this. "It shows foresight," she
said at length, "and a sense of social responsibility."

Lillian was silent for a moment. Then she pointed out:
"He said unspeakable things here."

"They are mutually exclusive terms."

"Let us call them obscenities, then. You may not have
caught them."

The old woman rose from her chair and arranged the
long skirt of her dove-gray ensemble, "Lillian, one must
know when to turn a deaf ear."

"I am apparently not in the know," Lillian said dryly.

"Perhaps it is an instinct." And suddenly she gave her
unique smile, which was quite yellow (for she retained her
own ancient teeth) but completely beguiling, and added:
"In any case, he is of my own generation, Lillian. That
counts for a great deal."

"He can't be more than sixty, aunt."

"It is close enough. Anyway, he is quite wrinkled. Also,
he is a man of integrity."

"How can you possibly know that?"

"It is my instinct." And gently touching her niece's
cheek, she said goodnight and went to her room, which
peacefully overlooked the back garden, away from the
street noises.

Undressing in her own smaller room, Lillian reflected,
not for the first time, that though it was Bedelia who had
remained unwed—Lillian herself having been married and
widowed during the war—it was she, Lillian, who felt
more the old maid, who seemed more dated, in a stale,

fusty way, with her tight 1950s hairdo, her plain wool suits
and practical life . . . but then, she led a
practical life . . . it was she who was trampled in the bus
queue and who sat down to a hectic switchboard, who
swept the increasingly filthy sidewalk and dealt with the
sullen butcher and careless paper boy—or tried to . . . it
seemed she was a middlewoman, a hybrid, too worldly to
partake of aunt's immense calm, too seclusive to sharpen
herself on the changing ways . . . aunt had sealed herself
off in a lofty, gracious world; she lived for it, she would
have died for it if it came to that . . . but what could she,
Lillian, die for? . . . she fit in nowhere, she thought, climbing into bed, and thirty years from now she would not have
aged into the rare creature aunt was—last survivor of a
fair, legendary breed, her own crimped hairdo as original
as the Edwardian pouf, her boxy suits as awesome as the
floor-sweeping gowns—no, she would just be a peculiar old
leftover in a room somewhere. For aunt was grande dame,
bluestocking, and virgin in one, and they didn't make that
kind anymore; they didn't make those eyes anymore, large,
hooded, a deep glowing violet. It was a hue that had passed.
. . . And she closed her own eyes, of candid, serviceable
gray, said the Lord's Prayer, and prepared to act as buffer
between her elite relative and the foul-mouthed old refugee.

Aunt Bedelia prepared the dinner herself, taking great
pains; then she creaked into her wet garden with an um-
brella and picked her finest blooms for a centerpiece; and
finally, over the knobbed, arthritic joint of her ring finger,
she twisted a magnificent amethyst usually reserved for
Christmas, Easter, and Bach's birthday. These touches Lillian expected to be lost on their wild-eyed guest, but Vladimir kissed the festive hand with a cavalier click of his
sandals, acknowledged the flowers with a noisy inhalation
of his large, hairy nostrils, and ate his food with admirable
if strained refinement. During coffee he capsized his cup,
but this was only because he and Bedelia were flying from
Bavarian spas and Italian sea resorts to music theory, Tur-
genev, and God knew what else—Lillian could hardly
follow—and then, urged by aunt, he jumped from the table,
rolled up the sleeves of his overalls, and flung himself into
Bach, while aunt, her fingers stiffly moving up and down
on her knee, threw back her head and entered some region
of flawless joy. At eleven o'clock Vladimir wrestled into his

red lumber jacket, expressed his delight with the evening, and slapped down the steps to his infirm 1938 Buick. Not one vulgar word had escaped his lips.

Nor in the seven following years of his friendship with Bedelia was this precedent ever broken. Even the night when some drunk sent an empty pint of muscatel crashing through the window, Vladimir's respect for his hostess was so great that all scurrility was plucked from his wrath. However, when he and Lillian happened to be alone together he slipped right back into the belching, offensive mannerisms for which he was known. She did not mention this to her aunt, who cherished the idea that he was very fond of Lillian.

"You know how he detests opera," the old lady would assure her, "and yet he has never alluded to the fact that you work at the Opera House and hold the form in esteem."

"A magnanimous gesture," Lillian said, smiling.

"For Vladimir, yes."

And after a moment's thought, Lillian had to agree. Her aunt apparently understood Vladimir perfectly, and he her. She wondered if this insight was due to their shared social origins, their bond of elevated interests, or their more baroque twinhood of eccentricity. Whatever it was, the couple thrived, sometimes sitting up till midnight with their sherry and sheet music, sometimes, when the Buick was well, motoring (Bedelia's term) into the countryside and then winding homeward along the darkening sea, in a union of perfect silence, as the old lady put it.

Bedelia died suddenly, with aplomb, under Toscanini's direction. Beethoven's Ninth was on the phonograph; the chorus had just scaled the great peak before its heart-bursting cascade into the finale; aunt threw her head back to savor the moment, and was gone.

The next morning Lillian called Vladimir. He shrieked, he wept, he banged the receiver on the table; and for ten days, helpless and broken, he spent every evening at the home of his departed love while Lillian, herself desolated, tried to soothe him. She felt certain he would never regain the strength to insult his clients again, much less strike anyone to the ground, but gradually he mended, and the coarseness, the irascibility flooded back, much worse than in the past.

For Bedelia's sake—of that Lillian was sure—he forced himself to take an interest in her welfare, which he would express in eruptions of advice whenever he telephoned. "You want to lead a decent life, Lillian, you give them hell! They sell you a bad cut of meat, throw it in the butcher's face! You get shortchanged, make a stink! You're too soft! Give them the finger, Lillian!"

"Yes, of course," she would murmur.

"For your aunt I was a gentleman, but now she's gone, who appreciates? A gentleman is a fool, a gentleman's balls are cut off! I know how to take care of myself, I am in an armored tank! And you should be too. Or find a protector. Get married!"

"Pardon?" she asked.

"Marry!"

"I have no desire to marry, Vladimir."

"Desire! Desire! It's a world for your desires? Think of your scalp? You need a protector, now Bedelia's gone!"

"Aunt was not my protector," she said patiently.

"Of course she was! And mine too!"

Lillian shifted her weight from one foot to the other and hoped he would soon run down.

"You want to get off the phone, don't you? Why don't you say, Vladimir get the shit off the phone, I'm busy! Don't be a doormat! Practice on me or you'll come to grief! What about that sow upstairs, have you given her hell yet? No, no, of course not! Jesus bleeding Christ, I give up!" And he slammed the receiver down.

Lillian had in fact complained. Allowing her new neighbor time to settle in, she had at first endured—through apparently rugless floorboards—the girl's music, her door slams, her crashing footfall which was a strange combination of scurry and thud, her deep hollow brays of laughter and shrieks of "You're *kidding*!" and "Fan*tas*tic!"—all this usually accompanied by a masculine voice and tread (varying from night to night, Lillian could not help but notice) until finally, in the small hours, directly above Bedelia's room, where Lillian now slept, ears stuffed with cotton, the night was crowned by a wild creaking of bedsprings and the racketing of the headboard against the wall. At last, chancing to meet her tormentor on the front steps (she was not the Amazon her noise indicated, but a small, thin creature nervously chewing gum with staccato snaps), Lillian decided to speak; but before she could, the girl cried: "Hi! I'm Jody—from upstairs?" with a quick, radiant smile that heartened the older woman in a way that the hair and hemline did not. Clad in a tiny, childish dress that barely reached her hip sockets, she might have been a prematurely worn twenty or an adolescent thirty—dark circles hung beneath the eyes and a deep line was etched between them, but the mouth was babyish, sweet, and the cheeks a glowing pink against the unfortunate mane of brassy hair, dark along its uneven part.

Having responded with her own name (the formal first *and* last) Lillian paused a courteous moment, then began: "I am glad to have this opportunity of meeting you; I've lived in this flat for twenty-four years, you see . . ." But the eyes opposite, heavily outlined with blue pencil, were already wandering under this gratuitous information. Brevity was clearly the password. "The point is"—restoring attention—"I would appreciate it if you turned down your music after ten P.M. There is a ruling."

"It bugs you?" the girl asked, beginning to dig turbulently through a fringed bag, her gum snaps accelerating with the search.

"Well, it's an old building, and of course if you don't have carpets . . ." She waited to be corroborated in this assumption, but now the girl pulled out her house key with fingers whose nails, bitten to the quick, were painted jet black. Fascinated, Lillian tried not to stare. "Not to worry," the girl assured her with the brief, brilliant smile, plunging the key into the door and bounding inside, "I'll cool it."

"There's something else, I'm afraid. When that door is slammed—"

But the finely arched brows rose with preoccupation; the phone was ringing down from the top of the stairs. "I dig, I dig. Look, hon, my phone's ringing." And closing the door softly, she thundered up the stairs.

After that the phonograph was lowered a little before midnight, but nothing else was changed. Lillian finally called the landlord, a paunchy, sweating man whom she rarely saw, and though she subsequently observed him disappearing into his unruly tenant's flat several evenings a week, the visits were apparently useless. And every time she met the girl, she was greeted with an insufferable "Hi! Have a nice day!"

Unfortunately, Lillian had shared some of her vexation with Vladimir, and whenever he dropped by—less to see her, she knew, than to replenish his memories of Bedelia— his wrath grew terrible under the commotion. On his last visit his behavior had frightened her. "Shut up!" he had screamed, shaking his fist at the ceiling. "Shut up, bitch! Whore!"

"Vladimir, please—this language, just because Bedelia's not here."

"Ah, Bedelia, Bedelia," he groaned.

"She wouldn't have tolerated it."

"She wouldn't have tolerated *that!* Hear the laugh—hee haw, hee haw! Braying ass! Bedelia would have pulverized her with a glance! None of this farting around you go in for!" His large head had suffused with red, his hands were shaking at his sides. "Your aunt was a genius at judging people—they should have lined up the whole fucking rotten city for her to judge!"

"It seems to me that you have always appointed yourself as judge," Lillian said, forcing a smile.

"Yah, but Vladimir is demented, you don't forget? He has it down in black and white! Ah, you think I'm unique, Lillian, but I am one of the many! I am in the swim!" He came over to her side and put his flushed head close, his small intense eyes piercing hers.

"You read yesterday about the girl they found in an alley not far from here, cut to small bits? Slash! Rip! Finito! And you ask why? Because the world, it is demented! A murder of such blood not even in the headlines and you ask why? Because it is commonplace! Who walks safe on his own street? It is why you need a husband!"

Lillian dropped her eyes, wondering for an embarrassed moment if Vladimir of all people could possibly be hinting at a marital alliance. Suddenly silent, he pulled a wadded handkerchief from his pocket with trembling fingers and wiped his brow. He flicked her a suspicious glance. "Don't look so coy. I'm not in the running. I loathe women— sticky! Full of rubbishy talk!" And once more he threw his head back and began bellowing obscenities at the ceiling.

"It's too much, Vladimir—please! You're not yourself!"

"I *am* myself!"

"Well then, I'm not. I'm tired, I have a splitting head-ache—"

"You want me to go! Be rude, good! I have better things

to do anyway!" And his face still aflame, he struggled into
his lumber jacket and flung out the door.

That night her sleep was not only disturbed by the noise,
but by her worry over the violence of Vladimir's emotions.
At work the next day she reluctantly inquired about her
friend, whose antics were usually circulated around the
staff but seldom reached her cubicle. For the first time in
years, she learned, the weird little Russian had gone right
over the edge, flapping newspapers in strangers' faces and
ranting about the end of civilization; storming out on tun-
ing jobs and leaving his tools behind, then furiously accus-
ing his clients of stealing them. The opinion was that if he
did not commit himself soon, someone else would do it for
him.

On the clamorous bus home that night, shoved as usual
into the rear, Lillian felt an overwhelming need for Bedelia,
for the sound of that clear, well-modulated voice that had
always set the world to rights. But she opened her door on
silence. She removed her raincoat and sat down in the
living room with the damp newspaper. People at work told
her she should buy a television set—such a good companion when you lived alone—but she had too long scorned
that philistine invention to change now. For that matter,
she seldom turned on the radio, and even the newspaper—
she ran her eyes over the soggy turmoil of the front page—
even the newspaper distressed her. Vladimir was extreme,
but he was right: everything was coming apart. Sitting
there, she thought she could hear the world's madness—its
rudeness, its litter, its murders—beat against the house
with the rain. And suddenly she closed her eyes under an
intolerable longing for the past: for the peaceful years she
had spent in these rooms with Bedelia; and before that, for
the face of her young husband, thirty years gone now; and
for even earlier days . . . odd, but it never seemed to rain in
her youth, the green campus filled the air with dizzying
sweetness, she remembered running across the lawns for no
reason but that she was twenty and the sun would shine
forever. . . .

She gave way to two large tears. Shaken, yet somehow
consoled, and at the same time ashamed of her self-
indulgence, she went into the kitchen to make dinner. But
as she cooked her chop she knew that even this small mea-
sure of comfort would be destroyed as soon as her neighbor

came banging through the door. Already her neck was tightening against the sound.

But there was no noise at all that night, not until 1 A.M. when the steady ring of the telephone pulled her groggily from bed.

"Listen, you'll kill me—it's Jody, I'm across the bay, and I just flashed on maybe I left the stove burners going."

"Who?" Lillian said, rubbing her eyes, "Jody? How did you get my number?"

"The phone book, why? Listen, the whole dump could catch fire, be a doll and check it out? The back door's unlocked."

Lillian felt a strange little rush of gratitude—that her name given to such seemingly indifferent ears on the steps that day, had been remembered. Then the feeling was replaced by anger; but before she could speak, the girl said, "Listen, hon, thanks a million," and hung up.

Clutching her raincoat around her shoulders, beaming a flashlight before her, Lillian nervously climbed the dark back stairs to her neighbor's door and let herself into the kitchen. Turning on the light, she stood aghast at what she saw: not flames licking the wall, for the burners were off, but grimed linoleum, spilled garbage, a sink of stagnant water. On the puddled table, decorated with a jar of blackened, long-dead daisies, sat a greasy portable television set and a pile of dirty laundry in a litter of cigarette butts, sodden pieces of paper, and the congealed remains of spare ribs. Hesitating, ashamed of her snoopiness, she peered down at the pieces of paper: bills from department stores, including Saks and Magnin's; scattered food stamps; handwritten notes on binder paper, one of which read "Jamie hony theres a piza in the frezzer I love U"—then several big hearts—"Jody." A long brown bug—a cockroach? was crawling across the note, and now she noticed another one climbing over a spare rib. As she stood cringing, she heard rain blowing through an open window somewhere, lashing a shade into frenzies. Going to the bedroom door, which stood ajar, she beamed her flashlight in and switched on the light. Under the window a large puddle was forming on the floor, which was rugless as she had suspected, though half carpeted by strewn clothes. The room was furnished only with a bed whose convulsed, mummy-brown sheets put her in mind of a pesthouse, and a deluxe television set in a rosewood cabinet; but the built-in bookcase was well

stocked, and, having shut the window, she ran her eyes
over the spines, curious. Many were cheap paperback thrill-
ers, but there was an abundance of great authors: Dostoevsky, Dickens, Balzac, Melville. It was odd, she puzzled,
that the girl had this taste in literature, yet could not spell
the simplest word and had never heard of a comma. As she
turned away, her eardrums were shattered by her own
scream. A man stood in the doorway.

A boy, actually, she realized through her fright; one of
Jody's more outstanding visitors, always dressed in one of
those Mexican shawl affairs and a battered derby hat, from
under which butter-yellow locks flowed in profusion, everything at the moment dripping with rain. More embarrassed
now than frightened—she had never screamed in her life,
or stood before a stranger in her nightgown, and neither
had Bedelia—she began pulsating with dignity. "I didn't
hear anyone come up the stairs," she indicted him.

"Little cat feet, man," he said with a cavernous yawn,
"Where's Jody? Who're you?"

She explained her presence, pulling the raincoat more
firmly together across her bosom, but unable to do anything about the expanse of flowered flannel below.

"Jody, she'd forget her ass if it wasn't screwed on," the
boy said with a second yawn. His eyes were watery and
red, and his nose ran. "If you'll excuse me," she said, going
past him. He followed her back into the kitchen and suddenly, with a hostlike warmth that greatly surprised her, he
asked, "You want some coffee?"

She declined, saying that she must be going.

At this he heaved a deep, disappointed sigh, which again
surprised her, and sank like an invalid into a chair. He was
a slight youth with neat little features crowded into the
center of his face, giving him, despite his woebegone expression, a pert, fledgling look. In Lillian's day he would
have been called a "pretty boy." He would not have been
her type at all; she had always preferred the lean profile.

"My name's Jamie," he announced suddenly, with a
childlike spontaneity beneath the film of langour; and he
proffered his hand.

Gingerly, she shook the cold small fingers.

"Hey, really," he entreated, "Stay and rap awhile."

"Rap?"

"Talk, man. Talk to me." And he looked, all at once, so

lonely, so forlorn, that even though she was very tired, she felt she must stay a moment longer. Pulling out a chair, she took a temporary, edge-of-the-seat position across the hideous table from him.

He seemed to be gathering his thoughts together. "So what's your bag?" he asked.

She looked at him hopelessly. "My bag?"

"You a housewife? You work?"

"Oh—yes, I work," she said, offended by his bold curiosity, yet grateful against her will to have inspired it.

"What's your name?" he asked.

He was speaking to her as a contemporary; and again, she was both pleased by this and offended by his lack of deference. "Lillian . . . Cronin," she said uncertainly.

"I'm Jamie," he laughed.

"So you mentioned." And thought—Jamie, Jody, the kinds of names you would give pet rabbits. Where were the solid, straightforward names of yesteryear—the Georges and Harolds, the Dorothys and Margarets? What did she have to say to a Jamie in a Mexican shawl and threadbare derby who was now scratching himself all over with little fidgety movements? But she said, breaking the long silence, which he seemed not to notice: "And what is *your* bag, if I may ask?"

He took several moments to answer. "I don't know, man . . . I'm a student of human nature."

"Oh? And where do you study?"

"Not me, man, that's Jody's scene . . . into yoga, alpha waves, the whole bit . . . even studies macramé and World Lit at jay cee . . ."

"Indeed? How interesting. I noticed her books."

"She's a towering intellect." He yawned, his eyes glassy with fatigue. He was scratching himself more slowly now.

"And does she work, as well?" Lillian asked, once more ashamed of her nosiness.

"Work?" he smiled. "Maybe you could call it that. . . ." But his attention was drifting away like smoke. Fumbling with a breadknife, he picked it up and languidly, distantly, speared a cockroach with the point. Then, with the side of the knife, he slowly, methodically, squashed the other one.

Averting her eyes from the massacre, Lillian leaned forward. "I don't mean to sound familiar, but you seem a quiet person. Do you think you might ask Jody to be a little less noisy up here? I've spoken to the landlord, but—" She saw the boy smile again, an odd, rueful smile that made her feel, for some reason, much younger than he. "You see—" she continued, but he was fading from her presence, slowly mashing his bugs to pulp and now dropping the knife to reach over and click on the food-spattered television set. Slouched, his eyes bored by what the screen offered, he nevertheless began following an old movie. The conversation appeared to be over.

Lillian rose. She was not accustomed, nor would Bedelia have been, to a chat ending without some mutual amenity. She felt awkward, dismissed. With a cool nod she left him and descended the splashing stairs to her own flat. Such a contrast the youth was of warmth and rudeness . . . and Jody, an illiterate studying Dostoevsky at college . . . food stamps lying hugger-mugger with bills from Saks . . . it was impossible to bring it all into focus; she felt rudderless, malfunctioning . . . how peculiar life had become . . . everything mixed up . . . a generation of fragments. . .

Climbing heavily back into bed, she wondered what Bedelia would have thought of Jody and Jamie. And she remembered how unkempt and disconcerting Vladimir had been, yet how her aunt had quickly penetrated to the valuable core while she, Lillian, fussed on about his bad language. No doubt Bedelia would have been scandalized by the filth upstairs, but she would not have been so narrowsouled as to find fault with spelling mistakes, first names, taste in clothing. . . . Bedelia might not have pulverized Jody with a glance, as Vladimir suggested, but instead seen some delicate tragedy in the worn cherubic features, or been charmed by the girl's invincible buoyancy . . . it was hard to tell with Bedelia, which facet she might consider the significant one . . . she often surprised you . . . it had to do with largeness of spirit. . . .

Whereas she, Lillian, had always to guard against stuffiness. . . . Still, she tried to hold high the torch of goodwill . . . too pompous a simile, of course, but she knew clearly and deeply what she meant . . . so *let* Vladimir rave on at her for refusing to shrink into a knot of hostility; what was Vladimir, after all? Insane. Her eyes opened in the dark as she faced what she had tried to avoid all day: that Vladimir had been wrenched off the tracks by Bedelia's death, and that it was Lillian's duty to enlighten him. But she winced at the thought . . . such a terrible thing to have to tell someone . . . if only she could turn to Bedelia . . . how

sorely she missed her . . . how sorely she missed George's
lean young face under his Army cap . . . youth . . . sunlight
. . . outside the rain still fell . . . she had only herself, and
the dark, unending rain. . . .

"Stop this brooding," she said aloud; if she had only
herself, she had better be decent company. And closing her
eyes she tried to sleep. But not until a gray watery dawn
was breaking did she drop off.

The opera house telephoned at three minutes past nine.
Leaden, taut-nerved, sourly questioning the rewards of her
long, exquisite punctuality, she pulled on her clothes, and,
burning eyes and empty stomach, hurried out of the house.
At work, though the board was busy, the hours moved
with monumental torpor. She felt increasingly unlike herself, hotly brimming over with impatience for all this
switchboard blather: calls from New York, Milan; Suther-
land with her sore throat, Pavarotti with his tight schedule
—did they really think that, if another *Rigoletto* were
never given, anyone would notice? She felt an urge to slur
this fact into the headphone, as befitted a truant traipsing
in at a quarter to ten, as befitted someone with minimally
combed hair and crooked seams and, even worse, with the
same underwear on that she had worn the day before. As if
a slatternly, cynical Lillian whom she didn't recognize had
squeezed slyly into prominence, a Lillian who half-
considered walking out on the whole tiresome business and
indulging in a lavish two-hour lunch downtown—let someone else serve, let someone else be polite.

Sandwiched into the bus aisle that night, she almost
smacked an old gentleman who crunched her right instep
under his groping heel; and as she creaked into the house
with her wet newspaper and saw that a motorcyclist had
been picked off on the freeway by a sniper, she had to fight
down a lip curl of satisfaction. Then, reflectively, still in
her raincoat, she walked to the end of the hall where an
oval mirror hung, and studied her face. It was haggard,
flinty, stripped of faith, scraped down to the cold, atavistic
bones of retaliation. She had almost walked off her job,
almost struck an old man, almost smiled at murder. A
feeling of panic shot through her; what were values if they
could collapse at the touch of a sleepless night? And she
sank the terrible face into her hands; but a ray of rational
thought lifted it again. "Almost." Never mind the queru-

lous inner tremble, at each decisive moment her principles
had stood fast. Wasn't a person entitled to an occasional fit
of petulance? There is such a thing as perspective, she told
herself, and in the meantime a great lust for steam and
soap had spread through her. She would scrub out the day
in a hot bath and in perfect silence, for apparently Jody
had not yet returned from across the bay. God willing, the
creature would remain away a week.

Afterward, boiled pink, wrapped in her quilted robe, she
felt restored to grace. A fine appetite raced through her,
along with visions of a tuna casserole which she hurried
into the kitchen to prepare, hurrying out again at the sum-
mons of the telephone. It was Vladimir, very excited, wanting to drop by. Her first response was one of blushing
discomfort: entertain Vladimir in her quilted bathrobe?
Her second she articulated: she was bone-tired, she was
going to bed right after dinner. But even as she spoke she
heard the remorseless door slam of Jody's return, and a
violent spasm twisted her features. "Please—next week," she
told Vladimir and hung up, clutching her head as tears of
rage and exhaustion burst from her eyes. Weeping, she
made a tuna sandwich, chewed it without heart, and sank
onto her unmade bed. The next morning, still exhausted,
she made an emergency appointment with her doctor, and
came home that night with a bottle of sleeping pills.

By the end of the week she was sick with artificial sleep,
there was an ugly rubber taste in her mouth, her eye sockets felt caked with rust. And it was not only the noise and
pills that plagued her: a second neighborhood woman had
been slashed to death by the rain man (the newspapers, in
their cozy fashion, had thus baptized the slayer). She had
taken to beaming her flashlight under the bed before saying
the Lord's Prayer; her medicinal sleep crackled with surreal visions; at the sullen butcher's her eyes were morbidly
drawn to the meat cleaver; and at work not only had she
upset coffee all over her lap, but she disconnected Rudolf
Bing himself in the middle of a sentence.

And never any respite from above. She had called the
landlord again, without audible results, and informed the
Board of Health about the cockroaches; their reply was that
they had no jurisdiction over cockroaches. She had stuck
several notes under Jody's door pleading with her to quiet
down, and had stopped her twice on the steps, receiving the
first time some capricious remark, and the second a sigh of

"Christ, Lilly, I'm trying. What d'you want?" Lilly! The gall! But she was gratified to see that the gum-snapping face was almost as sallow as her own, the circles under the eyes darker than ever, new lines around the mouth. So youth could crumble, too. Good! Perhaps the girl's insanely late hours were boomeranging, and would soon mash her down in a heap of deathlike stillness (would that Lillian could implement this vision). Or perhaps it was her affair with Jamie that was running her ragged. Ah, the costly trauma of love! Jealousy, misunderstanding—so damaging to the poor nervous system! Or so she had heard . . . she and George had been blessed with rapport . . . but try not to dwell on the past . . . yes, possibly it was Jamie who was lining the girl's face . . . Lillian had seen him a few times since their first meeting, once on the steps—he smiled, was pleasant, remembered her, but had not remembered to zip his fly, and she had hurried on, embarrassed—and twice in the back garden, where on the less drenching days she tended Bedelia's flowers, but without her aunt's emerald-green thumb . . . a rare sunny afternoon, she had been breaking off geraniums; Jody and Jamie lay on the grass in skimpy bathing suits, their thin bodies white, somehow poignant in their delicacy . . . she felt like a great stuffed mattress in her sleeveless dress, soiled hands masculine with age, a stevedore's drop of sweat hanging from her nose . . . could they imagine her once young and tender on her own bed of love? or now, with a man friend? As if everything closed down at fifty-seven, like a bankrupt hotel! —tearing off the head of a geranium—brash presumption of youth! But she saw that they weren't even aware of her, no, they were kissing and rolling about . . . in Bedelia's garden! "Here, what are you doing!" she cried, but in the space of a moment a hostile little flurry had taken place, and now they broke away and lay separately in charged silence, still taking no notice of her as she stood there, heart thumping, fist clenched. She might have been air. Suddenly, sick from the heat, she had plodded inside.

The next time she saw Jamie in the garden was this afternoon when, arriving home from work and changing into a fresh dress for Vladimir's visit, she happened to glance out her bedroom window. Rain sifted down but the boy was standing still, a melancholy sight, wrapped in a theatrical black cloak, the derby and Mexican shawl apparently having outlived their effectiveness as eyecatchers

. . . youth's eternal and imbecile need to shock . . . Jody
with her ebony fingernails and silly prepubescent hemlines;
and this little would-be Dracula with his golden sausage
curls, tragically posed in the fragile mist, though she noticed his hands were untragically busy under the cloak,
scratching as usual . . . or . . . the thought was so monstrous
that she clutched the curtain . . . he could not be standing
in the garden abusing himself; she must be deranged, suffering prurient delusions—she, Lillian Cronin, a decent, clean-
minded woman . . . ah God, what was happening, what
was happening? It was her raw nerves, her drugged and
hanging head, the perpetual din . . . even as she stood
there, her persecutor was trying on clothes, dropping shoes,
pounding from closet to mirror (for Lillian could by now
divine the activity behind each noise) while simultaneously
braying into the telephone receiver stuck between chin and
shoulder, and sketchily attending the deluxe television set,
which blared a hysterical melodrama . . .

Outside, the youth sank onto a tree stump, from which
he cast the upstairs window a long bleak look . . . they
must have had a lovers' quarrel, and the girl had shut him
out; now he brooded in the rain, an exile; or rather a
kicked puppy, shivering and staring up with ponderous woe
. . . then, eyes dropping, he caught sight of Lillian, and a
broad, sunny, candid smile flashed from the dismal coun-
tenance . . . odd, jarring, she thought, giving a polite nod
and dropping the curtain, especially after his rude impervi-
ousness that hot day on the grass . . . a generation of
fragments, she had said so before, though God knew she
never objected to a smile (with the exception of Jody's
grimace) . . . and walking down the hall away from the
noise, she was stopped woodenly by the sound of the girl's
doorbell. It was one of the gentlemen callers, who tore up
the stairs booming felicitations which were returned with
the inevitable shrieks, this commingled din moving into the
front room and turning Lillian around in her tracks. With
the door closed, the kitchen was comparatively bearable,
and it was time to eat anyway. She bought television dinners now, lacking the vigor to cook. She had lost seven
pounds, but was not growing svelte, only drawn. Even to
turn on the waiting oven was a chore. But slowly she got
herself into motion, and at length, pouring out a glass of
burgundy to brace herself for Vladimir's visit, she sat down
to the steaming, neatly sectioned pap. Afterward, dutifully

washing her glass and fork in the sink, she glanced out the window into the rain, falling in sheets now; the garden was dark and she could not be sure, but she thought she saw the youth still sitting on the stump. it was beyond her, why anyone would sit still in a downpour . . . but everything was beyond her, insurmountable . . . and soon Vladimir would arrive . . . the thought was more than she could bear, but she could not defer his visit again, it would be too rude. . . .

He burst in like a cannonball, tearing off his wet lumber jacket, an acrid smell of sweat blooming from his armpits; his jaws were stubbled with white, great bushes sprouted from his nostrils.

"You look terrible!" he roared.

Even though she had at the last moment rubbed lipstick into her pallid cheeks. She gave a deflated nod and gestured toward the relatively quiet kitchen, but he wanted the Bedelia-redolent front room, where he rushed over to the Steinway and lovingly dashed off an arpeggio, only to stagger back with his finger knifed up at the ceiling. "Still the chaos!" he cried.

"Please—" she said raggedly. "No advice, I beg of you."

"No advice? Into your grave they'll drive you, Lillian!" And she watched his finger drop, compassionately it seemed, to point at her slumped bosom with its heart beating so wearily inside. It was a small hand, yet blunt, virile, its back covered with coarse dark hair . . . what if it reached farther, touched her? . . . But spittle already flying, Vladimir was plunging into a maelstrom of words, obviously saved up for a week. "I wanted to come sooner, why didn't you let me? Look at you, a wreck! Vladimir knew a second one would be cut—he smells blood on the wind! He wants to come and pound on your door, to be with you, but no, he respects your wish for privacy, so he sits every night out front in his auto, watching!" Here he broke off to wipe his lips, while Lillian, pressing hard the swollen, rusty lids of her eyes, accepted the immense duty of guiding him to confinement. "And every night," he roared on, "while Vladimir sits, Bedelia plays 'Komm, Jesu, Komm,' it floats into the street, it is beautiful, beautiful—"

"Ah, Vladimir," broke pityingly from her lips.

Silence. With a clap of restored lucidity his fist struck his forehead. It remained tightly glued there for some time. When it fell away he seemed quite composed.

"I have always regretted," he said crisply, "that you resemble the wrong side of your family. All you have of Bedelia is a most vague hint of her cheekbones." Which he was scrutinizing with his small glittering eyes. Again, nervously, she sensed that he would touch her; but instead, a look of revulsion passed over his features as he stared first at one cheek, then the other. "You've got fucking gunk on! Rouge!"

With effort, she produced a neutral tone. "I'm not used to being stared at, Vladimir."

"Hah, I should think not," he snapped abstractedly, eyes still riveted.

Beast! Vile wretch! But at once she was shamed by her viciousness. From where inside her did it come? And she remembered that terrible day at work when a malign and foreign Lillian had pressed into ascendancy, almost as frightening a character change as the one she was seeing before her now, for Vladimir's peering eyes seemed actually black with hatred. "Stinking whore-rouge," he breathed; then with real pain, he cried: "Have you no thought for Bedelia? You have the blessing of her cheekbones! Respect them! Don't drag them through the gutter! My God, Lillian! My God!"

She said nothing. It seemed the only thing to do.

But now he burst forth again, cheerfully, rubbing his hands together. "Listen to Vladimir. You want a husband, forget the war paint, use what you have. Some intelligence. A good bearing—straighten the shoulders—and cooking talent. Not like Bedelia's, but not bad. Now, Vladimir has been looking around for you—"

"Vladimir," she said through her teeth.

"—and he has found a strong, healthy widower of fifty-two years, a great enjoyer of the opera. He has been advised of your virtues—"

"Vladimir!"

"Of course you understand Vladimir himself is out, Vladimir is a monolith—" A particularly loud thump shuddered the ceiling, and he jumped back yelling, "Shove it, you swine! Lice!"

"Vladimir, I do not want a man!" Lillian snapped.

"Not so! I sense sex boiling around in you!"

Her lips parted; blood rushed into her cheeks to darken the artificial blush. For certain, with the short, potent word, *sex*, his hands would leap on her.

"But you look a thousand years old," he went on. "It hangs in folds, your face. You must get rid of this madhouse upstairs! What have you done so far—not even told the landlord!"

"I *have*!" she cried; and suddenly the thought of confiding in someone loosened a stinging flood of tears from her eyes, and she sank into a chair. "He has come to speak to her . . . time and time again . . . he seems always to be there . . . but nothing changes. . . ."

"Ah, so," said Vladimir, pulling out his gray handkerchief and handing it to her. "The sow screws him."

She grimaced both at the words and the reprehensible cloth, with which she nevertheless dabbed her eyes. "I don't believe that," she said nasally.

"Why not? She's a prostitute. Only to look at her."

"You've seen her?" she asked, slowly raising her eyes. But of course, if he sat outside in his car every night . . .

"I have seen her," he said, revulsion hardening his eyes. "I have seen much. Even a bat-man with the face of a sorrowful kewpie doll. He pines this minute on the front steps."

"That's her boyfriend," Lillian murmured, increasingly chilled by the thought of Vladimir sitting outside all night, spying.

"Boyfriend! A hundred boyfriends she has, each with a roll of bills in his pocket!"

Tensely, she smoothed the hair at her temples. "Forgive me, Vladimir," she said gently, "But you exaggerate. You exaggerate everything, I'm afraid. I must point this out to you, because I think it does you no good. I really—"

"Don't change the subject! We're talking about her, upstairs!"

She was silent for a moment. "The girl is—too free, I suppose, in our eyes. But I'm certain that she isn't what you call her."

"And how do you come to this idiot conclusion?" he asked scornfully.

She lifted her hands in explanation, but they hung helplessly suspended. "Well," she said at last, "I know she reads Dostoevsky . . . she takes courses . . . and she cares for that boy in the cape, even if they do have their quarrels . . . and there's a quality of anguish in her face . . ."

"Anguish! I call it the knocked-out look of a female cretin who uses her ass every night to pay the rent. And

that pea-brain boyfriend outside, in his secondhand ghoul
costume to show how interesting he is! Probably he pops
pills and lives off his washerwoman mother, if he hasn't slit
her throat in a fit of irritation! It's the type, Lillian! Weak,
no vision, no guts! The sewers are vomiting them up by the
thousands to mix with us! They surround us! Slop! Shit!
Chaos! Listen to that up there! Hee-haw! Call that anguish? Even pleasure? No, I tell you what it is! Empty,
hollow noise—like a wheel spun into motion and never
stopped again! It's madness! The madness of our times!"

But as he whipped himself on, Lillian felt herself growing diametrically clear and calm, as if the outburst were
guiding her blurred character back into focus. When he
stopped, she said firmly, "Yes, I understand what you
mean about the wheel spinning. There is something pointless about them, something pitiful. But they're not from a
sewer. They're people, Vladimir, human beings like ourselves. . . ."

"Ah, blanket democracy! What else would you practice
but that piss-fart abomination?"

"I practice what Bedelia herself practiced," she replied
tartly.

"Ah," he sighed. "The difference between instinct and
application. Between a state of grace and a condition of
effort. Dear friend Lillian, tolerance is dangerous without
insight. And the last generation with insight has passed,
with the things it understood. Like the last generation of
cobblers and glass stainers. It is fatal to try to carry on a
dead art—the world has no use for it! The world will
trample you down! Don't think of the past, think of your
scalp!"

"No," she stated, rising and swaying with the lighthead-
edness that so frequently visited her now. "To live each
moment as if you were in danger—it's demeaning. I will
not creep around snarling like some four-legged beast. I am
a civilized human being. Your attitude shows a lack of
proportion, Vladimir; I feel that you really—"

A flash of sinewy hands; her wrists were seized and
crushed together with a stab of pain through whose shock
she felt a marginal heat of embarrassment, a tingling dis-
may of abrupt intimacy. Then the very center of her skull
was pierced by his shriek. "You *are* in danger! Can't you
*see*!" and he thrust his face at hers, disclosing the red veins
of his eyes, bits of sleep matted in the lashes, and the

immobile, overwhelmed look of someone who has seen the abyss and is seeing it again. Her heart gave the chop of an axe; with a wail she strained back.

His fixed look broke; his eyes grew flaring, kinetic. "One minute the blood is nice and cozy in its veins—the next, slice! and slice! and slice! Red fountains go up—a festival! Worthy of Handel! Oh marvelous, marvelous! The rain man—" Here he broke off to renew his grip as she struggled frantically to pull away. "The rain man, he's in ecstasies! Such founts and spouts, such excitement! Then at last it's all played out, nothing but puddles, and off he trots, he's big success! And it's big city—many many fountains to be had, all red as—as—red as—"

Her laboring wrists were flung aside; his hands slammed against her face and pressed fiercely into the cheeks.

"Vladimir!" she screamed, "It's Lillian—Lillian!"

The flared eyes contracted. He stepped back and stood immobile. Then a self-admonishing hand rose shakily to his face, which had gone the color of pewter. After a long moment he turned and walked out of the house.

She blundered to the door and locked it behind him, then ran heavily back into the front room where she came to a blank stop, both hands pressed to her chest. Hearing the sound of an engine starting, she wheeled around to the window and pinched back the edge of the shade. Through the rain she saw the big square car jerk and shudder, while its motor rose to a crescendo of whines and abruptly stopped. Vladimir climbed out and started back across the pavement. Her brain finally clicked: the telephone, the police.

With long strides she gained the hall where the telephone stood, and where she now heard the anticipated knock— but mild, rueful, a diminished sound that soon fell away. She moved on haltingly; she would call the police, yes—or a friend from work—or her doctor—someone, anyone, she must talk to someone, and suddenly she stumbled with a cry: it was Vladimir's lumber jacket she had tripped over, still lying on the floor where he had dropped it, his wallet sticking out from the pocket. Outside, the Buick began coughing once more, then it fell silent. A few moments later the shallow, timid knock began again. Without his wallet he could not call a garage, a taxi. It was a fifteen-block walk to his house in the rain. If only she could feel

Bedelia's presence beside her, look to the expression in the intelligent eyes. Gradually, concentrating on those eyes, she felt an unclenching inside her. She gazed at the door. Behind it Vladimir was Vladimir still. He had spoken with horrifying morbidity, and even hurt her wrists and face, but he was not the rain man. Bedelia would have seen such seeds. He had been trying to warn her tonight of the world's dangers, and in his passion had set off one of his numerous obsessions—with her fingertip she touched the rouged and aching oval of her cheek. Strange, tortured soul who had stationed himself out in the cold, night after night, to keep her from harm. Bending down, she gathered up the rough, homely jacket; but the knocking had stopped. She went back into the front room and again tweaked aside the shade. He was going away, a small decelerated figure, already drenched. Now he turned the corner and was lost from sight. Depleted, she leaned against the wall.

It might have been a long while that she stood there, that the noise from above masked the sound, but by degrees she became aware of knocking. He must have turned around in the deluge and was now, with what small hope, tapping on the door again. She hesitated, once more summoning the fine violet eyes, the tall brow under its archaic coiffure, which dipped in an affirmative nod. The jacket under her arm, Lillian went into the hall, turned on the porch light, and unlocked the door.

It was not Vladimir who stood there, but Jamie, as wet as if he had crawled from the ocean, his long curls limply clinging to the foolish cape, his neat little features stamped with despair, yet warmed, saved, by the light of greeting in his eyes. Weary, unequal to any visit, she shook her head.

"Jody?" she thought she heard him say, or more likely it was something else—the rain muffled his voice: though she caught an eerie, unnatural tone she now sensed was reflected in the luminous stare. With a sudden feeling of panic she started to slam the door in his face. But she braked herself, knowing that she was overwrought; it was unseemly to use such brusqueness on this lost creature because of her jangled nerves.

So she paused for one haggard, courteous moment to say, "I'm sorry, Jamie, it's late—some other time." And in that moment the shrouded figure crouched, and instantaneously, spasmlike, rushed up against her. She felt a huge but painless blow, followed by a dullness, a stillness deep inside her, and staggering back as he kicked the door shut behind them, she clung to the jamb of the front-room entrance and slowly sank to her knees.

She dimly comprehended the wet cloak brushing her side, but it was the room that held her attention, that filled her whole being. It had grown immense, lofty, and was suffused with violet, overwhelmingly beautiful. But even as she watched, it underwent a rapid wasting, paled to the faint, dead-leaf hue of an old tintype; and now it vanished behind a sheet of black as the knife was wrenched from her body.

# ROSS MACDONALD

# The Underground Man

## I

Before we reached Santa Teresa I could smell smoke. Then I could see it dragging like a veil across the face of the mountain behind the city.

Under and through the smoke I caught glimpses of fire like the flashes of heavy guns too far away to be heard. The illusion of war was completed by an old two-engine bomber which flew in low over the mountain's shoulder. The plane was lost in the smoke for a long instant, then climbed out trailing a pastel red cloud of fire retardant.

On the freeway ahead the traffic thickened rapidly and stopped us. I reached over to turn on the car radio but then decided not to. The woman beside me had enough on her mind without having to listen to fire reports.

At the head of the line, a highway patrolman was directing the movement of traffic from a side road onto the freeway. There were quite a few cars coming down out of the hills, many of them with Santa Teresa College decals. I noticed several trucks piled with furniture and mattresses, children and dogs.

When the patrolman let us pass, we turned onto the road that led to the hills. It took us in a gradual climb between

202

lemon groves and subdivisions toward what Jean described as Mrs. Broadhurst's canyon.

A man wearing a Forest Service jacket and a yellow hard hat stopped the Mercedes at the entrance to the canyon. Jean climbed out and introduced herself as Mrs. Broadhurst's daughter-in-law.

"I hope you're not planning to stay, ma'am. We may have to evacuate this area."

"Have you seen my husband and little boy?" She described Ronny—six years old, blue eyes, black-haired, wearing a light-blue suit.

He shook his head. "I've seen a lot of people leaving with their kids. It isn't a bad idea. Once the fire starts spilling down one of these canyons she can outrace you."

"How bad is it?" I said.

"It depends on the wind. If the wind stays quiet we could get her fully contained before nightfall. We've got a lot of equipment up on the mountain. But if she starts to blow—" He lifted his hand in a kind of resigned goodbye to everything in sight.

We drove into the canyon between fieldstone gate posts emblazoned with the name Canyon Estates. New and expensive houses were scattered along the canyonside among the oaks and boulders. Men and women with hoses were watering their yards and buildings and the surrounding brush. Their children were watching them, or sitting quietly in cars, ready to go. The smoke towering up from the mountain stood over them like a threat and changed the color of the light.

The Broadhurst ranch lay between these houses and the fire. We went up the canyon toward it, and left the county road at Mrs. Broadhurst's mailbox. Her private asphalt lane wound through acres of mature avocado trees. Their broad leaves were shriveling at the tips as if the fire had already touched them. Darkening fruit hung down from their branches like green hand grenades.

The lane broadened into a circular drive in front of a large and simple white stucco ranchhouse. Under the deep porch, red fuchsias dripped from hanging redwood baskets. At a red glass hummingbird feeder suspended among the baskets, a hummingbird which also seemed suspended was sipping from a spout and treading air.

The bird didn't move perceptibly when a woman opened the screen door and came out. She had on a white shirt and dark slacks which showed off her narrow waist. She moved across the veranda with rapid disciplined energy, making the high heels of her riding boots click.

"Jean darling."

"Mother."

They shook hands briefly like competitors before a match of some kind. Mrs. Broadhurst's neat dark head was touched with gray, but she was younger than I'd imagined, no more than fifty or so.

Only her eyes looked older. Without moving them from Jean's face, she shook her head from side to side.

"No, they haven't come back. And they haven't been seen in the area for some time. Who's the blond girl?"

"I don't know."

"Is Stanley having an affair with her?"

"I don't know, Mother." She turned to me. "This is Mr. Archer."

Mrs. Broadhurst nodded curtly. "Jean mentioned on the telephone that you're some kind of detective. Is that correct?"

"The private kind."

She raked me with a look that moved from my eyes down to my shoes and back up to my face again. "I've never set much store in private detectives, frankly. But under the circumstances perhaps you can be useful. If the radio can be believed, the fire has passed the Mountain House and left it untouched. Would you like to come up there with me?"

"I would. After I talk to the gardener."

"That won't be necessary."

"But I understand he gave your son a key to the Mountain House. He may know why they wanted it."

"He doesn't. I've questioned Fritz. We're wasting time, and I've already wasted a good deal. I stayed by the telephone until you and Jean got here."

"Where is Fritz?"

"You're persistent, aren't you? He may be in the lath house."

We left Jean standing white-faced and apprehensive in the shadow of the veranda. The lath house was in a walled garden behind one wing of the ranchhouse. Mrs. Broadhurst followed me in under the striped shadows cast by the roof.

"Fritz? Mr. Archer wants to ask you a question."

A soft-looking man in dungarees straightened up from the plants he was tending. He had emotional green eyes and a skittish way of holding his body, as if he was ready to avoid a threatened blow. There was a livid scar connecting his mouth and his nose which looked as if he had been born with a harelip.

"What is it this time?" he said.

"I'm trying to find out what Stanley Broadhurst is up to. Why do you think he wanted the key to the guest house?"

Fritz shrugged his thick loose shoulders. "I don't know. I can't read people's minds, can I?"

"You must have some idea."

He glanced uncomfortably at Mrs. Broadhurst. "Am I supposed to spit it all out?"

"Please tell the truth," she said in a forced tone.

"Well, naturally I thought him and the chick had hanky-panky in mind. Why else would they want to go up there?"

"With my grandson along?" Mrs. Broadhurst said.

"They wanted me to keep the boy with me. But I didn't want the responsibility. That's the way you get in trouble," he said with stupid wisdom.

"You didn't mention that before. You should have told me, Fritz."

"I can't remember everything at once, can I?"

"How was the boy behaving?" I asked him.

"Okay. He didn't say much."

"Neither do you."

"What do you want me to say? You think I did something to the boy?" His voice rose, and his eyes grew moist and suddenly overflowed.

"Nobody suggested anything like that."

"Then why do you keep at me and at me? The boy was here with his father. His father took him away. Does that make me responsible?"

"Take it easy."

Mrs. Broadhurst touched my arm. "We're getting nowhere."

We left the gardener complaining among his plants. The striped shadow fell from the roof, jailbirding him.

The carport was attached to an old red barn at the back of the house. Below the barn was a dry creekbed at the bottom of a shallow ravine which was thickly grown with oaks and eucalyptus. Band-tailed pigeons and sweet-voiced red-winged blackbirds were foraging under the trees and around a feeder. I stepped on fallen eucalyptus pods which looked like ornate bronze nailheads set in the dust.

An aging Cadillac and an old pickup truck stood under the carport. Mrs. Broadhurst drove the pickup, wrestling it angrily around the curves in the avocado grove and turning left on the road toward the mountains. Beyond the avocados were ancient olive trees, and beyond them was pasture gone to brush.

We were approaching the head of the canyon. The smell of burning grew stronger in my nostrils. I felt as though we were going against nature, but I didn't mention my qualms to Mrs. Broadhurst. She wasn't the sort of woman you confessed human weakness to.

The road degenerated as we climbed. It was narrow and inset with boulders. Mrs. Broadhurst jerked at the wheel of the truck as if it was a male animal resisting control. For some reason I was reminded of Mrs. Roger Armistead's voice on the phone, and I asked Mrs. Broadhurst if she knew the woman.

She answered shortly: "I've seen her at the beach club. Why do you ask?"

"The Armistead name came up in connection with your son's friend, the blond girl."

"How?"

"She was using their Mercedes."

"I'm not surprised at the connection. The Armisteads are *nouveaux riches* from down south—not my kind of people." Without really changing the subject, she went on: "We've lived here for quite a long time, you know. My grandfather Falconer's ranch took in a good part of the coastal plain and the whole mountainside, all the way to the top of the first range. All I have left is a few hundred acres."

While I was trying to think of an appropriate comment, she said in a more immediate voice: "Stanley phoned me last night and asked me for fifteen hundred dollars cash, today."

"What for?"

"He said something vague, about buying information. As you may or may not know, my son is somewhat hipped on the subject of his father's desertion." Her voice was dry and careful.

"His wife told me that."

"Did she? It occurred to me that the fifteen hundred dollars might have something to do with you."

"It doesn't." I thought of Al, the pale man in the dark suit, but decided not to bring him up right now.

"Who's paying you?" the woman said rather sharply.

"I haven't been paid."

"I see." She sounded as if she distrusted what she saw. "Are you and my daughter-in-law good friends?"

"I met her this morning. We have friends in common."

"Then you probably know that Stanley and she have been close to breaking up. I never did think that their marriage would last."

"Why?"

"Jean is an intelligent girl but she comes from an entirely different class. I don't believe she's ever understood my son, though I've tried to explain something about our family traditions." She turned her head from the road to glance at me. "Is Stanley really interested in this blond girl?"

"Obviously he is, but maybe not in the way you mean. He wouldn't have brought your grandson along—"

"Don't be too sure of that. He brought Ronny because he knows I love the boy, and because he wants money from me. Remember when he found I wasn't here, he tried to leave Ronny with Fritz. I'd give a lot to know what they're up to."

## II

At the base of a sandstone bluff where the road petered out entirely, she stopped the pickup and we got out.

"This is where we shift to shanks' mare," she said. "Ordinarily we could have driven around by way of Rattlesnake Road, but that's where they're fighting the fire."

In the lee of the bluff was a brown wooden sign, "Falconer Trail." The trail was a dusty track bulldozed out of the steep side of the canyon. As Mrs. Broadhurst went up ahead of me, she explained that her father had given the land for the trail to the Forest Service. She sounded as if she was trying to cheer herself in any way she could.

I ate her dust until I was looking down into the tops of the tallest sycamores in the canyon below. A daytime moon hung over the bluff, and we went on climbing toward it. When we reached the top I was wet under my clothes.

About a hundred yards back from the edge, a large weathered redwood cabin stood against a grove of trees. Some of the trees had been blackened and maimed where the fire had burned an erratic swath through the grove. The cabin itself was partly red and looked as if it had been splashed with blood.

Beyond the trees was a black hillside where the fire had browsed. The hillside slanted up to a ridge road and continued rising beyond the ridge to where the fire was now. It seemed to be moving laterally across the face of the mountain. The flames that from a distance had looked like artillery flashes were crashing through the thick chaparral like cavalry.

The ridge road was about midway between us and the main body of the fire. Toward the east, where the foothills flattened out into a mesa, the road curved down toward a collection of buildings which looked like a small college. Between them and the fire, bulldozers were crawling back and forth on the face of the mountain, cutting a firebreak in the deep brush.

The road was clogged with tanker trucks and other heavy equipment. Men stood around them in waiting attitudes, as if by behaving modestly and discreetly they could make the fire stay up on the mountain and die there, like an unwanted god.

As Mrs. Broadhurst and I approached the cabin I could see that part of its walls and roof had been splashed from the air with red fire retardant. The rest of the walls and the shutters over the windows were weathered gray.

The door was hanging open, with the key in the Yale lock. Mrs. Broadhurst walked up to it slowly, as if she dreaded what she might find inside. But there was nothing unusual to be seen in the big rustic front room. The ashes in the stone fireplace were cold, and might have been cold for years. Pieces of old-fashioned furniture draped with canvas stood around like formless images of the past.

Mrs. Broadhurst sat down heavily on a canvas-covered armchair. Dust rose around her. She coughed and spoke in a different voice, low and ashamed:

"I came up the trail a little too fast, I'm afraid."

I went out to the kitchen to get her some water. There were cups in the cupboard, but when I turned on the tap in the tin sink no water came. The butane stove was disconnected, too.

I walked through the other rooms while I was at it: two downstairs bedrooms and a sleeping loft which was reached by steep wooden stairs. The loft was lit by a dormer window, and there were three beds in it, covered with canvas. One of them looked rumpled. I stripped the canvas off it. On the heavy gray blanket underneath there was a Rorschach blot of blood which looked recent but not fresh.

I went down to the big front room. Mrs. Broadhurst had rested her head against the back of the chair. Her closed face was smooth and peaceful, and she was snoring gently.

I heard the rising roar of a plane coming in low over the mountain. I went out the back door in time to see its red spoor falling on the fire. The plane grew smaller, its roar diminuendoed.

Two deer—a doe and a fawn—came down the slope in a dry creek channel, heading for the grove. They saw me and rockinghorsed over a fallen log into the trees.

From the rear of the cabin a washed-out gravel lane overgrown with weeds meandered toward the ridge road. Starting along the lane toward the trees, I noticed wheel tracks in the weeds leading off toward a small stable. The wheel tracks looked new, and I could see only one set of them.

I followed them to the stable and peered in. A black convertible that looked like Stanley's stood there with the top down. I found the registration in the dash compartment. It was Stanley's all right.

I slammed the door of the convertible. A noise that sounded like an echo or a response came from the direction of the trees. Perhaps it was the crack of a stick breaking. I went out and headed for the partly burned grove. All I could hear was the sound of my own footsteps and a faint sighing which came from the wind in the trees.

Then I made out a more distant noise which I didn't recognize. It sounded like the whirring of wings. I felt hot wind on my face, and glanced up the slope.

The wall of smoke that hung above the fire was leaning out from the mountain. At its base the fire was burning more brightly and had changed direction. Outriders of flame were leaping down the slope to the left, the firemen were moving along the ridge road to meet them.

The wind was changing. I could hear it rattling now among the leaves—the same sound that had wakened me in West Los Angeles early that morning. There were human noises, too—sounds of movement among the trees.

"Stanley?" I said.

A man in a blue suit and a red hard hat stepped out from behind the blotched trunk of a sycamore. He was a big man, and he moved with a kind of clumsy lightness.

"Looking for somebody?" He had a quiet cool voice, which gave the effect of holding itself in reserve.

"Several people."

"I'm the only one around," he said pleasantly.

His heavy arms and thighs bulged through his business clothes. His face was wet, and there was dirt on his shoes. He took off his hard hat, wiping his face and forehead with a bandana handkerchief. His hair was gray and clipped short, like fur on a cannonball.

I walked toward him, into the skeletal shadow of the sycamore. The smoky moon was lodged in its top, segmented by small black branches. With a quick conjurer's motion, the big man produced a pack of cigarettes from his breast pocket and thrust it toward me.

"Smoke?"

"No thanks. I don't smoke."

"Don't smoke cigarettes, you mean?"

"I gave them up."

"What about cigars?"

"I never liked them," I said. "Are you taking a poll?"

"You might call it that." He smiled broadly, revealing several gold teeth. "How about cigarillos? Some people smoke them instead of cigarettes."

"I've noticed that."

"These people you say you're looking for, do any of them smoke cigarillos?"

"I don't think so." Then I remembered that Stanley Broadhurst did. "Why?"

"No reason, I'm just curious." He glanced up the mountainside. "That fire is starting to move. I don't like the feel of the wind. It has the feel of a Santa Ana."

"It was blowing down south early this morning."

"So I've heard. Are you from Los Angeles?"

"That's right." He seemed to have all the time he needed, but I was tired of fooling around with him. "My name is Archer. I'm a licensed private detective, employed by the Broadhurst family."

"I was wondering. I saw you come out of the stable."

"Stanley Broadhurst's car is in there."

"I know," he said. "Is Stanley Broadhurst one of the people you're looking for?"

"Yes, he is."

"License?"

I showed him my photostat.

"Well, I may be able to help you."

He turned abruptly and moved in among the trees along a rutted trail. I followed him. The leaves were so dry under my feet that it was like walking on cornflakes.

We came to an opening in the trees. The big sycamore which partly overarched it had been burned. Smoke was still rising from its charred branches and from the undergrowth behind it.

Near the middle of the open space there was a hole in the ground between three and four feet in diameter. A spade stood upright beside it in a pile of dirt and stones. Off to one side of the pile, a pickax lay on the ground. Its sharp tip seemed to have been dipped in dark red paint. Reluctantly I looked down into the hole.

In its shallow depth a man's body lay curled like a foetus, face upturned. I recognized his peppermint-striped shirt, glad rags to be buried in. And in spite of the dirt that stuffed his open mouth and clung to his eyes, I recognized Stanley Broadhurst, and I said so.

The big man absorbed the information quietly. "What was he doing here, do you know?"

"No. I don't. But I believe this is part of his family's ranch. You haven't explained what you're doing here."

"I'm with the Forest Service. My name's Joe Kelsey, I'm trying to find out what started this fire. And," he added deliberately, "I think I have found out. It seems to have flared up in this immediate area. I came across *this*, right there." He indicated a yellow plastic marker stuck in the burned-over ground a few feet from where we were standing. Then he produced a small aluminum evidence case and snapped it open. It contained a single half-burned cigarillo.

"Did Broadhurst smoke these?"

"I saw him smoke one this morning. You'll probably find the package in his clothes."

"Yeah, but I didn't want to move him until the coroner sees him. It looks as if I may have to, though."

He squinted uphill toward the fire. It blazed like a displaced sunset through the trees. The black silhouettes of men fighting it looked small and futile in spite of their tanker trucks and bulldozers. Off to the left the fire had spilled over the ridge and was pouring downhill like fuming acid eating the dry brush. Its smoke blew ahead of it and spread across the city toward the sea.

Kelsey took the spade and started to throw dirt into the hole, talking as he worked.

"I hate to bury a man twice, but it's better than letting him get roasted. The fire's coming back this way."

"Was he buried when you found him?"

"That's correct. But whoever buried him didn't do much of a job of covering up. I found the spade and the pick with the blood on it—and then the filled hole with loose dirt around. So I started digging. I didn't know what I was going to find. But I sort of had a feeling that it would be a dead man with a hole in his head."

Kelsey worked rapidly. The dirt covered Stanley's striped shirt and his upturned insulted face. Kelsey spoke to me over his shoulder:

"You mentioned that you were looking for several people. Who are the others?"

"The dead man's little boy is one. And there was a blond girl with him."

"So I've heard. Can you describe her?"

"Blue eyes, five foot six, 115 pounds, age about eighteen. Broadhurst's widow can tell you more about her. She's at the ranchhouse."

"Where's your car? I came out on a fire truck."

I told him that Stanley's mother had brought me in her pickup, and that she was in the cabin. Kelsey stopped spading dirt. His face was running with sweat, and mildly puzzled.

"What's she doing in there?"

"Resting."

"We're going to have to interrupt her rest."

Beyond the grove, in the unburned brush, the fire had

grown almost as tall as the trees. The air moved in spurts and felt like hot animal breath.

We ran away from it, with Kelsey carrying the spade and me carrying the bloody pick. The pick felt heavy by the time we reached the door of the cabin. I set it down and knocked on the door before I went in.

Mrs. Broadhurst sat up with a start. Her face was rosy. Sleep clung to her eyes and furred her voice:

"I must have dozed off, forgive me, but I had the sweetest dream. I spent—we spent our honeymoon here, you know, right in this cabin. It was during the war, quite early in the war, and traveling wasn't possible. I dreamed that I was on my honeymoon, and none of the bad things had happened."

Her half-dreaming eyes focused on my face and recognized the signs, which I couldn't conceal, of another bad thing that had happened. Then she saw Kelsey with the spade in his hands. He looked like a giant gravedigger blocking the light in the doorway.

Mrs. Broadhurst's normal expression, competent and cool and rather strained, forced itself down over her open face. She got up very quickly, and almost lost her balance.

"Mr. Kelsey? It's Mr. Kelsey, isn't it? What's happened?"

"We found your son, ma'am."

"Where is he? I want to talk to him."

Kelsey said in deep embarrassment: "I'm afraid that won't be possible, ma'am."

"Why? Has he gone somewhere?"

Kelsey gave me an appealing look. Mrs. Broadhurst walked toward him.

"What are you doing with that spade? That's my spade, isn't it?"

"I wouldn't know, ma'am."

She took it out of his hands. "It most certainly is. I bought it for my own use last spring. Where did you get hold of it, from my gardener?"

"I found it in the clump of trees yonder." Kelsey gestured in that direction."

"What on earth was it doing there?"

Kelsey's mouth opened and shut. He was unwilling or afraid to tell her that Stanley was dead. I moved toward her and told her that her son had been killed, probably with a pickax.

I stepped outside and showed her the pickax. "Is this yours, too?"

She looked at it dully. "Yes, I believe it is."

Her voice was a low monotone, hardly more than a whisper. She turned and began to run toward the burning trees, stumbling in her high-heeled riding boots. Kelsey ran after her, heavily and rapidly like a bear. He took her around the waist and lifted her off her feet and turned her around away from the fire.

She kicked and shouted: "Let me go. I want my son."

"He's in a hole in the ground, ma'am. You can't go in there now, nobody can. But his body won't burn, it's safe underground."

She twisted in his arms and struck at his face. He dropped her. She fell in the brown weeds, beating at the ground and crying that she wanted her son.

I got down on my knees beside her and talked her into getting up and coming with us. We went down the trail in single file, with Kelsey leading the way and Mrs. Broadhurst between us. I stayed close behind her, in case she tried to do something wild like throwing herself down the side of the bluff. She moved passively with her head down, like a prisoner between guards.

# III

Kelsey carried the spade in one hand and the bloody pickax in the other. He tossed them into the back of the truck and helped Mrs. Broadhurst into the cab. I took the wheel.

She rode between us in silence, looking straight ahead along the stony road. She didn't utter a sound until we turned at her mailbox into the avocado grove. Then she let out a gasp which sounded as if she'd been holding her breath all the way down the canyon.

"Where is my grandson?"

"We don't know," Kelsey said.

"You mean that he's dead, too. Is that what you mean?"

Kelsey took refuge in a southwestern drawl which helped to soften his answer. "I mean that nobody's seen hide nor hair of him, ma'am."

"What about the blond girl? Where is she?"

"I only wish I knew."

"Did she kill my son?"

"It looks like it, ma'am. It looks like she hit him over the head with that pickax."

"And buried him?"

"He was buried when I found him."

"How could a girl do that?"

"It was a shallow grave, ma'am. Girls can do about anything boys can do when they set their minds to it."

A whine had entered Kelsey's drawl under the pressure of her questioning and the greater pressure of her fear. Impatiently she turned to me:

"Mr. Archer, is my grandson Ronny dead?"

"No." I said it with some force, to beat back the possibility that he was.

"Has that girl abducted him?"

"It's a good assumption to work on. But they may simply have run away from the fire."

"You know that isn't so." She sounded as if she had crossed a watershed in her life, beyond which nothing good could happen.

I stopped the pickup behind my car on the driveway. Kelsey got out and offered to help Mrs. Broadhurst. She pushed his hands away. But she climbed out like a woman overtaken by sudden age.

"You can park the truck in the carport," she said to me. "I don't like to leave it out in the sun."

"Excuse me," Kelsey said, "but you might as well leave it out here. The fire's coming down the canyon, and it may get to your house. I'll help you bring your things out if you like, and drive one of your cars."

Mrs. Broadhurst cast a slow look around the house and its surroundings. "There's never been fire in this canyon in my lifetime."

"That means it's ripe," he said. "The brush up above is fifteen and twenty feet deep, and as dry as a chip. This is a fifty-year fire. It could take your house unless the wind changes again."

"Then let it."

Jean came to meet us at the door, a little tardily, as if she dreaded what we were going to say. I told her that her husband was dead and that her son was missing. The two women exchanged a questioning look, as if each of them was looking into the other for the source of all their troubles. Then they came together in the doorway and stood in each other's arms.

Kelsey came up behind me on the porch. He tipped his hard hat and spoke to the younger woman, who was facing him over Mrs. Broadhurst's shoulder.

"Mrs. Stanley Broadhurst?"

"Yes."

"I understand you can give me a description of the girl who was with your husband."

"I can try."

She separated herself from the older woman, who went into the house. Jean rested on the railing near the hummingbird feeder. A hummingbird buzzed her. She moved to the other side of the porch and sat on a canvas chair, leaning forward in a strained position and repeating for Kelsey her description of the blue-eyed blond girl with the strange eyes.

And you say she's eighteen or so?"

Jean nodded. Her reactions were quick but mechanical, as if her mind was focused somewhere else.

"Is—was your husband interested in her, Mrs. Broadhurst?"

"Obviously he was," she said in a dry bitter voice. "But I gathered she was more interested in my son."

"Interested in what way?"

"I don't know what way."

Kelsey switched to a less sensitive line of questioning. "How was she dressed?"

"Last night she had on a sleeveless yellow dress. I didn't see her this morning."

"I did," I put in. "She was still wearing the yellow dress. I assume you'll be giving all this to the police."

"Yessir, I will. Right now I want to talk to the gardener. He may be able to tell us how that spade and pick got up on the mountain. What's his name?"

"Frederick Snow—we call him Fritz," Jean said. "He isn't here."

"Where is he?"

"He rode Stanley's old bicycle down the road about half an hour ago, when the wind changed. He wanted to take the Cadillac, but I told him not to."

"Doesn't he have a car of his own?"

"I believe he has some kind of jalopy."

"Where is it?"

She shrugged slightly. "I don't know."

"Where was Fritz this morning?"

"I can't tell you. He seems to have been the only one here for most of the morning."

Kelsey's face saddened. "How does he get along with your little boy?"

"Fine." Then his meaning entered her eyes and darkened them. She shook her head as if to deny the meaning, dislodge the darkness. "Fritz wouldn't hurt Ronny, he's always been kind to him."

"Then why did he take off?"

"He said that he was worried about his mother. But I think he was scared of the fire. He was almost crying."

"So am I scared of the fire," Kelsey said. "It's why I'm in this business."

"Are you a policeman?" Jean said. "Is that why you're asking me all these questions?"

"I'm with the Forest Service, assigned to investigate the causes of fires." He dug into an inside pocket, produced the aluminum evidence case, and showed her the half-burned cigarillo. "Does this look like one of your husband's?"

"Yes it does. But surely you're not trying to prove that he started it. What's the point if he's dead?" Her voice had risen a little out of control.

"The point is this. Whoever killed him probably made him drop this in the dry grass. That means they're legally and financially responsible for the fire. And it's my job to establish the facts. Where does this man Snow live?"

"With his mother. I think their house is quite near here. My mother-in-law can tell you. Mrs. Snow used to work for her."

We found Mrs. Broadhurst in the living room, standing at a corner window which framed the canyon. The room was so large that she looked small at the far end of it. She didn't turn when we moved up to her.

She was watching the progress of the fire. It was in the head of the canyon now, slipping downhill like a loose volcano, and spouting smoke and sparks above the treetops. The eucalyptus trees behind the house were momentarily blanched by the gusty wind. The blackbirds and pigeons had all gone.

Kelsey and I exchanged glances. It was time that we went, too. I let him do the talking, since it was his territory and his kind of emergency. He addressed the woman's unmoving back:

"Mrs. Broadhurst? Don't you think we better get out of here?"

"You go. Please do go. I'm staying, for the present."

"You can't do that. That fire is really on its way."

She turned on him. Her face had sunk on its bones; it made her look old and formidable.

"Don't tell me what I can or can't do. I was born in this house. I've never lived anywhere else. If the house goes, I might as well go with it. Everything else has gone."

"You're not serious, ma'am."

"Am I not?"

"You don't want to get yourself burned, do you?"

"I think I'd almost welcome the flames. I'm very cold, Mr. Kelsey."

Her tone was tragic, but there was a note of hysteria running through it, or something worse. A stubbornness which could mean that her mind had slipped a notch, and stuck at a crazy angle.

Kelsey cast a desperate look around the room. It was full of Victorian furniture, with dark Victorian portraits on the walls, and several cabinets full of stuffed native birds under glass.

"Don't you want to save your things, ma'am? Your silver and bird specimens and pictures and mementos?"

She spread her hands in a hopeless gesture as if everything had long since run through them. Kelsey was getting nowhere trying to sell her back the pieces of her life.

I said:

"We need your help, Mrs. Broadhurst."

She looked at me in mild surprise. "My help?"

"Your grandon is missing. This is a bad time and place for a little boy to be lost—"

"It's a judgment on me."

"That's nonsense."

"So I'm talking nonsense, am I?"

I disregarded her angry question. "Fritz the gardener may know where he is. I believe you know his mother. Is that correct?"

Her answer came slowly. "Edna Snow used to be my housekeeper. You can't seriously believe that Fritz—" she stopped, unwilling to put her question into words.

"It would be a great help if you'd come along and talk to Fritz and his mother."

"Very well, I will."

We drove out the lane like a funeral cortege. Mrs. Broadhurst was leading in her Cadillac. Jean and I came next in the green Mercedes. Kelsey brought up the rear, driving the pickup.

I looked back from the mailbox. Sparks and embers were blowing down the canyon, plunging into the trees behind the house like bright exotic birds taking the place of the birds that had flown.

# TILLIE OLSEN

# Hey Sailor, What Ship?

## 1

The grimy light; the congealing smell of cigarettes that had been smoked long ago and of liquor that had been drunk long ago; the boasting, cursing, wheedling, cringing voices, and the greasy feel of the bar as he gropes for his glass.

*Hey Sailor, what ship?*

His face flaring in the smoky mirror. The veined gnawing. Wha's it so quiet for? Hey, hit the tune-box. (*Lennie and Helen and the kids.*) Wha time's it anyway? Gotta . . .

Gotta something. Stand watch? No, din't show last night, ain't gonna show tonight, gonna sign off. Out loud: Hell with ship. You got any friends, ship? then hell with your friends. That right, Deeck? And he turns to Deeck for approval, but Deeck is gone. Where's Deeck? Givim five bucks and he blows.

All right, says a nameless one, you're loaded. How's about a buck?

Less one buck. Company. But he too is gone.

And he digs into his pockets to see how much he has left.

Right breast pocket, a crumpled five. Left pants pocket, three, no, four collapsed one-ers. Left jacket pocket, pawn ticket, Manila; card, "When in Managua it's Marie's for

Hospitality"; union book; I.D. stuff; trip card; two ones, one five, accordion-pleated together. Right pants pocket, jingle money. Seventeen bucks. And the hands tremble.

Where'd it all go? and he lurches through the past. One hundred and fifty draw yesterday. No, day before, maybe even day 'fore that. Seven for a bottle when cashed the check, twenty to Blackie, thirty-three back to Goldballs, cab to Frisco, thirty-eight, thirty-nine for the jacket and the kicks (new jacket, new kicks, look good to see Lennie and Helen and the kids), twenty-four smackers dues and ten-dollar fine. That fine. . . .

*Hey,* to the barkeep, one comin' up. And he swizzles it down, pronto. Twenty and seven and thirty-three and thirty-nine. Ten-dollar fine and five to Frenchy at the hall and drinkin' all night with Johnson, don't know how much, and on the way to the paymaster. . . .

The paymaster. Out loud, in angry mimicry, with a slight scandihoovian accent, to nobody, nobody at all: Whaddaya think of that? Hafta be able to sign your name or we can't give you your check. Too stewed to sign your name, he says, no check.

Only seventeen bucks. Hey, to the barkeep, how 'bout advancing me fifty? Hunching over the bar, confidential, so he sees the bottles glistening in the depths. See? and he ruffles in his pockets for the voucher, P.F.E., Michael Jackson, thass me, five hundred and twenty-seven and eleven cents. You don' know me? Been here all night, all day. Bell knows me. Get Bell. Been drinkin' here twenty-three years, every time hit Frisco. Ask Bell.

But Bell sold. Forgot, forgot. Took his cushion and moved to Petaluma to raise chickens. Well hell with you. Got any friends? then hell with your friends. Go to Pearl's. (*Not Lennie and Helen and the kids?*) See what's new, or old. Got 'nuf lettuce for *them* babies. But the idea is visual, not physical. Get a bottle first. And he waits for the feeling good that should be there, but there is none, only a sickness lurking.

The Bulkhead sign bile green in the rain. Rain and the street clogged with cars, going-home-from-work cars. Screw 'em all. He starts across. Screech, screech, screech. Brakes jammed on for a block back. M. Norbert Jacklebaum makes 'em stop; said without glee. On to Pearl's. But someone is calling. Whitey, Whitey, get in here you stumblebum. And it is Lennie, a worn likeness of Lennie, so changed he gets in all right, but does not ask questions or answer them. (Are you on a ship or on the beach? How long was the trip? You sick, man, or just stewed? Only three or four days and you're feeling like this? *No*, no stopping for a bottle or to buy presents.)

He only sits while the sickness crouches underneath, waiting to spring, and it muddles in his head, *going to see Lennie and Helen and the kids, no presents for 'em, an' don't even feel good.*

*Hey Sailor, what ship?*

## 2

And so he gets there after all, four days and everything else too late. It is an old peaked house on a hill and he has imaged and entered it over and over again, in a thousand various places a thousand various times: on watch and over chow, lying on his bunk or breezing with the guys; from sidewalk beds and doorway shelters, in flophouses and jails; sitting silent at union meetings or waiting in the places one waits, or listening to the Come to Jesus boys.

The stairs are innumerable and he barely makes it to the top. Helen (Helen? so . . . grayed?), Carol, Allie, surging upon him. A fever of hugging and kissing. 'Sabout time, shrills Carol over and over again. 'Sabout time.

*Who is real and who is not?* Jeannie, taller than Helen suddenly, just standing there, watching. I'm in first grade now, yells Allie, now you can fix my dolly crib, Whitey, it's smashted.

You hit it just right. We've got stew, pressure cooker stuff, but your favorite anyway. How long since you've eaten? And Helen looks at him, kisses him again, and begins to cry.

Mother! orders Jeannie, and marches her into the kitchen.

Whassmatter Helen? One look at me, she begins to cry. She's glad to see you, you S.O.B.

Whassmatter her? She don't look so good.

You don't look so good either, Lennie says grimly. Better sit for a while.

Mommy oughta quit work, volunteers Carol; she's tired. All the time.

Whirl me round like you always do, Whitey, whirl me round, begs Allie.

Where did you go this time, Whitey? asks Carol. Thought you were going to send me stamps for my collection. Why didn't you come Christmas? Can you help me make a puppet stage?

Cut it, kids, not so many questions, orders Lennie, going up the stairs to wash. Whitey's got to take it easy. We'll hear about everything after dinner.

Your shoes are shiny, says Allie. Becky in my class got new shoes too, Mary Janes, but they're fuzzy. And she kneels down to pat his shoes.

Forgotten, how big the living room was. (And is he really here?) Carol reads the funnies on the floor, her can up in the air. Allie inspects him gravely. You got a new hurt on your face, Whitey. Sing a song, or say Thou Crown 'n Deep. And after dinner can I bounce on you?

Not so many questions, repeats Carol.

Whitey's gonna sit here. . . . Should go in the kitchen. Help your mommy.

Angry from the kitchen: Well, I don't care. I'm calling Marilyn and tell her not to come; we'll do our homework over there. I'm certainly not going to take a chance and let her come over here.

Shhh, Jeannie, shhh. He beg that, or Helen? The windows are blind with steam, all hidden behind them the city, the bay, the ships. And is it chow time already? He starts up to go, but it seems he lurched and fell, for the sickness springs at last and consumes him. And now Allie is sitting with him. C'mon, sit up and eat, Whitey, Mommy says you have to eat; I'll eat too. Perched beside him, pretty as you please. I'll take a forkful and you take a forkful. You're sloppy, Whitey—for it trickles down his chin. It does not taste; the inside of him burns. She chatters and then the plate is gone and now the city sparkles at him through the windows. Helen and Lennie are sitting there and somebody who looks like somebody he knows.

Chris, reminds Lennie. Don't you remember Chris, the grocery boy when we lived on Aerial way? We told you he's a M.D. now. Fat and a poppa and smug; aren't you smug, Chris?

I almost shipped with you once, Whitey. Don't you remember?

(Long ago. Oh yes, oh yes, but there was no permit to

be had; and even if there had been, by that time I didn't
have no drag.) Aloud: I remember. You still got the itch?
That's why you came round, to get fixed up with a trip
card?

I came around to look at you. But that was all he was
doing, just sitting there and looking.

Whassmatter? Don't like my looks? Get too beautiful
since you last saw me? Handsome new nose 'n everything.

You got too beautiful. Where can I take him, Helen?

Can't take me no place. M. Norbert Jacklebaum's fine.

You've got to get up anyhow, Whitey, so I can make up
the couch. Go on, go upstairs with Chris. You're in luck, I
even found a clean sheet.


He settles back down on the couch, the lean scarred
arms bent under his head for a pillow, the muscles ridged
like rope.

He's a lousy doc. Affectionately. Gives me a shot of B-1,
sleeping pills, and some bum advice. . . . Whaddaya think
of that, he remembered me. Thirteen years and he remembers me.

How could he help remembering you with all the hell his
father used to raise cause he'd forget his deliveries listening
to your lousy stories? You were his hero. . . . How do you
like the fire?

Your wood, Whitey, says Helen. Still the stuff you
chopped three years back. Needs restacking though.

Get right up and do it. . . . Whatdja call him for?

You scared us. Don't forget, your last trip up here was
for five weeks in Marine Hospital.

We never saw it hit you like this before, says Lennie.
After a five- six-week tear maybe, but you say this was a
couple days. You were really out.

Just catching up on my sleep, tha's all.

There is a new picture over the lamp. Bleached hills, a
fresh-ploughed field, red horses and a blue-overalled figure.

I got a draw coming. More'n five hundred. How's financial situation round here?

We're eating.

Allie say she want me to fix something? Or was it Carol?
Those kids are sure. . . . A year'n a half. . . . An effort to
talk, for the sleeping pills are already gripping him, and the
languid fire, and the rain that has started up again and

cannot pierce the windows. How *you* feeling, Helen? She looks more like Helen now.

Keeping my head above water. She would tell him later. She always told him later, when he would be helping in the kitchen maybe, and suddenly it would come out, how she really was and what was really happening, sometimes things she wouldn't even tell Lennie. And this time, the way she looked, the way Lennie looked. . . .

Allie is on the stairs: I had a bad dream, Mommy. Let me stay here till Jeannie comes to bed with me, Mommy. By Whitey.

What was your bad dream, sweetheart?

Lovingly she puts her arms around his neck, curls up. I was losted, she whispers, and instantly is asleep.

He starts as if he has been burned, and quick lest he wake her, begins stroking her soft hair. It is destroying, dissolving him utterly, this helpless warmth against him, this feel of a child—lost country to him and unattainable.

Sure were a lot of kids begging, he says aloud. I think it's worse.

Korea? asks Len.

Never got ashore in Korea. Yokohama, Cebu, Manila. (The begging children and the lost, the thieving children and the children who were sold.) And he strokes, strokes Allie's soft hair as if the strokes would solidify, dense into a protection.

We lay around Pusan six weeks. Forty-three days on that tub no bigger'n this house and they wouldn't give us no leave ashore. Forty-three days. Len, I never had a drop, you believe me, Len?

Felt good most of this trip, Len, just glad to be sailing again, after Pedro. Always a argument. Somebody says, Christ it's cold, colder'n a whore's heart, and somebody jumps right in and says, colder'n a whore's heart, hell, you ever in Kobe and broke and Kumi didn't give you five yen? And then it starts. Both sides.

Len and Helen like those stories. Tell another. Effort.

You should hear this Stover. Ask him, was you ever in England? and he claps his hands to his head and says, was I ever in England, Oh boy, was I ever in England, those limeys, they beat you with bottles. Ask him, was you ever in Marseilles and he claps his hands to his head and says, was I ever in Marseilles, Oh boy, was I ever in Marseilles, them frogs, they kick you with spikes in their shoes. Ask him, was you ever in Shanghai, and he says, was I ever in Shanghai, was I ever in Shanghai, man, they throw the crockery and the stools at you. Thass everyplace you mention, a different kind of beating.

There was this kid on board, Howie Adams. Gotta bring him up here. Told him 'bout you. Best people in the world, I says, always open house. Best kid. Not like those scenery bums and cherry pickers we got sailing nowadays. Guess what, they made me ship's delegate.

Well, why not? asks Helen; you were probably the best man on board.

A tide of peaceful drowsiness washes over the tumult in him; he is almost asleep, though the veined brown hand still tremblingly strokes, strokes Allie's soft pale hair.

Is that Helen? No, it is Jeannie, so much like Helen of years ago, suddenly there under the hall light, looking in at them all, her cheeks glistening from the rain.

Never saw so many peaceful wrecks in my life. Her look is loving. That's what I want to be when I grow up, just a peaceful wreck holding hands with other peaceful wrecks (For Len and Helen are holding hands). We really fixed Mr. Nickerson. Marilyn did my English, I did her algebra, and her brother Tommy, wrote for us "I will not" five hundred times; then we just tagged on "talk in class, talk in class, talk in class."

She drops her books, kneels down beside Whitey, and using his long ago greeting asks softly, Hey Sailor, what ship?, then turns to her parents. Study in contrasts, Allie's face and Whitey's, where's my camera? Did you tell Whitey I'm graduating in three weeks, do you think you'll be here then, Whitey, and be . . . all right? I'll give you my diploma and write in your name so you can pretend you got through junior high, too. Allie's sure glad you came.

And without warning, with a touch so light, so faint, it seems to breathe against his cheek, she traces a scar. That's a new one, isn't it? Allie noticed. She asked me, does it hurt? Does it?

He stops stroking Allie's hair a moment, starts up again desperately, looks so ill, Helen says sharply: It's late. Better go to bed, Jeannie, there's school tomorrow.

It's late, it's early. Kissing him, Helen, Lennie. Good night. Shall I take my stinky little sister upstairs to bed

with me whatever she's doing down here, or shall I leave
her for one of you strong men to carry?

Leaning from the middle stair: didn't know you were
sick, Whitey, thought you were like . . . some of the other
times. From the top stair: see you later, alligators.

Most he wants alone now, alone and a drink, perhaps
sleep. And they know. We're going to bed now too. Six
comes awful early.

So he endures Helen's kiss too, and Len's affectionate
poke. And as Len carries Allie up the stairs, the fire leaps
up, kindles Len's shadow so that it seems a dozen bent men
cradle a child up endless stairs, while the rain traces on the
windows, beseechingly, ceaselessly, like seeking fingers of
the blind.

*Hey Sailor, what ship? Hey Sailor, what ship?*

## 3

In his sleep he speaks often and loudly, sometimes moans,
and toward morning begins the trembling. He wakes into
an unshared silence he does not recognize, accustomed so
to the various voices of the sea, the multi-pitch of those
with whom sleep as well as work and food is shared, the
throb of engines, churn of the propeller; or hazed through
drink, the noises of the street, or the thin walls like ears—
magnifying into lives as senseless as one's own.

Here there is only the whisper of the clock (motor by
which this house runs now) and the sounds of oneself.

The trembling will not cease. In the kitchen there is a
note:

*Bacon and eggs in the icebox and coffee's made. The kids
are coming straight home from school to be with you.
DON'T go down to the front, Lennie'll take you tomorrow.
Love.*

Love.

The row of cans on the cupboard shelves is thin. So
things are still bad, he thinks, no money for stocking up.
He opens all the doors hopefully, but if there is a bottle, it
is hidden. A long time he stares at the floor, goes out into

the yard where fallen rain beads the grasses that will be
weeds soon enough, comes back, stares at his dampened
feet, stares at the floor some more (needs scrubbing, and
the woodwork can stand some too; well, maybe after I feel
better), but there are no dishes in the sink, it is all cleaner
than he expected.

Upstairs, incredibly, the beds are made, no clothes
crumpled on the floor. Except in Jeannie's and Allie's room:
there, as remembered, the dust feathers in the corners
and dolls sprawl with books, records, and underwear.
Guess she'll never get it clean. And up rises his old
vision, of how he will return here, laden with groceries, no
one in the littered house, and quickly, before they come,
straighten the upstairs (the grime in the washbasin), clean
the downstairs, scrub the kitchen floor, wash the hills of
dishes, put potatoes in and light the oven, and when they
finally troop in say, calmly, Helen, the house is clean, and
there's steak for dinner.

Whether it is this that hurts in his stomach or the burning chill that will not stop, he dresses himself hastily, argu-
ing with the new shoes that glint with a life all their own.
On his way out, he stops for a minute to gloss his hand
over the bookcase. Damn good paint job, he says out loud,
if I say so myself. Still stands up after fourteen years. Real
good that red backing Helen liked so much 'cause it shows
above the books.

*Hey Sailor, what ship?*

## 4

It is five days before he comes again. A cabbie precedes
him up the stairs, loaded with bundles. Right through, right
into the kitchen, man, directs Whitey, feeling good, oh
quite obviously feeling good. The shoes are spotted now, he
wears a torn Melton in place of the new jacket. Groceries,
he announces heavily, indicating the packages plopped
down. Steak. Whatever you're eating, throw it out.

Didn't I tell you they're a good-looking bunch? triumphantly indicating around the table. 'Cept that Lennie
hyena over there. Go on, man, take the whole five smackers.

Don't let him go, Whitey, I wanta ride in the cab, screams Allie.

To the top of the next hill and back, it's a windy curly round and round road, yells Carol.

I'll go too, says Jeannie.

*Shut up*, Lennie explodes, let the man go, he's working. Sit down, kids. Sit down, Whitey.

Set another plate, Jeannie, says Helen.

An' bring glasses. Got coke for the kids. We gonna have a drink.

I want a cab ride, Allie insists.

Wait till your mean old bastard father's not lookin'. Then we'll go.

Watch the language, Whitey, there's a gentleman present, says Helen. Finish your plate, Allie.

Thass right. Know who the gen'lmun is? I'm the gen'lmun. The world, says Marx, is divided into two classes. . .

Seafaring gen'lmun and shoreside bastards, choruses Lennie with him.

Why, Daddy! says Jeannie.

You're a mean ole bassard father, says Allie.

Thass right, tell him off, urges Whitey. Hell with waitin' for glasses. Down the ol' hatch.

*My* class is divided by marks, says Carol, giggling helplessly at her own joke, and anyway what about ladies? Where's *my* drink? Down the hatch.

I got presents, kids. In the kitchen.

Where they'll stay, warns Helen, till after dinner. Just keep sitting.

Course Jeannie over there doesn't care 'bout a present. She's too grown up. Royal highness doesn't even kiss old Whitey, just slams a plate at him.

Fork, knife, spoon too, says Jeannie, why don't you use them?

Good chow, Helen. But he hardly eats, and as they clear the table, he lays down a tenner.

All right, sailor, says Lennie, put your money back.

I'll take it, says Carol, if it's an orphan.

If you get into the front room quick, says Lennie, you won't have to do the dishes.

Who gives a shit about the dishes?

Watch it, says Helen.

Whenja start doin' dishes in this house after dinner anyway?

Since we got organized, says Lennie, always get things done when they're supposed to be. Organized the life out of ourselves. That's what's the matter with Helen.

Well, when you work, Helen starts to explain.

Lookit Daddy kiss Mommy.

Give me my present and whirl me, Whitey, whirl me, demands Allie.

No whirling. Jus' sat down, honey. How'd it be if I bounce you? Lef' my ol' lady in New Orleans with twenny-four kids and a can of beans.

Guess you think 'cause I'm ten I'm too big to bounce any more, says Carol.

Bounce everybody. Jeannie. Your mom. Even Lennie.

> What is life
> Without a wife (bounce)
> And a home (bounce bounce)
> Without a baby?

Hey, Helen, bring in those presents. Tell Jeannie, don't come in here, don't get a present. Jeannie, play those marimba records. Want marimba. Feel good, sure feel good. Hey, Lennie, get your wild ass in here, got things to tell you. Leave the women do the work.

Wild ass, giggles Allie.

Jeannie gets mad when you talk like that, says Carol. Give us our presents and let's have a cab ride and tell us about the time you were torpedoed.

Tell us Crown 'n Deep.

Go tell yourself. I'm gonner have a drink.

Down the hatch, Whitey.

Down the hatch.

Better taper off, guy, says Lennie, coming in. We want to have an evening.

Tell Helen bring the presents. She don't hafta be jealous. I got money for her. Helen likes money.

Upstairs, says Helen, they'll get their presents upstairs. After they're ready for bed. There's school tomorrow.

First we'll get them after dinner and now after we're ready for bed. That's not fair, wails Allie.

I never showed him my album yet, says Carol. He never said Crown 'n Deep yet.

It isn't fair. We never had our cab ride.

Whitey'll be here tomorrow, says Helen.

Maybe he won't, says Carol. He's got a room rented, he told me. Six weeks' rent in advance and furnished with eighteen cans of beans and thirty-six cans of sardines. All shored up, says Whitey. Somebody called Deeck stays there too.

Lef' my wile ass in New Orleans, twenty-four kids and a present of beans, chants Allie, bouncing herself up and down on the couch. And it's not *fair*.

Say good night to them, Whitey, they'll come down in their nightgowns for a good-night kiss later.

Go on, kids. Mind your momma, don't be like me. An' here's a dollar for you an' a dollar for you. An' a drink for me.

But Lennie has taken the bottle. Whass matter, doncha like to see me feelin' good? Well, screw you, brother, I'm supplied, and he pulls a pint out of his pocket.

Listen, Whitey, says Jeannie, I've got some friends coming over and . . . Whitey, please, they're not used to your kind of language.

That so? 'Scuse me, your royal highness. Here's ten dollars, your royal highness. Help you forgive?

Please go sit in the kitchen. Please, Daddy, take him in the kitchen with you.

Jeannie, says Lennie, give him back the money.

He gave it to me, it's mine.

Give it back.

All right. Flinging it down, running up the stairs.

Quit it, Whitey, says Lennie.

Quit what?

Throwing your goddam money around. Where do you think you are, down on the front?

'S better down on the front. You're gettin' holier than the dago pope.

I mean it, guy. And tone down that language. Let's have the bottle.

*No.* Into the pocket. Do *you* good to feel good for a change. You 'n Helen look like you been through the meat grinder.

Silence.

Gently: Tell me about the trip, Whitey.

Good trip. Most of the time. 'Lected me ship's delegate.

You told us.

Tell you 'bout that kid, Howie? Best kid. Got my gear off the ship and lef' it down at the hall for me.

Whaddaya think of that?

(Oh feeling good, come back, come back.)

Jeannie in her hat and coat. Stiffly. Thank you for the earrings, Whitey.

Real crystals. Best . . . Lennie, 'm gonna give her ten dollars. For treat her friends. After all, ain't she my wife?

Whitey, do I have to hear that story again? I was four years old.

Again? (He had told the story so often, as often as anyone would listen, whenever he felt good, and always as he told it, the same shy happiness would wing through him, how when she was four, she had crawled into bed beside him one morning, announcing triumphantly to her mother: I'm married to Whitey now, I don't have to sleep by myself any more.) Sorry, royal highness won't mention it. How's watch I gave you, remember?

(Not what he means to say at all. Remember the love I gave you, the worship offered, the toys I mended and made, the questions answered, the care for you, the pride in you.)

I lost the watch, remember? 'I was too young for such expensive presents.' You keep talking about it because that's the only reason you give presents, to buy people to be nice to you and to yak about the presents when you're drunk. Here's your earrings too. I'm going outside to wait for my friends.

Jeannie! It is Helen, back down with kids. Jeannie, come into the kitchen with me.

Jeannie's gonna get heck, says Carol. Geeeee, down the hatch. Wish *I* could swallow so long. Is my dresser set solid gold like it looks?

Kiss the dolly you gave me, says Allie. She's your grandchild now. You kiss her too, Daddy. I bet she was the biggest dolly in the store.

Your dolly can't talk. Thass good, honey, that she can't talk.

Here's my album, Whitey. It's got a picture of you. Is that really you, Whitey? It don't look like. . . .

Don't look, he says to himself, closing his eyes. Don't look. But it is indelible. Under the joyful sun, proud sea, proud ship as background, the proud young man, glistening hair and eyes, joyful body, face open to life, unlined.

Sixteen? Seventeen? Close it up, he says, M. Norbert Jacklebaum never saw the guy. Quit punchin' me.

Nobody's punchin' you, Whitey, says Allie. You're feeling your face.

*Tracing the scars, the pits and lines, the battered nose; seeking to find.*

Your name's Michael Jackson, Whitey, why do you always say Jacklebaum? marvels Allie.

Tell Crown 'n Deep. I try to remember it and I never can, Carol says, softly. Neither can Jeannie. Tell Crown 'n Deep, tell how you learnt it. If you feel like. Please.

Oh yes, he feels like. *When there is November in my soul,* he begins. No, wrong one.

Taking the old proud stance. The Valedictory, written the dawn 'fore he was executed by Jose Rizal, national hero of the Philippines. Taught me by Li'l Joe Roco, not much taller'n you, Jeannie, my first shipmate.

I'm Carol, not Jeannie.

Li'l Joe. Never got back home, they were puttin' the hatch covers on and . . . I only say it when it's special. Jose Rizal: El Ultimo Adiós. Known as The Valedictory, 1896.

> *Land I adore, farewell. . . .*
> *Our forfeited garden of Eden,*
> *Joyous I yield up for thee my sad life*
> *And were it far brighter,*
> *Young or rose-strewn, still would I give it.*
>
> *Vision I followed from afar,*
> *Desire that spurred on and consumed me,*
> *Beautiful it is to fall,*
> *That the vision may rise to fulfillment.*

Go on, Whitey.

> *Little will matter, my country,*
> *That thou shouldst forget me.*
> *I shall be speech in thy ears, fragrance and color,*
> *Light and shout and loved song. . . .*

Inaudible.

> *O crown and deep of my sorrows,*
> *I am leaving all with thee, my friends, my love,*
> *Where I go are no tyrants. . . .*

He stands there, swaying. Say good night, says Lennie. Whitey'll tell it all some other time. . . . Here, guy, sit down.

And in the kitchen.

You know how he talks. How can you let him? In front of the little kids.

They don't hear the words, they hear what's behind them. There are worse words than cuss words, there are words that hurt. When Whitey talks like that, it's everyday words; the men he lives with talk like that, that's all.

Well, not the kind of men I want to know. I don't go over to anybody's house and hear words like that.

Jeannie, who are you kidding? You kids use them all.

That's different, that's being grown-up, like smoking. And he's so drunk. Why didn't Daddy let me keep the ten dollars? It would mean a lot to me, and it doesn't mean anything to him.

It's his money. He worked for it, it's the only power he has. We don't take Whitey's money.

Oh no. Except when he gives it to you.

When he was staying with us, when they were rocking chair, unemployment checks, it was different. He was sober. It was his share.

He's just a Howard Street wino now—why don't you and Daddy kick him out of the house? He doesn't belong here.

Of course he belongs here, he's a part of us, like family. . . . Jeannie, this is the only house in the world he can come into and be around people without having to pay.

Somebody who brings presents and whirls you around and expects you to jump for his old money.

Remember how good he's been to you. To us. Jeannie, he was only a few years older than you when he started going to sea.

Now you're going to tell me the one about how he saved Daddy's life in the strike in 1934.

He knows more about people and places than almost anyone I've ever known. You can learn from him.

When's he like that anymore? He's just a Howard Street wino, that's all.

Jeannie, I care you should understand. You think Mr. Norris is a tragedy, you feel sorry for him because he talks

intelligent and lives in a nice house and has quiet drunks.
You've got to understand.

Just a wino. Even if it's whisky when he's got the money.
Which isn't for long.

To understand.

*In the beginning there had been youth and the joy of
raising hell and that curious inability to take a whore unless he were high with drink.*

*And later there were memories to forget, dreams to be
stifled, hopes to be murdered.*

Know who was the ol' man on the ship? Blackie Karns,
Kissass Karns hisself.

Started right when you did, Whitey.

Oh yes. (A few had nimbly, limberly clambered up.)
Remember in the war he was the only one of us would
wear his braid uptown? That one year I made mate? Know
how to deal with you, Jackson, he says. No place for you
on the ships any more, he says. My asshole still knows
more than all of you put together, I says.

What was it all about, Whitey?

Don't remember. Rotten feed. Bring him up a plate and
say, eat it yourself. Nobody gonna do much till we get
better. We got better.

This kid, overtime comin' to him. Didn't even wanta
beef about it. I did it anyway. Got fined by the union for
takin' it up. M. Norbert Jacklebaum fined by the union,
"conduct unbefitting ship's delegate" says the Patrolman,
"not taking it up through proper channels." (His old fine
talent for mimicry jutting through the blurred-together
words.)

These kids, these cherry pickers, they don't realize how
we got what we got. Beginnin' to lose it, too. Think anybody backed me up, Len? Just this Howie and a scenery
bum, Goldballs, gonna write a book. Have you in it, Jackson, he says, you're a real salt.

*Understand. The death of the brotherhood. Once, once
an injury to one is an injury to all. Once, once they had to
live for each other. And whoever came off the ship fat
shared, because that was the only way of survival for all of
them, the easy sharing, the knowing that when you needed,
waiting for a trip card to come up, you'd be staked.*

*Now it was a dwindling few, and more and more of*

*them winos, who shipped sometimes or had long ago ir-*
*revocably lost their book for nonpayment of dues.*

Hey, came here to feel good. Down the hatch. Hell with
you. You got any friends? Hell with your friends.

Helen is back. So you still remember El Ultimo, Whitey.
Remember when we first heard Joe recite it?

I remember.

*Remember too much, too goddam much. For twenty-*
*three years, the water shifting: many faces, many places.*

*But more and more, certain things the same. The gin*
*mills and the cathouses. The calabozas and jails and stock-*
*ades. More and more New York and Norfolk and New*
*Orleans and Pedro and Frisco and Seattle like the foreign*
*ports: docks, clip joints, hockshops, cathouses, skid rows,*
*the Law and the Wall: only so far shall you go and no*
*further, uptown forbidden, not your language, not your*
*people, not your country.*

*Added sometimes now, the hospital.*

What's going to happen with you, Whitey?

What I care? Nobody hasta care what happens to M.
Jacklebaum.

How can we help caring, Whitey? Jesus, man, you're a
chunk of our lives.

Shove it, Lennie. So you're a chunk of my life. So?

*Understand. Once they had been young together.*

*To Lennie he remained a tie to adventure and a world in*
*which men had not eaten each other; and the pleasure,*
*when the mind was clear, of chewing over with that tough*
*mind the happenings of the times or the queernesses of*
*people, or laughing over the mimicry.*

*To Helen he was the compound of much help given,*
*much support: the ear to hear, the hand that understands*
*how much a scrubbed floor, or a washed dish, or a child*
*taken care of for a while, can mean.*

*They had believed in his salvation, once. Get him away*
*from the front where he has to drink for company and for*
*a woman. The torn-out-of-him confession, the drunken end*
*of his eight-months-sober try to make a go of it on the*
*beach—don't you see, I can't go near a whore unless I'm*
*lit?*

*If they could know what it is like now, so casual as if it*
*were after thirty years of marriage.*

*Later, the times he had left money with them for plans:*

*fix his teeth, buy a car, get into the Ship Painters, go see his family in Chi. But soon enough the demands for the money when the drunken need was on him, so that after a few tries they gave up trying to keep it for him.*

*Later still, the first time it became too much and Lennie forbade the house to him unless he were "O.K."—"because of the children."*

*Now the decaying body, the body that was betraying him. And the memories to forget, the dreams to be stifled, the hopeless hopes to be murdered.*

What's going to happen with you, Whitey? Helen repeats. I never know if you'll be back. If you'll be able to be back.

He tips the bottle to the end. Thirstily he thinks: Deeck and his room where he can yell or sing or pound and Deeck will look on without reproach or pity or anguish.

I'm goin' now.

Wait, Whitey. We'll drive you. Want to know where you're shacked, anyway.

Go own steam. Send you a card.

By Jeannie, silent and shrunken into her coat. He passes no one in the streets. They are inside, each in his slab of house, watching the flickering light of television. The sullen fog is on his face, but by the time he has walked to the third hill, it has lifted so he can see the city below him, wave after wave, and there at the crest, the tiny house he has left, its eyes unshaded. After a while they blur with the myriad others that stare at him so blindly.

Then he goes down.

*Hey Sailor, what ship?*
*Hey Marinero, what ship?*

San Francisco   1953, 1955

---

*For Jack Eggan, Seaman.*   *1915–1938*
*Killed in the retreat across the Ebro, Spain.*

# ISHMAEL REED

# The Last Days of Louisiana Red

> *California, named for the negro*
> *Queen Califia*
> *California, The Out-Yonder State*
> *California, refuge for survivors*
> *of the ancient continent of*
> *Lemuria*
> *California, Who, one day, prophets*
> *say will also sink*

The story begins in Berkeley, California. The city of unfinished attics and stairs leading to strange towers.

Berkeley, California, was incorporated on April Fools' Day, 1878; it is an Aries town: Fire, Cardinal, Head (brain children who gamble with life, according to Carl Payne Tobey, author of *Astrology of Inner Space*).

Aries: activity, exaltation. PROPAGANDA. Self Assertiveness. Now, that would characterize Ed Yellings.

Ed Yellings was an american negro itinerant who popped into Berkeley during the age of Nat King Cole. People looked around one day and there he was.

When Osiris entered Egypt, cannibalism was in vogue. He stopped men from eating men. Thousands of years later when Ed Yellings entered Berkeley, there was a plague too, but not as savage. After centuries of learning how to be subtle, the scheming beast that is man had acquired the ability to cover up.

When Ed Yellings entered Berkeley "men were not eating men"; men were inflicting psychological stress on one another. Driving one another to high blood pressure, hardening of the arteries, which only made it worse, since the stabbings, rapings, muggings went on as usual. Ed Yellings, being a Worker, decided he would find some way to end Louisiana Red, which is what all of this activity was called. The only future Louisiana Red has is a stroke.

Ed gained a reputation for being not only a Worker but a worker too. No one could say that this loner didn't pay his way. He worked at odd jobs: selling tacos on University Avenue across the street from the former Santa Fe passenger station, now a steak joint; during the Christmas season peddling Christmas trees in a lot on San Pablo across the street from the Lucky Dog pet shop and the V.I.P. massage parlor.

He even worked in an outdoor beer joint on Euclid Street a few doors above the U.C. Corner.

Since he worked with workers, he gained a knowledge of the workers' lot. He knew that their lives were bitter. He experienced their surliness, their downtroddenness, their spitefulness and the hatred they had for one another and for their wives and their kids. He saw them repeatedly go against their own best interests as they were swayed and bedazzled by modern subliminal techniques, manipulated by politicians and corporate tycoons, who posed as their friends while sapping their energy. Whose political campaigns amounted to: "Get the Nigger."

Louisiana Red was the way they related to one another, oppressed one another, maimed and murdered one another, carving one another while above their heads, fifty thousand feet, billionaires flew in custom-made jet planes equipped with saunas tennis courts swimming pools discotheques and meeting rooms decorated like a Merv Griffin Show set. Like J. P. Morgan, who once made Millard Fillmore cool his heels, these men stood up powerful senators of the United States—made them wait and fidget in the lobby of the Mayflower Hotel.

The miserable workers were anti-negro, anti-chicano, anti-puerto rican, anti-asian, anti-native american, had forgotten their guild oaths, disrespected craftsmanship; produced badly made cars and appliances and were stimulated by gangster-controlled entertainment; turned out worms in the tuna fish, spiders in the soup, inflammatory toys, tumorous chickens, d.d.t. in fish and the brand new condominium built on quicksand.

What would you expect from innocent victims caught by the american tendency towards standardization, who monotonously were assigned to churning out fragments instead of the whole thing?

Sherwood Anderson, the prophet, had warned of the consequences of standardization and left Herbert Hoover's presence when he found that Hoover was a leveler: I don't care if my car looks like the other fellow's, as long as it gets me to where I'm going was how Hoover saw it.

Ed wanted to free the worker from Louisiana Red because Louisiana Red was killing the worker. It would be a holy occupation to give Louisiana Red the Business, Ed thought. Ed thought about these things a lot. Ed was a thinker and a Worker. After working at his odd jobs Ed would go to his cottage on Milvia Street and read up on botany theology music poetry corporation law american Business practices, and it was this reading as well as his own good instincts and experiences that led him to believe that he would help the worker by entering Business and recruiting fellow Workers. Not the primitive and gross businessmen of old who introduced the late movies on television, but the kind of Business people who made the circuit of 1890s America, contributing mystery and keeping their Business to themselves.

His reading directed him to an old company that was supposed to be the best in the Business. Their Board of Directors was very stringent; cruel, some would say. Ed passed their test and received his certificate from Blue Coal, the Chairman of the Board. Shortly afterwards he received an assignment from his new employers; they sent him to New Orleans on a mission to collect the effects of a certain astrologer, diviner and herbalist who had been done in by some pretty rough industrial spies working for the competition. Ed's assignment was to collect this man's bookkeeping and records and to continue this Businessman's Work. (His Board of Directors had distributed franchises all over the world; the New Orleans branch was one.)

Some say that it was after Ed returned from New Orleans that he abandoned the rarefied world of ideals and put his roots to Business; gave up being a short-order cook and handyman and became instead the head of a thriving "Gumbo" Business: Solid Gumbo Works.

He chose a very small staff of Workers—very small, because Ed had learned through bitter experience that if you go over a secret number you will run into an informer who leaks industrial secrets to industrial spies, or even worse a maniac who not only wishes to self-destruct but to bring down the whole corporation as well.

Ed rented an office on the Berkeley Marina and started making his Gumbo. He was deliberately cryptic about the kind of Gumbo he was into; it certainly wasn't "Soul Food."

Ed's Gumbo became the talk of the town, though people could only guess what Ed was up to in this city named for Bishop George Berkeley, the philosopher, who coined the phrase "Westward The Course Of Empire Takes Its Way."

When asked his purpose, Ed would merely answer that he had gone into the Gumbo Business.

Though no one could testify to having seen it or tasted it, Ed's Gumbo began making waves; though ordinary salesmen hated it, distributors wouldn't touch it and phony cuisinières gave it a bad name, no one could deny that, however unexplained, there was some kind of operation going on at Ed's Gumbo premises: cars could be seen arriving and departing; others got theirs through subscription.

Whatever Ed was selling, the people were buying, and rather than put his product on the shelves next to the synthetic wares of a poisonous noxious time, Ed catered to a sophisticated elite. In a town like Berkeley, as in any other american small town, superstitiousness and primitive beliefs were rife and so was their hideous Sister, gossip.

Ghosts too. The computer isn't to blame; the problems of The Bay Area Rapid Transit are due to the burial grounds of the Costanoan indians it disturbs as it speeds through the East Bay.

Ed was a Piscean, and so he had a whole lot of passion. Too much passion. It was all that passion that made him fall in love with the beautiful Ruby who had been Miss Atlantic City. Maybe it was those cowgirl clothes and

boots she wore the night he asked her to dance at Harry's,
the businessman's lunch place. (Its booths resembled those
of a victorian law office; it was dark inside all the time.
That's why exiled New Yorkers drank there: it reminded
them of home.)

Ed and Ruby danced all night to Al Green's singing of
The Oakland National Anthem. They danced so they didn't
even hear Percy, owner of the jackjohnson black derby and
'39 Pontiac, announce "Last Call."

It was all passion and no intellect that made him take
her home to his italianate cottage on Milvia and succumb
to her clamping squeezing sensual techniques. Before he
knew it he was in the vice.

Now, Solid Gumbo Works was becoming so prosperous
that when they were married they were able to move into a
fine old home in the Berkeley Hills equipped with fireplaces,
gaslight medallions, stained-glass windows, and rooms
with 12-foot ceilings; in the back was an old stable which
he had made into private rooms.

He didn't want to have children, but she was always
miscalculating her "phase of the moon"; she was always
talking that way as if influenced by forces in the remote
universe, like she was born of a comet or meteorite. How
else could you explain Ruby's strange power over people;
she always got her way. She could lie so cleverly that you
became convinced that it was the truth even though you
knew it was a lie. She would control people and abuse
them, but they always forgave her and loved her even
more.

Ed was no dummy. Nobody in the Business was a
dummy. He was patient; but after sifting the facts and
meditating to Doc John he decided to get rid of her. Doc
John was the head of the Old Co.'s western field office and
stood in an oil portrait on the wall behind Ed's desk in Ed's
study. He was a tall negro man who, in the painting, was
wearing a strange yellow top hat and red jacket and standing next to a handsome auburn-colored horse with a silver-
trimmed saddle on its back. In the painting's background
was the old steepled skyline of New Orleans.

Sometimes Ed's youngest daughter Minnie would
peek through his office's keyhole and see him there in that
black silk robe with the jet cross hanging on a chain
around his neck. Not the cross of anguish and suffering,

the *crux simplex*, but the oldest cross made of two straight lines which bisect each other at right angles.

There Ed would be kneeling, consulting with Doc John, while white peace candles burned on a long table of brilliant white linen in the center of which was a beautiful silver cup.

His problem wasn't difficult because Ruby Yellings wanted to leave too. Her husband would never discuss his Business with her. He spent most of his time at the Solid Gumbo Works. And she didn't like those people who worked with him. That Ms. Better Weather, Ed's assistant Worker, who sometimes wore a veil.

Ruby liked to spend her time at the Democratic Club. Though she ran for councilman and lost, she was building quite a machine. She was always flying from Berkeley to D.C. and partied with the black caucus.

One day Ed came home to find her closets empty and her valuables gone. There was a note on the dresser. She had run off with an up-and-coming Democrat and had gone for good to Washington, D.C., to enter national politics.

Ed was left behind with four children: Wolf, the oldest; Sister, the second; Street; and then the youngest, Minnie.

He wanted his children to believe in Labor, Work and Occupation.

He was successful with Wolf, who at an early age displayed cunning and self-reliance and the ability to finish projects he started. Sister was that way too. An industrious girl who was good with the needle, she sewed the clothes for the family. She was destined to become an internationally known fashion designer, famous for her eclectic prints.

Young Street was a disappointment. He walked about with a pugnacious swagger and was pretty much a bully until someone would give him a licking.

As for Minnie:

During the International Congress of Genetics held in Berkeley the week of August 20, 1973, an important paper was read whose prominence was overshadowed by the sensationalistic headline-grabbing race theories of a Berkeley geneticist. The tenure of this less heralded paper was that psychic as well as physical traits are inherited. Of course, we knew this all along, for didn't old folks used to speak of how so and so took after his mother or father or was the spitting image of some remote ancestor in "ways" as much as in physical appearance. How many of us have looked in the mirror and seen an unfamiliar pair of eyes staring out of our heads?

So it was with Minnie, the Yellings' youngest daughter. She was so much like her mother that they could have been twins, and she had her mother's "ways."

No! she wasn't going to wash the dishes; cleaning up your room was for the birds; if he didn't like what time she came in at night, that was his problem; she went out of her way to come on "field" just like her mother. The only person Minnie would mind was her Nanny, a hefty spread-out woman Ed hired after Ruby went east; what luck, Ed had thought at the time—Nanny had showed up asking for the job before he had placed the "help wanted" ad in the *Berkeley Gazette*. Nanny had come to them straight from New Orleans. Minnie loved this jolly, robust, happy-go-lucky creature.

Ed never spanked Minnie; he characterized spanking as "Louisiana Red"; he had a cryptic way of expressing himself. As the years went by he became weary of fighting with his youngest daughter and would try to appease her with gifts he'd never give the other children. When she reached her teens she was the only member of her set who owned a Porsche.

As time passed, more and more of Ed's hours were spent at the Solid Gumbo Works; the booming Business of his enterprise wouldn't allow him to spend as much time with his children.

The Berkeley Hills where they lived was located in the northern section of the town, called "White town." Negroes and poor whites lived in "Dark town" or "Bukra town" which was the area located below Grove Street in the "Flats." The area running through the border segments was referred to as "Japtown."

A good portion of the "Dark town" and "Bukra town" was located, you guessed it, across the railroad tracks which traveled across University Avenue. Ed liked it in the Berkeley Hills house, secluded by eucalyptus oak, bay and sycamore trees, even though, once, a cross was burned on his lawn. What luck, Ed had thought at the time. And, faithful to her promises, Nanny was good with the children and especially good with Minnie. They were always in a huddle, whispering.

* * *

Minnie still pouted and wise-cracked when Ed greeted her in the morning. She was rude to Ed's fellow Workers. Sometimes she'd get so angry she'd fly into Nanny Lisa's apron, whereupon Nanny Lisa would fix her some pancakes. That would make the child happy. She loved pancakes, especially topped with syrup. She would gobble them up, and Nanny would smile broadly—real broadly—and say, "That child loves to put away them flapjacks"; after which Nanny would bathe her and tuck her in, perhaps while singing a rousing version of "Take It Right Back," and other songs depicting negro men as brutish wayfaring louts. After the child was tucked in, Nanny would tell her those stories about the "Widow Paris," and her running combat with Doc John, a mean uppity diabolical smarty pants.

Minnie loved these "Louisiana Red" stories in which the Widow Paris, Marie, would always best Doc John; prevail over this no-account ruffian. (She liked Marie to win and would laugh her little chirren chitter when Doc John was brought down to size.)

Minnie was becoming suspicious of her father.

What was this Gumbo? She would ask Nanny about this Gumbo, and Nanny would cook it for her; but she knew that her dad wasn't in the restaurant business, so what kind of Gumbo was it? Nanny was as in the dark about the operation as she was. Once Minnie had seen her Nanny going through her dad's papers, and Nanny and Ed had a fight about it until Nanny had finally convinced the man that she was merely looking for some change to pay the paper boy. Her father was touchy and uptight. What did he have to hide? Why did he use the code "Gumbo" for what he was really up to?

Years passed. Minnie enrolled in the University of California at Berkeley in Rhetoric (they have a Ph.D. program) because she was good at that. Sister opened a boutique business on San Pablo. Wolf went into his father's Gumbo business, which was no surprise to Minnie; Wolf had been just like her father: secretive, taciturn, smart. Too godamn smart for Minnie's money. Bro. Street went to jail for busting one of his street companions on the head with a lead pipe.

Minnie stayed out a lot on Telegraph Ave. She'd go into the Mediterranean Restaurant for exotic coffee. It was

there that she met T Feeler, who was propounding the idea
known as "Moochism." Moochism was being whispered
about in cafés all over Berkeley; people had rallies about it.
The administration in Washington began bugging it; its
propaganda machine based in Berkeley and San Francisco
rivaled Ezra Pound's in the same places. Herb Caen's col-
umn dropped names from time to time: Big Sally, Rev.
Rookie, Cinnamon Easterhood and Maxwell Kasavubu.
The Moochers had lots of parties to acquaint people with
the idea; often T and Minnie would be the only "minori-
ties" present.

Moochers are people who, when they are to blame, say
it's the other fellow's fault for bringing it up. Moochers
don't return stuff they borrow. Moochers ask you to share
when they have nothing to share. Moochers kill their enemies like the South American insect which kills its foe by
squirting it with its own blood. God, do they suffer. "Look
at all of the suffering I'm going through because of you."
Moochers talk and don't do. You should hear them just the
same. Moochers tell other people what to do. Men Moochers blame everything on women. Women Moochers blame
everything on men. Old Moochers say it's the young's
fault; young Moochers say the old messed up the world
they have to live in. Moochers play sick a lot. Moochers
think it's real hip not to be able to read and write. Like
Joan of Arc the arch-witch, they boast of not knowing A
from B.
Moochers stay in the bathtub a long time. Though
Moochers wrap themselves in the full T-shirt of ideology,
their only ideology is Mooching.
Moochers aren't necessarily poor, though some are;
Moochers inject themselves between the poor and what
other people who are a little better off than the poor set
aside for the poor. Like the hoggish Freedmen's Bureau
crook, or the anti-poverty embezzler.
The highest order of this species of Moocher is the President, who uses the taxpayers' money to build homes all
over the world where he can be alone to contemplate his
place in history when history don't even want him. Moochers are a special order of parasite, not even a beneficial
parasite but one that takes—takes energy, takes supplies.
Moochers write you letters saying at once or at your earliest convenience, we are in a hurry, may I hear from you

soon, or please get right back to me—promptly. Moochers threaten to jump out of the window if you don't love them. The Moocher drug is heroin; the Moocher song is "Willow Weep for Me"; Moochers ask you for the same address over and over again. Moochers feel that generosity should flow one way: from you to them. You owe it to them. If you call a Moocher wrong, he will say, "I'm not wrong, you're paranoid." Freud gave the Moochers their greatest outs. Moochers talk so much about "integrity" when in fact they lead scattered, ragged lives.

Moochers are predators at the nesting grounds of industry.

Moochers decided to start an organization themselves:

T. Feeler had spent many years on Telegraph Ave. before meeting Minnie, and he was getting grey. He wore beret, boat jacket, sneakers and would bicycle about town calmly smoking his pipe.

T taught a course at U.C. Berkeley called "The Jaybird As An Omen In Afro-American Folklore." Just like him. T, Minnie and Maxwell Kasavubu, who was a "white" Literature instructor on loan from Columbia University, struck up quite a threesome. Kasavubu was writing a critical book on Richard Wright's masterpiece, *Native Son*, and had been teaching at U.C. Berkeley in the English Department. He wrote short stories in which he would cite all of the New York subway stops between the Brooklyn Ferry and Columbus Circle. This impressed his colleagues who like many members of the northern California cultural establishment felt inferior to New Yorkers. He derived his power from this and was able to get a job.

T would entertain Max and Minnie while they sat in the Mediterranean Café drinking Bianco. T tried to impress Maxwell Kasavubu, a real "right-on chap" as T would say, by showing off his knowledge of Old English.

Max would smile indulgently when T rattled on about obscure English poets, but one night Max got drunk at a faculty party and before the startled guests, including the Chairman of the Department, some kind of Bible devotee, announced: "T Feeler is destined to be the first nigger to be buried in Westminster Abbey."

The guests were too polite to laugh. They don't laugh in Berkeley anyway, they go around smiling all the time. T was embarrassed and went into the kitchen, only glancing from time to time into the main room where the party was taking place and where Max and Minnie were doing a pretty fierce grind. After a few beers T rose, went into the room and said: "Well, if I'm buried in Westminster Abbey, I hope I'm dressed in the manner of the bard."

The people laughed then. Minnie laughed too. T Feeler liked that, them laughing. Max came up to him and slapped him on the back.

In Berkeley, Moochism was becoming the thing to be. Books on Moochism appeared on the bookstore shelves, while the *Partisan Review* was hardly moving. The prose style was a little too "dudish" for this old-west town.

Minnie was happy about the outpouring of Moocher buttons. She was particularly pleased with one which read: "I Am A Moocher."

Minnie had risen in the Moochers' ranks, making quite a name for herself as orator and rhetorician. For her appearances she was provided with female bodyguards known as the Dahomeyan Softball Team who dressed in black knee-length pea jackets, dark pants and waffle stomper shoes. Sometimes they toted carbines.

There were Moocher songs, Moocher tie clips and Moocher bumper stickers; Wall Street predicted that Moochism would be one of the top thirty-five trends in the U.S. to succeed.

Minnie was content. She wriggled about Telegraph Ave. like a chicken without a neck. Then it happened.

Solid Gumbo Works had invented a Gumbo that became a cure for certain cancers. Crowds gathered, submitting their loved ones. Newsmen came. Gumbo came to be seen as a cure-all dish, and the health food stores were in trouble. The Co-ops had to slash prices to compete, and if this happened to these economical and consumer-minded stores you can imagine the panic at Safeways. The people didn't want to Mooch when they could have Gumbo, and so the Moocher recruits fell off. Minnie was even heckled.

Even though she was eighteen, she clung to the massive heaving bosom of her Nanny, and Nanny would rock her to sleep like she used to, staring at the child with her old shiny mammy eyes as she prayed to Saint Peter to look down on this chile. Outside, the Dahomeyan Softball Team, Minnie's crack bodyguards, would mill about as

Nanny issued hourly press bulletins on the state of Minnie's despondency. They were some fierce, rough-looking women led by this big old 6-foot bruiser they all called the "REICHSFÜHRER."

Ed, Wolf and some Workers came up to the house one night to discuss some Gumbo business and ran into this strange vigil. The Dahomeyan Softball Team camping out stared at the men angrily; Nanny was in the midst of telling Minnie one of those stories about Doc John, and how when Marie, by that time the "last American witch," finished with him, she had him eating out of her hand.

"What's wrong with Minnie?" Ed asked as he led the guests and Wolf into his study.

"Ah don't know, Mistuh Ed. Seems she haint feeling too good. I going to fix the child some buttermilk and put her to bed."

"I hope she feels better," Ed said as the company moved into Ed's private room.

Nanny undressed Minnie and put her to bed. When she was half asleep, she had the child drink some nice warm buttermilk. Minnie's body possessed all of the fertile peaks and valleys of young womanhood. Nanny stared at her a long time.

As Minnie climbed into bed, Nanny started to tell her the stories. Stories about Marie and how she had showed Doc John that he wasn't such a big deal. Minnie dozed off, smiling. She began to talk in her sleep. She was thinking of how better things would be if her father would just take a walk and not come back. Nanny shook her grey head sadly at the mutterings of this troubled teenager.

The next day Ed took off early. When he arrived home he told Nanny to fix him a rum and Coke. He went upstairs and climbed into bed.

Around the Bay it was April Fools' Day. A pig leaped from a truck in S.F. and was pursued by housewives waving meat cleavers and about to make mincemeat of it, until it was rescued by incredulous policemen, finally convinced that the farmer's bizarre tale was on the up and up. In the same town on the same day a man found a four-foot anaconda in his toilet bowl. A "bottomless" fight was being waged by café owners whose performers had been warned to cover up their Burgers. Rev. Rookie of the

Gross Christian Church preached a powerful jumpy sermon replete with strobes, bongos and psychedelic paraphernalia.

This was part of a three-day ceremony celebrating Minnie's ascension to Queen of the Moochers which ended with an old-fashioned torchlight parade to Provo Park in Berkeley. Sister went to hear Nina Simone at the Rainbow Sign on Grove St. that night.

A book called *White Dog*, on how to train dogs to check negroes, was on sale at The Show Dog, a pet shop at 1961 Shattuck Ave—"Whitetown." The North and South Hills Berkeley was getting ready. Dazed-eyed beasts big as horses trying to jump over the fence at negroes while their masters with those stupid-looking gardening hats on grinned at them.

The old feud was coming to a boil between the North and South Hills and their traditional enemies in the "Flats: niggertown. A councilman, popular among the University people and the "Flats," was recalled, unfairly many thought. People made comparisons to the Reconstruction days when many negro legislators were expelled from their seats and even lynched by the whites. There were more parallels than people thought. The councilman in question even wore a modern version of the post-Civil War clothes associated with the carpetbagger's nigger dandy: spats and such. The ex-councilman thought he was in New Haven; instead he was out here in Poker Flats, in Dry Gulch, in Tombstone. How did the old saying go? "There's no God nor Sunday west of Tombstone."

# TOM ROBBINS

# Another Roadside Attraction

Along their migratory routes, monarch butterflies stay nights in certain trees. The "butterfly trees," as they are called, are carefully chosen—although the criteria exercised in their selection are not known. Species is unimportant, obviously, for at one stopover the roosting tree may be a eucalyptus, at another a cedar or an elm. But, and this is what is interesting, they are always the same trees. Year after year, whether moving south or returning north, monarchs will paper with their myriad wings at twilight a single tree that has served as a monarch motel a thousand times before.

Memory? If so, it is genetic. For you see, the butterflies who journey south are not the ones who come back. Monarchs lay their eggs in sunny climes. Then they die. The hordes who flutter northward in spring are a succeeding generation. Yet, without hesitation, they roost in the same trees as did their ancestors.

Scientists have examined butterfly trees and found them chemically and physically identical to the trees surrounding them. Yet no other tree will do. Investigators have camouflaged a tree's color, altered its scent. The monarchs were not fooled. Another of nature's mysterious constants. A butterfly always knows when it is *there*.

\* \* \*

They found the zoo site on an October Sunday: a soft burpy day on which they crossed many bridges. Bridges over rivers and bridges over sloughs. The sky sagged like an udder. The air had a feel of heavy birds. Their motorcycle was a flash of overheated color in the damp green landscapes. At seventy miles an hour, it whined like a spinning top—and rattled Amanda's kidneys like dice in a box.

Amanda had peed in Seattle, she had peed in Everett. And now as they sped through the Skagit River Valley, she had to pee again. Already, she and John Paul were far behind the caravan that motored to Bellingham (near the Canadian border) where, on the campus of Western Washington State College, the circus was to unfurl its canvases for the last time. But when she rapped her code on Ziller's ribs, he dutifully braked the BMW and turned into the big fir-ringed parking lot of Mom's Little Dixie Bar-B-Cue. Luckily, Amanda's biological urgency became manifest on that rare stretch of Interstate 5 where the limited access rule had, for some reason, been suspended. Along that one fifteen-mile section of the Seattle-Vancouver Freeway (between Everett and Mount Vernon), there were scattered gas stations, general stores and restaurants. Not many, however, for this was farming country of almost unequaled lushness and the black juicy soil was far too valuable to be relegated to commerce.

The motorcycle engine died with a prolonged series of soft smoky gasps—like a dwarf choking on a burning rag. The couple dismounted. Only to discover that Mom's was closed. Not shuttered for the Sabbath but permanently shut down. Padlocked. Vacant. In a cobweb-frosted window corner a faded FOR RENT sign hung by one ear from a snipping of tape. So, while his young bride went around back to water the ferns, Ziller scrutinized the roadhouse—noted its spaciousness, its quaint but sturdy construction, the broad fields behind it, the grove in which it sat—and surmised that it was a likely edifice in which to house a zoo, a family and secret world headquarters.

"I am always voyaging back to the source," Ziller had said. He was a source-rer. Internally, he pursued the bright waters of his origins with whatever vehicles he could command. "In our human cells are recorded every single impulse of energy that has occurred since the beginning of time," Amanda had said. "The DNA genetic system is the one library in which it is really worthwhile to browse." Although *he* never said as much, Ziller seemed to find the key to that library in various mental disciplines, in capsules, powders, symbols, songs, rituals and vials. Externally, the source-search proceeded on a more obvious level. Ziller had pilgrimaged several times to Africa, place of his birth. Now, it was time to reassimilate the Pacific Northwest, the rained-on, clam-chawed land where he had lived his childhood. (Although it *could* be said that considering his books and films and daydreams and maps he was "in Africa" all those child-years, too. Or was it India?)

When Amanda returned, John Paul clasped her suspiciously moist fingers and led her across the Freeway—traffic was sparse and there was little danger of their being struck—to the edge of a lemonade-colored slough. Clotted with eelgrass and driftwood, the slough curled forlornly through the cropland like a moat that had been abandoned by its castle. The newlyweds stood with their backs to the water, stood on the muddy shoulder and gazed across four lanes of asphalt at the cafe, its two-story Cowboy Gothic facade silhouetted against the god's-belly clouds like the fortifications of a forbidden city. Amanda squeezed her husband's hand. She knew that they were there.

In the wash of the afternoon they perceived dimly that once, before the paint began to flake, the wood-frame facade of Mom's Little Dixie had been festooned with cartoon pigs, all wearing chef's hats and carrying steaming platters of barbecue and buns. Which caused Amanda to announce that she could never trust a pig that sold pork sandwiches. Which prompted Ziller to point out to her the parallels between such swine and businessmen everywhere.

On Monday evening, October 2, the Indo-Tibetan Circus & Giant Panda Gypsy Blues Band offered its final performance. And a rather good performance it was. Stimulated by sentiments of finality—in a short while Nearly Normal Jimmy would be taking the band to New York for a recording session and the troupers realized that the circus would probably never be reorganized—each performer uncorked hidden geysers of adrenalin and functioned at the summit of his potential.

Krishnalasa balanced himself on one thumb atop a twenty-five-watt bulb for sixty seconds. (Or was it atop a sixty-watt bulb for twenty-five seconds?) Master Ying swallowed (and disgorged unharmed) six frogs instead of the usual two. The monkey pipers blew until their faces turned black. Jugglers called for sharper blades, taller lampshades, additional marbles. With what clarity Elmer sang the Bhagavad-Gita, the Song Celestial, the ecstasy of the Divine One. Pursued by a gang of drooling amazons, the sugar-breasted Pammie led her yaks and goats to safety through the Tunnel of Hades. (The audience gasped as she braved the fire.) Clowns were stuffed into their suits like sausages. White mice dropped by toy parachutes from the wings of model airplanes. (One mouse broke a leg and was carried off in a tiny ambulance manned by a crew of parakeets.) In the center ring, a collection of paradoxes was exhibited. Déjà vu displays. Infinity chambers. Firecrackers. Chants. Cave paintings. Symbologies. Obscurities. Meditations. Inscrutabilities. Zen Yo-Yos. Kabuki kut-outs. Visions from the Tibetan *Book of the Dead*. Nuclear Phyllis roaring her scooter in and out among the blues chords looking for the peace that passeth all understanding. And so forth.

All this time Amanda lay napping, wrapped in a bulky tapestry. Outside her tipi, a dank October breeze raised goose pimples and flapped flags. The insect yammer of the crowd squirmed through the woven walls. Even into sleep the music followed her: she could hear her husband drumming, drumming as if freed from all the fetters that bind men to life. If she did not visibly respond it was because she was exhausted. Long insistent lines had formed before Amanda's booth that evening, and she had failed no one. Her trances had been crisp and short and accurate—almost staccato machine-gun glimpses of consciousness. And she had dazzled her clients with the data she had dredged from the cards. "I feel like a pressed duck, a squeezed grape," she sighed when it was over.

Now here was Nearly Normal awakening her. He brought a cucumber sandwich and a half-pint of milk. Good. Food would revive her. The bread slices collapsed like movie-set walls beneath her bite; the mayonnaise squished, the cucumber snapped tartly like the spine of an elf. She held aloft the milk carton and read aloud from it, "Four hundred U.S.P. units Vitamin D added per quart from activated ergosterol." Amanda winced before drinking. "Activated ergosterol? Jimmy, I'm not sure about this activated ergosterol. Do you suppose it could be a euphemism for strontium 90? Maybe it'll make me sterile?"

"That might be something less than a tragedy," said Nearly Normal. He patted her discreetly ballooning belly. "At any rate, the information on milk containers is highly educational. My first concepts of infinity were developed from looking at Pet milk cans when I was a kid. On the label there was a picture of a cow in a can, her big mooey head hanging out of one end of the can—another Pet milk can, naturally—and on the label of *that* can was the same cow in another Pet milk can. And that can also had a cow-in-can design on its label. And those cow cans, one inside the other, just went on, growing progressively smaller, as far as the eye could see. It walloped my little mind."

"They've changed the label," Amanda pointed out.

"Yeah. They have," sighed Jimmy as he left to return to the show. "To Madison Avenue even infinity is expendable."

\* \* \*

Off the Pacific shore of Washington State the Japanese Current—a mammoth river of tropical water—zooms close by the coast on a southernly turn. Its warmth is released in the form of billows of tepid vapor, which the prevailing winds drive inland. When, a few miles in, the warm vapor bangs head-on into the Olympic Mountain Range, it is abruptly pushed upward and outward, cooling as it rises and condensing into rain. In the emerald area that lies between the Olympics (the coastal range) and the Cascade Range some ninety miles to the east, temperatures are mild and even. But during the autumn and winter months it is not unusual for precipitation to fall on five of every seven days. And when it is not raining, still the gray is pervasive; the sun a little boiled potato in a stew of dirty dumplings; the fire and light and energy of the cosmos trapped somewhere far behind that impenetrable slugbelly sky.

Puget Sound may be the most rained-on body of water on earth. Cold, deep, steep-shored, home to salmon and lipstick-orange starfish, the Sound lies between the Cascades and the Olympics. The Skagit Valley lies between the Cascades and the sound—sixty miles north of Seattle, an equal distance south of Canada. The Skagit River, which formed the valley, begins up in British Columbia, leaps and splashes southwestward through the high Cascade wilderness, absorbing glaciers and sipping alpine lakes, running two hundred miles in total before all fish-green, driftwood-cluttered and silty, it spreads its double mouth like suckers against the upper body of Puget Sound. Toward the Sound end of the valley, the fields are rich with river silt, the soil ranging from black velvet to a blond sandy loam. Although the area receives little unfiltered sunlight, peas and strawberries grow lustily in Skagit fields, and more than half the world's supply of beet seed and cabbage seed is harvested here. Like Holland, which it in some ways resembles, it supports a thriving bulb industry: in spring its lowland acres vibrate with tulips, iris and daffodils; no bashful hues. At any season, it is a dry duck's dream. The forks of the river are connected by a network of sloughs, bedded with ancient mud and lined with cattail, tules, eelgrass and sedge. The fields, though diked, are often flooded; there are puddles by the hundreds and the roadside ditches could be successfully navigated by midget submarines.

It is a landscape in a minor key. A sketchy panorama where objects, both organic and inorganic, lack well-defined edges and tend to melt together in a silver-green blur. Great islands of craggy rock arch abruptly up out of the flats, and at sunrise and moonrise these outcroppings are frequently tangled in mist. Eagles nest on the island crowns and blue herons flap through the veils from slough to slough. It is a poetic setting, one which suggests inner meanings and invisible connections. The effect is distinctly Chinese. A visitor experiences the feeling that he has been pulled into a Sung dynasty painting, perhaps before the intense wisps of mineral pigment have dried upon the silk. From almost any vantage point, there are expanses of monochrome worthy of the brushes of Mi Fei or Kuo Hsi.

The Skagit Valley, in fact, inspired a school of neo-Chinese painters. In the Forties, Mark Tobey, Morris Graves and their gray-on-gray disciples turned their backs on cubist composition and European color and using the shapes and shades of this misty terrain as a springboard, began to paint the visions of the inner eye. A school of sodden, contemplative poets emerged here, too. Even the original inhabitants were an introspective breed. Unlike the Plains Indians, who enjoyed mobility and open spaces and sunny skies, the Northwest coastal tribes were caught between the dark waters to the west, the heavily forested foothills and towering Cascade peaks to the east; forced by the lavish rains to spend weeks on end confined to their longhouses. Consequently, they turned inward, evolving religious and mythological patterns that are startling in their complexity and intensity, developing an artistic idiom that for aesthetic weight and psychological depth was unequaled among all primitive races. Even today, after the intrusion of neon signs and supermarkets and aircraft industries and sports cars, a hushed but heavy force hangs in the Northwest air: it defies flamboyance, deflates extroversion and muffles the most exultant cry.

Yet one inhabitant of this nebulous and mystic land had had the audacity to establish a Dixie Bar-B-Cue. There is a colony of expatriated North Carolinians up in the timber country around Darrington: perhaps Mom was one of them. Her enterprise had not succeeded, obviously, and a disappointed and homesick Mom may have packed her curing salts and hot sauces and trucked on back to the red clay country where a good barbecue is paid the respect it deserves. At any rate, that aspect of the history of the cafe meant little to Amanda and John Paul Ziller for they were immune to the mystique of Southern pork barbecue. Neither had ever tasted the genuine article. Plucky Purcell had, of course, and he once remarked that "the only meat in the world sweeter, hotter and pinker than Amanda's twat is Carolina barbecue."

Prior to signing a lease for Mom's Little Dixie, Ziller had warned Amanda of the rigors of her new environment. He explained to his bride that there was seldom a thunderstorm in Skagit country—simply not enough heat—so no matter whether the influence storms had on her was good or ultimately evil, she could expect to be free of it as long as she resided in the Northwest. He told her that there would be butterflies in summer, but not nearly in the numbers to which she was accustomed in California and Arizona. Amanda knew, naturally, that cacti could not endure in these latitudes. And even their motorcycle would be impractical during the rainy season that lingered from October to May. "However," John Paul comforted her, "in those ferny forests"—he pointed to the alder-thatched Cascade foothills—"the mushrooms are rising like loaves. Like hearts they are pulsing and swelling; fungi of many hues, some shaped like trumpets and some like bells and some like parasols and others like pricks; with thick meat white as turkey or yellow as eggs; all reeking of primeval protein; and some contain bitter juices that make men go crazy and talk to God."

"Very well," said Amanda. "Mushrooms it will be." And it was.

Of the five thousand varieties of mushrooms that grow in the United States, approximately twenty-five hundred are found in western Washington. "I find those odds charming," said Amanda, salivating and lacing her boots.

Actually, there was little time for fungi those first few days at Mom's Little Dixie, although the Zillers did gather some meadow mushrooms on the golf course at Mount Vernon and filled another basket in a pasture on the river road.

The meadow mushroom (*Agaricus campestris* to Madame Goody) begins life looking like a slightly imperfect Ping-Pong ball and matures into a skullish white pancake. Its gills are pink when young, gradually turning chocolate. Shamefully, it admits to being a first cousin of the *Agaricus bisporus*, the mushroom found in the produce section of supermarkets, and of *Agaricus hortensis*, the kind one buys in tin cans. True fungus fanciers look upon those two traitors with withering disdain for only that pair among all the thousands have allowed themselves to be domesticated. The *campestris* has a much more interesting flavor than the supermarket sellouts, is less dull in color and less conservative in shape. But it suffers as a result of the weaklings in its family—its flavor could never inspire the odes or awed burps that the more noble varieties of wild mushrooms command. Still, when sautéed with minced onion in a sour cream sauce and served over rice, it is comfortably close to succulent, as the Zillers would readily attest. Anyway, the *campestris* would have to do for now: Amanda and John Paul hadn't the hours yet to devote to the deep-woods hunt. They were too busy cleaning house.

On the ground floor of Mom's Little Dixie there was an enormous L-shaped dining room defined by an enormous L-shaped counter, a huge kitchen, two fundamental toilets (sexually segregated) and a fair-sized windowless room that may have been used as a pantry. Upstairs (the stairs ascended from the rear of the kitchen), there was an apartment consisting of five spacious rooms and a bath. Out back, in the trees (remember that the cafe sat in a grove on the edge of croplands), there was a garage above which were two rooms that could be used for either storage or quarters.

With pails and mops and brooms and rags and an alchemicus of detergents, scouring powders and waxes (to which well-paid marketing experts had given names such as Pow, Rid, Thrill, and Zap—carefully chosen for their simple violence), Amanda and John Paul set out to clear all those compartments of dirt, dust and debris. Mon Cul was put to work washing windows and although easily distracted and prone to slope, the baboon did get them clean. Even Baby Thor had duties: emptying dustpans and fetching materials. With painting and decorating to follow, the project was destined to take weeks.

\* \* \*

"Magnificent!" exclaimed John Paul Ziller, pronouncing the word like he was a Kansas City intellectual describing the Louvre to his sister-in-law who'd called to tell him to bring his vacation slides over some other night because she'd burned the spaghetti sauce and the baby had colic. "Truly wondrous. Appraising it now I feel a bit like Bernard Berenson standing before Michelangelo's 'Temptation,' 'quaffing rare draughts of unadulterated energy' and itching to get his cultivated meathooks on the heroic buttocks of Eve. Though in truth, due to its humility and patience, it's less a Michelangelo than a Renoir: the roundness, the warmth, the rosy delight, the *joie de vivre*, the casual eroticism, the full and robust charm. It is at once a dramatically overflowing embodiment of the life force and an honest monument to the occasional genius of the plebeian palate."

With that blast of language, Ziller stepped back against a fir trunk to gain a slightly more distant perspective on the thirty-foot hot dog.

Amanda was shocked. She had never seen him like this: smiley, ebullient. Not once in the weeks she'd known him, worked and played with him, listened to his drums and flutes and plans, pored over his maps and charts, mingled her beauty and force with his, trapped explosive ribbons of his semen in her various bodily orifices, not once had he replaced his high jungle pride with such easy enthusiasm. It did not displease her, however. She walked to his side and stood with him, the better to admire the object of his excitement: the mighty mammoth king of weenies which he had painted in oils on thirty-four feet of plywood paneling.

"Note how the wrinkles in the bun—it's a steamed-soft bun, of course—fold dynamically, intuiting hidden movement as if they were folds in silks draped about a Renaissance Madonna. The texture of the bun is soft but not rubbery; it has the luster of a prairie moon. The sausage itself possesses a kind of peasant-folk serenity: it lounges in that bun as plump with confidence as a Polack bowling champion snoozing in a backyard hammock on the afternoon before the Greak Lakes regional finals. A simple fellow, the sausage, but the way his gentle contours catch the light and hold it gleaming, one senses something glorious in his spirit. I have molded his bulk—can you sense the physical participation of the artist in the formal objectification of the weenie's presence?—into a continuous volume that consumes vast quantities of space; it is three-dimensional, tactile, larger than life, as rotund and good-natured as Falstaff but not entirely devoid of Hamlet's rank. And what glamour is lent to the scene by the golden cloak of mustard, by the jazzy, jumpy play of flat patterns in the relish. Ahem."

Amanda licked her lips in amazement, more at the verbiage than at the inspiration of it, although it was indeed a hot dog of grand proportions. The panel was thirty-four feet long and nine feet high, the red hot was thirty feet in length and a little less than six feet in height and that weenie was not just loitering there in empty space. She perceived at the left end of the bun a green valley with cornfields and a river and some men in a boat on the river drinking beer and trolling for catfish; and across the river was a stadium with a baseball game in progress, probably a World Series because of all the dignitaries in the stands— political figures, movie stars and their counterparts in crime. In the twenty-four-inch space at the right end of the hot dog there was a brown-yellow plain with just a few thorny trees a-thirsting on it and a pride of lions resting in the stingy shade beneath one of those trees, and far in the distance, too far for the warm lions to bother with, a herd of wildebeests was kicking up dust, and even further in the distance Mt. Kilimanjaro jumped up like God's own sugar-tit, and in a modest encampment at the foot of the peak, E. Hemingway was cleaning his Weatherby 375 magnum (not trusting the native boys to handle such an instrument) and slurping his gin. In some mythic gesture of interracial world solidarity, the frankfurter bridged Africa and America in a manner that no United Nations mission or foreign aid program could hope to equal. It quickened the pulse. And reminded Amanda of John Paul's testimonial of a few days prior in which he professed that the sausage was one of the few achievements of Western technology that he could genuinely respect.

Up above that ambassador hot dog, in the night-blue sky above it, was to Amanda's eyes the most thrilling segment of the whole tableau: a skyful of vanilla stars and pastel planets and rushing comets and constellations (Jupiter was in the house of Gemini) and novae and nebulae and meteors dissolving in spittoons of fire and a tropical moon laid out against a cloud bank like a radioactive oyster on the half shell, and dominating the entire sidereal panorama was Saturn—silver and mysterious mushy omelet of ammonia and ice girded by its sharp gas rings like an avatar egg with a hip-hugger aura. And all this astronomical grandeur merely a backdrop for the mustard-draped shoulders of the cosmic colossal weenie, a sight to put a lump in the throat of the most unambitious Nebraska piglets, bar none.

The hot dog was to be erected on the roof of the road-house. Some workmen were coming from Mount Vernon with a crane. In a day or two, as soon as the paint was dry. It would be visible for miles.

The Zillers had reached no decision on the contents of the zoo. They were opposed to cages. Society was opposed to wild animals running loose in restaurants. The proper compromise evaded them. Amanda consulted the *I Ching*. She induced a trance. With no fit results. They had agreed to forget it for a while. In the meantime they could concentrate on what items they would sell in their shop, on what foods they would serve.

Something simple, they both insisted on simplicity. They had no intention of wasting their days cooking and washing dishes for tourist hordes. They shuddered at the thought. "Hot dogs," John Paul had suggested. "Good old-fashioned hot dogs. With steam-softened buns. We'll keep our buns in a steam cabinet the way they did when men were men and the sausage was the backbone of an empire. We'll offer fresh onions, raw or fried. A variety of mustards, catsups and relishes. Bacon, chopped nuts, melted cheese, sauerkraut—optional at additional cost, like whitewalls or power steering. The sausages we will carefully select for size and flavor; 100 per cent meat sausages (a little heavier on the beef than the pork), the best we can buy, the finest offspring of German technical expertise and American ingenuity."

Amanda was not at ease with the prospect of operating a hot dog stand. She was a vegetarian.

Due to the fact that she occasionally consumed milk and milk derivatives, she could not be considered a *strict* vegetarian. "Amanda," purists would scold, "milk is an animal product. How can you drink milk and still consider yourself a vegetarian?" And Amanda would answer, "The label states that this carton contains activated ergosterol. Have you ever heard of a cow that activated ergosterol?" But as vegetarians are a stubborn lot, the argument was never resolved.

At any rate, Amanda protested. "I shan't impose my beliefs on other people," she said, "but my conscience would turn purple were I, a vegetarian, to earn an income selling meat. There are limits to the decency of irony. Why, I'd feel like a Mormon." (Not that Amanda had any particular prejudice against Mormons, but she was a curious young woman, as many persons had established, and it confounded her curiosity that a denomination of nonsmoking teetotalers like the Mormons could justify supporting itself through the operation of supermarkets and drugstores in which alcoholic beverages and tobacco are prominent wares.)

John Paul was untroubled by any undue reverence for meat. "Look," he said, "the world is overrun with animals, great and small, fanged and feathered, all eating one another in happy harmony. Man is the party pooper. He'll eat pig flesh and pretend it's pork. He'll devour a chicken but not a kitten, a turkey but not a Turk. It isn't that he is principled, particularly. In fact, we all gut somebody every day. But it's sneaky, symbolic, unappetizing, ego-supportive, duty to God and country—never with a good pot roast in mind. No cheerful, honest cannibalism. Alas, alas."

Amanda was not much swayed by John Paul's remarks.

Incidentally, though, her vegetarian sentiments received a bit of a shake a few months later when Marx Marvelous said to her: "The cow became a sacred symbol to the Hindu because it gave milk and chops and hides. It nourished the babies and kept the old folks warm. Because it provided so many good life-supporting things, it was regarded as an embodiment of the Universal Mother, hence holy. Then it occurred to some monk or other, some abstract scholarly kook, as you would say, that gee, folks, since the cow is holy we maybe shouldn't be eating it and robbing its udder. So now the Hindu has got sacred cows up to here but no more milk and steaks. They starve in plain view of holy herds so big only Hopalong Cassidy could stop them if they took a notion to stampede. The spiritual man's beef against beef is the result of a classic distortion. It's another case of lost origins and inverted values." But that was Marx Marvelous and that came later.

For the present, they worked it out. They had to. While the interior of the cafe was now clean and freshly painted, the exterior had hardly been touched. A warning: the sky bulged like the sooty cheeks of an urban snowman—it hadn't rained yet but it wouldn't be long. The downpour was overdue. Action was required. So, Amanda reluctantly gave her consent to frankfurters and, in concession, John Paul agreed to a ban on dangerous fluids such as coffee and soda pop. For beverages they would serve the juices of fruits and vegetables. Amanda would squeeze them fresh in her automatic juicer. She had fun planning zesty combinations. Apple-papaya juice, for example. Carrot-orange. Spinach-tomato-cucumber. Good health to all! "People will think this a real funny place," said Ziller, "when they can't buy their coffee and Coca-Cola."

It was a funny place anyway. A roadside zoo with no animals. Except two garter snakes and a tsetse fly. And the tsetse fly was not even alive.

A trailer of rain fell for an hour at sunrise, but the afternoon was dry. The hot dog was erected on the roof of the cafe. It looked good. It could be seen for miles.

Ziller's magnificent sausage became a landmark in Skagit County. Directions were given in relation to it. "Turn right a couple hundred yards past the big weenie," some helpful farmer might say. From that time on, Mount Vernon school children would be obliged to compose annual essays on "The Sausage: Its Origin, Its Meaning and Its Cure."

To this day it hovers in plump passivity above the fertile fields. It is a perfect emblem for the people and the land.

A sausage is an image of rest, peace and tranquillity in stark contrast to the destruction and chaos of everyday life.

Consider the peaceful repose of the sausage compared with the aggressiveness and violence of bacon.

# THOMAS SANCHEZ

# The Washo Watched

*The Washo is a small tribe of about 500 Indians, living in the extreme Western part of Nevada, and Eastern California. They are usually a harmless people, with much less physical and mental development than the Paiutes, and more degraded morally. They are indolent, improvident, and much addicted to the vices and evil practices common in savage life. They manifest an almost uncontrollable appetite for intoxicating drinks. They are sensual and filthy, and are annually diminishing in numbers from the diseases contracted through their indulgences. A few have learned the English language and will do light work for a reasonable compensation. They spend the winter months about the villages and habitations of white men, from whom they obtain tolerable supplies of food and clothing. The spring, summer, and autumn months are spent in fishing about Washo and Tahoe lakes and the streams which flow through their country. They also gather grass seed and pine nuts, hunt rabbits, hares, and ducks. There is no suitable place for a reservation in the bounds of their territory, and, in view of their rapidly diminishing numbers and the diseases to which they are subjected, none is required.*

28th ANNUAL REPORT OF THE COMMISSIONER
OF INDIAN AFFAIRS TO
THE SECRETARY OF THE INTERIOR
(SUPERINTENDENT PARKER, 1866)

The Washo watched. The Washo watched through the trees. The Washo watched through the trees as *they* ate themselves. His chin lifted, head cocked rigid to one side as he watched through the leaves, the branches, the bark. The waiting winter light fell flat on the trees, on him, on *them*. The light hung in the branches, caught, glistening in the dead weight of snow that bent them down. The Washo watched between these trees pierced through the snow like spears being driven back, back into the snow that was as high as two men, one standing on the other, back into the frozen Earth. In this silence he heard a sound, a sound which did not come from *them*, a sound that was familiar to him, a sound that rushed over him watching down the slight slope of the mountain, a sound that crashed the silence of the trees, the silence of *them* on the higher snow packed in the lowness of the valley along the shore of the lake, a sound that was indifferent to what he was watching, a sound indifferent to all except the pure energy of its own existence, the sound of Geese. He looked up from *them* who were on the lake to the power in the Sky, the power of *Musege*, his brothers in nature who had secret medicine, strong medicine that many times was superior to his own, medicine which he had tried to capture, imitate, kill. He watched the *Power*, he watched it move in the Sky, the strength of the slick feathered wings digging into the coldness of the air in a seemingly effortless attempt of moving the Birds across the tops of trees, over the scene below. He watched the Birds as they moved off, long out of imaginary bow range. They seemed to be drifting slowly as if in a dream, but this was no dream, although it seemed like one for the air was sharp like the stoneknife at his side, it was a cold which he could not remember for any other winters, although he had heard his grandfather speak of one winter so cold that the frozen trees splintered like two boulders smashed into each other. Yet it was not only this cold; something seemed to suck him down, make it difficult to breathe, to move, the only thing easy was to watch, to wait. It was much like the feeling he had once before as a younger man, as if that feeling was a preparation for this.

The feeling came upon him one night as he lay asleep under his new Rabbit blanket with his two daughters and their mother that his Power had gone to another place; even the strength running deep in his bones fled. He awoke, tried to lift the softness of the blanket from his body, but could not, could not even raise his hands. He spoke loudly so that his two daughters and their mother would awake. Help me lift this blanket from us. All four tried to push together, it was of no use, they all lay back in their weakness, felt the heavy burden closing on their skin, weighting them down. In the morning when they awoke he asked if they remembered what had passed during the night. They did, but none could agree if it was true in the way of having taken place or true in the way of the dream. They did never again sleep in that *gadu*, even one more night. One thing he did know to be true as he watched down through the trees to the high snow by the lake shore, this was no dream. The body sprawled on the snow, split open, one of *them* standing over it with a hatchet hanging limp in his hand, the thickness of blood dripping slowly from the blade to the snow, each drop silently splashing red into the coldness, lightening into pink as it sought to touch all flakes with its warmth, its color. A boot smashed into the pinkish splotch of soiled snow, one of *them* bent over the body. Above the gash from the hatchet he plunged a thick knife, cut in along the heart, slashed the skin away over the ribs, leaving them exposed for an instant before he brought the butt of the knife down, breaking through. He yanked the broken bones away, once more cut in around the heart, this time freeing it, grabbing hold, the beat lingering in its firm flesh, pulsing weakly in his fist. He tugged it from its place, leaving a sucking hole, looked up around him, no one moved, their eyes tight on the meat clutched in the man's hand, sweat and saliva dripped onto the hair growing out from the bottom of his face, crystallizing into sharp chinks of ice. His head jerked looking from one to the other. Slowly he lifted the heart to his lips, the red slipping between his white cold fingers, moving down his wrists, splashed on the cracked leather boots. He opened his mouth, the smoke of his breath spurting in the air, the teeth clamped down on the warm meat. The one with the hatchet raised it high above his head, brought it down on the sprawled, heartless body, the blade sliced cleanly through the neck as if it were a slender log, sinking deep in

the snow. He picked up the head, his fingers locked in the
hair of the dripping globe, and tossed it away. Released, it
spun toward the lake. The others watched it float in the
quiet cold of morning air, then drop, landing softly on the
open whiteness; it did not roll, the eyes turned down in
the coldness, buried away from *them*. The people fell, as
if the head had severed the strings that held their bodies
rigid, the claws of their hands tearing the clothes from the
body beneath them, ripping into flesh. A sound exploded,
seeming to shake the snow from the trees, crashing up the
roll of slope where the Washo stood, stripping everything of
meaning in its path, driving into him like the jagged flint of
an arrowtip. He did not move, did not move as he watched,
as he heard the last whimper from the jagged, shouted cry
of pain from the one of *them* who was falling on the torn
body. It was as if *he* were falling, falling from a cloud, his
body felt hollow as it plunged, the rising Earth beating up,
straight, into his face, into the face of the woman as she
fell on the wet, ravaged body, her arms spread out stiff as
the hands beat into the snow, digging, trying to hang onto
the very coldness itself. One of *them* moved toward her, his
entire body straining against its own weight as he forced
the three long steps to come up to her, the big jacket
splitting open down the middle as he reached to pull a
knife tucked under his belt, its blade sparkling between the
clear winter light and the whiteness of the snow, caught,
glinting blindingly like the splashing rays of Sun in the
water of the lake. With one hand he yanked the woman up
by the hair, pulling her bloodstreaked face off the exposed
body. He put the knife to her throat; the arm stiffened as if
to slit open the neck of a wounded Deer. The man with the
hatchet moved, one leg came up, the boot hooking with a
crack under the jaw of the one with the knife, throwing
him backwards into the snow, almost pitching the long
knife from his hand. He raised his arm and brought the
hatchet down with a rush of air. The other one rolled over,
the hatchet slicing next to him, burying itself in the snow
up to the handle, he jabbed with the knife a single hard
stroke. The blade disappeared into the chest. The man
dropped, his hand still locked around the wooden handle of
the hatchet as the dead weight of his body hit the snow.
The one with the knife stood up, hot breath flaring from
his wide nostrils. He did notice a young boy move past him

to the body, lift an ax his own height and chop fiercely at the leg.

The Washo watched *them* moving slowly on the snow, clumsy, like Bears in water. He had been watching silently all morning, had seen, had seen them hunched, away from each other, mouths tearing at knots of flesh, faces smeared the color of a dying Sun. He had seen through the trees. He felt a hand on his shoulder, he turned and saw his brother. For a moment he felt ashamed, ashamed that he did not hear him approach, but then, he had been watching. He looked into his face, they did not speak, he too had seen, he too knew. They left, slowly, through the snow, they made their way up the slope of the mountain to the ridge and walked in silence away from the Sun.

On the top of the ridge it was easier to walk. He felt as his Deerhide wrapped feet pulled lightly out of the deep snow with each step that this winter must surely end; and when the waters ran once more it would wash away all of what he had seen, and when the Earth around the lake had again turned up black, free of its white burden, *they* would be gone. These things he thought as he walked ahead of his brother, away from the Sun, towards his people, towards his home on the Big Lake in the Sky, Tahoe. As they turned off the ridge and headed down into the first valley, soft bits of snow began to fall. The Indians pulled their Rabbit blankets closer about them and walked on. They had moved steadily from where they had come, never looking back. When the snow cleared the Sun had left the Sky; they followed the Stars, they knew from the night they could continue until the next afternoon. Then they would be home.

She sat naked from the waist up on the thick mat of branches. Her bent legs settled softly into the skins. She watched out the opening of the strong *galisdangal* her husband had built from cut limbs of trees, stacked close and tall, lashed with strips of Beaverhide to form a circle of protection against the mountain winds. Her brown eyes sunk deep in her blunt round face appeared aware of nothing, but she was watching. She was watching out across the small bay of the Big Lake, and behind it at the white wall of mountain. She had been watching this direction many days now. First she watched for her husband, and when finally he did not come his brother was sent. Now she watched for both. It was silent this day, as had been all the days of this winter; even the trees bent in silence under the winds. The only sound she could hear was the sucking of her baby. She held the weight of its body to her breast with one crooked arm, and watched. She gazed at the mountain waiting for only one thing, its white wall a backdrop for movements in her mind. Sitting, waiting for the small black shape of her husband on the white wall, she thought of him and how when the baby had finally come out and the old lady, her mother's cousin, had cut the cord from her body with a sharp wooden knife, his thin, hardset face cracked into smile, he placed an arrow in his bow, and shot it at the dull winter Sun. It sailed high, then fell, sticking up straight in the snow at his younger brother's feet. He looked at the arrow, turned and walked to the Lake Tahoe. Out a short distance on the ice the men followed him, each with a half hidden grin on his face, for he had to take the ritual bath after birth in icecold water. He brought out his knife, jabbed a circle in the white hard crust, finally breaking an opening large enough for his body. He turned towards the men, but his eyes did not meet theirs; he was looking over their heads, back at the *galisdangal*. He knew that his young wife was watching as he loosened the rawhide string of his leather breechcloth and let it fall, then jumped into the hole, the water splashing up above his waist. The men's laughter came like a cloudburst; laughing so hard they forgot themselves, toppled to the snow and rolled around in howling fits. His teeth began to chatter and he clenched them as he sank to his knees, his head going under water, his whole body submerged in freezing slush. As he climbed out from the hole the men found the strength to stand up and brush the snow from their almost naked bodies. He used the Deerskin breechcloth to wipe himself, then looped it back around his waist. He gently stooped, placed his knife at the rim of the hole, its thin stone blade facing inward in testimony as the traditional gift of birth for one of the men to take, then walked off. Some days later the piece of cord from the baby's belly fell to the ground. She told her husband he must go and hunt meat, for until now he had been forbidden to eat it. When he returned there would be the happiness of the babyfeast, and all but she would fill themselves on his killings. She must fast longer, to bring the

power of endurance upon the child. Before he left she
touched her hand to his face and spoke of how she was
sorry in her heart that the baby was in the winter and it
was expected of him to hunt in the snow, how she had
wished it had come like most others, when the pinenuts
were being gathered. It was bad for him as husband to
have to fast from meat and salt and not be allowed to sleep
at night until the cord fell. She could bear it, she was a
woman, but it was bad for a man to do without strength
during the white days. She must have done something to
bring the baby in the winter, she must have called down
some evil upon herself. The waterfall, she thought, that
must have been the evil power. But she did not tell him,
she only touched his face and spoke of her grief. How it
made her weep to bend his shoulders with her burdens.
Before he left he tied the newly fallen umbilical cord around
a stick and placed it at the right side of the child's
winnowing basket so that he would grow quickly and have
a powerful right hand. Since then, every day she had gone
to the place where he had buried the afterbirth of the child.
She stared at the frozen Earth, could see beneath it to that
part of her wrapped moistly in bark, waiting to grow again
within her stomach, to become heavy with flesh, to suck
at her breast, to walk the mountains and taste the spring
berries between its lips. She would gaze at the spot where
she knew it to be. She knew it was buried upright, and
wondered if in the spring he would return to dig it up and
rebury it facing down so that it would grow deep in the
black Earth and bring her the power to once more give him
a child.

She saw what she had been waiting for. The men outside
were shouting, their voices booming out across the flatness
of the Big Lake in celebration. Celebration was in her
heart; she hugged the child closer to her skin and waited
for the two distant figures that had appeared on the white
wall to make their way down to camp.

The man with the two Eagle feathers held tightly against
his head by a leather band stood watching in silence, his
bare feet planted firmly in the ankle deep snow. He watched
as his two youngest sons walked toward him through the
forest along the shore of the Big Lake. He knew this was
not right. Something was not as it should be. It was not
just the fact that his son with the new boychild had been

gone for more than fourteen nights' passing; it was greater than that. He hated the power of the feelings he had, he hated them because they were mostly right, like the time the sagebrush laughed when he was young, he had been right then too. He could not understand this power he had, he did not try to, he had been deceived for many years in believing that he could unravel this. Now he only hated it. He hated this winter. Not the cold, he could suffer that, he hated its silence, its length. Each day it challenged him, and each day he grew more bitter. It was the bitterness which allowed him to meet the challenge each day, the bitterness which allowed him to survive, and it was just that which he hated, for he knew it was the winter which gave him the strength to live through each day, only so it could challenge him again the next. But he did not fight. He had learned long ago that you cannot fight, you cannot fight for you are the only one that can be killed. You must wait and watch to survive. Only in this manner advantage can be taken of the situation, by surprising it and adopting its terms. Like the winter it is not something to be killed, it is impossible to capture its power, but it can be, in a miserable way, imitated. You can learn how to make your body grow cold with the winter, how to fill your mind with the warm image of spring Sun, a woman's flesh moving in the strong smell of a Rabbit blanket. Deceit is survival. You must look like the tree in the snow, dead and buried, but deep within the roots remain warm in hope, for spring always does come, winter always must pass, things do get better. But the old man could no longer take warmth from these thoughts. The cold had penetrated his roots, and now he met each day like the stone. The winter washed over him, it was only the fact that the winter did wash over him which held him together in bitterness.

As the Indian approached, his father loomed larger, he seemed a gray stone growing from the snow. He walked steadily toward him, his brother following in his footsteps. The men that had set up the cheer, which reached his ears from the surface of the Big Lake as he and his brother started down the last steep white mountainside, had fallen silent and stood behind the father, waiting for him to speak. He stopped at the edge of the camp and faced his father across the snow.

"Gayabuc," the old man's lips spoke the word after staring for some time into the face of his son. "You bring no

killings for the babyfeast." The son did not speak. Both
men were silent, facing each other with feet rooted in the
snow. "Do you not remember why you left the camp? Do
you not remember the boychild?"

"There will be no babyfeast for Gayabuc, for anyone,"
the Indian's words fell flat in the clearing.

"It is not the way," the old man stated.

"I have seen the way before me and followed it as I was
taught, but my eyes have now seen new things, things for
which I have no teaching, no power."

"For what new things are you without power?" the old
man asked in a low voice, knowing that once again his
feeling was right.

"Them."

The father looked at the son but the fear did not show in
his eyes. For many years now his people had heard that
others, others with skin like the snow, had come into the
high mountains from the desert, but he had not seen *them*,
none of his people had seen *them*. But there had been
many stories among other people. He himself had come
upon a Paiute not more than three summers past that made
much talk about seeing *them* and following *them* up into
the mountains, but never getting close enough to look *them*
in the face. *They* were tall men, tall as the men that came
long ago in his father's father's time and stole the children.
*Their* bodies were heavy. The women too, the animals,
wild stone-eyed beasts, were larger than both together. In
this he knew that the Paiute was not lying. For all the
stories spoke of *their* great size and strength, of how *they*
did not carry bows, but sticks, sticks from which fire would
burst and animals would fall. There was one story which
came from the desert that told of how the sticks had made
an Indian fall, an Indian, it was spoken true, that got too
close to *their* power, and who had looked in *their* faces.
This he had heard. He had no proof, but this he believed.
He believed all, because not having seen *them*, he had seen
*their* tracks some winters ago. They were tracks like no
animal would make; they were great in size, and deep. He
knew *they* must be heavy and he had no desire to follow
*them*, for he could sense that *their* path was evil. All of this
he spoke not to those of his camp, for he knew their way
was to be frightened and the stories which did reach their
ears had placed sorrow on their days. He spoke only to his
middle son; the oldest was dead. And when he was alive he

was not one to believe his father, so he spoke only to Gayabuc of *them*.

"Go to the mother of your son," he pointed to the *galisdangal* where she sat. "Go, Gayabuc."

The Indian did not move, his brother behind him did not move.

"Go, Gayabuc." The old man's voice came at his son again.

"I have seen *them* eat . . ."

The old man said nothing, he waited as his son fell silent, he waited, watching his face. He waited for what his son had no teaching, no power.

"I have seen *them* eat of *themselves*."

"Go to your *galisdangal*, Gayabuc."

"I have seen *them* eat the flesh from *their* own bodies."

"Go!"

He went. The Indian who would have no joyous baby-feast for his first boychild went. He turned from his father towards his wife, each foot leaving its soft black imprint in the snow as he walked up the rise to where she waited.

# DANNY SANTIAGO

# The Somebody

This is Chato talking, Chato de Shamrock, from the East-side in old L.A., and I want you to know this is a big day in my life because today I quit school and went to work as a writer. I write on fences or buildings or anything that comes along. I write my name, not the one I got from my father. I want no part of him. I write Chato, which means Catface, because I have a flat nose like a cat. It's a Mexi-can word because that's what I am, a Mexican, and I'm not ashamed of it. I like that language too, man. It's way better than English to say what you feel. But German is the best. It's got a real rugged sound, and I'm going to learn to talk it someday.

After Chato I write "de Shamrock." That's the street where I live, and it's the name of the gang I belong to, but the others are all gone now. Their families had to move away, except Gorilla is in jail and Blackie joined the navy because he liked swimming. But I still have our old arsenal. It's buried under the chickens, and I dig it up when I get bored. There's tire irons and chains and pick handles and spokes and two zip guns we made and they shoot real bullets but not very straight. In the good old days nobody cared to tangle with us. But now I'm the only one left.

Well, today started off like any other day. The toilet roars like a hot rod taking off. My father coughs and spits about nineteen times and hollers it's six-thirty. So I holler back I'm quitting school. Things hit me like that—sudden.

"Don't you want to be a lawyer no more," he says in Spanish, "and defend the Mexican people?"

My father thinks he is very funny, and next time I make any plans he's sure not going to hear about it.

"Don't you want to be a doctor," he said, "and cut off my leg for nothing someday?"

*"Due beast ine dumb cop,"* I tell him in German, but not very loud.

"How will you support me," he says, "when I retire? Or will you marry a rich old woman that owns a pool hall?"

"I'm checking out of this dump! You'll never see me again!"

I hollered at him, but already he was in the kitchen making a big noise in his coffee. I could be dead and he wouldn't take me serious. So I laid there and waited for him to go off to work. When I woke up again, it was way past eleven. I can sleep forever these days. So I got out of bed and put on clean jeans and my windbreaker and combed myself very neat because already I had a feeling this was going to be a big day for me.

I had to wait for breakfast because the baby was sick and throwing up milk on everything. There is always a baby vomiting in my house. When they're born, everybody comes over and says: *"Qué* cute!" but nobody passes any comments on the dirty way babies act or the dirty way they were made either. Sometimes my mother asks me to hold one for her but it always cries, maybe because I squeeze it a little hard when nobody's looking.

When my mother finally served me, I had to hold my breath, she smelled so bad of babies. I don't care to look at her any more. Her legs got those dark-blue rivers running all over them. I kept waiting for her to bawl me out about school, but I guess she forgot, or something. So I cut out.

Every time I go out my front door I have to cry for what they've done to old Shamrock Street. It used to be so fine, with solid homes on both sides. Maybe they needed a little paint here and there but they were cozy. Then the S.P. railroad bought up all the land except my father's place because he was stubborn. They came in with their wrecking bars and their bulldozers. You could hear those houses scream when they ripped them down. So now Shamrock

Street is just front walks that lead to a hole in the ground,
and piles of busted cement. And Pelón's house and Blackie's are just stacks of old boards waiting to get hauled
away. I hope that never happens to your street, man.

My first stop was the front gate and there was that sign
again, that big S wrapped around a cross like a snake with
rays coming out, which is the mark of the Sierra Street
gang, as everybody knows, I rubbed it off, but tonight
they'll put it back again. In the old days they wouldn't dare
to come on our street, but without your gang you're nobody. And one of these fine days they're going to catch up
with me in person and that will be the end of Chato de
Shamrock.

So I cruised on down to Main Street like a ghost in a
graveyard. Just to prove I'm alive, I wrote my name on the
fence at the corner. A lot of names you see in public places
are written very sloppy. Not me. I take my time. Like my
fifth-grade teacher used to say, if other people are going
to see your work, you owe it to yourself to do it right. Mrs.
Cully was her name and she was real nice, for an Anglo.
My other teachers were all cops but Mrs. Cully drove me
home one time when some guys were after me. I think she
wanted to adopt me but she never said anything about it. I
owe a lot to that lady, and especially my writing. You
should see it, man—it's real smooth and mellow, and curvy
like a blonde in a bikini. Everybody says so. Except one
time they had me in Juvenile by mistake and some doctor
looked at it. He said it proved I had something wrong with
me, some long word. The doctor was crazy, because I
made him show me his writing and it was real ugly like a
barb-wire fence with little chickens stuck on the points.
You couldn't even read it.

Anyway, I signed myself very clean and neat on that
corner. And then I thought, Why not look for a job someplace? But I was more in the mood to write my name, so I
went to the dime store and helped myself to two boxes of
crayons and some chalk and cruised on down Main, writing all the way. I wondered should I write more than my
name. Should I write, "Chato is a fine guy," or, "Chato is
wanted by the police"? Things like that. News. But I decided against it. Better to keep them guessing. Then I
crossed over to Forney Playground. It used to be our territory, but now the Sierra have taken over there like every-

place else. Just to show them, I wrote on the tennis court
and the swimming pool and the gym. I left a fine little trail
of Chato de Shamrock in eight colors. Some places I used
chalk, which works better on brick or plaster. But crayons
are the thing for cement or anything smooth, like in the
girls' rest room. On that wall I also drew a little picture the
girls would be interested in and put down a phone number
beside it. I bet a lot of them are going to call that number,
but it isn't mine because we don't have a phone in the first
place, and in the second place I'm probably never going
home again.

I'm telling you, I was pretty famous at the Forney by the
time I cut out, and from there I continued my travels till
something hit me. You know how you put your name on
something and that proves it belongs to you? Things like
schoolbooks or gym shoes? So I thought, How about that,
now? And I put my name on the Triple A Market and on
Morrie's Liquor Store and on the Zócalo, which is a beer
joint. And then I cruised on up Broadway, getting rich. I
took over a barber shop and a furniture store and the
Plymouth agency. And the firehouse for laughs, and the
phone company so I could call all my girl friends and keep
my dimes. And then there I was at Webster and Garcia's
Funeral Home with the big white columns. At first I
thought that might be bad luck, but then I said, Oh, well,
we all got to die sometime. So I signed myself, and now I
can eat good and live in style and have a big time all my
life, and then kiss you all good-bye and give myself the
best damn funeral in L.A. for free.

And speaking of funerals, along came the Sierra right
then, eight or ten of them down the street with that stupid
walk which is their trademark. I ducked into the garage
and hid behind the hearse. Not that I'm a coward. Getting
stomped doesn't bother me, or even shot. What I hate is
those blades, man. They're like a piece of ice cutting into
your belly. But the Sierra didn't see me and went on by. I
couldn't hear what they were saying but I knew they had
me on their mind. So I cut on over to the Boy's Club,
where they don't let anybody get you, no matter who you
are. To pass the time I shot some baskets and played a
little pool and watched the television, but the story was
boring, so it came to me, Why not write my name on the
screen? Which I did with a squeaky pen. Those cowboys

sure looked fine with Chato de Shamrock written all over them. Everybody got a kick out of it. But of course up comes Mr. Calderon and makes me wipe it off. They're always spying on you up there. And he takes me into his office and closes the door.

"Well," he says, "and how is the last of the dinosaurs?"

Meaning that the Shamrocks are as dead as giant lizards. Then he goes into that voice with the church music in it and I look out of the window.

"I know it's hard to lose your gang, Chato," he says, "but this is your chance to make new friends and straighten yourself out. Why don't you start coming to Boys' Club more?"

"It's boring here," I tell him.

"What about school?"

"I can't go," I said. "They'll get me."

"The Sierra's forgotten you're alive," he tells me.

"Then how come they put their mark on my house every night?"

"Do they?"

He stares at me very hard. I hate those eyes of his. He thinks he knows everything. And what is he? Just a Mexican like everybody else.

"Maybe you put that mark there yourself," he says. "To make yourself big. Just like you wrote on the television."

"That was my name! I like to write my name!"

"So do dogs," he says. "On every lamppost they come to."

"You're a dog yourself," I told him, but I don't think he heard me. He just went on talking. Brother, how they love to talk up there! But I didn't bother to listen, and when he ran out of gas I left. From now on I'm scratching that Boy's Club off my list.

Out on the street it was getting dark, but I could still follow my trail back toward Broadway. It felt good seeing Chato written everyplace, but at the Zócalo I stopped dead. Around my name there was a big red heart done in lipstick with some initials I didn't recognize. To tell the truth, I didn't know how to feel. In one way I was mad that anyone would fool with my name, especially if it was some guy doing it for laughs. But what guy carries lipstick? And if it was a girl, that could be kind of interesting.

A girl is what it turned out to be. I caught up with her at

the telephone company. There she is, standing in the shadows, drawing her heart around my name. And she has a very pretty shape on her, too. I sneak up behind her very quiet, thinking all kinds of crazy things and my blood shooting around so fast it shakes me all over. And then she turns around and it's only Crusader Rabbit. That's what we called her from the television show they had then, on account of her teeth in front.

When she sees me, she takes off down the alley, but in twenty feet I catch her. I grab for the lipstick, but she whips it behind her. I reach around and try to pull her fingers open, but her hand is sweaty and so is mine. And there we are, stuck together all the way down. I can feel everything she's got and her breath is on my cheek. She twists up against me, kind of giggling. To tell the truth, I don't like to wrestle with girls. They don't fight fair. And then we lost balance and fell against some garbage cans, so I woke up. After that I got the lipstick away from her very easy.

"What right you got to my name?" I tell her. "I never gave you permission."

"You sign yourself real fine," she says.

I knew that already.

"Let's go writing together," she says.

"The Sierra's after me."

"I don't care," she says. "Come on, Chato—you and me can have a lot of fun."

She came up close and giggled that way. She put her hand on my hand that had the lipstick in it. And you know what? I'm ashamed to say I almost told her yes. It would be a change to go writing with a girl. We could talk there in the dark. We could decide on the best places. And her handwriting wasn't too bad either. But then I remembered I had my reputation to think of. Somebody would be sure to see us, and they'd be laughing at me all over the Eastside. So I pulled my hand away and told her off.

"Run along, Crusader," I told her. "I don't want no partners, and especially not you."

"Who are you calling Crusader?" she screamed. "You ugly, squash-nose punk."

She called me everything. And spit at my face but missed. I didn't argue. I just cut out. And when I got to the first sewer I threw away her lipstick. Then I drifted over to the banks at Broadway and Bailey, which is a good spot for writing because a lot of people pass by there.

Well, I hate to brag, but that was the best work I've ever done in all my life. Under the street lamp my name shone like solid gold. I stood to one side and checked the people as they walked past and inspected it. With some you can't tell just how they feel, but with others it rings out like a cash register. There was one man. He got out of his Cadillac to buy a paper and when he saw my name he smiled. He was the age to be my father. I bet he'd give me a job if I asked him. I bet he'd take me to his home and office in the morning. Pretty soon I'd be sitting at my own desk and signing my name on letters and checks and things. But I would never buy a Cadillac, man. They burn too much gas.

Later a girl came by. She was around eighteen, I think, with green eyes. Her face was so pretty I didn't dare to look at her shape. Do you want me to go crazy? That girl stopped and really studied my name like she fell in love with it. She wanted to know me, I could tell. She wanted to take my hand and we'd go off together just holding hands and nothing dirty. We'd go to Beverly Hills and nobody would look at us the wrong way. I almost said "Hi" to that girl, and, "How do you like my writing?" But not quite.

So here I am, standing on this corner with my chalk all gone and only one crayon left and it's ugly brown. My fingers are too cold besides. But I don't care because I just had a vision, man. Did they ever turn on the lights for you so you could see the whole world and everything in it? That's how it came to me right now. I don't need to be a movie star or boxing champ to make my name in the world. All I need is plenty of chalk and crayons. And that's easy. L.A. is a big city, man, but give me a couple of months and I'll be famous all over town. Of course they'll try to stop me—the Sierra, the police, and everybody. But I'll be like a ghost, man. I'll be real mysterious, and all they'll know is just my name, signed like I always sign it, CHATO DE SHAMROCK with rays shooting out like from the Holy Cross.

# WILLIAM SAROYAN

# The Summer of the Beautiful White Horse

One day back there in the good old days when I was nine
and the world was full of every imaginable kind of magnifi-
cence, and life was still a delightful and mysterious dream,
my cousin Mourad, who was considered crazy by everybody who knew him except me, came to my house at four
in the morning and woke me up by tapping on the window
of my room.

Aram, he said.

I jumped out of bed and looked out the window.

I couldn't believe what I saw.

It wasn't morning yet, but it was summer and with day-
break not many minutes around the corner of the world it
was light enough for me to know I wasn't dreaming.

My cousin Mourad was sitting on a beautiful white
horse.

I stuck my head out of the window and rubbed my
eyes.

Yes, he said in Armenian. It's a horse. You're not dreaming. Make it quick if you want a ride.

I knew my cousin Mourad enjoyed being alive more
than anybody else who had ever fallen into the world by
mistake, but this was more than even I could believe.

In the first place, my earliest memories had been memories of horses and my first longings had been longings to ride.

This was the wonderful part.

In the second place, we were poor.

This was the part that wouldn't permit me to believe what I saw.

We were poor. We had no money. Our whole tribe was poverty-stricken. Every branch of the Garoghlanian family was living in the most amazing and comical poverty in the world. Nobody could understand where we ever got money enough to keep us with food in our bellies, not even the old men of the family. Most important of all, though, we were famous for our honesty. We had been famous for our honesty for something like eleven centuries, even when we had been the wealthiest family in what we liked to think was the world. We were proud first, honest next, and after that we believed in right and wrong. None of us would take advantage of anybody in the world, let alone steal.

Consequently, even though I could see the horse, so magnificent; even though I could *smell* it, so lovely; even though I could *hear* it breathing, so exciting; I couldn't *believe* the horse had anything to do with my cousin Mourad or with me or with any of the other members of our family, asleep or awake, because I *knew* my cousin Mourad couldn't have *bought* the horse, and if he couldn't have bought it he must have *stolen* it, and I refused to believe he had stolen it.

No member of the Garoghlanian family could be a thief.

I stared first at my cousin and then at the horse. There was a pious stillness and humor in each of them which on the one hand delighted me and on the other frightened me.

Mourad, I said, where did you steal this horse?

Leap out of the window, he said, if you want a ride.

It was true, then. He *had* stolen the horse. There was no question about it. He had come to invite me to ride or not, as I chose.

Well, it seemed to me stealing a horse for a ride was not the same thing as stealing something else, such as money. For all I knew, maybe it wasn't stealing at all. If you were crazy about horses the way my cousin Mourad and I were, it wasn't stealing. It wouldn't become stealing until we offered to sell the horse, which of course I knew we would never do.

Let me put on some clothes, I said.

All right, he said, but hurry.

I leaped into my clothes.

I jumped down to the yard from the window and leaped up onto the horse behind my cousin Mourad.

That year we lived at the edge of town, on Walnut Avenue. Behind our house was the country: vineyards, orchards, irrigation ditches, and country roads. In less than three minutes we were on Olive Avenue, and then the horse began to trot. The air was new and lovely to breathe. The feel of the horse running was wonderful. My cousin Mourad who was considered one of the craziest members of our family began to sing. I mean, he began to roar.

Every family has a crazy streak in it somewhere, and my cousin Mourad was considered the natural descendant of the crazy streak in our tribe. Before him was our uncle Khosrove, an enormous man with a powerful head of black hair and the largest mustache in the San Joaquin Valley, a man so furious in temper, so irritable, so impatient that he stopped anyone from talking by roaring, *It is no harm; pay no attention to it.*

That was all, no matter what anybody happened to be talking about. Once it was his own son Arak running eight blocks to the barber shop where his father was having his mustache trimmed to tell him their house was on fire. The man Khosrove sat up in the chair and roared, It is no harm; pay no attention to it. The barber said, But the boy says your house is on fire. So Khosrove roared, Enough, it is no harm, I say.

My cousin Mourad was considered the natural descendant of this man, although Mourad's father was Zorab, who was practical and nothing else. That's how it was in our tribe. A man could be the father of his son's flesh, but that did not mean that he was also the father of his spirit. The distribution of the various kinds of spirit of our tribe had been from the beginning capricious and vagrant.

We rode and my cousin Mourad sang. For all anybody knew we were still in the old country where, at least according to our neighbors, we belonged. We let the horse run as long as it felt like running.

At last my cousin Mourad said, Get down. I want to ride alone.

Will you let me ride alone? I said.

That is up to the horse, my cousin said. Get down.

The *horse* will let me ride, I said.

We shall see, he said. Don't forget that I have a way with a horse.

Well, I said, any way you have with a horse, I have also.

For the sake of your safety, he said, let us hope so. Get down.

All right, I said, but remember you've got to let me try to ride alone.

I got down and my cousin Mourad kicked his heels into the horse and shouted, *Vazire*, run. The horse stood on its hind legs, snorted, and burst into a fury of speed that was the loveliest thing I had ever seen. My cousin Mourad raced the horse across a field of dry grass to an irrigation ditch, crossed the ditch on the horse, and five minutes later returned, dripping wet.

The sun was coming up.

Now it's my turn to ride, I said.

My cousin Mourad got off the horse.

Ride, he said.

I leaped to the back of the horse and for a moment knew the awfulest fear imaginable. The horse did not move.

Kick into his muscles, my cousin Mourad said. What are you waiting for? We've got to take him back before everybody in the world is up and about.

I kicked into the muscles of the horse. Once again it reared and snorted. Then it began to run. I didn't know what to do. Instead of running across the field to the irrigation ditch the horse ran down the road to the vineyard of Dikran Halabian where it began to leap over vines. The horse leaped over seven vines before I fell. Then it continued running.

My cousin Mourad came running down the road.

I'm not worried about you, he shouted. We've got to get that horse. You go this way and I'll go this way. If you come upon him, be kindly. I'll be near.

I continued down the road and my cousin Mourad went across the field toward the irrigation ditch.

It took him half an hour to find the horse and bring him back.

All right, he said, jump on. The whole world is awake now.

What will we do? I said.

Well, he said, we'll either take him back or hide him until tomorrow morning.

He didn't sound worried and I knew he'd hide him and not take him back. Not for a while, at any rate.

Where will you hide him? I said.

I know a place, he said.

How long ago did you steal this horse? I said.

It suddenly dawned on me that he had been taking these early morning rides for some time and had come for me this morning only because he knew how much I longed to ride.

Who said anything about stealing a horse? he said.

Anyhow, I said, how long ago did you begin riding every morning?

Not until this morning, he said.

Are you telling the truth? I said.

Of course not, he said, but if we are found out, that's what you're to say. I don't want both of us to be liars. All you know is that we started riding this morning.

All right, I said.

He walked the horse quietly to the barn of a deserted vineyard which at one time had been the pride of a farmer named Fetvajian. There were some oats and dry alfalfa in the barn.

We began walking home.

It wasn't easy, he said, to get the horse to behave so nicely. At first it wanted to run wild, but as I've told you, I have a way with a horse. I can get it to want to do anything *I* want it to do. Horses understand me.

How do you do it? I said.

I have an understanding with a horse, he said.

Yes, but what sort of an understanding? I said.

A simple and honest one, he said.

Well, I said, I wish I knew how to reach an understanding like that with a horse.

You're still a small boy, he said. When you get to be thirteen you'll know how to do it.

I went home and ate a hearty breakfast.

That afternoon my uncle Khosrove came to our house for coffee and cigarettes. He sat in the parlor, sipping and smoking and remembering the old country. Then another visitor arrived, a farmer named John Byro, an Assyrian who, out of loneliness, had learned to speak Armenian. My mother brought the lonely visitor coffee and tobacco and he rolled a cigarette and sipped and smoked, and then at last, sighing sadly, he said, My white horse which was stolen last month is still gone. I cannot understand it.

My uncle Khosrove became very irritated and shouted, It's no harm. What is the loss of a horse? Haven't we all lost the homeland? What is this crying over a horse?

That may be all right for you, a city dweller, to say, John Byro said, but what of my surrey? What good is a surrey without a horse?

Pay no attention to it, my uncle Khosrove roared.

I walked ten miles to get here, John Byro said.

You have legs, my uncle Khosrove shouted.

My left leg pains me, the farmer said.

Pay no attention to it, my uncle Khosrove roared.

That horse cost me sixty dollars, the farmer said.

I spit on money, my uncle Khosrove said.

He got up and stalked out of the house, slamming the screen door.

My mother explained.

He has a gentle heart, she said. It is simply that he is homesick and such a large man.

The farmer went away and I ran over to my cousin Mourad's house.

He was sitting under a peach tree, trying to repair the hurt wing of a young robin which could not fly. He was talking to the bird.

What is it? he said.

The farmer, John Byro, I said. He visited our house. He wants his horse. You've had it a month. I want you to promise not to take it back until I learn to ride.

It will take you a *year* to learn to ride, my cousin Mourad said.

We could keep the horse a year, I said.

My cousin Mourad leaped to his feet.

What? he roared. Are you inviting a member of the Garoghlanian family to steal? The horse must go back to its true owner.

When? I said.

In six months at the latest, he said.

He threw the bird into the air. The bird tried hard, almost fell twice, but at last flew away, high and straight.

Early every morning for two weeks my cousin Mourad and I took the horse out of the barn of the deserted vineyard where we were hiding it and rode it, and every morning, when it was my turn to ride alone, leaped over grape vines and small trees and threw me and ran away. Nevertheless, I hoped in time to learn to ride the way my cousin Mourad rode.

One morning on the way to Fetvajian's deserted vineyard we ran into the farmer John Byro who was on his way to town.

Let me do the talking, my cousin Mourad said. I have a way with farmers.

Good morning, John Byro, my cousin Mourad said to the farmer.

The farmer studied the horse eagerly.

Good morning, sons of my friends, he said. What is the name of your horse?

*My Heart*, my cousin Mourad said in Armenian.

A lovely name, John Byro said, for a lovely horse. I could swear it is the horse that was stolen from me many weeks ago. May I look into its mouth?

Of course. Mourad said.

The farmer looked into the mouth of the horse.

Tooth for tooth, he said. I would swear it *is* my horse if I didn't know your parents. The fame of your family for honesty is well known to me. Yet the horse is the twin of my horse. A suspicious man would believe his eyes instead of his heart. Good day, my young friends.

Good day, John Byro, my cousin Mourad said.

Early the following morning we took the horse to John Byro's vineyard and put it in the barn. The dogs followed us around without making a sound.

The dogs, I whispered to my cousin Mourad. I thought they would bark.

They would at somebody else, he said. I have a way with dogs.

My cousin Mourad put his arms around the horse, pressed his nose into the horse's nose, patted it, and then we went away.

That afternoon John Byro came to our house in his surrey and showed my mother the horse that had been stolen and returned.

I do not know what to think, he said. The horse is stronger than ever. Better-tempered, too. I thank God.

My uncle Khosrove, who was in the parlor, became irritated and shouted, Quiet, man, quiet. Your horse has been returned. Pay no attention to it.

# WALLACE STEGNER

# New Almaden

Susan Ward came West not to join a new society but to
endure it, not to build anything but to enjoy a temporary
experience and make it yield whatever instruction it contained. She anticipated her life in New Almaden as she had
looked forward to the train journey across the continent—
as a rather strenuous outdoor excursion. The day she spent
resting with Oliver's sister Mary Prager in San Francisco
she understood to be the last day of the East, not the first
of the West. That sort of house, full of Oriental art, and
that hidden garden with its pampas grass and palms and
exotic flowers, were not for her, not yet. Mary Prager was
such a beauty, and Conrad Prager so formidably elegant,
that she wished she could introduce them to Augusta as
proof of the acceptability of Oliver's connections. Because
her trunks had not yet arrived, she had to wear Mary
Prager's clothes, which made her feel, in the strange garden
in the strange chilly air, like someone else—Mrs. Oliver
Ward, perhaps, wife of the young mining engineer who as
soon as he had established himself in his profession would
be able to provide such a house and life as this, preferably
near Guilford, Connecticut, or Milton, New York.

Nothing on the trip to New Almaden next day modified

her understanding that her lot at first would be hardship. It was intensely hot, the valley roads seen through the train windows boiled with white dust, Lizzie's usually silent baby cried and would not be comforted. In San Jose a stage with black leather curtains waited; they were the only passengers. But her anticipation of a romantic Bret Harte stage ride lasted only minutes. Dust engulfed them. She had Oliver draw the curtains, but then the heat was so great that they suffered at a slow boil. After three minutes she had Oliver open the curtains again halfway. They were thus insured both heat and dust, and were almost entirely cut off from the view.

By that time Susan cared nothing about the view, she only wanted to get there. Whenever Oliver caught her eye she made a point of smiling bravely; when he said abusive things about the weather she looked at her perspiring hands, and made mute faces of comic endurance. Now and then, as the stage rocked and threw them around among their luggage, she looked up into Lizzie's stony face and envied her patience.

It seemed a fantastically long twelve miles. Whatever conversation they attempted faded. They sat on, suffering. Susan was aware of brutal sun outside, an intolerable glare above and through their dust. Then after a long time—two hours?—she happened to glance out through the half-open curtains and saw the white trunk and pointed leaves of a sycamore going by. Their wheels were rolling quietly in sand. She thought the air felt cooler. "Trees?" she said. "I thought it would be all barren."

Oliver, sitting with his hands braced on his knees, looked altogether too vigorous and untired. He had evidently been keeping silent for her sake, not because he himself felt this jolting, dust-choked, endless ride a hardship. "Are you disappointed?" he said.

"If there are trees maybe there's a stream. Is there?"

"Not up at our place."

"Where do we get our water?"

"Why, the housewife carries it from the spring," he said. "It's only a half mile up the hill. Things are not as uncivilized out here as you think."

Lizzie's face, bent over the finally sleeping baby, showed the faintest shadow of a smile. It was not well advised of Oliver to make jokes before her. She was a jewel, tidy,

competent, and thoughtful, but she should not be spoiled
with familiarity. Susan watched the trees pass, dusty but
authentic.

The stage leveled off into what seemed a plain or valley.
She leaned to see. Ahead of them, abrupt as the precipices
up which little figures toil in Chinese paintings, she saw a
wild wooded mountainside that crested at a long ridge
spiky with conifers. She pulled the curtains wide. "But my
goodness!" she cried. "You called them *hills!*"

He laughed at her, as pleased as if he had made them by
hand. "You permiscus old consort," she said, "you deceived me. Don't tell me *anything*. I'm going to watch and
draw my own conclusions."

The road became a street, and no dust rose around their
wheels: she saw that it had been sprinkled. On one side of
them was a stream nearly lost among trees and bushes, on
the other a row of ugly identical cottages, each with a
patch of lawn like a shirtfront and a row of red geraniums
like a necktie. At the end of the street, below the wide
veranda of a white house, a Mexican was watering flowers
with a garden hose. She saw water gleam from the roadside
ditch, smelled wet grass. The oaks had been pruned so that
they went up high, like maples in a New England village.
Their shade lay across road and lawn.

"This must be the Hacienda," she said.

"Draw your own conclusions."

"I conclude it is. It's nice."

"Would you rather we were going to live down here?"

She thought that cool grass the most delicious thing
she had ever seen or smelled, but she appraised his tone
and said cautiously, "I haven't seen our place yet."

"No. But this looks good to you, does it?"

She considered, or pretended to. "It's lovely and cool,
but it looks as if it were trying to be something it isn't. It's
a little too *proper* to be picturesque, isn't it?"

Oliver took her hand and shook it. "Good girl. And too
close to too many people."

"Why? Aren't the manager and the others nice?"

"They're all right. I guess I prefer the Cousin Jacks and
Mexicans up at the camps."

They were going right through the Hacienda at a trot.
Some children scattered, turning to stare. A woman looked
out a door. "Aren't we stopping here?" she asked.

"I slipped Eugene a little extra to deliver you right to your gate."

"Ah," she said, "that'll be nicer," and leaned to the window to see as the stage tilted through dry oaks along a trail dug out of the hillside. But her mind worried a question. He thought of making her arrival as pleasant as possible, and as easy for her, and he didn't hesitate to spend money to do it, but he hadn't thought to send her the fare to cross the continent—not only Lizzie's fare, which he might have forgotten, but her own, which he shouldn't have. Not the least unknown part of her unknown new life was the man beside her. From the time she had bought the tickets out of her savings she had not been entirely free of fear.

Grandmother, I feel like telling her, have a little confidence in the man you married. You're safer than you think.

The road climbed, kinked back on itself and started a sweeping curve around a nearly bare hill. Ahead she saw five parallel spurs of mountain, as alike as the ridges of a plowed field but huge and impetuous, plunging down into the canyon. The first was very dark, the next less dark, the third hazed, the fourth dim, the fifth almost gone. All day there had been no sky, but now she saw that there was one, a pale diluted blue.

At the turn a battered liveoak leaned on limbs that touched the ground on three sides. To its trunk were nailed many boxes, each with a name painted or chalked on it: Trengove, Fall, Tregoning, Tyrrell. Across a gulch on the left she saw roofs and heard the yelling of children.

"Cornish Camp?"

"Draw your own conclusions."

"What are the boxes? Is there a newspaper?"

"Oh, Eastern effeteness," Oliver said. "Those are meat boxes. Every morning the meat wagon comes by and leaves Tregoning his leg of mutton and Trengove his soup bone and Mother Fall her pot roast. Tomorrow, if you want, I'll put up a box for Mother Ward."

"I don't think I should like everyone to know what I feed you," Susan said. "Doesn't anybody ever steal things?"

"Steals? This isn't the Hacienda."

"You don't *like* the Hacienda, do you?" she said. "Why not?"

He grunted.

"Well, I must say it's prettier than this."

"There I can't argue with you," he said. "It smells better, too."

The whole place had the air of having been dumped down the hillside—steep streets, houses at every angle white and incongruous or unpainted and shabby. Wash hung everywhere, the vacant lots were littered with cans and trash, dogs prowled and children screamed. At the water tank they slowed to pass through a reluctantly parting, densely staring tangle of men, boys, teamsters, cows, donkeys, mules. When Oliver leaned out and saluted some of them they waved, grinning, and stared with their hands forgotten in the air. Engineer and his new missus. She thought them coarse and cow-faced and strangely pale.

But they made sharp pictures, too: a boy hoisting a water yoke with a pail at each end, the pails sloshing silver over their rims; a teamster unyoking his mules; a donkey standing with his ears askew and his nose close to the ground, on his face a look of mournful patience that reminded her comically of Lizzie.

"Over there's Mother Fall's, where I lived," Oliver said, and pointed.

A white two-story house, square, blank, and ugly. Each window was a room, she supposed, one of them formerly his. The downstairs would smell of cabbage and grease. She could not even imagine living there. Her heart rose up and assured her that she would make him glad she had come.

"You said she was nice to you."

"Yes. A stout Cornish dame. She's been helping me get ready for you."

"I must call on her, I should think."

He looked at her a little queerly. "You sure must. If we don't have supper there tomorrow we'll never be forgiven."

Above and to the left, scattered down a long hogback ridge, the Mexican camp appeared. Its houses were propped with poles, timbers, ladders; its crooked balconies overflowed with flowers; in a doorway she saw a dark woman smoking a cigarette, on a porch a grandmother braided a child's hair. There were no white-painted cottages, but she thought this camp more attractive than the Cornish—it had a look of belonging, some gift of harmoniousness. The stage turned off to the right, below the camp, and left her craning, unsatisfied.

"Is there a Chinese Camp too?" she said.

"Around the hill and below us. We'll hear it a little, but we won't see it."

"Where's the mine?"

With his forefinger he jabbed straight down. "You don't see that either. Just a shaft house or a dump in a gulch here and there."

"You know what?" she said, holding the curtains back and watching ahead through the dusty little oaks, "I don't think you described this place very well."

"Draw your own conclusions," Oliver said. He offered a finger to Lizzie's baby, just waking up and yawning and focusing his eyes. The stage stopped.

The cottage she had imagined exposed on a bare hill among ugly mine buildlings was tucked back among live-oaks at the head of a draw. In her first quick devouring look she saw the verandas she had asked for and helped Oliver sketch, a rail fence swamped under geraniums. When she hopped out slapping dust from her clothes she saw that the yard showed the even tooth-marks of raking. He had prepared for her so carefully. But mostly what she felt in the moment of arrival was space, extension, bigness. Behind the house the mountain went up steeply to the ridge, along which now lay, as soft as a sleeping cat, a roll of fog or cloud. Below the house it fell just as steeply down spurs and canyons to tumbled hills as bright as a lion's hide. Below those was the valley's dust, a level obscurity, and rising out of it, miles away, was another long mountain as high as their own. Turning back the way she had come in, she saw those five parallel spurs, bare gold on top, darkly wooded in the gulches, receding in layers of blue haze. I know that mountain, old Loma Prieta. In nearly a hundred years it has changed less than most of California. Once you get beyond the vineyards and subdivisions along its lower slopes there is nothing but a reservoir and an Air Force radar station.

"Well," Oliver said, "come on inside."

It was as she had visualized it from his sketches, but much more finished—a house, not a picturesque shack. It smelled cleanly of paint. Its floors and wainscot were dark redwood, its walls a soft gray. The light was dim and cool, as she thought the light in a house should be. A breeze went through the rooms, bringing inside the smell of aro-

matic sun-soaked plants. The Franklin stove was polished
like a farmer's Sunday boots, water was piped into the
sink, the kitchen cooler held sacks and cans and let out a
rich smell of bacon. In the arch between dining room and
living room Oliver had hung his spurs, bowie, and six-
shooter. "The homey touch," he said. "And wait, there are
some little housewarming presents."

From the piazza he brought one of the packages that
had been part of their luggage down from San Francisco.
She opened it and pulled out a grass fan. "Fiji," Oliver
said. Next a large mat of the same grass, as finely woven as
linen, and with a sweet hay smell. "More Fiji." Next a
paper parasol that opened up to a view of Fujiyama.
"Japan," Oliver said. "Don't open it inside—bad luck." At
the bottom of the box was something heavy which, un-
wrapped, turned out to be a water jar with something in
Spanish written across it. "Guadalajara," Oliver said. "Now
you're supposed to feel that the place is yours. You know
what that Spanish means? It says, 'Help thyself, little
Tomasa.'"

There it sits, over on my window sill, ninety-odd years
later, without even a nick out of it. The fan and the parasol
went quickly, the mat lasted until Leadville and was
mourned when it passed, the olla has come through three
generations of us, as have the bowie, the spurs, and the
six-shooter. It wasn't the worst set of omens that attended
the beginning of my grandparents' housekeeping.

She was touched. Like the raked yard, the clean paint,
his absurd masculine decorations in the archway, his gifts
proved him what she had believed him to be. Yet the one
small doubt stuck in her mind like a burr in tweed. In a
small voice she said, "You'll spoil me."

"I hope so."

Lizzie came in with luggage in one hand and the baby in
her other arm. "Right through the kitchen," Oliver said.
"Your bed's made up. The best I could do for Georgie was
a packing box with a pillow in it."

"That will be fine, thank you," Lizzie said, and went
serenely on through.

Kind. He really was. And energetic. Within a minute he
was making a fire so that Susan could have warm water to
wash in. Then he said that he had a little errand at Mother
Fall's, and before she could ask him what he was off the
piazza and gone.

Susan took off her traveling dress and washed in the basin by the kitchen door. Below her were the tops of strange bushes, the steep mountainside tufted with sparse brown grass. Looking around the corner of Lizzie's room to the upward slopes, she saw exotic red-barked trees among the woods, and smelled the herb-cupboard smells of sage and bay. Another world. Thoughtfully she poured out the water and went inside, where Lizzie was slicing a round loaf she had found in the cooler. Even the bread here was strange.

"How does it seem, Lizzie? Is your room all right?"

"It's fine."

"Is it the way you imagined it?"

"I don't know that I imagined it much."

"Oh, I did," said Susan. "All wrong."

She looked at Lizzie's room, clean and bare; went out through the dining room where her gifts lay on the table and read the inscription on the olla: Help thyself, Tomasita. Out on the piazza she sat in the hammock and looked out over the green and gold mountain and thought *how strange, how strange.*

Rocks clattered in the trail, and Oliver came in sight with a great black dog padding beside him. He made it sit down in front of the hammock. "This is Stranger. We figure he's half Labrador and half St. Bernard. He thinks he's my dog, but he's mistaken. From now on he goes walking with nobody but you. Shake hands, Stranger."

With great dignity Stranger offered a paw like a firelog, first to Oliver, who pushed it aside, and then to Susan. He submitted to having his head stroked. "Stranger?" Susan said. "Is that your name, *Stranger?* That's wrong. You're the one who lives here, *I'm* the stranger."

Oliver went inside and came out with a piece of buttered bread. "Give him something. You're to feed him, always, so he'll get attached to you."

"But it's you he likes," Susan said. "Look at the way he watches every move you make."

"Just the same, he's going to learn to like *you.* That's what we got him for, to look after you. If he doesn't, I'll make a rug of him. You hear that, you?"

The dog rolled his eyes and twisted his head back, keeping his bottom firmly on the boards. "Here, Stranger," Susan said, and broke off a piece of bread. The dog's eyes rolled down to fix on it. She tossed it, and he slupped it out of the air with a great sucking sound that made them both laugh. Over his broad black head Susan looked into Oliver's eyes. "You *will* spoil me."

"I hope so," he said for the second time.

Then she couldn't keep the question back any longer. "Oliver."

"Yes."

"Tell me something."

"Sure."

"I don't want you to be angry."

"Angry? At *you*?"

"It seems so petty. I shouldn't even mention it. I only want us to start without a single shadow between us."

"My God, what have I done?" Oliver said. Then a slow mulish look came into his face, a look like disgust or guilt or evasion. She stared at him in panic, remembering what his mother had said of him: that when he was put in the wrong he would never defend himself, he would only close up like a clam. She didn't want him to close up, she wanted to talk this out and be rid of it. Blue as blue stones in his sunburned face, his eyes touched hers and were withdrawn. Miserably she stood waiting. "I know what it is," he said. "You needn't tell me."

"You didn't just forget, then."

"No, I didn't forget."

"But *why*, then?"

He looked over her head, he was interested in the valley. She could see shrugging impatience in his shoulders. "It isn't the money," she said. "I had the money, and there was nothing I would rather have spent it for than coming to you. But your letter never even mentioned it. I thought perhaps . . . I don't know. It shamed me before Father. I hated it that he had to send me off to someone he would think didn't know . . ."

"What my duty was?" Oliver said, almost sneering. "I knew."

"Then why?"

Impatiently he turned, he looked down at her directly. "Because I didn't have it."

"But you said you had something saved."

He swung an arm. "There it is."

"The house? I thought the mine agreed to pay for that."

"Kendall did. The manager. He changed his mind."

"But he *promised*!"

"Sure," Oliver said. "But then somebody overspent on one of the Hacienda cottages and Kendall said no more renovations."

"But that's unfair!" she said. "You should have told Mr. Prager."

His laugh was incredulous. "Yes? Run crying to Conrad?"

"Well then you should just have stopped. We could have lived in it as it was."

"I could have," Oliver said. "You couldn't. I wouldn't have let you."

"Oh, I'm sorry!" she said. "I didn't understand. I've been such an expense to you."

"It seems to me I've been an expense to you. How much did you spend for those tickets?"

"I won't tell you."

They stared at each other, near anger. She forgave him everything except that he hadn't explained. One word, and she would have been spared all her doubts about him. But she would certainly not let him pay her back. The hardship would not be all his. He was looking at her squarely, still mulish. She wanted to shake him. "You great . . . Why couldn't you have told me?"

She saw his eyebrows go up. His eyes, as they did when he smiled, closed into upside-down crescents. Young as he was, he had deep fans of wrinkles at the corners of his eyes that gave him a look of always being on the brink of smiling. And now he *was* smiling. He was not going to be sullen. They were past it.

"I was afraid you'd be sensible," he said. "I couldn't stand the thought of this place sitting here all ready for you and you not in it."

Supper was no more than bread and butter, tea from Augusta's samovar, and a left-over bar of chocolate. The dog lay at their feet on the veranda. Along the ridge with its silvery comb of fog the sky faded from pale blue to steely gray, and then slowly flushed the color of a ripe peach. The trees on the crest—redwoods, Oliver said— burned for a few seconds and went black. Eastward down the plunging mountainside the valley fumed with dust that was first red, then rose, then purple, then mauve, then gray, finally soft black. Discreet and quiet, Lizzie came out and got the tray and said good night and went in again. They sat close together in the hammock, holding hands.

"I don't believe this is me," Oliver said.

"Thee mustn't doubt it."

"Theeing?" he said. "Now I know I'm one of the family."

A shiver went through her from her hips up to her shoulders. At once he was solicitous. "Cold?"

"Happy, I think."

"I'll get a blanket. Or do you want to go in?"

"No, it's beautiful out here."

He got a blanket and tucked her into the hammock as if into a steamer chair. Then he sat down on the floor beside her and smoked his pipe. Far down below, in the inverted sky of the valley, lights came on, first one, then another, then many. "It's like sitting in the warming oven and watching corn pop down on the stove," Susan said.

Sometime later she held up her hand and said, "Listen!" Fitful on the creeping wind, heard and lost and heard again, came a vanishing sound of music—someone sitting on porch or balcony up in the Mexican camp and playing the guitar for his girl or his children. Remembering nights when Ella Clymer had sung to them at Milton, Susan all but held her breath, waiting for the rush of homesickness. But it never came, nothing interrupted this sweet and resting content. She put out a hand to touch Oliver's hair, and he captured it and held the fingers against his cheek. The bone of his jaw, the rasp of his beard, sent another great shiver through her.

They sat up a good while, watching the stars swarm along the edge of the veranda roof. When they finally went to bed I hope they made love. Why wouldn't they, brought together finally after eight years, and with only a two-week taste of marriage? I am perfectly ready to count the months on Grandmother. Her first child, my father, was born toward the end of April 1877, almost precisely nine months after her arrival in New Almaden. I choose to believe that I was made possible that night, that my father was the first thing they did together in the West. The fact that he was accidental and at first unwanted did not make him any less binding upon their lives, or me any less inevitable.

In the night she may have heard the wind sighing under the eaves and creaking the stiff oaks and madrones on the hillside behind. She may have heard the stealthy feet of raccoons on the veranda, and the fumble and rush as Stranger rose and put the intruders out. She may have waked and listened to the breathing beside her, and been shaken by unfamiliar emotions and tender resolves. Being who she was, she would have reasserted to herself beliefs about marriage, female surrender, communion of the flesh and union of the spirit that would have been at home in a Longfellow poem. She could have both written and illustrated it. When I catch Grandmother thinking in this fashion I shy away and draw the curtains, lest I smile. It does not become a historian to smile.

# JOHN STEINBECK

# Flight

About fifteen miles below Monterey, on the wild coast, the
Torres family had their farm, a few sloping acres above a
cliff that dropped to the brown reefs and to the hissing
white waters of the ocean. Behind the farm the stone mountains stood up against the sky. The farm buildings huddled
like little clinging aphids on the mountain skirts, crouched
low to the ground as though the wind might blow them
into the sea. The little shack, the rattling, rotting barn were
grey-bitten with sea salt, beaten by the damp wind until they
had taken on the color of the granite hills. Two horses, a
red cow and a red calf, half a dozen pigs and a flock of
lean, multicolored chickens stocked the place. A little corn
was raised on the sterile slope, and it grew short and thick
under the wind, and all the cobs formed on the landward
sides of the stalks.

Mama Torres, a lean, dry woman with ancient eyes, had
ruled the farm for ten years, ever since her husband tripped
over a stone in the field one day and fell full length on a
rattlesnake. When one is bitten on the chest there is not
much that can be done.

Mama Torres had three children, two undersized black
ones of twelve and fourteen, Emilio and Rosy, whom
Mama kept fishing on the rocks below the farm when the

sea was kind and when the truant officer was in some
distant part of Monterey County. And there was Pepé, the
tall smiling son of nineteen, a gentle, affectionate boy, but
very lazy. Pepé had a tall head, pointed at the top, and
from its peak, coarse black hair grew down like a thatch all
around. Over his smiling little eyes Mama cut a straight
bang so he could see. Pepé had sharp Indian cheek bones
and an eagle nose, but his mouth was as sweet and shapely
as a girl's mouth, and his chin was fragile and chiseled. He
was loose and gangling, all legs and feet and wrists, and he
was very lazy. Mama thought him fine and brave, but she
never told him so. She said, "Some lazy cow must have got
into thy father's family, else how could I have a son like
thee." And she said, "When I carried thee, a sneaking lazy
coyote came out of the brush and looked at me one day.
That must have made thee so."

Pepé smiled sheepishly and stabbed at the ground with
his knife to keep the blade sharp and free from rust. It was
his inheritance, that knife, his father's knife. The long
heavy blade folded back into the black handle. There was a
button on the handle. When Pepé pressed the button, the
blade leaped out ready for use. The knife was with Pepé
always, for it had been his father's knife.

One sunny morning when the sea below the cliff was
glinting and blue and the white surf creamed on the reef,
when even the stone mountains looked kindly, Mama
Torres called out the door of the shack, "Pepé, I have a
labor for thee."

There was no answer. Mama listened. From behind the
barn she heard a burst of laughter. She lifted her full long
skirt and walked in the direction of the noise.

Pepé was sitting on the ground with his back against a
box. His white teeth glistened. On either side of him stood
the two black ones, tense and expectant. Fifteen feet away
a redwood post was set in the ground. Pepé's right hand lay
limply in his lap, and in the palm the big black knife
rested. The blade was closed back into the handle. Pepé
looked smiling at the sky.

Suddenly Emilio cried, "Ya!"

Pepé's wrist flicked like the head of a snake. The blade
seemed to fly open in midair, and with a thump the point
dug into the redwood post, and the black handle quivered.
The three burst into excited laughter. Rosy ran to the post
and pulled out the knife and brought it back to Pepé. He

closed the blade and settled the knife carefully in his listless palm again. He grinned self-consciously at the sky.

"Ya!"

The heavy knife lanced out and sunk into the post again. Mama moved forward like a ship and scattered the play.

"All day you do foolish things with the knife, like a toybaby," she stormed. "Get up on thy huge feet that eat up shoes. Get up!" She took him by one loose shoulder and hoisted at him. Pepé grinned sheepishly and came halfheartedly to his feet. "Look!" Mama cried. "Big lazy, you must catch the horse and put on him thy father's saddle. You must ride to Monterey. The medicine bottle is empty. There is no salt. Go thou now, Peanut! Catch the horse."

A revolution took place in the relaxed figure of Pepé. "To Monterey, me? Alone? *Sí*, Mama."

She scowled at him. "Do not think, big sheep, that you will buy candy. No, I will give you only enough for the medicine and the salt."

Pepé smiled. "Mama, you will put the hatband on the hat?"

She relented then. "Yes, Pepé. You may wear the hatband."

His voice grew insinuating, "And the green handkerchief, Mama?"

"Yes, if you go quickly and return with no trouble, the silk green handkerchief will go. If you make sure to take off the handkerchief when you eat so no spot may fall on it. . . ."

"*Sí*, Mama. I will be careful. I am a man."

"Thou? A man? Thou art a peanut."

He went into the rickety barn and brought out a rope, and he walked agilely enough up the hill to catch the horse.

When he was ready and mounted before the door, mounted on his father's saddle that was so old that the oaken frame showed through torn leather in many places, then Mama brought out the round black hat with the tooled leather band, and she reached up and knotted the green silk handkerchief about his neck. Pepé's blue denim coat was much darker than his jeans, for it had been washed much less often.

Mama handed up the big medicine bottle and the silver coins. "That for the medicine," she said, "and that for the salt. That for a candle to burn for the papa. That for *dulces* for the little ones. Our friend Mrs. Rodriguez will give you dinner and maybe a bed for the night. When you go to the church say only ten Paternosters and only twenty-five Ave Marias. Oh! I know, big coyote. You would sit there flapping your mouth over Aves all day while you looked at the candles and the holy pictures. That is not good devotion to stare at the pretty things."

The black hat, covering the high pointed head and black thatched hair of Pepé, gave him dignity and age. He sat the rangy horse well. Mama thought how handsome he was, dark and lean and tall. "I would not send thee now alone, thou little one, except for the medicine," she said softly. "It is not good to have no medicine, for who knows when the toothache will come, or the sadness of the stomach. These things are."

"Adios, Mama," Pepé cried. "I will come back soon. You may send me often alone. I am a man."

"Thou art a foolish chicken."

He straightened his shoulders, flipped the reins against the horse's shoulder and rode away. He turned once and saw that they still watched him, Emilio and Rosy and Mama. Pepé grinned with pride and gladness and lifted the tough buckskin horse to a trot.

When he had dropped out of sight over a little dip in the road, Mama turned to the black ones, but she spoke to herself. "He is nearly a man now," she said. "It will be a nice thing to have a man in the house again." Her eyes sharpened on the children. "Go to the rocks now. The tide is going out. There will be abalones to be found." She put the iron hooks into their hands and saw them down the steep trail to the reefs. She brought the smooth stone *metate* to the doorway and sat grinding her corn to flour and looking occasionally at the road over which Pepé had gone. The noonday came and then the afternoon, when the little ones beat the abalones on a rock to make them tender and Mama patted the tortillas to make them thin. They ate their dinner as the red sun was plunging down toward the ocean. They sat on the doorsteps, and watched the big white moon come over the mountain tops.

Mama said, "He is now at the house of our friend Mrs. Rodriguez. She will give him nice things to eat and maybe a present."

Emilio said, "Some day I too will ride to Monterey for medicine. Did Pepé come to be a man today?"

Mama said wisely, "A boy gets to be a man when a man is needed. Remember this thing. I have known boys forty years old because there was no need for a man."

Soon afterwards they retired, Mama in her big oak bed on one side of the room, Emilio and Rosy in their boxes full of straw and sheepskins on the other side of the room.

The moon went over the sky and the surf roared on the rocks. The roosters crowed the first call. The surf subsided to a whispering surge against the reef. The moon dropped toward the sea. The roosters crowed again.

The moon was near down to the water when Pepé rode on a winded horse to his home flat. His dog bounced out and circled the horse yelping with pleasure. Pepé slid off the saddle to the ground. The weathered little shack was silver in the moonlight and the square shadow of it was black to the north and east. Against the east the piling mountains were misty with light; their tops melted into the sky.

Pepé walked wearily up the three steps and into the house. It was dark inside. There was a rustle in the corner.

Mama cried out from her bed. "Who comes? Pepé, is it thou?"

"*Sí*, Mama."

"Did you get the medicine?"

"*Sí*, Mama."

"Well, go to sleep, then. I thought you would be sleeping at the house of Mrs. Rodriguez." Pepé stood silently in the dark room. "Why do you stand there, Pepé? Did you drink wine?"

"*Sí*, Mama."

"Well, go to bed then and sleep out the wine."

His voice was tired and patient, but very firm. "Light the candle, Mama. I must go away into the mountains."

"What is this, Pepé? You are crazy." Mama struck a sulphur match and held the little blue burr until the flame spread up the stick. She set light to the candle on the floor beside her bed. "Now, Pepé, what is this you say?" She looked anxiously into his face.

He was changed. The fragile quality seemed to have gone from his chin. His mouth was less full than it had been, the lines of the lips were straighter, but in his eyes the greatest change had taken place. There was no laughter

in them any more, nor any bashfulness. They were sharp
and bright and purposeful.

He told her in a tired monotone, told her everything just
as it had happened. A few people came into the kitchen of
Mrs. Rodriguez. There was wine to drink. Pepé drank
wine. The little quarrel—the man started toward Pepé and
then the knife—it went almost by itself. It flew, it darted
before Pepé knew it. As he talked, Mama's face grew stern,
and it seemed to grow more lean. Pepé finished. "I am a
man now, Mama. The man said names to me I could not
allow."

Mama nodded. "Yes, thou art a man, my poor little
Pepé. Thou art a man. I have seen it coming on thee. I
have watched you throwing the knife into the post, and I
have been afraid." For a moment her face had softened,
but now it grew stern again. "Come! We must get you
ready. Go. Awaken Emilio and Rosy. Go quickly."

Pepé stepped over to the corner where his brother and
sister slept among the sheepskins. He leaned down and
shook them gently. "Come, Rosy! Come, Emilio! The
mama says you must arise."

The little black ones sat up and rubbed their eyes in the
candlelight. Mama was out of bed now, her long black
skirt over her nightgown. "Emilio," she cried. "Go up and
catch the other horse for Pepé. Quickly, now! Quickly."
Emilio put his legs in his overalls and stumbled sleepily out
the door.

"You heard no one behind you on the road?" Mama
demanded.

"No, Mama. I listened carefully. No one was on the
road."

Mama darted like a bird about the room. From a nail on
the wall she took a canvas water bag and threw it on the
floor. She stripped a blanket from her bed and rolled it into
a tight tube and tied the ends with string. From a box
beside the stove she lifted a flour sack half full of black
stringy jerky. "Your father's black coat, Pepé. Here, put it
on."

Pepé stood in the middle of the floor watching her activity. She reached behind the door and brought out the rifle,
a long 38-56, worn shiny the whole length of the barrel.
Pepé took it from her and held it in the crook of his elbow.
Mama brought a little leather bag and counted the car-

tridges into his hand. "Only ten left," she warned. "You must not waste them."

Emilio put his head in the door. " '*Qui 'st 'l caballo*, Mama."

"Put on the saddle from the other horse. Tie on the blanket. Here, tie the jerky to the saddle horn."

Still Pepé stood silently watching his mother's frantic activity. His chin looked hard, and his sweet mouth was drawn and thin. His little eyes followed Mama about the room almost suspiciously.

Rosy asked softly, "Where goes Pepé?"

Mama's eyes were fierce. "Pepé goes on a journey. Pepé is a man now. He has a man's thing to do."

Pepé straightened his shoulders. His mouth changed until he looked very much like Mama.

At last the preparation was finished. The loaded horse stood outside the door. The water bag dripped a line of moisture down the bay's shoulder.

The moonlight was being thinned by the dawn and the big white moon was near down to the sea. The family stood by the shack. Mama confronted Pepé. "Look, my son! Do not stop until it is dark again. Do not sleep even though you are tired. Take care of the horse in order that he may not stop of weariness. Remember to be careful with the bullets—there are only ten. Do not fill thy stomach with jerky or it will make thee sick. Eat a little jerky and fill thy stomach with grass. When thou comest to the high mountains, if thou seest any of the dark watching men, go not near to them nor try to speak to them. And forget not thy prayers." She put her lean hands on Pepé's shoulders, stood on her toes and kissed him formally on both cheeks, and Pepé kissed her on both cheeks. Then he went to Emilio and Rosy and kissed both of their cheeks.

Pepé turned back to Mama. He seemed to look for a little softness, a little weakness in her. His eyes were searching, but Mama's face remained fierce. "Go now," she said. "Do not wait to be caught like a chicken."

Pepé pulled himself into the saddle. "I am a man," he said.

It was the first dawn when he rode up the hill toward the little canyon which let a trail into the mountains. Moonlight and daylight fought with each other, and the two warring qualities made it difficult to see. Before Pepé had gone a hundred yards, the outlines of his figure were misty; and long before he entered the canyon, he had become a grey, indefinite shadow.

Mama stood stiffly in front of her doorstep, and on either side of her stood Emilio and Rosy. They cast furtive glances at Mama now and then.

When the grey shape of Pepé melted into the hillside and disappeared, Mama relaxed. She began the high, whining keen of the death wail. "Our beautiful—our brave," she cried. "Our protector, our son is gone." Emilio and Rosy moaned beside her. "Our beautiful—our brave, he is gone." It was the formal wail. It rose to a high piercing whine and subsided to a moan. Mama raised it three times and then she turned and went into the house and shut the door.

Emilio and Rosy stood wondering in the dawn. They heard Mama whimpering in the house. They went out to sit on the cliff above the ocean. They touched shoulders. "When did Pepé come to be a man?" Emilio asked.

"Last night," said Rosy. "Last night in Monterey." The ocean clouds turned red with the sun that was behind the mountains.

"We will have no breakfast," said Emilio. "Mama will not want to cook." Rosy did not answer him. "Where is Pepé gone?" he asked.

Rosy looked around at him. She drew her knowledge from the quiet air. "He has gone on a journey. He will never come back."

"Is he dead? Do you think he is dead?"

Rosy looked back at the ocean again. A little steamer, drawing a line of smoke sat on the edge of the horizon. "He is not dead," Rosy explained. "Not yet."

Pepé rested the big rifle across the saddle in front of him. He let the horse walk up the hill and he didn't look back. The stony slope took on a coat of short brush so that Pepé found the entrance to a trail and entered it.

When he came to the canyon opening, he swung once in his saddle and looked back, but the houses were swallowed in the misty light. Pepé jerked forward again. The high shoulder of the canyon closed in on him. His horse stretched out its neck and sighed and settled to the trail.

It was a well-worn path, dark soft leaf-mould earth

strewn with broken pieces of sandstone. The trail rounded
the shoulder of the canyon and dropped steeply into the
bed of the stream. In the shallows the water ran smoothly,
glinting in the first morning sun. Small round stones on the
bottom were as brown as rust with sun moss. In the sand
along the edges of the stream the tall, rich wild mint grew,
while in the water itself the cress, old and tough, had gone
to heavy seed.

The path went into the stream and emerged on the other
side. The horse sloshed into the water and stopped. Pepé
dropped his bridle and let the beast drink of the running
water.

Soon the canyon sides became steep and the first giant
sentinel redwoods guarded the trail, great round red trunks
bearing foliage as green and lacy as ferns. Once Pepé was
among the trees, the sun was lost. A perfumed and purple
light lay in the pale green of the underbrush. Gooseberry
bushes and blackberries and tall ferns lined the stream, and
overhead the branches of the redwoods met and cut off the
sky.

Pepé drank from the water bag, and he reached into the
flour sack and brought out a black string of jerky. His
white teeth gnawed at the string until the tough meat
parted. He chewed slowly and drank occasionally from the
water bag. His little eyes were slumberous and tired, but
the muscles of his face were hard set. The earth of the trail
was black now. It gave up a hollow sound under the walking hoofbeats.

The stream fell more sharply. Little waterfalls splashed
on the stones. Five-fingered ferns hung over the water and
dripped spray from their fingertips. Pepé rode half over in
his saddle, dangling one leg loosely. He picked a bay leaf
from a tree beside the way and put it into his mouth for a
moment to flavor the dry jerky. He held the gun loosely
across the pommel.

Suddenly he squared in his saddle, swung the horse from
the trail and kicked it hurriedly up behind a big redwood
tree. He pulled up the reins tight against the bit to keep the
horse from whinnying. His face was intent and his nostrils
quivered a little.

A hollow pounding came down the trail, and a horseman rode by, a fat man with red cheeks and a white
stubble beard. His horse put down its head and blubbered
at the trail when it came to the place where Pepé had

turned off. "Hold up!" said the man and he pulled up his horse's head.

When the last sound of the hoofs died away, Pepé came back into the trail again. He did not relax in the saddle any more. He lifted the big rifle and swung the lever to throw a shell into the chamber, and then he let down the hammer to half cock.

The trail grew very steep. Now the redwood trees were smaller and their tops were dead, bitten dead where the wind reached them. The horse plodded on; the sun went slowly overhead and started down toward the afternoon.

Where the stream came out of a side canyon, the trail left it. Pepé dismounted and watered his horse and filled up his water bag. As soon as the trail had parted from the stream, the trees were gone and only the thick brittle sage and manzanita and chaparral edged the trail. And the soft black earth was gone, too, leaving only the light tan broken rock for the trial bed. Lizards scampered away into the brush as the horse rattled over the little stones.

Pepé turned in his saddle and looked back. He was in the open now: he could be seen from a distance. As he ascended the trail the country grew more rough and terrible and dry. The way wound about the bases of great square rocks. Little grey rabbits skittered in the brush. A bird made a monotonous high creaking. Eastward the bare rock mountaintops were pale and powder-dry under the dropping sun. The horse plodded up and up the trail toward a little V in the ridge which was the pass.

Pepé looked suspiciously back every minute or so, and his eyes sought the tops of the ridges ahead. Once, on a white barren spur, he saw a black figure for a moment, but he looked quickly away, for it was one of the dark watchers. No one knew who the watchers were, nor where they lived, but it was better to ignore them and never to show interest in them. They did not bother one who stayed on the trail and minded his own business.

The air was parched and full of light dust blown by the breeze from the eroding mountains. Pepé drank sparingly from his bag and corked it tightly and hung it on the horn again. The trail moved up the dry shale hillside, avoiding rocks, dropping under clefts, climbing in and out of old water scars. When he arrived at the little pass he stopped and looked back for a long time. No dark watchers were to

be seen now. The trail behind was empty. Only the high
tops of the redwoods indicated where the stream flowed.

Pepé rode on through the pass. His little eyes were
nearly closed with weariness, but his face was stern, relentless and manly. The high mountain wind coasted sighing
through the pass and whistled on the edges of the big
blocks of broken granite. In the air, a red-tailed hawk
sailed over close to the ridge and screamed angrily. Pepé
went slowly through the broken jagged pass and looked
down on the other side.

The trail dropped quickly, staggering among broken
rock. At the bottom of the slope there was a dark crease,
thick with brush, and on the other side of the crease a little
flat, in which a grove of oak trees grew. A scar of green
grass cut across the flat. And behind the flat another mountain rose, desolate with dead rocks and starving little black
bushes. Pepé drank from the bag again for the air was so
dry that it encrusted his nostrils and burned his lips. He
put the horse down the trail. The hooves slipped and struggled on the steep way, starting little stones that rolled off
into the brush. The sun was gone behind the westward
mountain now, but still it glowed brilliantly on the oaks
and on the grassy flat. The rocks and the hillsides still sent
up waves of the heat they had gathered from the day's
sun.

Pepé looked up to the top of the next dry withered ridge.
He saw a dark form against the sky, a man's figure standing on top of a rock, and he glanced away quickly not to
appear curious. When a moment later he looked up again,
the figure was gone.

Downward the trail was quickly covered. Sometimes the
horse floundered for footing, sometimes set his feet and
slid a little way. They came at last to the bottom where the
dark chaparral was higher than Pepé's head. He held up his
rifle on one side and his arm on the other to shield his face
from the sharp brittle fingers of the brush.

Up and out of the crease he rode, and up a little cliff.
The grassy flat was before him, and the round comfortable
oaks. For a moment he studied the trail down which he
had come, but there was no movement and no sound from
it. Finally he rode out over the flat, to the green streak, and
at the upper end of the damp he found a little spring
welling out of the earth and dropping into a dug basin
before it seeped out over the flat.

Pepé filled his bag first, and then he let the thirsty horse drink out of the pool. He led the horse to the clump of oaks, and in the middle of the grove, fairly protected from sight on all sides, he took off the saddle and the bridle and laid them on the ground. The horse stretched his jaws sideways and yawned. Pepé knotted the lead rope about the horse's neck and tied him to a sapling among the oaks, where he could graze in a fairly large circle.

When the horse was gnawing hungrily at the dry grass, Pepé went to the saddle and took a black string of jerky from the sack and strolled to an oak tree on the edge of the grove, from under which he could watch the trail. He sat down in the crisp dry oak leaves and automatically felt for his big black knife to cut the jerky, but he had no knife. He leaned back on his elbow and gnawed at the tough strong meat. His face was blank, but it was a man's face.

The bright evening light washed the eastern ridge, but the valley was darkening. Doves flew down from the hills to the spring, and the quail came running out of the brush and joined them, calling clearly to one another.

Out of the corner of his eye Pepé saw a shadow grow out of the bushy crease. He turned his head slowly. A big spotted wildcat was creeping toward the spring, belly to the ground, moving like thought.

Pepé cocked his rifle and edged the muzzle slowly around. Then he looked apprehensively up the trail and dropped the hammer again. From the ground beside him he picked an oak twig and threw it toward the spring. The quail flew up with a roar and the doves whistled away. The big cat stood up: for a long moment he looked at Pepé with cold yellow eyes, and then fearlessly walked back into the gulch.

The dusk gathered quickly in the deep valley. Pepé muttered his prayers, put his head down on his arm and went instantly to sleep.

The moon came up and filled the valley with cold blue light, and the wind swept rustling down from the peaks. The owls worked up and down the slopes looking for rabbits. Down in the brush of the gulch a coyote gabbled. The oak trees whispered softly in the night breeze.

Pepé started up, listening. His horse had whinnied. The moon was just slipping behind the western ridge, leaving the valley in darkness behind it. Pepé sat tensely gripping his rifle. From far up the trail he heard an answering whinny and the crash of shod hooves on the broken rock. He jumped to his feet, ran to his horse and led it under the trees. He threw on the saddle and cinched it tight for the steep trail, caught the unwilling head and forced the bit into the mouth. He felt the saddle to make sure the water bag and the sack of jerky were there. Then he mounted and turned up the hill.

It was velvet dark. The horse found the entrance to the trail where it left the flat, and started up, stumbling and slipping on the rocks. Pepé's hand rose up to his head. His hat was gone. He had left it under the oak tree.

The horse had struggled far up the trail when the first change of dawn came into the air, a steel greyness as light mixed thoroughly with dark. Gradually the sharp snaggled edge of the ridge stood out above them, rotten granite tortured and eaten by the winds of time. Pepé had dropped his reins on the horn, leaving direction to the horse. The brush grabbed at his legs in the dark until one knee of his jeans was ripped.

Gradually the light flowed down over the ridge. The starved brush and rocks stood out in the half light, strange and lonely in high perspective. Then there came warmth into the light. Pepé drew up and looked back, but he could see nothing in the darker valley below. The sky turned blue over the coming sun. In the waste of the mountainside, the poor dry brush grew only three feet high. Here and there, big outcroppings of unrotted granite stood up like mouldering houses. Pepé relaxed a little. He drank from his water bag and bit off a piece of jerky. A single eagle flew over, high in the light.

Without warning Pepé's horse screamed and fell on its side. He was almost down before the rifle crash echoed up from the valley. From a hole behind the struggling shoulder, a stream of bright crimson blood pumped and stopped and pumped and stopped. The hooves threshed on the ground. Pepé lay half stunned beside the horse. He looked slowly down the hill. A piece of sage clipped off beside his head and another crash echoed up from side to side of the canyon. Pepé flung himself frantically behind a bush.

He crawled up the hill on his knees and one hand. His right hand held the rifle up off the ground and pushed it ahead of him. He moved with the instinctive care of an

animal. Rapidly he wormed his way toward one of the big
outcroppings of granite on the hill above him. Where the
brush was high he doubled up and ran, but where the cover
was slight he wriggled forward on his stomach, pushing the
rifle ahead of him. In the last little distance there was no
cover at all. Pepé poised and then he darted across the
space and flashed around the corner of the rock.

He leaned panting against the stone. When his breath
came easier he moved along behind the big rock until he
came to a narrow split that offered a thin section of vision
down the hill. Pepé lay on his stomach and pushed the rifle
barrel through the slit and waited.

The sun reddened the western ridges now. Already the
buzzards were settling down toward the place where the
horse lay. A small brown bird scratched in the dead sage
leaves directly in front of the rifle muzzle. The coasting
eagle flew back toward the rising sun.

Pepé saw a little movement in the brush far below. His
grip tightened on the gun. A little brown doe stepped dain-
tily out on the trail and crossed it and disappeared into the
brush again. For a long time Pepé waited. Far below he
could see the little flat and the oak trees and the slash of
green. Suddenly his eyes flashed back at the trail again. A
quarter of a mile down there had been a quick movement
in the chaparral. The rifle swung over. The front sight
nestled in the v of the rear sight. Pepé studied for a moment and then raised the rear sight a notch. The little
movement in the brush came again. The sight settled on it.
Pepé squeezed the trigger. The explosion crashed down the
mountain and up the other side, and came rattling back.
The whole side of the slope grew still. No more movement.
And then a white streak cut into the granite of the slit and
a bullet whined away and a crash sounded up from below.
Pepé felt a sharp pain in his right hand. A sliver of granite
was sticking out from between his first and second knuckles and the point protruded from his palm. Carefully he
pulled out the sliver of stone. The wound bled evenly and
gently. No vein nor artery was cut.

Pepé looked into a little dusty cave in the rock and
gathered a handful of spider web, and he pressed the mass
into the cut, plastering the soft web into the blood. The
flow stopped almost at once.

The rifle was on the ground. Pepé picked it up, levered a
new shell into the chamber. And then he slid into the brush

on his stomach. Far to the right he crawled, and then up the hill, moving slowly and carefully, crawling to cover and resting and then crawling again.

In the mountains the sun is high in its arc before it penetrates the gorges. The hot face looked over the hill and brought instant heat with it. The white light beat on the rocks and reflected from them and rose up quivering from the earth again, and the rocks and bushes seemed to quiver behind the air.

Pepé crawled in the general direction of the ridge peak, zig-zagging for cover. The deep cut between his knuckles began to throb. He crawled close to a rattlesnake before he saw it, and when it raised its dry head and made a soft beginning whirr, he backed up and took another way. The quick grey lizards flashed in front of him, raising a tiny line of dust. He found another mass of spider web and pressed it against his throbbing hand.

Pepé was pushing the rifle with his left hand now. Little drops of sweat ran to the ends of his coarse black hair and rolled down his cheeks. His lips and tongue were growing thick and heavy. His lips writhed to draw saliva into his mouth. His little dark eyes were uneasy and suspicious. Once when a grey lizard paused in front of him on the parched ground and turned its head sideways he crushed it flat with a stone.

When the sun slid past noon he had not gone a mile. He crawled exhaustedly a last hundred yards to a patch of high sharp manzanita, crawled desperately, and when the patch was reached he wriggled in among the tough gnarly trunks and dropped his head on his left arm. There was little shade in the meager brush, but there was cover and safety. Pepé went to sleep as he lay and the sun beat on his back. A few little birds hopped close to him and peered and hopped away. Pepé squirmed in his sleep and he raised and dropped his wounded hand again and again.

The sun went down behind the peaks and the cool evening came, and then the dark. A coyote yelled from the hillside. Pepé started awake and looked about with misty eyes. His hand was swollen and heavy; a little thread of pain ran up the inside of his arm and settled in a pocket in his armpit. He peered about and then stood up, for the mountains were black and the moon had not yet risen. Pepé stood up in the dark. The coat of his father pressed on his arm. His tongue was swollen until it nearly filled his mouth. He wriggled out of the coat and dropped it in the brush, and then he struggled up the hill, falling over rocks and tearing his way through the brush. The rifle knocked against stones as he went. Little dry avalanches of gravel and shattered stone went whispering down the hill behind him.

After a while the old moon came up and showed the jagged ridge top ahead of him. By moonlight Pepé traveled more easily. He bent forward so that his throbbing arm hung away from his body. The journey uphill was made in dashes and rests, a frantic rush up a few yards and then a rest. The wind coasted down the slope rattling the dry stems of the bushes.

The moon was at meridian when Pepé came at last to the sharp backbone of the ridge top. On the last hundred yards of the rise no soil had clung under the wearing winds. The way was on solid rock. He clambered to the top and looked down on the other side. There was a draw like the last below him, misty with moonlight, brushed with dry struggling sage and chaparral. On the other side the hill rose up sharply and at the top the jagged rotten teeth of the mountain showed against the sky. At the bottom of the cut the brush was thick and dark.

Pepé stumbled down the hill. His throat was almost closed with thirst. At first he tried to run, but immediately he fell and rolled. After that he went more carefully. The moon was just disappearing behind the mountains when he came to the bottom. He crawled into the heavy brush feeling with his fingers for water. There was no water in the bed of the stream, only damp earth. Pepé laid his gun down and scooped up a handful of mud and put it in his mouth, and then he spluttered and scraped the earth from his tongue with his finger, for the mud drew at his mouth like a poultice. He dug a hole in the stream bed with his fingers, dug a little basin to catch water; but before it was very deep his head fell forward on the damp ground and he slept.

The dawn came and the heat of the day fell on the earth, and still Pepé slept. Late in the afternoon his head jerked up. He looked slowly around. His eyes were slits of wariness. Twenty feet away in the heavy brush a big tawny mountain lion stood looking at him. Its long thick tail

waved gracefully, its ears were erect with interest, not laid
back dangerously. The lion squatted down on its stomach
and watched him.

Pepé looked at the hole he had dug in the earth. A half
inch of muddy water had collected in the bottom. He tore
the sleeve from his hurt arm, with his teeth ripped out a
little square, soaked it in the water and put it in his mouth.
Over and over he filled the cloth and sucked it.

Still the lion sat and watched him. The evening came
down but there was no movement on the hills. No birds
visited the dry bottom of the cut. Pepé looked occasionally
at the lion. The eyes of the yellow beast drooped as though
he were about to sleep. He yawned and his long thin red
tongue curled out. Suddenly his head jerked around and his
nostrils quivered. His big tail lashed. He stood up and
slunk like a tawny shadow into the thick brush.

A moment later Pepé heard the sound, the faint far
crash of horses' hooves on gravel. And he heard something
else, a high whining yelp of a dog.

Pepé took his rifle in his left hand and he glided into the
brush almost as quietly as the lion had. In the darkening
evening he crouched up the hill toward the next ridge.
Only when the dark came did he stand up. His energy was
short. Once it was dark he fell over the rocks and slipped
to his knees on the steep slope, but he moved on and on up
the hill, climbing and scrabbling over the broken hillside.

When he was far up toward the top, he lay down and
slept for a little while. The withered moon, shining on his
face, awakened him. He stood up and moved up the hill.
Fifty yards away he stopped and turned back, for he had
forgotten his rifle. He walked heavily down and poked
about in the brush, but he could not find his gun. At last
he lay down to rest. The pocket of pain in his armpit had
grown more sharp. His arm seemed to swell out and fall
with every heartbeat. There was no position lying down
where the heavy arm did not press against his armpit.

With the effort of a hurt beast, Pepé got up and moved
again toward the top of the ridge. He held his swollen arm
away from his body with his left hand. Up the steep hill he
dragged himself, a few steps and a rest, and a few more
steps. At last he was nearing the top. The moon showed the
uneven sharp back of it against the sky.

Pepé's brain spun in a big spiral up and away from him.

He slumped to the ground and lay still. The rock ridge top was only a hundred feet above him.

The moon moved over the sky. Pepé half turned on his back. His tongue tried to make words, but only a thick hissing came from between his lips.

When the dawn came, Pepé pulled himself up. His eyes were sane again. He drew his great puffed arm in front of him and looked at the angry wound. The black line ran up from his wrist to his armpit. Automatically he reached in his pocket for the big black knife, but it was not there. His eyes searched the ground. He picked up a sharp blade of stone and scraped at the wound, sawed at the proud flesh and then squeezed the green juice out in big drops. Instantly he threw back his head and whined like a dog. His whole right side shuddered at the pain, but the pain cleared his head.

In the grey light he struggled up the last slope to the ridge and crawled over and lay down behind a line of rocks. Below him lay a deep canyon exactly like the last, waterless and desolate. There was no flat, no oak trees, not even heavy brush in the bottom of it. And on the other side a sharp ridge stood up, thinly brushed with starving sage, littered with broken granite. Strewn over the hill there were giant outcroppings, and on the top the granite teeth stood out against the sky.

The new day was light now. The flame of the sun came over the ridge and fell on Pepé where he lay on the ground. His coarse black hair was littered with twigs and bits of spider web. His eyes had retreated back into his head. Between his lips the tip of his black tongue showed.

He sat up and dragged his great arm into his lap and nursed it, rocking his body and moaning in his throat. He threw back his head and looked up into the pale sky. A big black bird circled nearly out of sight, and far to the left another was sailing near.

He lifted his head to listen, for a familiar sound had come to him from the valley he had climbed out of; it was the crying yelp of hounds, excited and feverish, on a trail.

Pepé bowed his head quickly. He tried to speak rapid words but only a thick hiss came from his lips. He drew a shaky cross on his breast with his left hand. It was a long struggle to get to his feet. He crawled slowly and mechanically to the top of a big rock on the ridge peak. Once there, he arose slowly, swaying to his feet, and stood erect. Far below he could see the dark brush where he had slept. He braced his feet and stood there, black against the morning sky.

There came a ripping sound at his feet. A piece of stone flew up and a bullet droned off into the next gorge. The hollow crash echoed up from below. Pepé looked down for a moment and then pulled himself straight again.

His body jarred back. His left hand fluttered helplessly toward his breast. The second crash sounded from below. Pepé swung forward and toppled from the rock. His body struck and rolled over and over, starting a little avalanche. And when at last he stopped against a bush, the avalanche slid slowly down and covered up his head.

# JOSÉ ANTONIO VILLAREAL

# Pocho

It was 1940 in Santa Clara, and, among other things, the Conscription Act had done its part in bringing about a change. It was not unusual now to see soldiers walking downtown or to see someone of the town in uniform. He was aware that people liked soldiers now, and could still remember the old days, when a detachment of cavalry camped outside the town for a few days or a unit of field artillery stayed at the university, and the worst thing one's sister could do was associate with a soldier. Soldiers were common, were drunkards, thieves, and rapers of girls, or something, to the people of Santa Clara, and the only uniforms with prestige in the town had been those of the CCC boys or of the American Legion during the Fourth of July celebration and the Easter-egg hunt. But now everybody loved a soldier, and he wondered how this had come about.

There were the soldiers, and there were also the Mexicans in ever-increasing numbers. The Mexican people Richard had known until now were those he saw only during the summer, and they were migrant families who seldom remained in Santa Clara longer than a month or two. The orbit of his existence was limited to the town, and actually to his immediate neighborhood, thereby preventing his association with the Mexican family which lived on the other side of town, across the tracks. In his wanderings into San Jose, he began to see more of what he called "the race." Many of the migrant workers who came up from southern California in the late spring and early summer now settled down in the valley. They bought two hundred pounds of flour and a hundred pounds of beans, and if they weathered the first winter, which was the most difficult, because the rains stopped agricultural workers from earning a living, they were settled for good.

As the Mexican population increased, Richard began to attend their dances and fiestas, and, in general, sought their company as much as possible, for these people were a strange lot to him. He was obsessed with a hunger to learn about them and from them. They had a burning contempt for people of different ancestry, whom they called Americans, and a marked hauteur toward México and toward their parents for their old-country ways. The former feeling came from a sense of inferiority that is a prominent characteristic in any Mexican reared in southern California; and the latter was an inexplicable compensation for that feeling. They needed to feel superior to something, which is a natural thing. The result was that they attempted to segregate themselves from both their cultures, and became truly a lost race. In their frantic desire to become different, they adopted a new mode of dress, a new manner, and even a new language. They used a polyglot speech made up of English and Spanish syllables, words, and sounds. This they incorporated into phrases and words that were unintelligible to anyone but themselves. Their Spanish became limited and their English more so. Their dress was unique to the point of being ludicrous. The black motif was predominant. The tight-fitting cuffs on trouserlegs that billowed at the knees made Richard think of some longforgotten pasha in the faraway past, and the fingertip coat and highly lustrous shoes gave the wearer, when walking, the appearance of a strutting cock. Their hair was long and swept up to meet in the back, forming a ducktail. They spent hours training it to remain that way.

The girls were characterized by the extreme shortness of their skirts, which stopped well above the knees. Their jackets, too, were fingertip in length, coming to within an inch of the skirt hem. Their hair reached below the shoul-

der in the back, and it was usually worn piled in front to
form a huge pompadour.

The pachuco was born in El Paso, had gone west to Los
Angeles, and was now moving north. To society, these
zootsuiters were a menace, and the name alone classified
them as undesirables, but Richard learned that there was
much more to it than a mere group with a name. That in
spite of their behavior, which was sensational at times and
violent at others, they were simply a portion of a confused
humanity, employing their self-segregation as a means of
expression. And because theirs was a spontaneous, and not
a planned, retaliation, he saw it as a vicissitude of society,
obvious only because of its nature and comparative suddenness.

From the leggy, short-skirted girls, he learned that their
mores were no different from those of what he considered
good girls. What was under the scant covering was as
inaccessible as it would be under the more conventional
dress. He felt, in fact, that these girls were more difficult to
reach. And from the boys he learned that their bitterness
and hostile attitude toward "whites" was not merely a lark.
They had learned hate through actual experience, with
everything the word implied. They had not been as lucky
as he, and showed the scars to prove it. And, later on,
Richard saw in retrospect that what happened to him in
the city jail in San Jose was due more to the character of a
handful of men than to the wide, almost organized attitude
of a society, for just as the zootsuiters were blamed en
masse for the actions of a few, they, in turn, blamed the
other side for the very same reason.

As happens in most such groups, there were misunder-
standings and disagreements over trivia. Pachucos fought
among themselves, for the most part, and they fought hard.
It was not unusual that a quarrel born on the streets or
backalleys of a Los Angeles slum was settled in the Santa
Clara Valley. Richard understood them and partly sympa-
thized, but their way of life was not entirely justified in his
mind, for he felt that they were somehow reneging on life;
this was the easiest thing for them to do. They, like his
father, were defeated—only more so, because they really
never started to live. They, too, were but making a show of
resistance.

Of the new friends Richard made, those who were native

to San Jose were relegated to become casual acquaintances, for they were as Americanized as he, and did not interest him. The newcomers became the object of his explorations. He was avidly hungry to learn the ways of these people. It was not easy for him to approach them at first, because his clothes labeled him as an outsider, and, too, he had trouble understanding their speech. He must not ask questions, for fear of offending them; his deductions as to their character and makeup must come from close association. He was careful not to be patronizing or in any way act superior. And, most important, they must never suspect what he was doing. The most difficult moments for him were when he was doing the talking, for he was conscious that his Spanish was better than theirs. He learned enough of their vernacular to get along; he did not learn more, because he was always in a hurry about knowledge. Soon he counted a few boys as friends, but had a much harder time of it with the girls, because they considered him a traitor to his "race." Before he knew it, he found that he almost never spoke to them in English, and no longer defended the "whites," but, rather, spoke disparagingly of them whenever possible. He also bought a suit to wear when in their company, not with such an extreme cut as those they wore, but removed enough from the conservative so he would not be considered a square. And he found himself a girl, who refused to dance the faster pieces with him, because he still jittered in the American manner. So they danced only to soft music while they kissed in the dimmed light, and that was the extent of their lovemaking. Or he stood behind her at the bar, with his arms around her as she sipped a Nehi, and felt strange because she was a Mexican and everyone around them was also Mexican, and felt stranger still from the knowledge that he felt strange. When the dance was over, he took her to where her parents were sitting and said goodnight to the entire family.

The orchestra had blared out a jazzedup version of "Home, Sweet Home" and was going through it again at a much slower tempo, giving the couples on the dancefloor one last chance for the sensual embraces that would have to last them a week. Richard was dancing with his girl, leading with his leg and holding her slight body close against his, when one of his friends tapped him on the shoulder.

"We need some help," he said. "Will you meet us by the door after the dance?" The question was more of a command, and the speaker did not wait for an answer. The dance was over, and Richard kissed the girl goodbye and joined the group that was gathering conspicuously as the people poured out through the only exit.

"What goes?" he asked.

"We're going to get some guys tonight," answered the youth who had spoken to him earlier. He was twenty years old and was called the Rooster.

The Mexican people have an affinity for incongruous nicknames. In this group, there was Tuerto, who was not blind; Cacarizo, who was not pockmarked; Zurdo, who was not left-handed; and a drab little fellow who was called Slick. Only Chango was appropriately named. There was indeed something anthropoidal about him.

The Rooster said, "They beat hell out of my brother last night, because he was jiving with one of their girls. I just got the word that they'll be around tonight if we want trouble."

"Man," said Chango, "we want a mess of trouble."

"Know who they are?" asked the Tuerto.

"Yeah. It was those bastards from Ontario," said the Rooster. "We had trouble with them before."

"Where they going to be?" asked Richard.

"That's what makes it good. Man, it's going to be real good," said the Rooster. "In the Orchard. No cops, no nothing. Only us."

"And the mud," said the Tuerto. The Orchard was a twelve-acre cherry grove in the new industrial district on the north side of the city.

"It'll be just as muddy for them," said the Rooster. "Let's go!"

They walked out and hurriedly got into the car. There were eight of them in Zurdo's sedan, and another three were to follow in a coupé. Richard sat in the back on Slick's lap. He was silent, afraid that they might discover the growing terror inside him. The Rooster took objects out of a gunnysack.

"Here, man, this is for you. Don't lose it," he said. It was a doubled-up bicycle chain, one end bound tightly with leather thongs to form a grip.

Richard held it in his hands and, for an unaccountable reason, said, "Thank you." Goddamn! he thought. What the hell did I get into? He wished they would get to their destination quickly, before his fear turned to panic. He had no idea who it was they were going to meet. Would there be three or thirty against them? He looked at the bludgeon in his hand and thought, Christ! Somebody could get killed!

The Tuerto passed a pint of whiskey back to them. Richard drank thirstily, then passed the bottle on.

"You want some, Chango?" asked the Rooster.

"That stuff's not for me, man. I stick to yesca," he answered. Four jerky rasps came from him as he inhaled, reluctant to allow the least bit of smoke to escape him, receiving the full force of the drug in a hurry. He offered the cigarette, but they all refused it. Then he carefully put it out, and placed the butt in a small matchbox.

It seemed to Richard that they had been riding for hours when finally they arrived at the Orchard. They backed the car under the trees, leaving the motor idling because they might have to leave in a hurry. The rest of the gang did not arrive; the Rooster said, "Those sons of bitches aren't coming!"

"Let's wait a few minutes," said the Tuerto. "Maybe they'll show up."

"No, they won't come," said the Rooster, in a calm voice now. He unzipped his pants legs and rolled them up to the knees. "Goddamn mud," he said, almost good-naturedly. "Come on!" They followed him into the Orchard. When they were approximately in the center of the tract, they stopped. "Here they come," whispered the Rooster.

Richard could not hear a thing. He was more afraid, but had stopped shaking. In spite of his fear, his mind was alert. He strained every sense, in order not to miss any part of this experience. He wanted to retain everything that was about to happen. He was surprised at the way the Rooster had taken command from the moment they left the dance-hall. Richard had never thought of any one of the boys being considered a leader, and now they were all following the Rooster, and Richard fell naturally in line. The guy's like ice, he thought. Like a Goddamn piece of ice!

Suddenly forms took shape in the darkness before him. And just as suddenly he was in the kaleidoscopic swirl of the fight. He felt blows on his face and body, as if from a distance, and he flayed viciously with the chain. There was a deadly quietness to the struggle. He was conscious that some of the fallen were moaning, and a voice screamed,

"The son of a bitch broke my arm!" And that was all he heard for a while, because he was lying on the ground with his face in the mud.

They half-dragged, half-carried him to the car. It had bogged down in the mud, and they put him in the back while they tried to make it move. They could see headlights behind them, beyond the trees.

"We have to get the hell out of here," said the Rooster. "They got help. Push! Push!" Richard opened the door and fell out of the car. He got up and stumbled crazily in the darkness. He was grabbed and violently thrown in again. They could hear the sound of a large group coming toward them from the Orchard.

"Let's cut out!" shouted the Tuerto. "Leave it here!"

"No!" said the Rooster. "They'll tear it apart!" The car slithered onto the sidewalk and the wheels finally got traction. In a moment, they were moving down the street.

Richard held his hands to his head. "Jesus!" he exclaimed. "The cabrón threw me with the shithouse."

"It was a bat," said the Rooster.

"What?"

"He hit you with a Goddamn baseball bat!"

They took Richard home, and the Rooster helped him to his door. "Better rub some lard on your head," he told him.

"All right. Say, you were right, Rooster. Those other cats didn't show at all."

"You have to expect at least a couple of guys to chicken out on a deal like this," said the Rooster. "You did real good, man. I knew you'd do good."

Richard looked at his friend thoughtfully for a moment. In the dim light, his dark hair, Medusalike, curled from his collar in back almost to his eyebrows. He wondered what errant knight from Castile had traveled four thousand miles to mate with a daughter of Cuahtémoc to produce this strain. "How did you know?" he asked.

"Because I could tell it meant so much to you," said the Rooster.

"When I saw them coming, it looked like there were a hundred of them."

"There were only about fifteen. You're okay, Richard. Any time you want something, just let me know."

Richard felt humble in his gratification. He understood the friendship that was being offered. "I'll tell you,

Rooster," he said. "I've never been afraid as much as I was tonight." He thought, If he knows this, perhaps he won't feel the sense of obligation.

"Hell, that's no news. We all were."

"Did we beat them?" asked Richard.

"Yeah, we beat them," answered the Rooster. "We beat them real good!"

And that, for Richard Rubio, was the finest moment of a most happy night.

And yet oddly, despite the chances he took, it was while in the company of his childhood friends that Richard became involved with the police. It happened so suddenly that he had no chance to prepare himself for the experience.

Ricky had a car now, and the gang was going to get him skirts for it as a sort of a present. They searched all over San Jose until they found a car with a set that would look good on Ricky's, but they had not even started to take them off when two night watchmen, on their way home from work somewhere, stopped them. The men really had nothing to hold them on, because they had not done anything yet, but Richard knew they did not need a reason.

The guards had them lined up against the firehouse when the squadcars arrived. The lead car had not yet come to a complete stop when the rear door opened and the first cop jumped out. He kept moving toward them in one motion, and as Richard was the closest to him, he got it first, in the face, and the back of his head hit the brick wall and he slid down to the sidewalk. The guys jumped the cop then, crying and swinging, but it was a futile attack, because the rest of the officers were out of the cars by then, and they simply beat them to pieces. They were thrown into the back of the cars bodily, and were lucky they did not hit the side of the car as they went through the door. They were hit and jabbed in the ribs all the way to the city jail. The cars went down a ramp into the cellar of the joint, and they were pushed and dragged into a large room. First all their belongings were taken from them and put in individual paper bags, and then a big man in plain clothes came in.

Richard asked where he could lodge a complaint against the officers for beating them, but the detective just grinned.

"Resisting arrest," someone said.

The plainclothesman went into the buddybuddy act with them, and laughed as if the whole thing were a great joke.

"What were you going to do to the car, fellows?" he asked almost jovially.

They did not answer him. One of the cops went over to Ricky and hit him under the ear, and, when he fell, gave him the boots.

"Goddamn pachucos!" he said.

"Now," said the detective, "maybe one of you other guys wants to tell me."

They remained silent, and were all given another beating. Richard's head ached, and he was frightened. He remembered that when he was a kid, a friend of the family had been picked up for drunkenness, and was later found dead in his cell under mysterious circumstances. He realized he must say something—anything.

"We weren't doing anything," he said. "Just fooling around town when those guards hollered at us, and we stopped to see what they wanted."

"How about the girls? Had any idea in mind about the girls?"

"What girls?"

"The two girls walking by—don't make out you don't know what I'm talking about. You Goddamn bastards think you can come here and just take a clean white girl and do what you want! Where you from, anyway? Flats? Boyle Heights?" He really thought they were from Los Angeles.

"We're from Santa Clara and we don't run around raping girls." The detective slapped him with the back of his hand. He looked at him for a minute and said:

"Don't give me that crap. You little bastards give us more trouble than all the criminals in the state. . . . God, I wish we had a free hand to clean out our town of scum like you! Now, you're going to tell me! What were you doing by that car?"

Richard decided to keep silent, like the others, and the detective left the room. Then a cop began taking them one by one. Ricky was half-carried into the other room, and Richard began to think about how rough it all was. Strange how the police thought they were zootsuiters. Hell, they all had on Levis and wore their hair short.

Ricky was brought back almost immediately, and Richard could see by the stubborn expression on his face that

he had not said a word. He could also see that he was
frightened, too, but still game as hell. They took one of the
others in, but he also came out almost immediately, and
the cop motioned to Richard. He knew then that the detective would not waste time with the others, because while
they had been silent, he had at least answered some of the
questions. But he did not really know what to expect.

"Sit down, kid." The detective's approach was different
this time. "Tell me all about it." Richard almost laughed,
because now he was being conned; and he suddenly realized that this was the last of it and the detective would
not hold them, because he had nothing to keep them on.

"There isn't anything to tell," he said, and the officer
made a little joke about how Richard was the only one
who would speak up, and how that showed he was not
afraid, like the others—though he knew all along it was
just the opposite. And Richard knew that he knew this, but
now he was over his fear and talked to him calmly, not
with the voice he had earlier, when he was near cracking
up. The thought of what he must have sounded like shamed
him so he damn near puked. "Look, sir," he said. "What
are you holding us for, anyway? You want us to tell you
we did something we didn't, but I don't know what it is.
And then knocking hell out of us like that . . ."

"You resisted arrest."

"Not in here we didn't resist arrest. How come these
guys been batting us around like that? You must be a
bunch of sadists, all of you. What if one of us dies, or
something?"

"I don't know what you're talking about," said the detective. He asked the cop at the door, "You see anyone get hit
around here?"

"No. He's crazy," he answered.

"See?" The detective thought he was a real actor. "Now,
look. You tell me what you were doing, and I'll see that
you get a break."

"Nothing, I told you."

"All right, then, don't tell me about tonight. But how
about on other nights? What have you guys been up to? A
little stealing, maybe? Where do you get your marihuana?
You been maybe jumping a nice little gringa out in Willow
Glen? We haven't got the bastard that pulled that one yet!"
He stopped, because his anger was becoming obvious in

spite of himself. He said casually, "You know about that, don't you?"

"No."

"Well, then, you heard about it."

"No. I haven't."

"You read the papers, no?"

"Only the sports page—the rest of it's a lot of bull and I don't have time for it."

He did not believe him. "You can't tell me that," he said. "You must read the papers sometimes."

"Sure, sometimes I'll glance at the first page, but I don't even do that very much. I just take the second section and read the sports. Maybe when this happened that you're talking about, I didn't look at the front page."

"Hell, no wonder you people are almost illiterate. How you going to know how to vote when you get old enough?"

"I don't want to vote. I just want to get out of here." He was beginning to feel sick, really sick, and his kidneys hurt him so that he was sure he would be passing blood for a week.

"You have to want to vote—it's one right you're guaranteed." He seemed to be a little sorry about that.

"If that's so," said Richard, "then it's my right to not vote if I don't want to vote, isn't it?"

The man dropped it. "This little girl I was telling you about . . . she was walking home from the movies, and three Mexicans pulled her behind a hedge and had some fun."

He seemed to want to keep talking, so Richard asked, "How do you know they were Mexicans?"

"She saw them."

"Yeah, but did she see their birth certificates? Maybe they were Americans?"

The detective looked at him for such a long time that he thought, Oh-oh, I did it this time, but the man had decided a while ago not to use force again. "You're a wise little bastard," he finally said. "Talk pretty good English, too, not like most 'chucos." Again he tried hard not to show his anger, but his voice was loud once more. "You know what I mean when I say Mexican, so don't get so Goddamn smart. She said they were Mexican, that's how we know. Maybe it was your gang."

Richard felt good, because he was certain the detective

was going to have to let them go, so he really began to act smart. "We're not a gang," he said. "That is, not a gang the way you mean, only a gang like kids' gangs are, because we grew up together and we played cops-and-robbers, you know. And funny how we used to fight because we all wanted to be the good guys, but now I don't think it was such a good idea, because I just got a pretty good look at the good guys." That jolted the detective a little, and he looked almost embarrassed.

"We have a job to do," he said, explaining everything. "Now, you're sure you guys didn't have anything to do with that?" He said it real cutelike, a sneak punch, and for a moment Richard thought that he would ask where he had been on such-and-such a night, but the detective just smiled his friendly smile.

"I'm sure," Richard said, and smiled right back at him, and one side of his face was so numb that he knew it was not smiling like the other side. "I'm the only Mexican— like you say Mexican—in the bunch," he said. "And the others are Spanish, and one is Italian. Besides, I don't know any 'chucos well enough to run around with them."

"Let me see your hands." He looked and was satisfied. "No tattoos. But that's a bad-looking wart you got there."

"I've been playing with frogs," he said sarcastically, but the detective appeared to miss it.

"Better have it taken care of," he said with honest concern. "You still say you don't come from down south?"

"Call up the Santa Clara police, and they'll tell you about me. About all of us."

He was sent into the other room then, and after a while an officer returned their wallets and things and told them they could go. The detective stopped Richard at the door and said:

"So you're going to be a college boy?"

"I guess so." So he *had* checked up.

"Drop in and see me sometime. We can use someone like you when you get older. There are a lot of your people around now, and someone like you would be good to have on the side of law and order."

Jesus Christ! Another one, thought Richard. Aloud he said, "No, thanks. I don't want to have anything to do with you guys."

"Think about it. You have a few years yet. There's a lot you can do for your people that way."

His sincerity surprised Richard. He seemed to mean it. "No," he answered. "I'm no Jesus Christ. Let 'my people' take care of themselves."

"You were defending them a while ago."

"I was defending myself!" *Stupid!*

But who the hell were his people? He had always felt that all people were his people—not in that nauseating God-made-us-all-equal way, for to him that was a deception; the exact opposite was so obvious. But this man, in his attitude and behavior, gave him a new point of view about his world.

Painfully, they walked across town to Ricky's car and somehow made it home. He could not sleep. Things were going on around him that he did not know about. He was amazed at his naïveté. Hearing about Mexican kids being picked up by the police for having done something had never affected him in any way before. Even policemen had never been set aside in his mind as a group. In Santa Clara, where he knew the town marshal and his patrolmen, and always called them by their first names, he did not think of them as cops but as people—in fact, neighbors. One evening had changed all that for him, and now he knew that he would never forget what had happened tonight, and the impression would make him distrust and, in fact, almost hate policemen all his life. Now, for the first time in his life, he felt discriminated against. The horrible thing that he had experienced suddenly was clear, and he cried silently in his bed.

In México they hang the Spaniard, he thought, and here they would do the same to the Mexican, and it was the same person, somehow, doing all this, in another body—in another place. What do they do, these people? That detective, when he is not slapping a face or cajoling or entreating for a confession of some unsolved crime—what does he do when he is not doing this horrible thing he calls a job? Does he have a home, a hearth? A wife upon whom he lavishes all the tenderness in him, whom he holds naked —the only way—to his own nakedness, and in his nakedness is he then real? Or perhaps even—Jesus Christ, NO! NOT CHILDREN! A man like that have children! The wonder of that!

And the guys—they had not said anything, but the way they had looked at him for having stayed in the office so long with that man. "Man," that is truly the worst thing he could possibly call him at this moment. They had been afraid that he had betrayed their trust. Once, on the silent ride home, he had almost exclaimed, "Look, you bastards, I didn't cop out on you. He tried to con me and I conned *him*, and he had to let us go." But he was hurt and a little resentful, and decided they were not worth it. And now they were thinking that if he had not been there, they would not have been accused by association, and therefore not beaten. They were right, of course. And, in a way he had betrayed them, but they did not know this. He had kept his mouth shut, not because of the code but because by co-operating with the police he would have implicated himself. But the guys' loyalty to an unwritten law transcended the fact that they had been at the point of committing a criminal offense, and so much so that they actually forgot this fact. And he knew that from this moment things would not be the same for them again. Something had happened to their relationship, particularly to his relationship with Ricky. More than ever he knew they could never be friends again, because somehow he represented an obstacle to the attainment of certain goals Ricky had imposed upon his life.

He stopped crying then, because it was not worth crying for people. He withdrew into his protective shell of cynicism, but he recognized it for what it was and could easily hide it from the world.

# SHAWN WONG

# All in the Night Without Food

The night train stopped at the edge of the ocean, the engine steaming into the waves that lapped against the iron wheels. The ocean was humbled in front of the great steaming engine, its great noise was iron; the moonlight on the ocean gave the sea its place, made the water look like waves of rippling steel. There was a low mumble heard beneath the sound of the waves whose constant voice muted itself against fine sand; the voices of the men came towards me. I could not see their faces smeared with soot, charcoal faces. Their voices moved past me, towards the ocean, yet I was not afraid, I knew them. They had worked all day on the railroad, but at night they built the great iron engine that brought them to the sea's edge, pointed them home, the way west. They climbed down from the engine, faces black with soot, disguised, to dive into the ocean and swim home, but the moonlight hit the waves and made the surf like bones, white in their faces. Their swimming was useless, their strokes made in a desert of broken bones, of bone hitting bone, hollow noises to men who believed in home and hollow noises to men whose black faces held in their souls. But the engine waited in the iron night. And by morning the sun came up like the hot pulsating engine, the earth steams dry as I walk and kneel and wash my face

with the earth's breathing, and the Chinamen rise all
around me, their faces clean and grim, rising like swiftly
rising steam to walk farther into their forest.

They go back to work, their eyes red with sea salt, their
hands red from swimming with the broken bone sea. The
black from the iron rails comes off in their hands.

I run through a thick night, that night of black soot
mixing with my sweat to drip like black tears from my
face; my heart is the engine's red iron and if I stop running
I will be burned. Now the night driver is me. The old night
train filled with Chinamen, my grandfathers, fathers, all
without lovers, without women, struggling against black
iron with hands splintered from coarse crossties. I am the
night driver. Angry. Moving out of a narrow side road at
ninety. One bump. The jump of my headlights. With my
father's spirit I am driving at night. No music. No more
dreams. Soundlessly, air cooled, short breaths, this drive is
mourning. There is only the blur of the white line, the
white guard rail at the edges of my sight as I outrun the
yellow glare of lights, an ache at the temples and a pulse in
the white of my palms, knowing what is in front of me. I
am speaking to the road with the green lights of the instru-
ments touching my face, no dreams, just talk, like an
ocean's talk, constant, muted against sand, immediate, suf-
focating. My fingers moving from the steering wheel,
through glass, to grab at the blurs of white, one hundred
miles an hour of white engine scream, my hands lifting
myself out of my seat to stoop over and grab at the bleached
bones of the road. I reach out to take the road in my
hands, the blur of bones, no blood, someone speaks and I
do not recognize the voice. Piano music rising in my ears
like the winds that move across the plains and sweep like
rivers, its waves of voice nearing my ear. The memorized
picture fades and I am again speaking to myself with my
lovers there, mother and father, and I remind myself what
I call them. They begin to move. I give her all my weight,
my father gives me his hand to hold saying, "We have to
run, hold on." And I hold on for the chase, flying, my feet
touching ground every six feet, like giants marching over
the earth, my father, the track star, the running giving me
all the soul of his green grave, the name is marble, the
name of blue mountains, air sirens of our home, thinking
of lovers.

I was never old enough to write a letter to my father to tell him how he had shaped my life. So on a night like this I write him a letter. Standing there on the beach, the night train easing up to me, the engine blacker than the night, blowing steam out to sea. So I write. Dear Father, I am now at home. At our home on the range, our place. It is April. Tonight I remember a humid night in Guam when I held your forehead in my small hands as I rode on your shoulders. My hands felt your ears, the shape of your chin, and the shape of your nose until you became annoyed and placed my hands back on your forehead and shifted my weight on your shoulders. Like a blind man, I remember your face in the darkness. I remember you now with urgency. In this night here I heard the same sounds of a tropical night; the clicking of insects, the scrape of a lizard's claws on the screen door. Because I am now the same age as you are, Father, I remember how you showed me the buttonholes and buttons of my clothes, the loops needed to tie my shoes. I do not remember whether you admired me then, or remarked to yourself how much I looked like you, or felt satisfied that I would grow into the athlete you were. Tonight I took a long look into your face and saw you smiling. You are twenty-eight years old. At fifteen when my mother died, I thought my terror would increase with age. The terror that I would not be like you, the terror that I would never admit where my home stood rooted. A woman I love, Father, told me that identity is a word full of the home. Identity is a word that whispers, not whispers, but *gets* you to say, "ever, ever yours."

The night train is beside me, spewing steam. I hear iron gates and doors opening and closing, I feel the heat of the engine beside me. The cold ocean waves boil against the hot iron beneath the engine. The waves wet my shoes and my pants at the ankles. The train fills the whole night. It is a wall between the dry beach and the edge of the ocean. Under the legend of this train, the heart of this country lies in immoveable granite mountains, and lies in the roots of giant trees. Those roots are sharp talons in the earth of my country. I stand my ground and wave the train on. The train inches by me, heaving up steam, heat, sand, and sea water. The last thing I remember doing tonight is raising my hand to signal the train on. I walk back to the dock where I am making my stand in the night and see the train

gather speed, feel it brush by me. I count every car pulled
by the engine until all the noise of the night is gone.

Now I have the loneliness of fathers. To work from my
soul, the heart speaking, not in self-pity, since the dream of
Great-Grandfather, whose crying left scars on his face,
pledges a feeling and commitment that gives like my father's giving to his lover, my mother. Dear Father, I say, I
write, I sing, I give you my love, this is a letter whispering
those words, "ever, ever yours." But, you are dead. There
is nothing that keeps me, no voice, except that voice
plagued by memory and objects of no value, a watch, a
ring, a sweater, no movement, "keep it close to the skin," I
say to myself. Father, I have dreams of departures, people
leaving me, of life losing ground. I cannot control the
blood that rushes to my head in the night and makes my
dreams red.

I am driving at night and the whine of the car's engine
rips through second and third gears. The straight at last,
that familiar white blur. A shift at a hundred and ten,
deafening my ears. The night is crowded with people blackness, the night is a city street, people jumping for the side
of the road at the whites of my lights. The chase in wet
city streets is my mind in this lonely night. No sound
except for the building whine of my engine, my knees go
weak, no blood there. I am too busy for fear, checking oil,
rpm's, engine heat, speed at a glance, hands and arms
working meticulously at the wheel, correcting for wind
gusts.

I am pointing the car's sloping blue nose at a hundred
into the blur of moons. What my eye sees becomes a
scream, the scream of moonlight. I take my hands off the
road, out of the ocean of bones, my sight returns to that
yellow glare of headlights, the car slows to a stop, trembling like the blood at my knees. I move across America
picking up ghosts.

In the late nights of Spring, 1957, my mother drove
home from Oak Knoll Naval Hospital, thrashing the night
traffic, pushing the little car through its gears, and somehow returned home away from the sleepless daze and the
edge of crash. She came home joking about amazing dog
stories, traveling across the desert, oceans, freezing mountains all in the night without food. Her driving at night
seemed to her like swimming the currents of a flooded
street, her eyes unfocused on the black night, still seeing

the white hospital bed, father's pale skin and the light in the hospital's solarium that signaled his dying.

And one night she came home early, not joking, not ready to gather me up in her arms to play. She asked what color I wanted my room painted. And in her blank expression I knew that father had died. I started crying. She became angry, not looking at me, and started calling out colors.

I had said before that I am violent, that I had become a father to myself. But it was my mother that controlled my growing until she too died eight years after my father's death. Not a startling revelation except when I saw her burial, and I discovered that she had shaped the style of my manhood in accordance with her own competitive and ambitious self. I grew up watching my mother's face for direction, the movements of her body. The features of her face shaped the style of my manhood. She was thirty-two years old when father died and I was seven, and when I think of her now I remember her as a young woman and how her growing kept pace with mine. She would not let me be present at my father's funeral, she did not want to be the object of everyone's pity, the mother of a fatherless child, and she did not want my childhood shaped around the ceremony and ritual of a funeral. And now, after I had witnessed her dying in another hospital eight years later and became the prominent figure at her funeral, I did not cry, I did not want everyone's pity for an orphaned fifteen-year-old boy, but kept my eyes on the casket, kept my hands in my pockets and walked quickly through the ceremony of her death.

After she died, I was no longer anyone's son. By my mother's arrangement I was to go off and live with my uncle and aunt until I was eighteen, then I could decide for myself what I wanted to do with my life. They lived along the California coast by a large lagoon. My uncle kept my mother's old Volkswagen there until I turned sixteen and learned how to drive. I suffered from dreams in that car. I remembered a lot of life driving around in my mother's car.

After my father's death, my mother took me to Carmel on weekends and only there, while I played on the beach and she walked along the ocean's edge, did she show her despair. I knew she brought me to the white sandy beaches of Carmel because it reminded her of our last happy days

as a family on Guam. She merely wished that I should
continue my uninterrupted childhood from one beach to
another. But I had already lost my role as a child at the
age of seven when I noticed her desperate efforts and private despair. A child doesn't accept tragedy in the same
light as an adult because in the fantasy world of the hero
in books and movies, the hero has no weaknesses other
than his own mortality, and, sometimes even that is ques-
tionable. So, out of my vacated childhood, I wanted to
show my mother that I had accepted father's death and
needed her real life around me. From the popular war hero
and cowboy I inherited a melodramatic strength, a hero's
arrogance, I was able to take care of myself, and her death
further enhanced that strength. I grew up out of the ruin of
a childhood, yet the fantasies and myths a child believes in
fathered me through those years. When I entered high
school, I entered with a stoic, not passive, acceptance of
the stereotyped insane adolescent years. Whether I had
known or not, I had grown beyond those years and the
social life of a teenager was a blank. There were no dates,
no dances, just swimming and water polo practice. I was a
poor student because that role did not fit into the concep-
tion of myself, but the direct test of my physical abilities
did.

My mother had brought me beyond those years. I lost
myself, my role as a student, and could not grasp anything
that was irrelevant to my sensibilities, my sense of tragedy,
but competition. The need to compete filled my life, especially when my mother was dying and slipping from my
grip. I brought to her bedside the water polo awards, the
swimming medals of my ambitious life. But she saw that I
was now like my father, the track star, the basketball and
ice hockey player, and whether I had then realized it or not
did not matter to her. She had succeeded in forming me
into her notion of manly style, and in her eyes, I had
simply become her husband's son. She must have seen the
hints of his sensibility in my personality and their own
conspicuously romantic past, because in the middle of a
perfect recovery, she died in the night.

A few days after my father died, my mother opened a
flower shop. She taught me the flower business until I was
able to assist her and prepare the flowers for weddings,
assemble corsages, and make flower arrangements for all
occasions. When customers wanted something "exotic,"

like one of those "Japanese modernistic" flower arrangements, my mother would smile and take their order and charge them appropriately for a custom-made, one-of-a-kind arrangement dug out of our supposed, misty, oriental heritage. She always let me make those floral arrangements, and I worked like a demented Dr. Frankenstein in his laboratory, twisting ti leaves into circles, shredding leaves into fountains of green splinters amid pieces of wood and stone, and arranging three lone but strategically placed flowers known by all to symbolize sun, moon, and earth. The customers were always pleased by the work of art, never knowing that a fourteen-year-old kid wearing a letterman's jacket, jeans, and black tennis shoes was behind the creation.

In the evening following her funeral I stood in the darkened store, silent except for the refrigerator fans cooling the flowers. I did not cry at her funeral, and now standing in the tomb of her energies I wanted to cry for my loss, but with almost no sleep in the three days following her death, I simply felt a moment of relief away from the relatives and friends. I walked up to the display refrigerator and opened the door to turn off the fluorescent lights. That cold, sweet air pushed out at me and I started to get sick. I shut off the fans of the refrigerator, but the air still filtered out as I backed away from the opened door.

Three mornings a week she had sent me with the driver to the flower market, and to me it had been the fulfillment of the childish gesture of bringing flowers home to mother. Except I brought home several hundred of the finest, hothouse grown flowers. And it was on those mornings that I felt vibrant and alive, stepping into the warehouse where the growers set up tables, piled high with flowers. The air was so thick that it soaked into my clothes and stayed with me for hours afterwards. After she died, it was that thick, sweet smell of the flower market that froze me on the edge of shock, made me sick to my stomach. That same smell followed my mother when she came out with the flowers from the storage refrigerator into the dusty smells of the warm storefront. Holidays for everyone else became hectic labor all night long for us. Mother's Day was always the worst. We boxed roses and made corsages all night long until we finished the day's orders. And, at the end of all this, we would go home without a single flower for my own mother, and she would always say, when I pointed out the lack of flowers in our home, "We spend more time at the shop and that's where the flowers are. Besides I've told you that 'the cobbler's son has no shoes.' "

After my mother died, I never wanted to be alone. I was in competition with everyone except myself. I was driving at night. I was driving with my father. When I was three, he had decided it was time he and his family saw America. He drove a brown, clattering, stubborn Hillman Minx across the country and back, across the plains of America, into big cities like Chicago and New York. I slept most of the way and only remember a day in New York, a day in Washington, D.C. at the Lincoln Monument, a store in Oklahoma where he bought me a slingshot, and I remember standing at the rim of the Grand Canyon. And when we came home, he never spoke of that journey again while I was growing up except to say that "we had done it."

Until my father died he had brought me up on all the childhood heroes. He indulged me in my fantasies and fascinations with planes, cars, cowboys, comic book heroes, and trains. He took me down to Berkeley's Aquatic Park two or three times a week to watch the trains pull into the factories bordering the lake. We sat in the car parked under a tree watching the trains for hours at a time. My father sat in the back seat of the car and napped, smoked and read the newspaper while I stood up on the front seat watching for trains. My father always read every page of the paper, beginning with the first page and ending on the last page of the financial section. If stories were continued on other pages, he wouldn't turn to them until he had read all the stories in between. He read the paper as people do riding on a crowded bus, folding it lengthwise and reading half of the paper at a time instead of holding it at arm's length.

The box-cars were too far away from me to read the names on the sides, so while they were pulling in or pulling out, I called out the names of states and big cities I knew. I always called the caboose "Berkeley," for our hometown. And after a while if I saw that a train was leaving, I'd wake my father up and make him rush to a crossing gate so that I could see, up close, the sides of the cars, listen to them building up speed, hear the rhythm of the iron wheels keeping time with the ringing bell at the crossing gate in front of us. On Guam, the bombers at the Air Force base

took the place of the trains. My father and I would stand
at the end of the runway as I plugged my ears, clenched
my teeth, wrinkled my face into what must have looked
like an expression of great pain, as the bombers thundered
off the runway about a hundred feet over us, shaking the
ground and blowing two-hundred-mile-an-hour dust at us.

I remember those bombers like friends. My father took
pictures of them for the family album. The B-47's made a
lot of noise with their jet engines, and I always liked to see
them land and watch their chutes pop out of their tails.
But, there was no real detail to the B-47's; they were sleek,
fast, and efficient-looking. There were no names on the B-
47's like "Rosie" or "Betty Sue," just numbers. The old B-
29's were turned into weather planes and their tails were
painted orange. Before the B-47's came to Guam, the base
was filled with a kid's closest friend—the B-36. It looked
like a giant toothpick, with a bubble cockpit up front, a
straight back tail and swept wings. It killed the enemy by
making him laugh. It looked like a silver boat with six
outboard engines on the rear of the wings. It was like a
kid's drawing of fancy planes, except this one flew.

And when my father took pictures of those planes for
me, and when he waited hours for those trains to pass by
Aquatic Park, he encouraged my enthusiasm and imagination. At night, when the trains were no longer visible, he
drove me down to Emeryville to see the enormous "Sher-
win Williams' Paints Cover the Earth" neon sign, watching
the red lights pour down over the earth out of the giant,
green lit paint can. He walked with me. He towed me up
and down the sidewalks in a red wagon. He kept pace with
my youth. He was Bobby to me. And when he died, my
mother knew she had to tell me about his youth, and the
lives of my grandfathers as he had told her. She had to tell
me who kept pace with his youth, what was the grief that
shaped his sensibility, and who struggled to make a place
for him, for me. She had to make me more than just her
husband's son. She had to more than make me understand
his sensibility, but rather make me realize it on my own,
and sometime in my life simply say that "I am the son of
my father."

When the nurse dropped my mother's thick, green jade
bracelet into my hands, the circle of green stone moved in
my hands, turned red. I could not let go of it. It was the

sound of her heart. She has no shape for me now, only my echo, and she kept my youth like cool, green jade—fatherless. She had a lover two years after my father died who moved like a ghost around my mother, loving her like artificial heat, dry, stifling, a silent heat that kept me secret in my play. No heroes, only that dark love, that dry, heated love, the smell of exhausted and warmed car heat, stifling my breath for some air outside the windows. I stayed cool by putting my ear to the window and listening to the highway air, my cheek pressed against the glass. It felt like ice in the windy forest of friends, my heroes climbing, fighting, shooting, running alongside the car, waving frantically, calling me into the forest to join their gang, ride their train, and I forgot the ceaseless hum of the car's heater. I was running on iron wheels, my face in the wind, breathing frozen air and white engine steam, the fear of my mother's lover towards him moved me and made me run in my dreams, pointless, frantic, running nowhere, just to run and feel my own secret and the pain of breath. It is only when I wake that I am frightened, feeling that somehow I have progressed, leaving myself behind at the same time. I am violent. I give myself names to prove the fantasy, but the dream eludes me. *I commit myself to love, saying it is there, but never going further to grasp loving. My real life eludes action. It leaves me a father to myself.*

She thought that now the nights of crying could be solved by this new love. Yet her grief was still overpowering her; she held onto her grief for her dead husband and lover, crying at nights, taking her well-kept grief out of its hiding place to cry herself to sleep. I would hear her moaning and crying. Only in the first days after my father's death did I cry silently into my pillow, my lover, my hero gone, his name whispered on my lips as I cried; then one day I stopped crying for him, resolved to make my life like his; it gave me strength. And it was my resolution not to cry anymore that always drove me to my mother to comfort her in her grief. Her grief became my duty. I watched her tears fall to the pillow, asking her not to cry, impatient, knowing that all her strength was leaving her, and somehow I thought if I put my mouth to the tear-stained pillow and sucked the tears from the white case, her energy would pass to me in the warm salt of those tears. And when she died, I was mad that she had failed me. She had no longer wanted to stand by my side. I was alone, but I did not cry.

My sleep tore me apart, but gave her flesh back to me in pieces, her voice with no substance, and, finally, nothing but a hollow sound would wake me, her jade bracelet knocking against the house as she moved around, cleaning, cooking, writing. It had become for me, in those dreams, the rhythmic beating of her heart. There was no need for me to put my head against her chest to hear the beating of her heart, that cold stone, jade in my eyes, filled my youth and kept time with the unsteady beating of my own heart.

# HISAYE YAMAMOTO

# Yoneko's Earthquake

Yoneko Hosoume became a freethinker on the night of March 10, 1933, only a few months after her first actual recognition of God. Ten years old at the time, of course she had heard rumors about God all along, long before Marpo came. Her cousins who lived in the city were all Christians, living as they did right next door to a Baptist church exclusively for Japanese people. These city cousins, of whom there were several, had been baptized en masse, and were very proud of their condition. Yoneko was impressed when she heard of this and thereafter was given to referring to them as "my cousins, the Christians." She, too, yearned at times after Christianity, but she realized the absurdity of her whim, seeing that there was no Baptist church for Japanese in the rural community she lived in. Such a church would have been impractical, moreover, since Yoneko, her father, her mother, and her little brother Seigo, were the only Japanese thereabouts. They were the only ones, too, whose agriculture was so diverse as to include blackberries, cabbages, rhubarb, potatoes, cucumbers, onions, and canteloupes. The rest of the countryside there was like one vast orange grove.

Yoneko had entered her cousins' church once, but she could not recall the sacred occasion without mortification.

346

It had been one day when the cousins had taken her and Seigo along with them to Sunday school. The church was a narrow, wooden building mysterious-looking because of its unusual bluish-gray paint and its steeple, but the basement schoolroom inside had been disappointingly ordinary, with desks, a blackboard, and erasers. They had all sung "Let Us Gather at the River" in Japanese. This goes:

> *Mamonaku kanata no*
> *Nagare no soba de*
> *Tanoshiku ai-masho*
> *Mata tomodachi to*
>
> *Mamonaku ai-masho*
> *Kirei-na, kirei-na kawa de*
> *Tanoshiku ai-masho*
> *Mata tomodachi to.*

Yoneko had not known the words at all, but always clever in such situations, she had opened her mouth and grimaced nonchalantly to the rhythm. What with everyone else singing at the top of his lungs, no one had noticed that she was not making a peep. Then everyone had sat down again and the man had suggested, "Let us pray." Her cousins and the rest had promptly curled their arms on the desks to make nests for their heads, and Yoneko had done the same. But not Seigo. Because when the room had become so still that one was aware of the breathing, the creaking, and the chittering in the trees outside, Seigo, sitting with her, had suddenly flung his arm around her neck and said with concern, "Sis, what are you crying for? Don't cry." Even the man had laughed and Yoneko had been terribly ashamed that Seigo should thus disclose them to be interlopers. She had pinched him fiercely and he had begun to cry, so she had had to drag him outside, which was a fortunate move, because he had immediately wet his pants. But he had been only three then, so it was not very fair to expect dignity of him.

So it remained for Marpo to bring the word of God to Yoneko, Marpo with the face like brown leather, the thin mustache like Edmund Lowe's, and the rare, breathtaking smile like white gold. Marpo, who was twenty-seven years old, was a Filipino and his last name was lovely, something like Humming Wing, but no one ever ascertained the spelling of it. He ate principally rice, just as though he were Japanese, but he never sat down to the Hosoume table, because he lived in the bunkhouse out by the barn and cooked on his own kerosene stove. Once Yoneko read somewhere that Filipinos trapped wild dogs, starved them for a time, then, feeding them mountains of rice, killed them at the peak of their bloatedness, thus insuring themselves meat ready to roast, stuffing and all, without further ado. This, the book said, was considered a delicacy. Unable to hide her disgust and her fascination, Yoneko went straightway to Marpo and asked, "Marpo, is it true that you eat dogs?", and he, flashing that smile, answered, "Don't be funny, honey!" This caused her no end of amusement, because it was a poem, and she completely forgot about the wild dogs.

Well, there seemed to be nothing Marpo could not do. Mr. Hosoume said Marpo was the best hired man he had ever had, and he said this often, because it was an irrefutable fact among Japanese in general that Filipinos in general were an indolent lot. Mr. Hosoume ascribed Marpo's industry to his having grown up in Hawaii, where there is known to be considerable Japanese influence. Marpo had gone to a missionary school there and he owned a Bible given him by one of his teachers. This had black leather covers that gave as easily as cloth, golden edges, and a slim purple ribbon for a marker. He always kept it on the little table by his bunk, which was not a bed with springs but a low, three-plank shelf with a mattress only. On the first page of the book, which was stiff and black, his teacher had written in large swirls of white ink, "As we draw near to God, He will draw near to us."

What, for instance, could Marpo do? Why, it would take an entire, leisurely evening to go into his accomplishments adequately, because there was not only Marpo the Christian and Marpo the best hired man, but Marpo the athlete, Marpo the musician (both instrumental and vocal), Marpo the artist, and Marpo the radio technician:

(1) As an athlete Marpo owned a special pair of black shoes, equipped with sharp nails on the soles, which he kept in shape with the regular application of neatsfoot oil. Putting these on, he would dash down the dirt road to the highway, a distance of perhaps half a mile, and back again. When he first came to work for the Hosoumes, he undertook this sprint every evening before he went to get his supper but, as time went on, he referred to these shoes less and less and, in the end, when he left, he had not touched

them for months. He also owned a muscle-builder sent him by Charles Atlas which, despite his unassuming size, he could stretch the length of his outspread arms; his teeth gritted then and his whole body became temporarily victim to a jerky vibration. (2) As an artist, Marpo painted larger-than-life water colors of his favorite movie stars, all of whom were women and all of whom were blonde, like Ann Harding and Jean Harlow, and tacked them up on his walls. He also made for Yoneko a folding contraption of wood holding two pencils, one with lead and one without, with which she, too, could obtain double-sized likenesses of any picture she wished. It was a fragile instrument, however, and Seigo splintered it to pieces one day when Yoneko was away at school. He claimed he was only trying to copy Boob McNutt from the funny paper when it failed. (3) As a musician, Marpo owned a violin for which he had paid over one hundred dollars. He kept this in a case whose lining was red velvet, first wrapping it gently in a brilliant red silk scarf. This scarf, which weighed nothing, he tucked under his chin when he played, gathering it up delicately by the center and flicking it once to unfurl it—a gesture Yoneko prized. In addition to this, Marpo was a singer, with a soft tenor which came out in professional quavers and rolled r's when he applied a slight pressure to his Adam's apple with thumb and forefinger. His violin and vocal repertoire consisted of the same numbers, mostly hymns and Irish folk airs. He was especially addicted to "The Rose of Tralee" and the "Londonderry Air." (4) Finally, as a radio technician who had spent two previous winters at a specialists school in the city, Marpo had put together a bulky table-size radio which brought in equal proportions of static and entertainment. He never got around to building a cabinet to house it and its innards of metal and glass remained public throughout its lifetime. This was just as well, for not a week passed without Marpo's deciding to solder one bit or another. Yoneko and Seigo became a part of the great listening audience with such fidelity that Mr. Hosoume began remarking the fact that they dwelt more with Marpo than with their own parents. He eventually took a serious view of the matter and bought the naked radio from Marpo, who thereupon put away his radio manuals and his soldering iron in the bottom of his steamer trunk and divided more time among his other interests.

However, Marpo's versatility was not revealed, as it is here, in a lump. Yoneko uncovered it fragment by fragment every day, by dint of unabashed questions, explorations among his possessions, and even silent observation, although this last was rare. In fact, she and Seigo visited with Marpo at least once a day and both of them regularly came away amazed with their findings. The most surprising thing was that Marpo was, after all this, a rather shy young man meek to the point of speechlessness in the presence of Mr. and Mrs. Hosoume. With Yoneko and Seigo, he was somewhat more self-confident and at ease.

It is not remembered now just how Yoneko and Marpo came to open their protracted discussion on religion. It is sufficient here to note that Yoneko was an ideal apostle, adoring Jesus, desiring Heaven, and fearing Hell. Once Marpo had enlightened her on these basics, Yoneko never questioned their truth. The questions she put up to him, therefore, sought neither proof of her exegeses nor balm for her doubts, but simply additional color to round out her mental images. For example, who did Marpo suppose was God's favorite movie star? Or, what sound did Jesus' laughter have (it must be like music, she added, nodding sagely, answering herself to her own satisfaction), and did Marpo suppose that God's sense of humor would have appreciated the delicious chant she had learned from friends at school today:

> There ain't no bugs on us,
> There ain't no bugs on us,
> There may be bugs on the rest of you mugs,
> But there ain't no bugs on us?

Or, did Marpo believe Jesus to have been exempt from stinging eyes when he shampooed that long, naturally wavy hair of his?

To shake such faith, there would have been required a most monstrous upheaval of some sort, and it might be said that this is just what happened. For early on the evening of March 10, 1933, a little after five o'clock this was, as Mrs. Hosoume was getting supper, as Marpo was finishing up in the fields alone because Mr. Hosoume had gone to order some chicken fertilizer, and as Yoneko and Seigo were listening to Skippy, a tremendous roar came out of nowhere and the Hosoume house began shuddering vio-

lently as though some giant had seized it in his two hands
and was giving it a good shaking. Mrs. Hosoume, who
remembered similar, although milder experiences, from her
childhood in Japan, screamed, *"Jishin, jishin!"* before she
ran and grabbed Yoneko and Seigo each by a hand and
dragged them outside with her. She took them as far as the
middle of the rhubarb patch near the house, and there they
all crouched, pressed together, watching the world about
them rock and sway. In a few minutes, Marpo, stumbling
in from the fields, joined them, saying, "Earthquake, earthquake!", and he gathered them all in his arms, as much to
protect them as to support himself.

Mr. Hosoume came home later that evening in a stranger's car, with another stranger driving the family Reo. Pallid, trembling, his eyes wildly staring, he could have been
mistaken for a drunkard, except that he was famous as a
teetotaler. It seemed that he had been on the way home
when the first jolt came, that the old green Reo had been
kissed by a broken live wire dangling from a suddenly
leaning pole. Mr. Hosoume, knowing that the end had
come by electrocution, had begun to writhe and kick and
this had been his salvation. His hands had flown from the
wheel, the car had swerved into a ditch, freeing itself from
the sputtering wire. Later, it was found that he was left
permanently inhibited about driving automobiles and permanently incapable of considering electricity with calm-
ness. He spent the larger part of his later life weakly,
wandering about the house or fields and lying down frequently to rest because of splitting headaches and sudden
dizzy spells.

So it was Marpo who went back into the house as
Yoneko screamed, "No, Marpo, no!" and brought out the
Hosoumes' kerosene stove, the food, the blankets, while
Mr. Hosoume huddled on the ground near his family.

The earth trembled for days afterwards. The Hosoumes
and Marpo Humming Wing lived during that time on a
natural patch of Bermuda grass between the house and the
rhubarb patch, remembering to take three meals a day and
retire at night. Marpo ventured inside the house many
times despite Yoneko's protests and reported the damage
slight: a few dishes had been broken; a gallon jug of mayonnaise had fallen from the top pantry shelf and spattered
the kitchen floor with yellow blobs and pieces of glass.

Yoneko was in constant terror during this experience.

Immediately on learning what all the commotion was
about, she began praying to God to end this violence. She
entreated God, flattered Him, wheedled Him, commanded
Him, but He did not listen to her at all—inexorably, the
earth went on rumbling. After three solid hours of silent,
desperate prayer, without any results whatsoever, Yoneko
began to suspect that God was either powerless, callous,
downright cruel, or nonexistent. In the murky night, under
a strange moon wearing a pale ring of light, she decided
upon the last as the most plausible theory. "Ha," was one
of the things she said tremulously to Marpo, when she was
not begging him to stay out of the house, "you and your
God!"

The others soon oriented themselves to the catastrophe
with philosophy, saying how fortunate they were to live in
the country where the peril was less than in the city and
going so far as to regard the period as a sort of vacation
from work, with their enforced alfresco existence a sort of
camping trip. They tried to bring Yoneko to partake of this
pleasant outlook, but she, shivering with each new quiver,
looked on them as dreamers who refused to see things as
they really were. Indeed, Yoneko's reaction was so notable
that the Hosoume household thereafter spoke of the event
as "Yoneko's earthquake."

After the earth subsided and the mayonnaise was mopped
off the kitchen floor, life returned to normal, except that
Mr. Hosoume stayed at home most of the time. Sometimes,
if he had a relatively painless day, he would have supper
on the stove when Mrs. Hosoume came in from the fields.
Mrs. Hosoume and Marpo did all the field labor now,
except on certain overwhelming days when several Mexicans were hired to assist them. Marpo did most of the
driving, too, and it was now he and Mrs. Hosoume who
went into town on the weekly trip for groceries. In fact,
Marpo became indispensable and both Mr. and Mrs.
Hosoume often told each other how grateful they were for
Marpo.

When summer vacation began and Yoneko stayed at
home, too, she found the new arrangement rather incon-
venient. Her father's presence cramped her style: for instance, once when her friends came over and it was decided to make fudge, he would not permit them, saying
fudge used too much sugar and that sugar was not a play-
thing; once when they were playing paper dolls, he came

along and stuck his finger up his nose and pretended he was going to rub some snot off onto the dolls. Things like that. So, on some days, she was very much annoyed with her father.

Therefore when her mother came home breathless from the fields one day and pushed a ring at her, a gold-colored ring with a tiny glasslike stone in it, saying, "Look, Yoneko, I'm going to give you this ring. If your father asks where you got it, say you found it on the street." Yoneko was perplexed but delighted both by the unexpected gift and the chance to have some secret revenge on her father, and she said, certainly, she was willing to comply with her mother's request. Her mother went back to the fields then and Yoneko put the pretty ring on her middle finger, taking up the loose space with a bit of newspaper. It was similar to the rings found occasionally in boxes of Crackerjack, except that it appeared a bit more substantial.

Mr. Hosoume never asked about the ring; in fact, he never noticed she was wearing one. Yoneko thought he was about to, once, but he only reproved her for the flamingo nail polish she was wearing, which she had applied from a vial brought over by Yvonne Fournier, the French girl two orange groves away. "You look like a Filipino," Mr. Hosoume said sternly, for it was another irrefutable fact among Japanese in general that Filipinos in general were a gaudy lot. Mrs. Hosoume immediately came to her defense, saying that in Japan, if she remembered correctly, young girls did the same thing. In fact, she remembered having gone to elaborate lengths to tint her fingernails: she used to gather, she said, the petals of the red *tsubobana* or the purple *kogane* (which grows on the underside of stones), grind them well, mix them with some alum powder, then cook the mixture and leave it to stand overnight in an envelope of either persimmon or sugar potato leaves (both very strong leaves). The second night, just before going to bed, she used to obtain threads by ripping a palm leaf (because real thread was dear) and tightly bind the paste to her fingernails under shields of persimmon or sugar potato leaves. She would be helpless for the night, the fingertips bound so well that they were alternately numb or aching, but she would grit her teeth and tell herself that the discomfort indicated the success of the operation. In the morning, finally releasing her fingers, she would find the nails shining with a translucent red-orange color.

Yoneko was fascinated, because she usually thought of her parents as having been adults all their lives. She thought that her mother must have been a beautiful child, with or without bright fingernails, because, though surely past thirty, she was even yet a beautiful person. When she herself was younger, she remembered, she had at times been so struck with her mother's appearance that she had dropped to her knees and mutely clasped her mother's legs in her arms. She had left off this habit as she learned to control her emotions, because at such times her mother had usually walked away, saying, "My, what a clinging child you are. You've got to learn to be a little more independent." She also remembered she had once heard someone comparing her mother to "a dewy, half-opened rosebud."

Mr. Hosoume, however, was irritated. "That's no excuse for Yoneko to begin using paint on her fingernails," he said. "She's only ten."

"Her Japanese age is eleven, and we weren't much older," Mrs. Hosoume said.

"Look," Mr. Hosoume said, "if you're going to contradict every piece of advice I give the children, they'll end up disobeying us both and doing what they very well please. Just because I'm ill just now is no reason for them to start being disrespectful."

"When have I ever contradicted you before?" Mrs. Hosoume said.

"Countless times," Mr. Hosoume said.

"Name one instance," Mrs. Hosoume said.

Certainly there had been times, but Mr. Hosoume could not happen to mention the one requested instance on the spot and he became quite angry. "That's quite enough of your insolence," he said. Since he was speaking in Japanese, his exact accusation was that she was *nama-iki*, which is a shade more revolting than being merely insolent.

"*Nama-iki, nama-iki?*" said Mrs. Hosoume. "How dare you? I'll not have anyone calling me *nama-iki!*"

At that, Mr. Hosoume went up to where his wife was ironing and slapped her smartly on the face. It was the first time he had ever laid hands on her. Mrs. Hosoume was immobile for an instant, but she resumed her ironing as though nothing had happened, although she glanced over at Marpo, who happened to be in the room reading a newspaper. Yoneko and Seigo forgot they were listening to the radio and stared at their parents, thunderstruck.

"Hit me again," said Mrs. Hosoume quietly, as she ironed. "Hit me all you wish."

Mr. Hosoume was apparently about to, but Marpo stepped up and put his hand on Mr. Hosoume's shoulder. "The children are here," said Marpo, "the children."

"Mind your own business," said Mr. Hosoume in broken English. "Get out of here!"

Marpo left, and that was about all. Mrs. Hosoume went on ironing, Yoneko and Seigo turned back to the radio, and Mr. Hosoume muttered that Marpo was beginning to forget his place. Now that he thought of it, he said, Marpo had been increasingly impudent towards him since his illness. He said just because he was temporarily an invalid was no reason for Marpo to start being disrespectful. He added that Marpo had better watch his step or that he might find himself jobless one of these fine days.

And something of the sort must have happened. Marpo was here one day and gone the next, without even saying good-bye to Yoneko and Seigo. That was also the day the Hosoume family went to the city on a weekday afternoon, which was most unusual. Mr. Hosoume, who now avoided driving as much as possible, handled the cumbersome Reo as though it were a nervous stallion, sitting on the edge of the seat and hugging the steering wheel. He drove very fast and about halfway to the city struck a beautiful collie which had dashed out barking from someone's yard. The car jerked with the impact, but Mr. Hosoume drove right on and Yoneko, wanting suddenly to vomit, looked back and saw the collie lying very still at the side of the road.

When they arrived at the Japanese hospital, which was their destination, Mr. Hosoume cautioned Yoneko and Seigo to be exemplary children and wait patiently in the car. It seemed hours before he and Mrs. Hosoume returned, she walking with very small, slow steps and he assisting her. When Mrs. Hosoume got in the car, she leaned back and closed her eyes. Yoneko inquired as to the source of her distress, for she was obviously in pain, but she only answered that she was feeling a little under the weather and that the doctor had administered some necessarily astringent treatment. At that, Mr. Hosoume turned around and advised Yoneko and Seigo that they must tell no one of coming to the city on a weekday afternoon, absolutely no one, and Yoneko and Seigo readily assented. On the way home, they passed the place of the encounter with the collie, and Yoneko looked up and down the stretch of road but the dog was nowhere to be seen.

Not long after that, the Hosoumes got a new hired hand, an old Japanese man who wore his gray hair in a military cut and who, unlike Marpo, had no particular interests outside working, eating, sleeping, and playing an occasional game of *goh* with Mr. Hosoume. Before he came Yoneko and Seigo played sometimes in the empty bunkhouse and recalled Marpo's various charms together. Privately, Yoneko was wounded more than she would admit even to herself that Marpo should have subjected her to such an abrupt desertion. Whenever her indignation became too great to endure gracefully, she would console herself by telling Seigo that, after all, Marpo was a mere Filipino, an eater of wild dogs.

Seigo never knew about the disappointing new hired man, because he suddenly died in the night. He and Yoneko had spent the hot morning in the nearest orange grove, she driving him to distraction by repeating certain words he could not bear to hear: she had called him Serge, a name she had read somewhere, instead of Seigo; and she had chanted off the name of the tires they were rolling around like hoops as Goodrich Silver-TO-town, Goodrich Silver-TO-town, instead of Goodrich Silver-town. This had enraged him, and he had chased her around the trees most of the morning. Finally she had taunted him from several trees away by singing "You're a Yellow-streaked Coward," which was one of several small songs she had composed. Seigo had suddenly grinned and shouted, "Sure!", and walked off, leaving her, as he intended, with a sense of emptiness. In the afternoon, they had perspired and followed the potato-digging machine and the Mexican workers, both hired for the day, around the field, delighting in unearthing marble-sized, smooth-skinned potatoes that both the machine and the men had missed. Then, in the middle of the night, Seigo began crying, complaining of a stomach ache. Mrs. Hosoume felt his head and sent her husband for the doctor, who smiled and said Seigo would be fine in the morning. He said it was doubtless the combination of green oranges, raw potatoes, and the July heat. But as soon as the doctor left, Seigo fell into a coma and a drop of red blood stood out on his underlip, where he had evidently bit it. Mr. Hosoume again fetched the doctor, who was this time very grave and wagged his head, saying several times, "It looks very bad." So Seigo died at the age of five.

Mrs. Hosoume was inconsolable and had swollen eyes in the morning for weeks afterwards. She now insisted on visiting the city relatives each Sunday, so that she could attend church services with them. One Sunday, she stood up and accepted Christ. It was through accompanying her mother to many of these services that Yoneko finally learned the Japanese words to "Let Us Gather at the River." Mrs. Hosoume also did not seem interested in discussing anything but God and Seigo. She was especially fond of reminding visitors how adorable Seigo had been as an infant, how she had been unable to refrain from dressing him as a little girl and fixing his hair in bangs until he was two. Mr. Hosoume was very gentle with her and when Yoneko accidentally caused her to giggle once, he nodded and said, "Yes, that's right, Yoneko, we must make your mother laugh and forget about Seigo." Yoneko herself did not think about Seigo at all. Whenever the thought of Seigo crossed her mind, she instantly began composing a new song, and this worked very well.

One evening, when the new hired man had been with them a while, Yoneko was helping her mother with the dishes when she found herself being examined with such peculiarly intent eyes that, with a start of guilt, she began searching in her mind for a possible crime she had lately committed. But Mrs. Hosoume only said, "Never kill a person, Yoneko, because if you do, God will take from you someone you love."

"Oh, that," said Yoneko quickly, "I don't believe in that, I don't believe in God." And her words tumbling pell-mell over one another, she went on eagerly to explain a few of her reasons why. If she neglected to mention the test she had given God during the earthquake, it was probably because she was a little upset. She had believed for a moment that her mother was going to ask about the ring (which, alas, she had lost already, somewhere in the flumes along the canteloupe patch).

# AL YOUNG

# Sitting Pretty

Maybe it was on accounta it was a full moon. I dont know. It's a whole lotta things I use to be dead certain about— like, day follow night and night follow day—things I wouldnt even bet on no more. It's been that way since me and Squirrel broke up and that's been yeahbout fifteen-some-odd years ago, *odd* years—July the Fourth.

If I was to wake up tomorrow and read in the headlines where it say it aint gon be no more full moons cause the atmosphere done got too polluted or somethin like that, it wouldnt hardly faze me none.

I'd just lay back and figger, well, maybe by men all the time goin up there foolin round with the moon and stuff, that maybe they done messed that up too the way they done the air and water so cant no full moon get over no more without undue difficulty.

I'd just shake my head, move on to the sports page or the comics and figger another good thing done come to a close.

But this full moon, this big old yella-lookin full moon was up there shinin its ass off, just big enough to fit in her bedroom window which was pretty big. She got one of them fancy places, you know, real big with nice rugs down

358

on the floor feel like you steppin in deep velvet when you walk out barefoot to go to the bathroom.

I'd seen her before, lotsa times in Adamo's. She'd come in there lookin like royalty and order up seventy or eighty dollars wortha booze and snacks just like that! I mean, no pain whatsoever. I'd be up there at the counter next to her countin out my little quarters and dimes and pennies to pay for my fifth of Eyetalian Swiss Colony Port, hopin the man let me slide if I'm a coupla cent short, and she just whip out her fancy BankAmericard, sign, and the clerk flag a boy to tote her stuff out and load it in that white Mercedes she drive.

Then one night she come in there, got her dark shades on with a expensive rag tied round her head. Her long dress was draggin the floor. While she chargin up some vodka, some Wild Turkey and one of them teensie cans of caviar cost fifteen dollars, I checked her peepin over the topa her sunglasses at me but I didnt pay it much mind cause one of the integral aspects of my personal philosophy is to be cool. Even when jive get way outta hand I tries my best to maintain my cool. You ask anybody that know me well—Willie G., the Professor, Broadway, Miz Duchess, any of em—and theyll tell you how I strives to comport myself with coolness and discretion dont care what the situation.

She grin at me while I'm still buyin my wine and head on out the store with her purchase. She was walkin kinda shaky, weavin a little like she done already had a few. She slow down and turn my way and say, "Hi!"

"How you doin tonight?" I say, kinda wonderin what a old woman like her see in a old man like me. Probly just bein friendly, I tell myself.

Next thing I know, I'm walkin out the store with my bottle under my arm when I hear this voice, the same woman settin up in her fancy sedan got her head stuck out the window. "Do you have the time?"

"You talkin to me?"

"Yes, yes, what time do you have?"

I walks up to the car and say, "I don't wear no watch, lady, but the clock in the liquor store say nine-fifteen."

I was bout to walk on off—it's only ten minutes by foot to my room at the Blue Jay—when I hear her hollerin after me again.

"Mister, could you give me a hand? . . . Please? . ."

Now, this here where the full moon come in. I look up in the sky and shonuff it's a giant-size for-real full moon hangin up there over the whole scene, and I know for a fact that when it's a full moon out people gon naturally start cuttin the fool and clownin and carryin on.

See, moon in Latin is *luna*, you know, same as in Spanish so that's where we get the word *lunatic* from. I dont think I need to go into it any deeper than that. I studies these things. The Professor gimme this big dictionary for a present a coupla years back. I be steady readin round in it to enhance my word power. I cut this article out the *National Enquirer* that maintain how you can succeed and develop yourself and transformate your whole personality by buildin up your vocabulary.

Anyway, I see it's gon be one of them old off-the-wall summertime nights. I ease back up to the car and ask her what's the matter.

She turnt her head to one side and cough some, then she commence to grinnin again. What with the moon so bright and the neon light flashin off the liquor store sign upside her face she didnt look all that old. She kinda red in the face and her skin a little rough-lookin from drinkin too much. Up close I can see she dark-complected somethin long the order of a Mexican or a Portuguese or one of them Creoles I use to know a whole lot of back south when I was livin on the Coast.

"I'll tell you the truth, honey," she say like we old friends or somethin. "I'm a little . . . I'm a little bit, well, too tipsy to drive home and I was wondering if you could—"

She let out a belch in the middle of what she was bout to tell me and I could smell garlic all mixed up with liquor and stuff but I didnt even bat an eye.

"You need somebody to drive you home. That what you tryna say?"

"In a word—yes!"

I just looked at the woman. Just so happen I had other plans.

"Please, pleeeease," she starts whinin in that halfway-beggin—halfway-playin kinda way some women'll do when they after you to do somethin and they half tore-up. She slump down in the seat with the backa her neck against the leather headrest and shut her eyes real tight like she either fixin to break down and cry or else do somethin outrageous.

Now, me, I dont go for people goin into they crazy numbers up outta the blue, dont care who it is. You put me up round the Queen of England or the King of the Zulus or the Head Mucky-Muck of the Eskimos and I'm ready to get my hat the minute they start puttin me thru any kinda unforeseen, elaborate or unnecessary changes.

I looked at this drunk woman. I looked at her real hard and I looked at my wine all bagged up so nice and I'm thinkin to myself: Well now, Sidney J. Prettymon, here you stand once again on the threshold of destiny, temptation and fate.

Now, that's *bad!* Lemme run thru that one again so yall can savor it. . . .

Here you stand on the threshold of destiny, temptation and fate. Should you run the risk of drivin this drunk woman home to a neighborhood that probly aint too use to seein no niggers—and what you gon do once you get her there, walk back home?—or should you just mind your own business, go drink your wine, climb in bed and study the next chapter of your 90 *Days to a More Powerful Vocabulary?*

My better mind told me to get my butt home. Yet and still I hated seein anybody in this kinda predicament, stranded *and* wasted. I asked her where she live at.

"Atherton . . . on Primrose Path. You mean you . . . youre gonna drive me?"

"Naw, that aint what I said. I just wanted to know—"

"Listen, I'll make it worth your while if you do get me to my place. I'll send you home in a taxi, OK?"

She opened the door and slid over.

It was a good old comfortable shift car like that raggedy Plymouth I'd been gettin round in until I parked it in one of them tow-away zones up in San Francisco a little while back. Went in to holler at this old frienda mine and when I come back out theyd done shonuff towed that damn pile of junk away. Cost too much to get it back so I just let it stay over there at the garage where theyd hauled it. I got enough problems anyway. Got fifty unpaid parkin tickets and I was tireda slippin round thru the streets scared any minute some cop gon jump up in my chest talkin bout, *I got a warrant for your arrest!*

"What's your name?" she say.

"Sitting Pretty," I say.

"No," she say, "I wanna know your name."

"Sitting Pretty *is* my name. What's yours?"

"Marguerite."

"Glad to meetcha, Marguerite. You gotta gimme some directions."

She start tellin me how to get to her place but keep on slurrin her words and gettin all mixed up. I keep tryna imagine what it look like to the public with me at the wheel and her up next to me in that shiny white Mercedes-Benz drivin down El Camino Real at nine o'clock at night.

Every time she get her directions mixed up, insteada reachin out and touchin my shoulder or my arm the way most people would, she reach over and lay her hand on my johnson. I mean, she dont just touch it, she rub it kinda.

I just looked at Marguerite and back at the road again.

I started laughin to myself at the way the moon was shinin down thru the windshield and thought about my white port right there in my coat pocket just itchin for me to twist the cap off and get at it.

First thing she done after we got to the house was to ask me to make myself comfortable on this giant couch, musta been ten feet long if it was one inch.

"You can stay a minute, cant you?" she say. "I'll fix you a drink. What do you like?"

I set back, taken out my bottle and plunked it on the coffee table. "Don't put yourself to no trouble, ma'am, I brung my own. Wine bout the only thing I fool with anymore."

"Well then, save yours, Ive got wine up the kazoo. What's your pleasure—burgundy, gamay, zinfandel, dry riesling?"

"Port, port will do, just a little glass with maybe some ice if you got any."

"I've got just the thing—some delicious tawny port my husband had shipped over from Funchal last fall. It's so good I even serve it over ice cream sometimes for dessert."

Wine and ice cream? Funchal? Her husband? What kinda inordinate setup was I steppin into? I know rich people the weirdest of all—they can afford to be—but, I swear, I couldnt get a good fix on where this broad was comin from.

"Relax," she say, "I have to make a trip to the little girl's room and then I'll be back with the best port youve ever tasted on that sweet tongue of yours. You just relax."

So that's what I done. I laid back and closed my eyes and figgered what the hell, I'm in the shit now. I'd have me one expensive drink and then ask the woman for my cab fare home. I'm the kinda dude can relax anywhere. Gimme a minute and I can relax in it. Unlax is what I call it. Gimme five minutes and I'm dead asleep like somebody done hypmatized me.

A hour coulda oozed by or maybe just a minute or two. I got off into one of them things where you kinda dead but you still alive, I mean, you be dreamin funny little unto-gether things, things that sorta mean somethin the moment you dreamin em but they keep changin and meltin into somethin else. Yet at the same time all this be happenin it still look like you wide awake and keepin tracka what's goin on in the room you settin in only that's parta the dream too.

Next thing I know, I'm openin my eyes and it's this little white poodle dog got a red ribbon tied round his neck layin up in a easy chair cross the room lookin at me like I'm stone crazy. It was hate at first sight. I cant stand a damn poodle with they high-strung ways. It's people starvin and scufflin and here they is round here chompin on steaks and tranquilizers and got charge accounts at the beauty parlor and shit. I got hot but that damn dog, I must admit, was cool. He just set there, stylin out, starin at me. Some slick white boy on the record player was imitatin the blues, probly knockin down a coupla grand a week.

Marguerite come in the room with a trayfulla stuff—two big ice-tea-lookin glasses of drinks, a coupla bottles, a bowl of ice and some corn chips.

Good gracious alive! She got on one of them see-thru nightgowns and, even tho I didnt really wanna see what all she got to present, I couldnt help focusin in on her fine behind, that pudgy protudin puddin belly, them hips she got on her, them big sturdy legs and the way it all got to wobblin when she walked.

"Desirée!" she shout, reachin for the dog. "Desirée, I want you to meet a very nice man."

The dog leap on her lap and she pat him some with one hand while she liftin her glass with the other'n. She taken a

big swig and then she and the dog kiss one another on the
mouth. They do that a coupla times before I just up and
quit lookin at em and knock back a good stiff slug myself.
That funnystyle wine she laid on me wasn't half bad. It
taste more bitterish than what I was use to, a little more
heavy and serious, guess you could say, so I reckon it was
spose to be more sophisticated.

"Desirée, I want you to meet Mr. Standing Pat. He
drove mummy home out of the kindness of his heart because mumsy-wumsy was a wee bit tipsy and. . . . Do you
like dogs, Standing Pat?"

My stomach was startin do flip-flops. I taken a really big
swallow and looked the woman dead in the eye. "It aint
Standing Pat, it's Sitting Pretty," I tell her.

"O do forgive me . . . I'm really embarrassed. I . . . I
knew it had something to do with being OK or something
like that but . . . O please dont . . . I hope you wont think
I'm making fun or anything. Do you like Desirée?"

"Aw, I guess he all right."

"She."

"Hunh?"

"Desirée is a she. . . . My little bitch . . . My widdle
bitchy-witchy thoroughbred . . ." Here she go huggin and
kissin on the dog again, rubbin its forehead up against her
forehead. "Poor little thing. She's been fixed so she cant
really get into all the delicious trouble her mumsy-wumsy
gets into. She doesnt even know what it's all adout."

By now I'm ready to throw up for real. I take a cigarette
out the wooden box of em on the coffee table and light
up.

"Ah, what a wonderful idea. Would you light one for me
too?" She snap her fingers and the dog jump down outta
her lap and land on the floor lookin shame. "Time for
babies to be in bed. Go back to your room and go to
sleep!"

Desirée do like she told and disappear.

Marguerite go to smokin on the cigarette I lit for her and
talkin all outta her head. She light another cigarette offa
that one and talk till both our drinks is drained.

Talk, talk, talk about her problems, all the crazy things
she done been thru, includin her husband—his third marriage, her fourth. He work for some big research outfit and
spend pretty much all his time on the road but pull down a
whole heapa bread, like enough to set me up for the next

decade. She liked that, him bein off someplace mosta the
time. That's how come she married him.

"What he be researchin?" I ask her.

"Damned if I know. He doesnt really like to talk about
it. O he's a character, a regular goddam character, that
Harry. Works for this division called Urban Systems. I
think it has something to do with, you know, efficiency,
getting city things to work more smoothly, that sort of
thing, but that's just a guess. All I really know is the
government's backing the Institute's research and I'm well
informed enough to know that whatever the government's
behind is apt to be sneaky and dangerous. I dont quiz him
too closely. What do you do?"

The question hit me like a missile. I wasnt ready for it.
Aint nobody asked me nothin like that since I moved into
the Blue Jay.

"You dont have to tell me if you dont want to," she say.
"Just being curious. I'm always curious about us."

"About . . . us?"

"Yeah, you know. . . . We have to sort of keep tabs on
one another."

"I dont understand."

She ease over on the couch and throw both her arms
round my neck.

"I'm a sister, silly! Cant you tell?"

"A sister? How you mean?"

She commence to whisperin somethin in my left ear all
sloppy but I cant make out a word she sayin. She draw her
head back and laugh and then start slidin her big old fat
wet tongue round in my ear and up and down alongside
my jaw and chin. Then she tease the corners of my mouth,
stabbin and lickin round the edges. Before I know it, she
done slipped that thing dead in my mouth. Taste like whiskey and cigarette smoke only it's soft and real warm,

By this time my johnson is turning flip-flops.

Now, my johnson got its own ideas bout things. Its got
its philosophy and I got mine. We been friends goin on
fifty-five years but a long time ago we drew a line whereupon it was agreed we was gon follow our own separate
paths. I wasnt spose to get in mister johnson's way and vice
versa. We still tryna make it work.

Imagination is a wonderful thing—and all I mean by
imagination is the way stuff look when you pull back from

it and give it some reflectin room—but when you come
right smack back on down on the ground to the stone nit-
nat, then you into that other world, this so-call reality, you
wanna call it that. I never much cared for it myself. It just
dont make much sense.

When I be up there in my room at the Blue Jay, readin
or drinkin or just listenin in on some of the talk shows on
my little transistor, mister johnson and me'll start havin
fantasies and reminiscin bout all the good times we done
been thru together—thrills and spills and intimate moments you might say. It be somethin like that old record
Howlin Wolf use to have out bout how he done enjoyed
things that kings and queens will never have and can never
get and dont even know about. *"And women?"* he say.
*"Great kooklymookly!!!"*

But out here in this whatchacall reality is this Marguerite, bout as drunk as the moon is full, massagin my
thighs and belly and erogenous zones and even got her old
juicylip mouth down round my crotch breathin hot air thru
my britches, got poor mister johnson and me both twitchin
and steamin.

I really hadnt been in the mood up until then. I really
didnt like the broad all that much after I'd done seen for
myself how bad she strung out behind alcohol—and I aint
no one to talk! Watchin her kissin on that dog was what
done it tho, plus the fact I'd done been thru a hard week, got
in a argument with Aristotle, my son. He a lawyer. Got a
pretty good practice goin up in Oakland with a coupla
other sharp young dudes. It really hurt me some of the
stuff he said—bout how I never encouraged him or his
sister and how I walked off and left they mother and them
stranded to make ends meet. He dont really understand
how it really went down. If it's the last thing I do I gotta
make him and Cornelia see how I am not the irresponsible
villain they mama Squirrel like to make me out to be.

"Uh, excuse me please. Excuse me, lady, I mean, Marguerite, but, like . . ."

"Something the matter, honey?" She look up, all teeth or
dentures—I couldnt tell which—and her head go to weavin
round while she starin at me like she fixin to work some
kinda spell or put me in a trance. She dont look all that
repulsive when she grin. Fact, that grin probly knock
maybe ten years off her age which I calculated to be—by
conservative estimate—somethin like forty-seven, forty-

nine, pushin the hell outta fifty at any rate. Considerin all the changes I done been thru behind women and this thing they got about never gettin outta they teens or twenties, I sure as hell wasnt gon ask her how old she was.

I take another look at her head-on like I'm some kinda cold-blooded official the City done sent out to do a little appraisin. That good-quality wine was openin my eyes. I can see she got dark hair only it's sorta reddish when you look at it close with the light from the ultramodern lamp shinin in backa her.

Mister johnson gigglin.

"I could use another little teensie-weensie," she say. "How about you?"

"Suit yourself. I'm fine, thank you."

"But your glass is empty." She drop some more cubes in and head for the bathroom. "Excuse me again. Gotta tinkle, you know. Help yourself. I'll bring more ice."

It was already enough ice still stacked up to build some pint-size Eskimo a igloo but she snatch the bowl anyway and carry it off with her.

I set there gazin at that luxurious tushie of hers—Jewish word for what we use to call totches in my day—and relax like the world bout to come to a close, watchin it wobble off in the distance again.

It's a whole lotta things I could say about that night. All I kept thinkin was what that old Alabama guvnor use to say: "Let's put the hay down on the ground so the goats can get at it."

She didnt have shade or curtain or venetian blind the first on her bedroom window. Didn't need none, I guess, on accounta all you could see when you looked out was plants and shrubbery. That full moon still shinin down like movie projector light. Fact, I felt like I was in some movie.

Willie G. and Broadway and them all the time tellin me how wild these little young girls spose to be, be boppin round here you can see they titties bouncin and some of em, from what I hear, dont even wear no draws. Wait till I tell em bout this monster I lucked up on. Naw, on second thought, I wasnt gon tell em nothin!

We got to tusslin and jammin so hard round there on that big round bed of hers until at one point I thought I was gon have a heart attack.

The Professor was right. I need to get more physical

exercise, joggin maybe or swimmin at the Y. She even taught me some things I didnt even know people did.

The woman literally picked the seeds outta my watermelon and put a pillow up under my head.

One thing tho kept gettin on my nerves—that damn dog was up under the bed and every time Marguerite get to moanin and cryin and squealin and carryin on, the dog start yippin and howlin and runnin round the room.

"Cant we put, uh, Desirée out?"

"Why? She bugging you?"

"Somethin terrible."

"OK, tell you what. I'll put Desirée out if you'll take your socks off."

"Well . . . I really dont think you want me to do that."

"Well then, Desirée stays. Besides, this is her room as much as it is mine. That's just like a brother. Always trying to boss his women around."

"You must be stone crazy, you *got* to be!"

She just push me down and climb back on and laugh.

I had to laugh myself.

Poor mister johnson too tired to even crack a smile.

\* \* \*

I went down to the California Department of Human Resources and picked up my last two unemployment checks. Somethin sinister bout that place. I dont dig it at all. Take the name they call it by—human resources—like I'm some kinda walkin, breathin coal mine or oil field or electrical plant or somethin!

They got me classified there as a janitor, maintenance engineer, but they aint been able to help me find job the first in six months. Now my benefits done run out and I was feelin glad about it in a funny sorta way. Time to knuckle back down and get on a schedule again. A hundred forty dollars wasnt gon carry me that far into the future when here I was needin to buy some clothes, some shoes, get a haircut. After I paid my fifty-dollar room rent and set aside that dollar a day it take to keep me in port, that didnt leave too much for eatin much less anything else.

At Walgreen's on University Avenue they was outta *National Enquirer*s, so I hung around the newsstand readin this article in *Psychology Today* about how psychiatrists done finally got around to studyin how people have to play different kindsa roles to keep theyself together. Masks they call em. A joker be one way when he round his wife and kids, another way when he be on the job, another way when he with somebody from a different social or ethnic background—and like that. They tickle me these professors and headshrinkers and things. They all the time comin up with some new discovery I done pieced together and peeped forty years ago. Yet and still I like to check em out and see where they heads at from time to time. Every once in a while they will hit on somethin worth worryin over or thinkin about. People need they masks, heh! Aint a black person in the world dont already know that. *Been* knowin it, had to know it to keep functionin.

"What you doin lookin at that magazine all hard like that, Sitting Pretty? You know you cant read."

It was Willie G. done tipped up behind me, bustin into that loud laugh like he always do in public places.

"Hey, where you been, Willie? I been keepin a eye out for you."

"Had to go down to L.A. to visit my sister. She got the flu and I fooled around down there and ended up catchin it myself."

"The flu in the summertime?"

"Where you been, Sit? You know these people out here in California keep some kinda flu or disease going around. Get me mad. They always tryna blame it on somebody else, some other race—the Asian flu, the Hong Kong flu— when it aint nothin but that good old, aggravatin California plague."

I picked up a Palo Alto *Times* to check the want ads and we went down the street to the Ocean Cafe to get a sammich and some coffee. Willie G. wanted his beer, a big cold glassa Slitz.

It's quite a few people in there I recognize from the Blue Jay but I dont really know em to speak to. The Blue Jay the kinda place where it's always people comin and goin. Me and Willie, the Duchess and the Professor done bout been there long as anybody, goin on two and a half years. The Duchess been there a lot longer, ten years maybe. A lotta peripatetic types come thru there, if you know what I mean.

Wing Lee come out from the kitchen and run the new waitress off when he see me and Willie settin down at the counter. He own the place.

"Well, well, so it's that time again!" Wing Lee say,

noticin I had the classified section of the paper out. "You look around for a job again."

"Yeah, Wing, you know bout anything?"

Wing in his early sixties but look younger'n me or Willie G. We bout the same height—five-ten—which is pretty tall for a Chinese dude. He keep trim and healthy, not like me. I probly weigh two hundred to his one seventy-five which is what the doctor say I oughtta slim down to.

"You wanna come to work for me again? My dishwasher and cook help is moving up to Portland."

I didnt know if I was ready to go thru them changes again. I'd worked in the Ocean Cafe kitchen durin a bad spell over a year ago. I got plenty to eat and all but couldnt make no money and got bored pretty quick.

"I'll have to think about it."

"OK, you think about it but, remember, I got to know by day after tomorrow. You want coffee and a grilled cheese on whole wheat, right? And what you like, Mistah Gee?"

While Wing was off gettin our orders I told Willie all about the Plymouth and the fight with my boy and how I had to get some kinda job right away. He sipped on his Slitz and listen careful, shakin his head and frownin. That's how come I like Willie G. Now, he one outrageous Negro and do a lotta crazy stuff that'd get me killed shonuff but he quiet with his shit. He keep it cooled down, somethin Broadway aint gon never learn to do. Willie give you the shirt off his back and then turn around and go steal another one for hisself.

"Why cant you go back to work for Sam?"

"Mmmm, I dont know. Sam kinda funny and sometimey, you know. I dont mind workin for him when he in a good mood but—aw, we be cleanin up and washin these places down at night and, you know, I like to have me a little taste in the evenin. I mean, I can take care of stuff OK. You dont see me stumblin round sloppy drunk or wasted or anything like that but Sam, well, he just dont want you to be drinkin or smellin like you been drinkin or actin funny or lookin funny or nothin!"

"I understand. I met him, remember? Straight-line nigger. But I can understand where he comin from. He's a family man, a church man, finally struggled up and got that janitorial service goin, took his son into the business, got two trucks and contracts with a lotta these good solid

businesses round the area here—banks and some of these
bigger stores. I know he had to hustle his butt off to get to
that point. Shoot, I wouldnt want anybody fuckin up a
good thing either if I'd done worked as hard as he has to
build it up."

"Yeah, I know."

"You gotta learn to compromise, Sit. I mean, you know
me. I like to go out and cut the fool with the best of em
but I know how to ease up and act right when it come to
earnin bread."

"You still on vacation?"

"Unh-hunh. Got a week and a half to go. It's kinda slow
right now over at the wreckin yard and bein round that jive
all the time is startin to get to me—old nasty, rusted-out,
smashed-up cars and parts and broken glass and grease and
shit. Getcha down after while. I'd go back to cleanin and
polishin cars on that Ford lot in Redwood City in a minute
if I could get on again. At least be around some new-lookin
merchandise for a change."

"Yeah, Willie, but I was talkin on the radio to my man
Ed Jason the other day bout how people done stopped
buyin up all these big-ass Detroit cars like they use to.
Cant afford em no more. Gas costin too much and them
smog devices aint exactly helpin what little mileage you do
get. You better think about gettin on at one of these Dat-
sun lots or Toyota lots cause them's the cars that's movin
right now."

"It aint that bad yet but I have been thinkin ahead. My
sister—the one in L.A.—done put this supermarket idea in
my head and I been thinkin bout it seriously."

"Supermarket idea?"

"That's right, goin to supermarket school and learnin
how to check out groceries. You gotta put out a little
money to put yourself thru but it's worth it in the end. You
get to be a checker and the pay aint bad."

"That would drive me nuts."

"But look at it this way. You know if I get backstage in
one of them markets, I aint gon never starve. I'm gonna get
me some groceries some kinda way."

We laugh over that and Wing Lee come back with our
sammiches. He push his chef's hat back on his baldin
head—the only clue that he got a little age on him—and
reach back under his apron and take his wallet out.

"Look at that," he say real proud, got his billfold open

to a color picture of two little Chinese babies, couldnt be more'n a few weeks old, wrapped up in blankets, they eyes all squinched shut.

"My first great-grandchildren. Twins. What you thinka that?"

Willie and me smile and reach cross the counter, shakin Wing's hand and pattin him on the back.

"That's wonderful," I say. "I got twins too but they just my grandchildren."

"Ah but you dont know what this really mean," Wing say. "We Chinese we dont have twins too often. Use to be considered a curse back in the old country, so I guess we just stopped having them. Me, I never believe in all that superstition hogwash. I think it's sign of a great blessing, so I am happy. You looking today at a very happy man. I never thought I would live to see such a thing—and my own great-grandchildren."

I felt happy for the man but started gettin depressed at the same time.

"You two eat up. This one is on me, OK? But you got to tell me if you still want the job."

Wing disappeared again and I told Willie I wish I was in a position to do more for my own family.

"You cant win," he say.

"How you mean?"

"You all the time complainin about how you done failed your wife and kids and grandkids, and I'm still wonderin if it's too late for me to still have any."

"Too late? You just now turnt forty. You can still have kids."

"O I know that. I know I'm still a good stickman and all that. I just wonder if I could stand that bein a father and a husband-plus-a-provider scene. That's like doin time, man."

"Wrong. It's worse than doin time, but it's still somethin a man oughtta should go thru."

"Why?"

"I dont know. Maybe just so he can know what real freedom is all about."

"You feel free?"

"Dont I look free to you?"

"I'm gonna do you a favor, Sit, and not answer that. But I do think you should check Sam out again. He pays pretty good, dont he?"

"Best job I ever had since I moved down here."

Willie G. swallowed the last drop of beer and hold his empty bottle up for the girl to bring him another'n.

"What would you like to be if it wasn't anything holdin you back, Sitting Pretty?"

"You mean . . . anything?"

"Anything."

"A radio announcer or a disc jockey or somethin long that line."

"That how come you always listenin to these talk shows and phonin in and stuff?"

"Hadnt thought much about it but your analysis is probly correct. I even got a few fans already just from callin into Ed Jason's show on KRZY. Some people wrote in letters and postcards sayin how much they like that old dude Sitting Pretty, say I be *tellin* it! One old joker down in San Jose say he dont go for me tho, but I can tell he just one of them redneck reactionaries, dont like to hear a nigger that can articulate and express hisself persuasively."

Willie lookin at me all incredulous, smirkin kinda.

"I got the letters and things up in my room you dont believe me. The station forwards em on to me. I'll show em to you."

"I believe you, I believe you!" Willie start shoutin, bobbin his head up and down a little too much, bout to go into his boisterous public thing again.

People was beginnin to look over at us.

Elsie, a poor old colored woman you always see walkin round downtown all day long, settin down at the other enda the counter. It's ninety degrees outside and she got a heavy black sweater on. She turn on her stool and holler cross the room, "Attaboy, Willie G., you tell em, sweetnin!"

"Aw, keep it down, Willie," I tell him, "else people'll be thinkin we crazy."

He straighten his tie, brush a little brew off the collar of his shortsleeve shirt and say, "And we cant have em thinkin *that* now can we, Sitting Pretty?"

* * *

Willie G. might know all about cars, how to rip em apart and put em back together, but he one of the scariest drivers I ever had the displeasure of ridin with.

He slouch all down in his seat, use his left hand to steer while he be steady twistin the radio knob and smokin with his right. He dont signal when he change lanes and he *keep* changin lanes. It aint nothin for him to just all of a sudden

shoot from the slow lane straight over to the fast—no turn
signal, no hand out the window, nothin—just zip right over
there in fronta some big monster truck and then speed up
till he right on topa the car in fronta him and tailgate the
hell outta it and honk his horn, really mash on it, so that
either the lead car gotta get out his way or else he gon
zoom back into the lane to the right and try and overtake
the sucker just so he can feel like he the leader of the pack
or some fool nonsense.

All the time this mess is goin on, he got the radio blastin
or either he reachin and feelin round the topa the dashboard or up under or back round behind the seat tryna find
some particular eight-track cassette to shove in this new
tape dohickey he done just had installed. It's tape cartridges scattered all over the front and back seats along
with girlie magazines, old racin forms, newspaper, rags,
rusty car parts, tools, Coke bottles, Dr Pepper and Slitz
cans, cigarette and candy wrappers, potato chip bags, old
Colonel Sanders take-out boxes with dried-up chicken
bones stickin up outta em, mitchmatch socks and shoes,
spare neckties, shirts and britches all crumpled up, cans of
Maine sardines unopened, half-eaten ice cream cones,
orange peels, coils and coils of used dental floss, LP al-
bums with no jackets all warped outta shape by the sun,
Vicks inhalers, Christmas tree branches, a paira psychedelic women's underpants and aint really no tellin what-all
since buried down underneath all that is stuff I cant even
make heads or tails outta.

What it is is a miniature version of the city dump, a
travelin nuthouse on radial tires. This rebuilt Chrysler
jacked up so high off the ground with the shocks he put in
until if you wasn't careful to check yourself right close
when you opened the door to step out you was subject to
fall to your death. I mean, sail right to the pavement and
dash your silly brains out!

The racket from the radio and tapes so damn loud you
gotta holler and shout and even scream just to be heard.

"JUST A MINUTE NOW," Willie G. shriek while I'm
tryna tell him bout Marguerite and Squirrel and how much
it mean to me to be ridin up to talk over this deal, whatever it was, with my man Ed Jason. "HOLD ON, SIT, I
GOT SOMETHIN YOU JUST *GOTS* TO LISTEN TO!
IF I CAN JUST LOCATE THE DURN TAPE—"

Now, here he go feelin and fumblin round the floor

again, aint lookin at the road or nothin, swervin all in and outta the lane.

My throat sore from shoutin and my nerves—every single one of em done shriveled up and collapsed. I just flat out give up.

For some reason, dont ask me why, I'd got up that mornin feelin like, well, Marguerite she goodlookin and educated and even sensitive when she lighten up on that bourbon, plus she consider herself some kinda soul sister and *love* to whip on me all that well-aged exquisite what the late Mr. Ian Fleming refer to as Pussy Galore. You ever see that picture, *Goldfinger*? Yet and still, behind all that, I still found it hard to fill her in on what's been happenin with me all this time I been away from my family. How come? I dont rightly know but it worried me all in my sleep, so I figgered I'd lay the whole thing on Willie G. drivin in that mornin.

Facta business, wasnt nothin much to tell. After you hit thirty, twenty years dont really seem like no time. Look like it flash past faster'n you can swat at a gnat. That great Persian poet, old Omar Khayyam, he did write them lines that go: 'The bird of time hath but a little ways to fly, and lo the bird is on the wing,' now, didnt he?

I was gon tell all this to Willie G. I tried, I swear, only he never heard a word I said. All that stuff about carryin luggage out at the airport, drivin a Yellow Cab in Oakland, breathin them chemicals in a drycleanin plant, parkin cars for fancy San Francisco restaurants, cleanin up nightclubs after hours with this insane joker call hisself Black Buddha, jack-leg bartendin with a pistol closeby at a joint call Booker's T Club up there round Marin City, bein the janitor for a TV station in San Jose—which, combined with bein round clubs and bars, I learned a little somethin bout showbiz—not to mention short-term gigs such as substitute mail carryin, short-order cookin and dishwashin at places like Wing Lee's Ocean Cafe, plus workin for people like Sam. Damn!

That's what make time go by so quick. Just to tell about that'd take more'n a book and that dont include all the women I got messed up with, the hassles with people, the drinkin too much, the times I spent throwin the shoppin news and puttin junk advertizements up on people's porches just to keep up my room rent and wine habit which, as you might guess, got outta control from time to time even

tho it's really pretty regulated now. All them times I was
ready to give up but didnt, them evil dawns and afternoons—how you gon tell somebody was raised by professors the shit you been thru? How you gon explain it? On
what basis? Aint no way they can comprehend it, dont care
how many library books they done laid up in and pondered
and empathized with.

Willie G. grinnin and I can see his mouth movin as he
jam another cartridge in the tape mechanism but I cant
make out what he sayin to save my life. What I really need
now is for Miz Duchess to be there with us. She claim she
can read lips when she feel like it.

Luckily it's a slow tune he put on, a ballad, got soft
violins and stuff in the background in place of all that car-
shakin bammity-blam-boom give a deaf-mute a headache.
He still play it loud but I can kinda hear myself think for a
change.

"What's this?"

"Roberta Flack. Man, she sure can sing, cant she?"

"Say, Willie, I know it aint none of my business but
dont you ever throw nothin away?"

"Be with you in a second, Sit."

He cut over two lanes to the right and almost got smashed
by a Greyhound bus. I'm bout to lose every bit of my
breakfast.

"What was that all about?"

"Sorry, man, but I had to get outta that lane or else
we'da ended up way over on Van Ness Avenue."

"But that's where I wanna go. The station's not too far
from there."

"Is that right? I thought you told me it was downtown."

"Well . . . Actually you can get there from downtown
pretty quick. At least you done got me to San Francisco."

"Just relax, Sit, a few minutes aint gon make that much
difference. Now, what were you sayin to me back there?"

"Aw, nothin, it wasnt important. But—would you tell
me this? Well, it's two things I wanna know really. First
off, what's the significance of all them neckties you keep in
the back seat?"

"No big thing. I just like to change ties whenever the
mood hits me. I know it's strange but that's just me. I'll be
drivin someplace and suddenly I'll pull over and put a fresh
tie on, spruce up my image. Ties is it. I see a broad I
wanna impress and *shhhoomp!* I whip my dark tie off and

throw on my bright multicolored can-you-dig-it tie. You know, it was one time a tie saved my life. Way back in the sixties when the Watts riot broke out, I was toolin round down there in L.A. lookin for a job, had my sharkskin suit on, beautiful shirt and this respectable tie, lookin like I'm really together, you see. I didnt know the riot was goin on but, like, the closer I get toward Watts I start noticin how hostile the niggers on the streets is lookin at me at them stoplights. So finally I pull into a Texaco station, black-owned, you know, and while I'm gettin a fill-up I ask the dude how come people actin up so funny when they see me. He say, 'O that's easy. You must aint heard bout the riots yet. These kids probly think you with the Establishment because you are dressed rather clean and bourgie, if you dont mind my sayin so.' That's all I needed to hear, Sit. Shoot, I took my jacket off, my shoes, unbuttoned my shirt and let it hang open to my navel, found some old plastic thongs in the backa the short, put *them* on, combed my hair all every whichway until it looked all nappy and fucked-up, took the purplest tie I could find and wound it round my forehead. Shit, after that I drove clean thru Watts past flamin buildins, fire trucks, niggers bustin windows to get em a leather coat—and not one of them clowns ever even looked at me except to flash me the victory sign or somethin, heh heh!"

We rollin off the freeway now and Willie really crackin up. He laugh and snort and bang on the dashboard until it's tears seepin out the corners of his eyes. I'm still wishin he would look at where he goin some.

Roberta Flack singin bout how she taste just like a woman, and a light rain startin to come down. I sorta laugh a little myself just to keep Willie company.

He go to havin another laughin fit and keep it up till we pull up in fronta the KRZY studios. I keep on forgettin how crazy Willie G. really is.

"Here you go, Sit. Hope you get back OK. I'm runnin over here to check on this security-guard job but I wont be headin back for a good day or two. There's this chick stay over here in Twin Peaks I use to fix cars for her mother. Watch your step comin out now!"

I kick some calcified french fries and well-gnawed bobby-cue sparerib bones out the way, open the door and take a deep breath before I make the big leap.

"HEY," Willie G. come shoutin after me as he pullin

off, "TELL THEM PEOPLE YOU GOT A GOOD FRIEND THAT WOULDNT MIND BEIN ON THE RADIO TOO, HEAR?"

Two old ladies hobblin down the sidewalk, leanin up against one another, stop and turn around to look at him like he *got* to be tripped out.

I'm cool and pretend like I dont even know the fool. If it hadna been for me concentratin on circlin that damn car with white light before gettin in it, I might not be here today to tell yall all this.

# Contributors

**Alice Adams (1926-   )**

Alice Adams was born in Fredericksburg, Virginia, and grew up in Chapel Hill, North Carolina. Educated at Radcliffe, she moved to San Francisco in the early 1950s and has lived in California ever since. She is best known for her short stories, which have appeared in *The New Yorker, The Atlantic Monthly, Redbook* and *The Paris Review*, and which have been collected in *Beautiful Girl* (1979). Between 1971 and 1978 she had a story included in each year's O. Henry Awards collection. She has also written three novels, *Careless Love, Families and Survivors*, which was nominated for the 1976 National Book Critics Circle Award, and *Listening to Billie* (1978).

**M. F. Beal (1937-   )**

Mary F. Beal was born in New York City. She studied at Barnard and in the writing program at the University of Oregon where she received an M.F.A. in 1970. Since then she has lived on the west coast. Her short fiction has appeared in *New American Review* and *The Atlantic*. "Gold" was included in Martha Foley's *Best American Short Stories* 1972. She has also written two novels, *Amazon One* (1975) and *Angel Dance* (1977). A Founder Member of the Womens Resource Center

379

in Lincoln County, Oregon, she has taught writing and literature at California State University, Fresno.

## Gina Berriault

Gina Berriault was born and grew up in Long Beach, California. Since the 1950s she has been living and writing in the San Francisco Bay Area. Her highly praised short fiction has appeared in *Esquire, The Paris Review, Mademoiselle, Contact,* and was collected in her book. *The Mistress and Other Stories* (1965). Her stories have been included in numerous anthologies, among them Martha's Foley's *Best American Short Stories* and three O. Henry Awards collections. Hiram Haydn has said of her work, "The light she casts into the inner recesses of apparently ordinary people makes one feel that there is no such thing as an ordinary person." She has also written three novels, *Descent* (1960), *Conference of Victims* (1962), and *The Son* (1966). Former recipient of a Radcliffe Institute Fellowship, she is an Assistant Professor in Humanities at San Francisco State University.

## Richard Brautigan (1935- )

Richard Brautigan was born in Tacoma, Washington, growing up there and in Portland, Oregon. He has been living in the San Francisco Bay Area since the 1950s, writing the whimsical and unorthodox works that made him a counterculture hero and one of America's most widely read authors. His first published novel was *A Confederate General in Big Sur* (1964). The book that made him famous was *Trout Fishing in America* (1967). Since then he has published numerous works of prose and poetry, among them *In Watermelon Sugar* (1968), *Rommel Drives Deeper into Egypt* (1970), *Revenge of the Lawn* (1971), *The Hawkline Monster* (1974), and *Dreaming of Babylon* (1977), a parody of the west coast detective novel.

## Raymond Carver (1938- )

Raymond Carver was born in Clatskanie, Oregon, and grew up in and around Yakima, Washington, an area where several of his stories are set. He has distinguished himself as both a poet and short story writer, winning numerous honors, including a Joseph Henry Jackson Award, an NEA Grant, a Guggenheim Fellowship and a National Book Award Nomination for his first collection of stories, *Will You Please Be Quiet, Please* (1976). *Furious Seasons* (1977) was his second collection. These stories—previously published in *Esquire, Chicago Review, Carolina Quarterly, Harpers Bazaar,* and elsewhere—map out a literary world Carver has made his own. It is partly regional— as Gary Fisketjon noted in the *Village Voice,* "Carver has roots somewhere, or most places, between northern California and the Washington–British Columbia border"—and partly the spare, unmistakable style that digs into the underside of coast-to-coast neighborhood living with uncanny precision. Carver has taught at Iowa Writers Workshop, at the University of Texas, El Paso, and for the University of California. He has also published three volumes of poetry.

### Raymond Chandler (1888-1959)

Raymond Chandler was born in Chicago, but spent most of his youth in England, where he attended Dulwich School and later worked as a journalist for *The Westminster Gazette* and *The Spectator.* During World War I he served with the Canadian Expeditionary Force in France, and then with the R.A.F. After the war he settled in southern California, and worked as an oil company executive, until the Depression put an end to his business career. He was over forty when he turned to writing mystery stories, which first appeared in *Black Mask* magazine. He was 51 when his first novel, *The Big Sleep,* was published in 1939. By that time he was established as a master of the modern detective story, characterized by the hard-boiled private eye he and Dashiell Hammett developed. His novels brought him to the attention of movie producers, and during the 1940s he also became a successful screen writer. Among his other novels—all featuring the L.A.-based private detective, Phillip Marlowe—are *Farewell, My Lovely* (1940), *Lady in the Lake* (1943), and *The Long Goodbye* (1953).

### Leonard Gardner (1933- )

Leonard Gardner was born in Stockton, California. The town, fields, and waterways of the upper San Joaquin Valley provide settings for his stories as well as for *Fat City* the novel (1969), nominated for a National Book Award in 1970, and *Fat City* the John Huston film (1972), for which Gardner also wrote the script. He has received numerous awards for his fiction, including the Joseph Henry Jackson Award, a Saxton Fellowship and a Guggenheim grant. His work has appeared in *Esquire, Genesis West, The Southwest Review, The Paris Review* and *The Red Clay Reader.* He studied in the writing program at San Francisco State and now lives in San Francisco.

### Jack Kerouac (1922-1969)

Jack Kerouac was born in Lowell, Massachusetts. His family background was French-Canadian. In New York City during the 1940s, he attended Columbia, the New School for Social Research, and met some of the writers—Allen Ginsberg, William Burroughs, etc.—who would become, with him, the nucleus of the Beat Generation. His first novel, *The Town and the City* (1950) was a formal, traditionally conceived account of his own growing up. In the 1950s he traveled to the west coast, working at numerous jobs, and he discovered "spontaneous prose," the headlong rushing first-person narrative that energized such now-famous works as *On the Road* (1957), *The Subterraneans* (1958), and *Big Sur* (1962). In the introduction to *Lonesome Traveller* (1960), Kerouac said of himself, "Always considered writing my duty on earth. Also the preachment of universal kindness, which hysterical critics have failed to notice beneath frenetic activity of my true-story novels about the 'beat' generation. Am actually not 'beat' but strange solitary crazy Catholic mystic. . . ."

### Ken Kesey (1935-    )

Ken Kesey was born in La Junta, Colorado. He grew up in and around Springfield, Oregon, graduated from the University of Oregon in 1957, and then went to Stanford for graduate work. His enormously successful first novel, *One Flew Over the Cuckoo's Nest* (1962) later became the basis for an award-winning film. *Sometimes a Great Notion* (1964) was his second novel. In both these books he taps deeply into the cultural history and potent landscape of his native region and also makes daring and exciting use of experimental narrative devices in order to penetrate complex realms of consciousness. Together with his renegade and notoriously publicized life—which became the subject of Tom Wolfe's *Electric Koolaid Acid Test* in 1968—these books made him one of the cult heroes of the 1960s, a situation that has sometimes blurred the appreciation for what he achieved in his fiction. For several years he has been living near Eugene, Oregon, producing a variety of works which include a good portion of *The Last Supplement to the Whole Earth Catalog* (1971), *Garage Sale* (1971), and short fiction in *Esquire, The Northwest Review,* and in his own magazine, *Spit in the Ocean.*

## Maxine Hong Kingston (1940-  )

Maxine Hong Kingston was born in Stockton, California, and educated at the University of California, Berkeley. Her parents immigrated to the United States from a small village in China in the 1930s. She drew upon this background—the dreams, the legends, the cultural collisions—for her first book, *The Woman Warrior* (1976). A richly textured narrative that moves between memoir and fable, this book received the 1978 Anisfield-Wolf Award in Race Relations. Kay Boyle has said of it, "Thank God for a woman's book that has the vitality to take one far, far away from the domestic grievances of American suburbia, wooing one into the wit, and the love, and grief of another place entirely." Her work has appeared in *New West, Viva, American Heritage* and *The New York Times Sunday Magazine*. She now lives in Honolulu, where she has taught at the Pacific Institute and the University of Hawaii.

## William Kittredge (1932-  )

William Kittredge was born in Portland, Oregon, and spent a number of years in and around the ranch country in the eastern part of the state. His short stories are deliberately western in flavor, often using the myths and cliches of the region as a means for exploring realities of contemporary life. They have appeared in a number of magazines, including *The Atlantic, Tri-Quarterly, Carolina Quarterly, The Antioch Review*, and *The Iowa Review*. Eight were gathered in his first collection, *The Van Gogh Field and Other Stories* (1978), which won the St. Lawrence Award for short fiction. He has received a Wallace Stegner Fellowship at Stanford, as well as an NEA Writing Grant. He attended Oregon State University, and is now an Associate Professor of English at the University of Montana in Missoula, where he heads the creative writing program.

## Ella Leffland (1931-  )

Ella Leffland was born in Martinez, California, and attended San Jose State University. Her short stories have appeared in *The New Yorker, Cosmopolitan, The Quarterly Review of Literature, Epoch*, and *Best American Short Stories*. "Last Courtesies" appeared in *Harpers* in 1976 and was awarded First Prize in the 1977 O. Henry Awards collection. She has also written three novels, *Mrs. Munck* (1970), *Out of Season*

(1974), and *Rumors of Peace* (1979), the story of a teenaged girl experiencing the repercussions of World War II in a northern California town. She lives in San Francisco.

### Ross Macdonald (1915- )

Ross Macdonald is the pen name of Kenneth Millar, who was born in San Francisco. Educated in Canada, and at the University of Michigan, he has lived in Santa Barbara, California, since the late 1940s. Lew Archer, his Los Angeles-based private detective, has now been featured in some nineteen novels, including *Moving Target* (1965) which became the movie *Harper*, *The Goodbye Look* (1969), *The Underground Man* (1971), and *The Blue Hammer* (1976). Speaking of the world Archer inhabits, Millar said in a 1972 *Esquire* interview:

> Southern California is a recently born world center. It has become a world center, in the sense that London and Paris are world centers, just in the last twenty-five years, since the war, on the basis of new technology. It's become the center of an originative style. It differs from other centers in that the others have been there for a long time and have more or less established a life-style and a civility which keep things pretty much under control. And they have established a relationship with the natural world, centuries old, which hasn't changed much. Here in California, what you've got is an instant megalopolis superimposed on a background which could almost be described as raw nature. What we've got is the twentieth century right up against the primitive.

One of America's most popular and highly respected mystery writers, and a past president of the Mystery Writers of America, Millar received a Ph.D. in literature from the University of Michigan in 1951, with a dissertation on Samuel Taylor Coleridge.

### Tillie Olsen (1913- )

Tillie Olsen was born in Omaha, Nebraska. Her formal education ended "almost through high school." In 1933 she moved to San Francisco and has lived in northern California since then. Her early writing efforts were interrupted by the demands of raising and supporting a family. She was over forty when she returned to fiction and embarked upon a career that has met with widespread critical success and brought her numerous honors. In 1955 she won a Stegner Fellowship to Stanford, and later received a Ford Foundation Grant, an NEA Writing Grant, and an O. Henry First Prize in 1961 for her best known piece of fiction, the novella "Tell Me A Riddle." This was also the title piece of the story collection first published in 1961. "Hey Sailor, What Ship?" appeared in that collection, after being included in Martha Foley's *Best American Short Stories* 1957. Among her other works are *Yonnondio*, an unfinished novel she began in the 1930s, published in 1974, and *Silences* (1978), an extended essay on women and writing.

### Ishmael Reed (1938-  )

Ishmael Reed was born in Chattanooga, Tennessee. In New York City he founded the *East Village Other* and wrote his first novel, *The Freelance Pallbearers* (1967). He moved to Berkeley in 1968. Both a novelist and widely anthologized poet, Reed has also become an influential figure in west coast publishing. With Al Young he founded the Berkeley-based *Yardbird Reader* and its successor, *Y'bird*, farsighted multi-racial journals aiming to dissolve the barriers that tend to keep writers separated into their ethnic groups. His writing—which he has called "Neo-hoodooism"—is a stimulating and entirely original mix of black experience, national legend, African imagery and wild leaps of language. *The Last Days of Louisiana Red* (1974) received the 1975 Rosenthal Foundation Award from the American Academy of Arts and Letters. His other novels are *Yellow Back Radio Broke Down* (1969), *Mumbo Jumbo* (1972), and *Flight to Canada* (1976). He has also written two volumes of poetry, *Conjure* (1972) and *Chattanooga* (1973), and a collection of essays, *Shrovetide in Old New Orleans* (1978).

### Tom Robbins (1936-  )

Tom Robbins was born in Blowing Rock, North Carolina, and was reared in a small town near Richmond, Virginia. A former student of art and religion, he received a degree from the Richmond Professional Institute, a school of art, drama and music. He later worked as a newspaperman. Sometime during the 1960s he arrived in Seattle, where he worked for a while as an art reviewer for *The Seattle Times*. For several years he has lived in a small fishing village near Puget Sound, north of Seattle, the area which provides the setting and much of the imagery for his first novel, *Another Roadside Attraction* (1971). His second novel was *Even Cowgirls Get the Blues* (1976).

386 Contributors

### Thomas Sanchez (1944- )

Thomas Sanchez was born in Oakland, California. He holds a B.A. and M.A. from San Francisco State College, where he studied in the writing program and later taught for three years. His first novel, *Rabbit Boss* (1973), is an ambitious, lyrical panorama spanning one hundred years of western experience. It was followed by *Zoot Suit Murders* (1978), a novel set in the Los Angeles barrio during the period of the World War II Zoot Suit Riots. He has also written for *Esquire* and *The Los Angeles Times*. He now lives near Santa Barbara.

### Danny Santiago

Danny Santiago is a Chicano and a native of Los Angeles. The rest of it, he keeps to himself. "When it comes to biography," he says, "I am *muy burro*, as we say in Spanish, which means worse than mulish." "The Somebody" appeared in *Redbook* in 1970, and was included in Martha Foley's *Best American Short Stories* 1971.

### William Saroyan (1908- )

William Saroyan was born in Fresno, California, and grew up in the midst of a large Armenian family. He left high school at fifteen and worked at a variety of jobs. While living in San Francisco he wrote the stories for his first book, *The Daring Young Man on the Flying Trapeze* (1934). It was an instant critical and popular success, soon followed by more story collections, *Inhale and Exhale* (1936), *Love, Here Is My Hat* (1938), and *My Name Is Aram* (1940). His play, *The Time of Your Life*, set in "Nick's Pacific Street Saloon," San Francisco, won a Pulitzer Prize in 1940, as well as the New York Drama Critics Circle Award. During a career that spans fifty years he has written over thirty books—novels, story collections, rambling works of memoir and opinion—and a dozen plays. In the opening pages of his first book, in a story called "Seventy Thousand Assyrians," Saroyan voiced an attitude toward writing that fittingly introduces himself and his life's work: "I am out here in the far west, in San Francisco, in a small room on Carl Street, writing a letter to common people, telling them in simple language things they already know. I am merely making a record, so if I wander around a little, it is because I am in no hurry and because I do not know the rules. If I have any desire at all, it is to show the brotherhood of man."

**Wallace Stegner (1909-   )**

Wallace Stegner was born in Lake Mills, Iowa. One of America's most distinguished men of letters, he is the author of some thirty works of fiction, biography, criticism and personal memoir. His literary realm in very general terms has been the American West—its past and present, literature, landscape and preservation. He grew up in Saskatchewan and Salt Lake City, where he attended the University of Utah, receiving his B.A. there and later, after a stint in the graduate writing program at Iowa, a Ph.D. in literature. The Canadian prairie and the Rocky Mountain region has provided materials for some of his strongest work, such as the novels *On a Darkling Plain* (1940), *The Big Rock Candy Mountain* (1943) and most recently, *Recapitulation* (1979). He taught at Utah and at Harvard, before moving to California in 1945 to take a post at Stanford, where he established the Stegner Fellowships program and for twenty-five years headed the Stanford Writing Center. Since the early 1960s his fiction has frequently emerged from California—its history, as well as the contemporary scene —in such works as *All the Little Live Things* (1967), *Angle of Repose* (1971), which won the Pulitzer Prize in 1972, and *Spectator Bird*, which received the National Book Award in 1977.

**John Steinbeck (1902-1968)**

John Steinbeck was born in Salinas, California. Generally regarded as one of the foremost American writers of the twentieth century, he was awarded the Nobel Prize for Literature in 1962. His formal education was sketchy. He attended Stanford intermittently in the 1920s but never finished. His first novel, *Cup of Gold,* an historical romance, appeared in 1929. His next two books, *Pastures of Heaven* (1932) and *To a God Unknown* (1934) announce the intense involvement with the landscape of central California that would permeate his later and more important works. His first popular success, *Tortilla Flat* (1935), was followed by three powerful novels that probed the plight of the working man and forever linked Steinbeck with the proletarian struggles of the 1930s—*In Dubious Battle* (1936), *Of Mice and Men* (1937), which became a successful stage play and then a film, and *The Grapes of Wrath* (1939) which became an immensely popular film. Also active as a film writer, Steinbeck adapted some of his own fiction for the screen—*The Red Pony, The Pearl*—and wrote the script for *Viva Zapata!* (1952), once again voicing his deep concern for matters of social justice. *East of Eden*, one of the major American novels to come from the west coast, and the novel Steinbeck considered his masterwork, was published in 1952.

### José Antonio Villareal

José Antonio Villareal was born in California's Imperial Valley. He grew up in the Santa Clara Valley, served with the U.S. Army during World War II, and was educated at the University of California. His first novel, *Pocho*, is based on his own experiences as the son of immigrant parents, starting out in the fields and orchards of California, then seeking to define himself as a man of Mexican origins in American society. Published by Doubleday in 1959, *Pocho* is regarded as the first Chicano novel—the first novel about Mexican American experience written by a Mexican American. (*Pocho* means a person of Mexican descent born in the U.S.) His second novel, *The Fifth Horseman* (1974) deals with the Mexican revolution. Villareal has also worked as a journalist in southern California.

### Shawn Wong (1949- )

A fourth-generation Californian, Shawn Wong was born in Oakland. He holds a B.A. from the University of California and an M.F.A. from the writing program at San Francisco State. He has taught there and at Mills College. "All In The Night Without Food" is taken from his first novel, *Homebase* (1979), which like most Asian American fiction is intensely family-centered. A generous-spirited, lyrical work, it maps the generations that have given the narrator his life and dimensions and history. Wong is also an active editor and reviewer. He co-edited the most comprehensive collection of Asian American writing to date, *Aiiieeeee* (1974). His work has appeared in *Yardbird Lives* and *The Bulletin for Concerned Asian Scholars*. He lives in Seattle.

### Hisaye Yamamoto (1921- )

Hisaye Yamamoto was born in Redondo Beach, California. Her parents were farmers, immigrants from Japan. Her stories grow out of her own farming community experiences, illuminating the interplay between races and the unique nature of Japanese American sensibility. During World War II she and her family were sent to the Colorado River Relocation Center, near Poston, Arizona, one of ten internment camps for

Japanese Americans. Some of her early writings appeared in the camp paper, *The Poston Chronicle*. After the war she returned to southern California, where she still lives, and began to write the short stories that were soon appearing in *Kenyon Review, Partisan Review, Harpers, Furioso* (later *Carleton Miscellany*), and *Arizona Quarterly*. In 1950 she received a John Hay Whitney Fellowship. In 1952 "Yoneko's Earthquake" was included in Martha Foley's *Best American Short Stories*. In the early 1960s she put aside fiction writing in order to devote more time to her family.

## Al Young (1939-    )
Al Young was born in Ocean Springs, Mississippi. He grew up in the South and in Detroit, years which provided material for his first novel, *Snakes* (1970). After attending the University of Michigan he moved to Berkeley in the early 1960s and received a B.A. from the University of California. His subsequent novels, *Who Is Angelina* (1975) and *Sitting Pretty* (1976), combine a wise understanding of black American experience with a clear-eyed, often comic view of the fast-shifting scene in contemporary California. A writer of amazing versatility, Young has written on jazz for Fantasy records, he has written a film script on the life of Dick Gregory, he has published three volumes of poetry, and he has also been active as a west coast magazine and small-press editor, collaborating with Ishmael Reed on the pioneering Yardbird Publishing Co. Formerly a Jones Lecturer in Writing at Stanford, he has received numerous honors, including a Joseph Henry Jackson Award, NEA grants, and a Guggenheim Fellowship. He lives in the San Francisco Bay area.

# ABOUT THE EDITOR

JAMES D. HOUSTON was born in San Francisco in 1933 and currently teaches fiction writing at the University of California at Santa Cruz. Whether he is writing fiction, nonfiction or movie scripts, Houston invariably imparts a distinctly "California" consciousness to his work, all of which deals in some way with the experience of living on the West Coast. In 1966, he was awarded a Wallace Stegner Fellowship at Stanford University, resulting in *Gig* which won the coveted Joseph Henry Jackson Award for fiction. Houston later collaborated with his wife, Jeanne Wakatsuki Houston on *Farewell to Manzanar*. The script the Houstons wrote for the television movie that followed was nominated for an Emmy and was awarded the Humanitas and Christopher prizes. Houston is also the author of a novel, *Continental Drift,* and editor of *California Heartland*.